# DATA GAMES

## H. I. WEISBERG

Causalytics Books

ISBN-13: 9798631721760
ISBN-10: 1477123456

Cover design by: Robin Zucker
Library of Congress Control Number: 2018675309
Printed in the United States of America

Facts are stubborn things,
but statistics are more pliable.

Mark Twain

I only believe in statistics
that I doctored myself.

Winston Churchill

# CHAPTER 1

Friday, August 7

The email was unusual. Its arrival in my inbox was heralded by the usual annoying "ping" sounding late on a sultry summer afternoon. At that moment, I was catching up on some paperwork in my office. The sender was David Parker, the president of Innovative Scientific Research, a small but highly successful scientific consulting practice. ISR specialized in providing expert, and very discreet, research in complex legal matters, such as product liability or intellectual property litigation. Ordinarily, such research was undertaken behind-the-scenes and rarely culminated in public disclosure of the resulting technical reports. Consequently, while highly regarded among the cognoscenti customarily involved in such arcane matters, the firm had almost no public visibility.

I had worked on about a dozen projects for Dave's outfit over the past few years. More often than not, these were rather pedestrian undertakings: critical reviews of data analyses presented by statistical experts in ongoing litigation. The client, usually a law firm representing a pharmaceutical company, wished to know whether any holes could be poked in the analyses performed by statisticians working for opposing counsel. As a professor of biostatistics at Boston University, I usually found these projects interesting, as well as fairly lucrative. Finding subtle errors that had been overlooked by others was a kind of statistical detective work. Crossing swords with opposing statisticians who had committed egregious errors or outright distortions was especially gratifying.

Usually, these projects involved only a day or two of my time. On a few occasions, however, my work had resulted in a formal expert report submitted to the court, followed by a deposition under oath. In most of these cases, a settlement was ultimately reached prior to trial; in two of them, I wound up testifying in court. Fortunately, both cases ended successfully for David's client, so I had become his go-to statistical expert.

Dave's cryptic email invited me to meet him that night at eight o'clock to discuss a potential new case. Now, ordinarily he would have provided more detail about the case and tried to set up a phone call to discuss some particulars. Moreover, such a brusque meeting proposal out of the blue, and well after normal business hours, was unprecedented. My first impulse was to pick up my cellphone and call him for some additional explanation. But then I hesitated. Perhaps this was merely a prank message or phishing attempt, not from David at all. I wrote back: "For real?" A minute later came the reply: "Yes, similar to ACORN."

ACORN was an acronym we had used for a litigation support project we had worked on together about three years before. It was a highly confidential critique of a published article by a Columbia professor that had turned out to involve academic fraud. Our client, Starbucks, suspected (hoped, actually) that a well-publicized study linking consumption of black coffee with throat cancer was somehow defective. I was able to prove that some of the data had actually been fabricated in order to achieve apparent statistical significance. The tipoff was a subtle inconsistency between two of the statistics presented in the article. Anyway, the case was settled quietly, with the researcher "voluntarily" resigning from his university post.

The mention of this project, known to only a handful of people, convinced me that the email was almost certainly authentic. But I wondered about the rush to meet and the hush-hush tone. I phoned my wife Valerie to tell her I would be home late, then continued to work on an article being prepared for submission to a statistical journal.

At 7:20, I left my office at B.U. and crossed Commonwealth Avenue to catch the MBTA Green Line trolley. Shortly after, it braked to a halt with a grating screech, as metal wheels ground against the ancient trolley track. I boarded and, twenty minutes later, emerged from the underground station and walked over to the Prudential Center entrance. The Pru, as all Bostonians and many tourists know, is a Boston landmark comprising a large indoor shopping mall replete with upscale stores and restaurants. It also includes entrances for two residential towers and an office building, 111 Huntington Avenue, my destination.

This building is home to several of Boston's elite law firms. Thus, it is an ideal location for ISR, which is tucked away unobtrusively in a corner of the twelfth floor. The door sports the letters ISR along with a stylish logo in maize and blue, the iconic colors of Dave's alma mater, the University of Michigan. The door was closed and locked, so I rang the doorbell. After a short interval, Dave opened the door and ushered me in.

"Hi, Ken, so good of you to come on short notice," he said, somehow sparking the image of a character in one of those British detective dramas on public television. I resisted the urge to reply with something like: "Think nothing of it, old sport, always glad to lend a hand." But Dave wasn't in the mood for our usual light banter. Instead, I just nodded and followed him down the hall. The office suite was completely deserted, lending it an aura of mystery, as I followed Dave in silence.

We arrived at the main conference room, which had a magnificent view of Boston's Back Bay neighborhood, with its elegant, beautifully restored, Victorian brickfront buildings, and the Charles River beyond. Across the Charles, I knew, were Harvard and MIT. At this hour, though, their campus buildings could be perceived only dimly in the fading light of a late-summer evening. I could just make out the iconic B.U. boathouse, where two men were returning their rowing shell. The scene was so familiar, but I was accustomed to observing it in full daylight. The effect of this unusual perspective evoked a haunting sense that something out of the ordinary was about to begin.

Upon entering the room, I was greeted by a rather tall, wiry man with sandy hair that was beginning to thin. I immediately pictured him as a former oarsman for a college crew team, which our exchange of pleasantries confirmed was in fact true. We traded anecdotes about our respective rowing careers, his much more impressive than mine. He seemed a bit younger than me, perhaps in his mid to late thirties. He was wearing a white shirt with the sleeves rolled up. His jacket and tie had been slung carelessly over the chair beside him. I sensed instinctively that he was an attorney who had been working under stress since early morning, also a correct observation.

He held out his hand as he approached, and looked me in the eyes with great intensity and an expression that suggested we had met before. Indeed, he looked vaguely familiar. "I doubt you remember me," he said, "but we actually have met, though we were never formally introduced. Do you remember your testimony at the Acerbin trial three years ago?"

"Sure," I replied. He was referring to the drug at the center of the ACORN case. I noted Dave nodding, as if encouraging me to go on. "That was quite a grilling. Wait a minute. Were you in the courtroom that day? I know you weren't the lawyer who gave me such a hard time on cross-examination, but…"

"Yeah, I was that guy sitting right behind the two lead attorneys who were trying the case. I was a senior associate in the firm then; my job was to understand the nuts and bolts of the statistical issues. I'm the bastard who fed them all those tricky questions that made you squirm a bit."

"Uh huh, I do remember you now. But I don't think I like you much," I kidded.

"I really can't blame you, but you acquitted yourself very well, and your side did win that case ultimately," he said with a wry smile. "And that brings us to why we are here tonight in this rather unorthodox get-together. The cloak-and-dagger routine was my doing, by the way, but soon you'll understand the reason for it. First, let me introduce myself formally. My name is Hal Farenheit, and please spare me the temperature jokes. Believe me, I've heard them all. Anyway, I'm currently a partner at the law firm of Cooley & Lerner. As you may know, we represent several of the world's major pharmaceutical companies. It's in connection with one of these clients that I contacted Dave here yesterday." He glanced over at Dave.

Dave nodded in confirmation and began to explain. "Hal told me his firm's client had encountered a problem that required some statistical expertise. It might or might not eventually entail the need to testify either before the FDA or in court. The potential harm to their client could be catastrophic. Their immediate need is for an initial review of certain technical material. Some of this stuff is pharmacological, the typical biochemical type analyses I and my colleagues have performed for his firm in the past. But, a critical element of the problem relates to biostatistics. He asked me if I knew a statistician with impeccable credentials, knowledge of clinical trials methodology and the ability to think outside the box. Of course, I thought of you immediately." He glanced over with an exaggerated smile.

"Oh, and he also emphasized that it should be someone I knew well and could trust implicitly. When I mentioned your name, he mentioned that he knew a bit about you. Until this meeting, I didn't know what he meant."

"Okay," I said, "but what about the urgency, and the secrecy?"

"Getting there. Hal told me that we needed to move on this quickly. Could we possibly meet with you tonight? He wanted me to contact you, but give you only a minimum of information. In fact, he drafted the email I sent."

"If you choose to become involved," added Hal, "we'll need to keep any communications absolutely private. In fact, before we go any further, I need you to sign a nondisclosure agreement. It's the standard one you have signed before on projects with ISR, with one added wrinkle."

"What's that?" I said, my voice betraying the suspicion I was feeling. "Some punitive indemnity clause?"

"No, no, nothing like that," replied Hal. It pertains to the usual proviso that you must not disclose any confidential information we provide to you *unless* you are required by a court order. Of course, this is a necessary exception, but we have added a provision. If you are ever requested to provide such confidential information, you must immediately notify me, or my designee."

"Of course," I interjected, "I would ordinarily do that anyway. I understand that you would need the heads up, so you could object if necessary."

"I know, but the client is insisting on this, and all of our consultants, including Dave, have accepted it."

"That's right," Dave confirmed.

"All right, I guess that will be okay for me too. I skimmed through the two-page document he handed me and signed it.

"Good, now I can give you some more details about the situation. Then, you can decide whether to proceed with the next step. Incidentally, we are willing to pay double your usual hourly rate, since you will have to make this your priority over the next few weeks."

"Actually," I said, "that should work, since classes at B.U. don't begin until after Labor Day." At this point I was getting really intrigued, but also a little apprehensive. What was I getting myself into?

"Before we go any further, there's one thing I need to know."

"Shoot," Hal said.

"Who is your client? I need to be sure that I don't have any potential conflict of interest."

"Sure, I understand. The client is PhireBreak Pharmaceuticals. Are you familiar with them?"

"I've heard of them, of course. I believe they're one of the largest bioengineering companies, and have a recently approved blockbuster drug. And no, I have never done any work that involved their products. By the way, how did they come up with that name?"

"So the 'ph' deliberate mis-spelling pertains to pharma, of course. The 'firebreak' idea, supposedly, comes from an epiphany experienced by one of the founders while evacuating his house in the wake of a California forest fire. He realized that metastatic cancer is like a wildfire, and a drug to curtail the blaze was like a firebreak to keep it from spreading."

"Very clever."

"Of course, some cynics think the story's apocryphal and was actually dreamed up by their PR agency. Anyway, the company was started by two boy-geniuses, one from Harvard and one from Stanford. They had invented some new technology for enhancing the cancer-fighting properties of certain chemical compounds. Anyway, despite its brilliant scientific research, the company was in serious financial difficulty until it was rescued from the brink of bankruptcy about ten years ago. The new ownership group had shrewdly purchased a major interest in several biotech start-ups around the world. PhireBreak turned out to be a big winner. Three years ago, it went public and is now worth a fortune."

"Hmm, interesting."

"The PhireBreak headquarters is, naturally, right here in Kendall Square," he continued, pointing in the direction of M.I.T.'s campus. He was referring to the Kendall Square area of Cambridge, adjacent to M.I.T. and minutes from Harvard. Formerly a run-down, semi-industrial, low-rent district, it has been transformed by the booms in high-tech and bioscience. Now, it is filled with gleaming office towers, restaurants, and hotels catering to the needs of these burgeoning industries.

"So that's how your law firm became involved?" I ventured.

"Right, actually one of our specialties, and mine in particular, is helping pharma companies stay out of trouble. Or, when necessary, to *get* out of trouble. We are currently representing several companies with offices in Kendall Square on a variety of issues ranging from garden-variety regulatory compli-ance to class-action products-liability litigation."

"Interesting," I said. "So where does this particu-lar case fit in?"

"That's a very interesting question," replied Hal, "If I knew the answer, I might not be here talking to you guys."

# CHAPTER 2

Friday, August 7

**H**al rose and stretched before continuing to explain the situation. "First, I need to give you some background. Then, I'll tell you exactly why we need your assistance. At that point, you can decide whether you want to continue on the project. If you decide to work with us, you'll be on the clock. If not, we can part company, you'll receive $5,000 for participating in this meeting, and you will never mention that we met or what we discussed here to anyone. Okay?"

"Sure but I do have some conditions. First, I assume it may be necessary to examine certain statistical analyses. That would include not only the reported results, but also the underlying data and computer code used to generate the results. To help me with this, I want to bring in a statistical computing specialist, Hector Peres. As Dave well knows, Hector and I have collaborated on many 'forensic' statistical projects."

"Yes, Hector's a brilliant programmer. I can vouch for him without hesitation," said Dave.

"Will he be available?" Hal asked.

"For double his normal rate? I'm quite sure he can make time," I replied, smiling.

"Okay, then, what's your second condition?"

I inhaled deeply, and pushed on. "I will need a letter of authorization, signed by the CEO of PhireBreak, permitting me unfettered access to any document, computer code, or data that pertains to the case."

Hal whistled softly. "That's pushing it a bit, but I think in this case it shouldn't be a problem. Any other requests?"

"Not really, except I'd like to take a fifteen-minute break to use the bathroom and then call my wife to tell her not to wait up tonight. Oh, and maybe we could break out that single malt Dave hides in the credenza there."

"Now you're talking," said Dave.

Taking a strategic bathroom break to mull things over is a practice I have developed when I'm not confident I know what's really going on. I reflected on our conversation as I walked down the hall to the men's room. I was intrigued by what I was hearing but needed to know more before fully engaging. Before I returned to the conference room, I called Valerie to check in. When I got back to the conference room. Dave had broken out the scotch and some glasses. He was returning from a small refrigerator with a plastic cup full of ice cubes for our drinks. We resumed the discussion, while sipping Dave's twenty-year old scotch. After downing a couple of ounces, my mood was considerably more relaxed. "So what's this all about?" I asked.

"As you know," Hal began, "about two years ago, in 2024 I believe, the Data Transparency Act was passed by Congress. This legislation was intended to make personal data collected in research projects more widely available for bona fide research purposes. It's patterned after the Freedom of Information Act. In principle, it's a fine idea. Unfortunately, this law has caused some headaches for pharma companies." He paused slightly, looked as if he was considering whether to say more, and then just shrugged slightly before continuing.

"Under the Data Transparency Act, a pharmaceutical manufacturer can be forced to share virtually all the data underlying a clinical trial upon request by any qualified institution. The DTA works rather like the Freedom of Information Act, except that the institution requesting the data has to reimburse the data provider for any costs incurred in producing the data. Of course, there's a great deal of fine print regarding certain restrictions to preserve patient confidentiality and the pharma company's intellectual property. These requirements can be complex, and potentially involve costly litigation."

"Good business for your firm, no doubt," I quipped. He smiled in mock condescension.

"Anyway," he continued, "about two years ago,

a group in the clinical epidemiology department at Yale Med School got hold of the data behind the Velex FDA application. You know about Velex, right?"

"In general," I replied.

"Velex became a sensation soon after it was approved by the FDA about five years ago. The pivotal study that formed the main basis for FDA approval of the drug was nothing short of spectacular. Velex was a non-opioid painkiller that was found to be as effective as the most popular opioids, but without the addictive potential or any major side effects. Pfeffer Pharmaceuticals, its inventor and manufacturer, invested heavily in promoting it by mounting an aggressive ad campaign, and expanding their facilities to ramp up production. To do all this rapidly, they borrowed heavily, expecting to reap the rewards quickly. Pfeffer's stock went through the roof. For months, it was the darling of Wall Street."

"Yes, but then things went south, somehow."

"Exactly, lightning struck, in the form of a twelve-page article in the *Journal of the American Medical Association.* The Yale researchers had found that Velex apparently wasn't quite so miraculous after all. Yes, it reduced pain, and no, it was not addictive. But, as with most medications, Mother Nature exacts a price for these benefits, and for Velex it was a steep one. The risk of a myocardial infarction...a heart attack, was found to be nearly doubled."

"I see. So Velex might save you from an opioid

overdose only to give you a heart attack. I know how these scenarios usually unfold. First, there are media reports. Then, the plaintiff attorneys smell blood. Litigation ensues, the company denies and defends; it becomes a PR nightmare. Investors begin to get nervous, creditors freak out, sales plummet etc. The beleaguered company's stock slides, and the company is lucky to escape bankruptcy, perhaps being ultimately bought out in a fire sale by another pharma willing to take a chance that it might be possible to tweak the chemical so that the adverse effect problem goes away."

"That's pretty close, actually, except for the ending. You're not gonna believe this one. The white knight, or maybe black knight in this tale, was a hedge fund, not a rival pharma company. They bought the company for about a third of its pre-debacle peak valuation. But, here's the kicker. The hedge fund had made a big play selling Pfeffer stock short a few weeks before the article came out. So they essentially ended up paying for the company out of the profits from the short-selling. Overall, it cost them practically zilch to acquire an asset that's potentially worth many billions."

"Pretty slick," I said, "but what does that have to do with your client's situation?"

"Nothing directly. Think of it as a cautionary tale. Pfeffer was the first big casualty of the Data Transparency Act. Now, the whole industry is freaking out over this. Was this a one-off, or the canary in the coal mine? Which brings me to why we're here.

One of the DTA provisions concerns any re-analyses of a company's clinical trial data that are published. A final draft of a proposed research article reporting the study results must be sent to the company for review at least sixty days before publication. The company can suggest any corrections or clarifications they deem necessary and write a commentary to be published along with the article itself."

He paused for a drink of water, then got up and stretched. Meanwhile, I thought about what he was telling me.

"So, to protect the company from potentially getting completely screwed, they get a heads-up and a chance to rebut." I began to see where this was heading. "And now, you're going to tell me that something like this is about to go down, right?"

"Last year, PhireBreak received approval for a new blockbuster medication. The approval was based mainly on the results of a large-scale clinical trial. The trial confirmed the impressive success evident in preliminary testing, so the FDA expedited the approval process, and the drug was approved in record time. It is our understanding, though it's not yet publicly known, that a group of researchers at Johns Hopkins have now re-analyzed the data from the trial."

"So what's the problem?"

"Three days ago, we were contacted by an expert we've worked with on some previous cases. She suggested that something, uh...complicating might be coming down the pike. Her information came from a conversation at an academic conference last week. She was chatting with a friend from grad school who is now at Johns Hopkins. Apparently, the guy let slip...after several margaritas, that his colleagues were re-analyzing the clinical trial. He wouldn't share any specifics, but was bragging about how their study would make a big splash. He told her to keep an eye on *The Lancet* in a few months. As you know, Ken, a featured article in that medical journal would immediately garner worldwide attention. Depending on what the article contains, this could spell big trouble."

"Now, this might mean nothing," Hal said, sounding doubtful, "but after the Pfeffer fiasco, we don't want to take any chances. So here's what I would like to propose. When we do receive the manuscript from Johns Hopkins, we will immediately send it to you for a thorough critical review. In the meantime, we'll send you copies of all previously published and unpublished reports that pertain to the product. That will give you some background."

"Sounds good," I said. "Just one more question."

"Yes?"

"Before I sign on the dotted line, can you tell me what product we're talking about?"

Hal looked straight at me with his piercing hazel eyes and hesitated for just a moment before answering. "Certainly, Ken, we are talking about Caliximabab, better known under its brand name, Verbana."

"*Whoa!* isn't that the one I keep hearing ads for every time I turn on the TV? It's supposed to be the next big thing in cancer treatment, right?"

"Exactly. Verbana is the newest immunotherapy wonder-drug. These are drugs that can strengthen the body's own immune system in highly selective ways to recognize and attack cancer cells. Verbana employs an array of novel biochemical tricks that PhireBreak researchers have pioneered. It's been shown to be extraordinarily effective against lung and colon cancers, and is currently being tested against a wide array of other cancers. If it proves as effective against the other major cancers, it could save millions of lives annually. Needless to say, it's poised to become one of the most lucrative drugs ever. So you can understand why we need to stay on top of any potentially complicating developments."

"Indeed, I do."

Shortly after that, the meeting broke up. As we left Dave's office suite and headed toward the elevator, Hal told me I would receive the background material within a few days. I could begin immediately thereafter to get up to speed. I told him I'd get right on it.

Soon, I was on the Green Line trolley heading toward home. It was ten thirty, and only two fellow passengers shared the car with me. Both decamped before I reached my stop at the Newton Centre station. From there, it was a pleasant stroll to our three-bedroom colonial on a tree-lined street about a half-mile from the village center. Newton Centre is one of thirteen villages that comprise the City of

Newton, home to about ninety-thousand inhabitants. Its excellent school system and proximity to Boston were the reasons Val and I chose it as our home. Now, as I strode wearily through its deserted streets, past its renovated Victorian houses and well-kept lawns, I wondered what the hell I was getting myself into.

.

# CHAPTER 3

Saturday, August 8

The next morning, I awoke much later than usual, even for a Saturday morning. It took me a while to shake off the cobwebs, as I was slightly hung over from the previous evening's libations. After brushing my teeth, shaving, and a quick shower, I came downstairs to find Valerie at the stove, cooking up an omelette, which smelled deliciously of grilled onions and mushrooms. "Ah, finally," she remarked, "I thought we would have to eat without you."

Meanwhile, Sam, our nine-year old, intent on a video game, ignored my appearance. "Hi, buddy," I said, tousling his hair, to which he responded by exclaiming "hey, no, dad" without taking his eyes off the screen. "Ah, a scene of modern domestic bliss," I said.

"So, Ken, what was the big deal that kept you so late last night?" Valerie asked, her tone betraying slight annoyance.

"It may turn out to be quite a *big* deal, but I can't tell you any details. I had an impromptu meeting at David Parker's office with a white-shoe attorney. He wants me to look at some data about a clinical trial that may, possibly, lead to some big-time litigation. I had to sign an NDA on the spot. It could be nothing much, or perhaps end up being our ticket to a bigger house. You know it's very hard to predict how these things will go, but I have a feeling this could be something pretty momentous."

She sighed: "I suppose that means our vacation on the Vineyard may need to be cancelled?" We had been spending the last two weeks in August on Martha's Vineyard for the past few years. We loved it there and five years ago had purchased a small cottage in Chilmark, one of the quaint villages on the island. During most of the summer months we rented it out, but always kept two weeks open for ourselves. The house itself had only two bedrooms and was about a mile from the town beach but, even so, purchasing it had only been possible because Val had inherited some money from an uncle with whom she had been close.

"Not really," I said, as she handed me a platter of eggs. I set the table as she grabbed the toast, and we simultaneously shouted for Sam to join us. "First, I don't expect to get anything from the lawyers for a couple of weeks. Second, if necessary, I should be able to work from the Vineyard for at least part of the time during the two weeks. The wi-fi connection at our cottage is pretty good. ... *Sam*, get over here, *now!*"

Val seemed mostly mollified. Sam finally joined us, and we enjoyed our breakfast in relative peace and tranquility. Val seemed rather contemplative, then asked: "Were you serious about that larger house?" This had begun to become a topic of discussion a few weeks ago when we discovered, quite unexpectedly, that Val had become pregnant.

"Well, semi-serious anyway, but don't get your hopes up."

The remainder of that day was pretty idyllic. We accompanied Sam to the birthday party of a friend in our neighborhood. Besides the usual excess of sugar-laden foods, popping balloons, brightly wrapped gifts, etc., the friend's parents had rented a pony for the afternoon to provide rides around their backyard. This turned out to be a great hit, though punctuated by some minor mishaps related to overly rambunctious riders. Meanwhile, Val and I schmoozed with the other parents.

One of these turned out to be Carl Vitale, an oncologist at the Mass General Hospital who also taught at the Harvard Medical School. I knew him casually through our children, who attended the same elementary school. After some vapid neighborhood gossip, I couldn't resist picking his brain a bit regarding immunotherapy. Of course, I disclosed nothing about my motive for being particularly interested in that topic. Carl was happy to hold forth on his area of expertise, expounding on the rapid advances being made and his group's role in some of them. Then, out of the blue, he surprised me by mentioning that he'd been one of the clinical investigators on the major Verbana trial.

Very large clinical trials typically involve many different medical centers, or "sites," in order to recruit a sufficient cohort of patients. I casually inquired about Carl's site.

"You must have been one of the main study centers," I said.

"Oh, yes, we wound up with seventy-four patients after screening out those who failed the inclusion criteria. There were thirty-seven who received Verbana and thirty-seven who got pills that contained conventional medication. Of course, we didn't know which was which. To be honest, I always feel a little funny, knowing that some patients weren't receiving what I believed would turn out to be a much superior alternative."

"Which it did," I commented. "But it must be quite gratifying to know you contributed so much to Verbana's success," I remarked.

"Yeah, I'd feel even better if I could've wangled some stock options, though." We both knew he was kidding, as that would be highly illegal.

After we walked home from the party, Sam conked out immediately. Val and I relaxed on our back porch. I read the Boston Globe, while she enjoyed the latest mystery novel by her current favorite author. For dinner, I cooked some hamburgers on the grill, nursing a light beer. Idyllic. While I was flipping the burgers, it suddenly occurred to me that I might really need Hector on this project fairly soon, and I didn't know what his availability might be. I decided to give him a call after dinner.

Now, Saturday evening might seem like an odd time to call a business associate, but Hector is also a friend and he's extremely laid back. Plus, I knew that his girlfriend, Dana, was out of town visiting her parents, so he would probably be home reading or working. Dana is slender, athletic, and fanatically health-conscious. Hector is, well, less so, his last serious exercise, when he was a soccer goalie in college, being about a decade behind him. When she is home, they tend to bicker about dietary issues, and rarely go out for lavish dining. Her temporary absence therefore offered Hector an irresistible temptation to indulge his gastronomic preferences. If he wasn't at home, he would most probably be at his favorite Brazilian restaurant.

Hector was raised in several countries and speaks four languages with varying degrees of proficiency. His father emigrated from Portugal to the States for graduate school at Purdue. There he met Hector's mother, who was a graduate student in classical languages and literature. His father became a civil engineer working for an international engineering company. When Hector was young, his family lived in South America for several years, and he became fluent in both Spanish and Portuguese. He can also get by in Italian, thanks to a year spent in Florence. Hector loves food in general, and Brazilian cuisine in particular. It was around six thirty when I got around to calling him. He picked up after a couple of rings, and I could hear the background bustle of voices, music and clattering dishes.

"Hey, Hector," I began, you're at *Feijoada*, aren't you? Sorry to bother you."

"That's okay dude," he replied. "I've only had one drink so far and I'm currently waiting for a savory repast that Dana would definitely not approve of. What's up?"

"I'll make this fast," I offered. "Are you potentially available for what might turn out to be a huge case at double your normal rate? If so, I would probably need you to start in a couple of weeks. This would have to be your top priority, so if it causes a problem I need to know, so I can make other arrangements. A simple yes or no will do for now."

"Haha," he responded, "you're joking, right?"

"Actually, I am perfectly serious. Please, just say you can do this, and further details will eventually follow when I know more myself. Then, you can enjoy your decadent feast, and I can turn on the Sox game."

"Well, I'll need to think about this. Hmm, double my rate, you say. Okay dude, for *you*, I'll make time. Oops, here comes the food. Let's talk soon. Bye."

After hanging up, I grabbed another cold beer from the fridge and settled down to watch a few innings of baseball: Yankees vs. Red Sox. The first few innings were uneventful, with a scattering of hits and no runs scored. Then, there was a very close play involving a Red Sox player sliding head-first into home and being called out. The image of this play will forever be etched on my mind, because of what happened next. My concentration on the TV screen was interrupted by the buzzing of my cell-phone. I didn't recognize the number, but picked up, wondering who would be calling at this time.

It was Hal Farenheit.

"Hi, Ken...sorry to bother you, but there's been a development." He sounded tense.

"Uh, what kind of development?" I asked, fearing that my promising new project might be having the plug pulled. This sort of one-eighty reversal was not uncommon in my experience of working with at-torneys. I was resigned.

"I'd rather you form your own opinion," he said. "I'm going to email you a link to an article that was just published online in a medical trade magazine called *ClinScan*. Are you familiar with it?"

"No, not at all. Are you?"

"Yeah, it's one of a dozen such publications we monitor, since we have so many pharma clients. This one tends to focus on issues related to clinical trials, especially when there are problems. Please take a look at the article and call me right back."

"I will."

I went over to my laptop, retrieved the email and clicked on the link. The headline was a stunner: *New Research Raises Questions about Anti-Cancer Drug*. The reporter was Alex Bleven. I recognized the name from somewhere but couldn't place it. The article was only three paragraphs long. It mentioned that Johns Hopkins researchers had recently discovered some "potential complications" regarding the effects of Verbana. Although the full implications of their findings were unclear, it was possible that the drug's benefits might be "compromised" in certain patients. The final paragraph alluded to something called the Kreutzfeld hypothesis. It was all rather vague, but certainly not good news for my new client.

After reading the article, I called Hal back, and he picked up after one ring. "What do you think?" he asked.

I paused for a few seconds to collect my thoughts. "Well, I have a lot of questions, but a couple of things jump to mind. First, who tipped the press off? Second, why did this come out now? Also, how does this affect my involvement?"

"All excellent questions, and I can't answer the first two...yet. As for the third, it's certainly going to accelerate our need to assess what we are dealing with. So, Ken, you'd better buckle up your seatbelt. Any other questions?"

"Yeah, what the hell is the Kreutzfeld hypothesis?"

# CHAPTER 4

Wednesday, August 12

"The Kreutzfeld hypothesis," began Dave Parker, is a highly controversial theory that was proposed about ten years ago by Prof. Noah Kreutzfeld of the University of Pennsylvania." He was addressing a small gathering in a conference room in the offices of Cooley & Lerner LLP the following Wednesday morning. Once again, I was in 111 Huntington, but this time on the thirty-sixth floor, in the far more sumptuously decorated suite occupied by Cooley & Lerner's Boston office. Eight expensive-looking leather chairs were arranged around a large antique burled walnut table. I gazed out through an enormous picture window at the now clearly visible Charles River, and about two dozen sailboats gliding slowly near the B.U. boathouse. "Probably students just learning the ropes," I mused.

In addition to me and Dave, Hal was there from Cooley & Lerner along with a young associate named Robert Shin, who held a Master of Public

Health degree from Johns Hopkins along with his
J.D. from Harvard. Also present were Selwyn Washington, Executive VP and General Counsel of Phire-
Break; Carolyn Cummings, the company's Medical
Director and Chief Research Scientist; and Justin
Osborne, VP and Director of Public Relations. Carolyn held an M.D. from UPenn along with a Ph.D. in
microbiology from Stanford. Justin held a Ph.D. in
psychology from Tulane and an M.B.A. from Columbia. The average IQ in the room was somewhere
north of 150. The mood was serious.

Dave continued his lecture. "When immunotherapy was first coming online, there were some skep-
tics who counseled caution. Tinkering with the immune system is obviously a tricky business. Even
simply revving up the system globally can have
undesirable consequences, such as increasing the
risk of certain auto-immune diseases, for example
rheumatoid arthritis. Therapeutic agents that can
modify an immune response in more subtle and
selective ways can have other unintended consequences. Several such adverse effects from immunotherapy have been discovered recently. These have
all been restricted to specific organs. For example,
inflammation of the pituitary gland was one of the
first such adverse effects to be identified."

He paused briefly.

"Is that what's being suggested here?" asked Carolyn, sounding incredulous.

"As far as I know," Dave responded, "Kreutzfeld
has argued that certain immunotherapeutic drugs

can cause *behavioral* problems. So, perhaps, they're alleging that Verbana may have had a neurological effect of some kind, such as increasing the risk of Parkinson's disease."

"Does that seem plausible? Could Verbana have had such an effect?" asked Hal Farenheit.

"After years of testing in dozens of clinical trials, nothing like that has ever been found. Eventually, the furor died down, and now Kreutzfeld is widely regarded as kind of a crank. But he still has some supporters."

At this point, Selwyn Washington, the ranking officer of the group, took charge. "Thanks for the briefing, Dave. Let me say a few things about why I asked you all to come here today."

Washington was fifty-three years old and exuded gravitas. In the Naval academy he had been one of the relatively few African-American midshipmen, and was a starting tailback on the Navy football team, despite carrying only 170 pounds on a wiry six-foot frame. He had gone on to a distinguished career in military intelligence, retiring from the Navy after fifteen years, having attained the rank of rear admiral, to seek his fortune in the private sector. After three years of Cornell law school he found his way into the pharma industry and rapidly climbed the corporate ladder.

"First of all, thanks for coming on such short notice. This article in *ClinScan* raises a lot of questions, but it doesn't give us much to go on. It may be a false alarm. However, it *may* be a shot across the bow, if you'll forgive my Naval metaphor. And part of my responsibility is to be fully aware of any potential threats to PhireBreak, especially to our flagship product. So here are three questions I'd like to discuss with you to begin anticipating a possible threat and, developing counter-measures, if necessary. Of course, nothing we discuss here today leaves this room."

He went to the large whiteboard and wrote the following:

Who leaked the information and why?

What exactly will be alleged by the Johns Hopkins team?

How valid is the scientific basis for these allegations?

"We need to learn as much as we can as soon as we can to answer these questions. Anybody want to comment on what we know, or suspect, and how we can find out more?"

"Before we get into that, I have a question," I piped up, before anyone else could speak. Unconsciously, I stood up and began slowly pacing back and forth. "Why am I here? All the rest of you have worked for, or along with, PhireBreak for many years. You are insiders. I seem to be the only new kid on the team. Surely, you have some very capable statisticians in senior positions within the company and connections with some renowned academics. Why isn't one of *them* here instead?"

"A fair question," replied Selwyn. "You are correct that we have all worked together for years. I know these folks well. I respect their abilities and trust them all completely. If there was someone in the company with those attributes, I would certainly consider him or her. Unfortunately, all of our senior statisticians were hired within the last two years. The market for such talent is so tight right now that it's been difficult to hold onto the best and brightest. Plus, to be frank, some of the possible candidates for this assignment are, shall we say, ... lacking in creativity. They are highly proficient at dotting all the i's and crossing the t's required by the FDA's rigid requirements, but we also need someone who can think outside the box."

I noticed some nodding of heads in agreement around the table.

"Okay, but what about academia? Haven't you worked with some very capable and creative academic statisticians?"

Selwyn interlocked his finger, reversed his hands and stretched his arms straight out ahead, while locking eyes with me. "Ah, that would present a different set of issues. You see, at this stage we're not at all sure which way the wind is blowing. Maybe we will have to confront some, ah, ...dirty laundry. Or perhaps we will need to undermine the analyses performed by other well-regarded researchers, possible even some of their own colleagues. We don't want to expose these valuable human resources yet to any of this before we know exactly how and why it may be necessary. We want someone who will be completely honest with us and ruthless in pursuit of the truth, wherever it might lead. That might be hard for these other outside experts to provide, or it might even compromise the work they're doing for us on other matters. And that's why we picked you, Dr. Wheeler. Did we choose wisely?"

This was my first encounter with Selwyn's very direct manner, and it took me aback. I searched my mind for several seconds for a suitable riposte, but came up empty. Finally, I just said: "Ruthless pursuit of the truth is what you'll get. *That*, I can promise you."

"Good," he said with a slight smile. "Now, why don't we take a fifteen-minute coffee break and then address the questions at hand."

During the break, I chatted with the others. Everyone was cordial, but with Carolyn I did sense a certain coolness. I had the impression she was not thrilled about adding an outsider to the team. Perhaps it was just that I was intruding on her turf, as the PhireBreak statistical group was included in her domain.

When we reconvened, Selwyn pointed us to the first of his three questions. "Okay, who wanted this story out and why? Any takers?"

To my surprise, it was Osborne who spoke first. I had somehow expected Hal to take the bit. The PR chief had said very little so far, but projected an air of quiet confidence as he spoke with deliberation. His relaxed manner and slight southern drawl, by way of a Louisiana upbringing I learned later, was quite disarming.

"Let me take a crack at that," he said. "There are always two general possibilities for a leak like this, what I call a push or a pull. A *pull* is driven by the media. Investigative reporters are always sniffin' around like hound dogs, tryin' to dig up some dirt. It's possible that Alex Bleven managed to connect somehow with a source involved in the Hopkins study and drew somethin' out. I've had to deal with him before, and he seems to be quite good at that," he offered, parenthetically. "Fancies himself a sort of crusader for exposin' corporate wrongdoing. That might be the best case for us, actually."

"On the other hand, this could be a *push*, meanin' that someone with an agenda is stokin' the fire. It would have to be someone with inside information. There are several possibilities. It could be the researchers themselves, tryin' to promote themselves, but that seems unlikely. It could be a competitor of ours, lookin' to throw some shade over our product to improve their own market position. But then, how did they know about the study's results? It could even be an unethical investment fund that somehow got wind of this and is tryin' to make a quick score by sellin' us short. But that could be a risky play, as market manipulation and insider trading are watched very closely these days. Finally, and perhaps most plausible, there is the plaintiff bar. Those sharks are quite organized, and well-funded, these days and like nothin' better than a potential products liability case, if that's where this could lead."

"I would tend to lean in that direction too," said Hal. "If I'm not mistaken, Bleven was the one who first broke the Velex story. Is that right, Justin?" he asked," and Osborne nodded in agreement. "We always suspected that one of the firms involved in that litigation had tipped him off. I hope to hell they're not involved here, but we have to consider that angle. After all, they have their tentacles everywhere, so news about a study like this might have surfaced and then Bleven carried the ball."

"Okay, said Selwyn," addressing Hal. I'd like you and Justin to coordinate on finding out whatever you can about this, especially the plaintiff possibility. The last thing we want is a major lawsuit. Now, what about the second question? Carolyn, you have any thoughts?"

Carolyn did not seem at all happy. "Frankly, I'm really pissed about this. Where do these Hopkins assholes come off trashing our studies? We analyzed this data eight ways from Sunday, and found no hint of a problem. Our results were verified by academic experts and the FDA's finest. If the Hopkins group had a quibble, why not come to us ahead to hash it out. I refuse to believe that there's anything wrong with our results. Verbana works just fine and will ultimately save millions of lives."

"Okay, Carolyn, no need to get defensive," said Selwyn. "I'm sure we'll get to the bottom of this, and straighten it all out. We're really not sure what we are even dealing with. Dave, what's your read?"

"Well, I've already talked about the Kreutzfeld hypothesis, which, personally, I think is a crock. But the statement regarding the effect being 'compromised' is intriguing. This could imply that the effect is weakened in some way, or perhaps that it's offset by some adverse event that was missed by everyone previously. I seriously doubt that either conclusion is correct, but at least the basic efficacy of the drug may not be in question."

"I think it might pay to ask whether our original source is willing to make some discreet inquiries," added Hal. "Perhaps she can get some clarification on this point. If not, we'll probably just have to wait until the draft manuscript is sent to us and the sixty-day clock is ticking for us to respond."

"That may be a few weeks for all we know. I hate to wait that long," said Osborne.

"Then, let's try to shake some bushes," said Selwyn, glancing toward Hal. "Okay, now for the big question, which I realize is quite premature. Could they possibly be right?"

I looked over at Carolyn and Dave, hoping one of them would tackle this first, but noticed that all eyes had suddenly turned towards me. I took a deep breath and exhaled slowly. Again, I unconsciously stood up. I decided to be as diplomatic as possible without being dishonest.

"Well, from my limited understanding so far, it seems highly unlikely that anything critical managed to slip through the various levels of internal and external expert review. However, contrary to some opinion, statisticians are human. Mistakes can be made. It's possible that something was missed, but very doubtful that whatever that might be would alter the risk-benefit trade-off materially. So one possibility is that the potential problem is real but of minor importance." I noticed Carolyn nodding, ever so slightly, to signal cautious approval.

"It's also possible that the Hopkins researchers have made a methodological error. There are many ways that I have seen a statistical analysis go awry, usually but not always inadvertently." I smiled.

"Sometimes the wrong statistical method is chosen, sometimes the right method is applied incorrectly, sometimes an error is made in the computer programming. I have even seen a case in which a clerical error in writing up the study report turned out to be the problem. All we know at this point is that their reported analyses will differ in some respect from...those in the Verbana new drug application."

It struck me at this point that I had narrowly sidestepped the trap of calling them "our analyses," a natural tendency, but important to avoid. As an outside expert, my objectivity is of paramount importance. I have witnessed a couple of disasters that occurred when an expert "went native." Their excessive zeal to help the client actually impaired their judgment and wound up backfiring.

"The first thing I will need to find out is exactly *how* they do differ. Answering that question will, no doubt, then lead to further questions about *why* they differ?"

At this point, Selwyn consulted his smartwatch and said, "I guess that's a good place to stop for now. I'd like you all to follow up on what we discussed and let's tentatively schedule the next meeting for two weeks from today, same time, same place. In the meantime, if there are important new developments, I'll keep you informed, and we may need to meet earlier."

Everyone began to head for the door, but Hal beckoned for me and Dave to come over. Would you two guys come with me to my office for a moment?" he said. We walked down the hall to Hal's office. He closed the door behind him and went to his desk, opened a side drawer and pulled out two flash drives. He handed us each one of the drives.

"Each of these contains nearly a terabyte of data pertaining to the Verbana trials. I believe they contain everything you might need and probably much more. We want you to start digging into this as quickly as possible, so you'll be ready when the draft article arrives from Hopkins. Oh, and I almost forgot," he said, "here's that letter you asked for, Ken. Please check it to make sure you're satisfied."

I took an envelope from him, and opened the letter. It was on beautifully embossed PhireBreak letterhead, and signed by the CEO herself. "This I might have to frame," I thought, but simply said: "Yep, looks good."

# CHAPTER 5

Friday, August 14

T he ensuing two days were filled with preparations for our vacation. Fortunately, most
of the shopping and packing duties were
handled by Val, who had taken some time off from
her veterinary practice. I absolutely hate such activities, and was able to use the pretext of an urgent
need to start sorting through the mountain of information contained on the flash drive.

At this stage, I was just trying to get a handle on
the contents of the drive. I figured that most of the
material could be put aside for now, and I would
download just the most relevant parts onto my
laptop. This would include the published articles
related to the main clinical trial plus any of the earl-
ier-stage trials. In addition to the published articles
that described the study results, I also downloaded
a variety of documents related to the research process.

The final published articles can be regarded as only the tip of a very large iceberg. In order to satisfy the FDA and its counterparts in other countries, a great deal of information regarding how exactly the research had been planned and implemented had to be maintained and submitted, along with the final results. The total volume of all this material could be enormous. In the days before computerization, I am told, a large truck would be needed to transport the fully documented drug application's paperwork to the FDA headquarters. Nowadays, everything can be contained in a two-ounce flash drive like the one Hal had handed me.

I was particularly interested in three kinds of documents that are produced as a matter of course in a clinical trial. First, there is, for each clinical trial, the study *protocol*. This is the master plan that is written prior to carrying out the clinical trial. Second, there is the *statistical analysis plan*, which is the even more specific and technical blueprint for analyzing the data that will result from the study. Third on my list was the *clinical study report*. This mammoth document is a comprehensive final summation of the entire study. It often runs to several hundred pages and includes much more detail about the data and the various statistical tabulations and analyses than can be squeezed into a few journal articles.

By Saturday, when we were scheduled to head for our two weeks on the Vineyard, I had pretty much accomplished my goal of downloading all the potentially relevant documents onto my laptop. Equally important, I had organized them in a way that would enable me to find what I needed quickly to answer any questions that might arise from my initial reviews of the published journal articles. Now, I was looking forward to digging into it all and, I hoped, being able to reassure PhireBreak that their studies rested on solid ground.

The plan for the vacation was that I would be left in peace during the mornings after breakfast to work. Val would keep Sam occupied outside the house, or sometimes leave him with me as long as he could keep himself busy, quietly. Then, the afternoons would be devoted to family activities, preferably outdoors on or near the ocean if the weather cooperated. Miniature golf and riding the antique carousel at Oak Bluffs were particular favorites of Sam. He was also on a mission to find the best ice cream cone on the island. That quest would require some serious research, as there were many options.

It was also understood that on Tuesday of the second week, I would return home to Newton in the afternoon, stay overnight, and attend the meeting at Cooley & Lerner the following morning. Then, I would get back to the Vineyard by Wednesday evening. This also had the advantage of enabling me to pick up some delicacies at Whole Foods and Trader Joe's. These were not obtainable on the island. One of the charming, but inconvenient, aspects of Martha's Vineyard is that no chain stores are allowed. Unfortunately, the charming old New

England ambience this regulation is intended to preserve was entirely lost on Sam. The treats from the mainland helped put a lid on his complaints.

Sam was also looking forward to spending time with his grandmother. For the past few years, Val's mother, Jean, had come out to stay with us for a few days. Fred, her father, did not especially enjoy the Vineyard, so he preferred to stay home in Connecticut to "work." We suspected that he spent more time on the golf course with his buddies while Jean was away than at his accounting firm's office. This year, we thought the middle of week two would be a good time for her visit, since Jean could be there to help out while I was "off-island" for my meeting. Also, while the area near the cottage is quite safe, I felt better about not leaving Val alone, just in case there was a problem.

By nine a.m. on Saturday, we were all packed up and ready to depart. We decided to take two cars, one of which would be left at the offsite parking lot near the ferry terminal at Woods Hole on Cape Cod. For the other, we had made a reservation on the ferry well in advance, since it was high season. When I came back on the ferry Tuesday as a walk-on, I would retrieve my car for the trip up to Newton, and Val would still have a car on the island.

Martha's Vineyard is about twenty miles long and six miles wide, and contains six towns, each with a distinct character. Chilmark is about fifteen miles from the ferry terminal at Vineyard Haven. It is in the sparsely settled "up-island" area, with many rolling meadows and wooded areas, and some fairly rugged terrain. The town center is quite small, the only place to shop for food and supplies is a general store, and there is only one restaurant. The relatively small town beach is spectacular, but we also like to frequent the much larger beaches located "down-island." For these reasons, having a car is essential for travel around the island.

Our first week of vacation worked out pretty much as planned. In the mornings I immersed myself in the virtual landscape of data and statistics, and in the afternoons in the gorgeous physical landscape all around. Val caught up on her reading, visited several local markets, both farmers' and flea, and spent much quality time with Sam. At the end of the week, she also managed to discover a couple of beautiful summer outfits at her favorite Edgartown boutique. When I gasped in mock horror at the price-tag, she reminded me that since I was about to make us rich, I had no right to complain. I smiled, but at this point I was beginning to wonder just how long and lucrative the project would be.

My impression so far, was that the research had been performed to a very high professional standard. I couldn't imagine how the Johns Hopkins team had managed to find anything major to quibble about. "Perhaps," I thought, "this tempest would be contained in the proverbial teapot." But how wrong I was.

The extent of my naivete became clear just after a lovely Sunday brunch at the iconic Black Dog Tavern, one of our favorite Vineyard Haven eateries. We were contentedly strolling over to the nearby pier to watch the eponymous canines torment the local seagulls, when my phone buzzed. "Ken, it's Hal. Hope you're enjoying your vacation. Sorry to interrupt. Can you talk?" He sounded excited.

"Okay, sure, what's up?"

"Here's the deal. We got the manuscript of the article last night. Haven't had time to digest the details, but the bottom line is that they supposedly found a statistically significant effect for, you'll never believe this, *dementia*. Carolyn tells me there's no mention of dementia in the protocol for the Verbana clinical trial. That implies they must have concocted a new endpoint to use as the outcome variable in their re-analysis. They claim that the magnitude of this purported adverse effect could offset substantially the benefits of Verbana, although more research is necessary to determine exactly how large the impact might be. They're calling for either a suspension of sales, or at least a black-box warning, at least until further research indicates it is no longer warranted."

"Wow," I said, my mental wheels turning. "Even a black-box warning on Verbana's label would potentially dampen sales considerably. Also, it might take years until this cloud could be lifted, even if the drug is ultimately exonerated. The first thing I need to do is read the article."

"Of course," said Hal, "and it should be in your inbox before we sign off. One other surprise, though, that I think you'll find intriguing."

"Yeah, what's that?"

"One of the co-authors is Noah Kreutzfeld."

"Oh!"

"Indeed. By the way, I spoke with Selwyn and the meeting on Wednesday remains as planned. It should be interesting."

"Right, see you then."

"See you then."

I must have looked a bit stunned and distracted, because Val asked whether I was all right. I filled her in on the basic situation. "I guess, you'll be even busier now," she said ruefully. "Who knew being married to a statistician could be so exciting?"

When we got back to our cottage, we decided to spend some time at the Chilmark beach, open only to town residents and guests. Coming here was bittersweet, as the beach is doomed to vanish within a decade as erosion implacably wears it away. As I gazed out at the gorgeous turquoise water being roiled by a stiff breeze, I couldn't stop thinking ahead about my next steps. First, I needed to read the article carefully and see if anything jumped out. After that, I would need to formulate a plan for unraveling exactly what the Hopkins researchers had done. That would involve attempting to recreate their analyses and, for that, I would need assistance from Hector. I decided it was time to give him a call, which I promptly did when we got back to the cottage.

Although it was mid-afternoon, He sounded

groggy. "Did I wake you?"

"No, I've been up for hours. Well, an hour, anyway. I just need one more cup of coffee to be fully conscious." Hector takes his coffee in the Brazilian style: strong, black, and in tiny espresso cups with lots of sugar. He despises the "insipid swill" that, he claims, generally passes for coffee in America. I tend to agree, but, lacking the time or patience to brew my own espresso, I've made my peace with Starbucks.

I assumed that Hector had been out until late the night before, and was gradually recovering.

"Just gulp another cup down," I said, "I need your full attention."

"Why, what's happening? Something on that new case you mentioned?"

"Yes, it looks like we may have to swing into action soon. I need you to help me dig into the data underlying a big clinical trial. I have a meeting Wednesday morning, by which time I hope to know a lot more. I'm coming back Tuesday afternoon from the Vineyard, and I'd like to meet you for dinner that night. I could give you some more details, and you can help me get ready for the meeting. Will that work?"

"Sure, where do you want to meet?"

"How about the Thai restaurant in Wellesley where we've been to before, say around seven?"

"Sure, see you there."

"Yeah, see you. Bye"

Over the next two days, I dug into the draft

article. On the surface it seemed quite rigorous, though the motivating theory was highly speculative. This theory implied that Verbana was likely to increase the frequency of a new syndrome characterized by a rapid mental decline similar to Alzheimer's. They even gave this new condition a catchy name: hyper-immune dementia, or HID. This was a particularly unfortunate acronym as it brought to mind both AIDS and HIV.

The Kreutzfeld hypothesis provided the biological rationale supporting this conjectural HID. Supposedly, Verbana can affect the lymphocytes, the white blood cells that are involved in an immune response. The result is a possible increase in the level of inflammation in the brain. The details of this argument involve various complex biochemical processes that to me were completely incomprehensible. My limited knowledge of biochemistry was derived from a single college course taken two decades ago. Dealing with the relevant current science was the province of Dave Parker and his associates. My job was to focus on the data and statistical analyses. I drew up a list of questions about how and why certain methodological decisions had been made and whether the statistical analyses were appropriate. But at this stage I had no clue about whether the findings were trustworthy. Only one thing was certain. PhireBreak was sitting on a keg of dynamite that had better be defused, and soon.

# CHAPTER 6

Tuesday, August 25

Around two p.m. on Tuesday, Valerie dropped me at the ferry terminal. A half-hour later I boarded the ferry and found a seat outside on the top deck. It was a beautiful day, and I enjoyed the forty-minute trip over to Woods Hole. From there it was a twenty-minute walk to pick up my car, and I reached Newton in another ninety minutes. After parking my eight-year old BMW in the driveway, I picked up the weekly Newton Chronicle, entered the house and looked around. Everything was just as we had left it, meaning immaculate, as if ready to be shown by a realtor. That was Val. If a burglar had come in to rob us and saw that the place was a mess, she would be more concerned about the latter than the former. Actually, I genuinely appreciated her obsessive tidiness, which compensated for my own slovenliness.

I still had three hours until I was scheduled to

meet Hector in Wellesley, about a half hour away. I was about to plop down in my favorite chair with the newspaper, when the doorbell rang. Slightly annoyed, I went to the door and beheld a diminutive man in his seventies holding a large cloth shopping bag. It took me a few seconds to recognize our neighbor, Joe Silverman, who had apparently decided to let his beard grow since I'd seen him last. I'd forgotten that he had volunteered to take in the mail while we were away.

"Hi, Ken" he said. "I saw your car pull in. Here's the mail. I threw out the fliers and some obvious junk mail, like Valerie asked me to. This is the rest of it."

"Thanks, Joe," I said.

"No problem," he responded. "Are you all back?"

"No, Joe, just me. I had some business to attend to, but plan to go back tomorrow night. Then, we'll all be back on Saturday. Did we miss anything exciting while we've been gone?"

I asked, just to be neighborly. I knew that Joe, who was retired, kept a close eye on local happenings and loved to gossip about them.

"Well, not really, though I did hear from Cathy that the Morrises are putting their house on the market soon." Cathy, Joe's wife, was a realtor.

"Really," I replied, feigning a modicum of interest in this prosaic development. In fact, I barely knew the Morris family, who lived several doors down from us. Is Cathy going to get the listing?" I asked, attempting to be sociable.

"Yeah, I think so. Apparently, Sid's being transferred to an office in New Hampshire."

"Oh," I said. "Well thanks again, Joe. Say hi to Cathy."

Joe hesitated for a second, no doubt hoping to prolong the conversation, but then just said "Will do," as he smiled, and started to walk away.

As I was about to sit down once again, my phone rang. It was Val, and she sounded upset.

"Hi, dear," she began, "everything is okay, but we had a bit of excitement here."

"What kind of excitement are you talking about?"

"I'm still a bit rattled," she continued, "but wanted you to know that Sam is fine and there's nothing to worry about." Now, I was really starting to get worried.

"Okay, just calm down and tell me what happened."

"Well, after I dropped you off, I decided to do a little shopping. I was actually in a shop on the wharf trying on a sweatshirt when my mom called. She was frantic. It seems that an hour before, Sam had been accidentally locked in the bathroom. The lock must have jammed somehow. He couldn't get out and started shouting for her to open the door, which she couldn't do. She started to panic. She tried to call me, but I was in a dead zone and didn't get the call. You know how spotty the phone service can be, especially near the water. Then, she decided to call 9-1-1, but couldn't remember the address for the cottage. Fortunately, Sam suggested that the police could probably locate her phone, so she made the call. Then Sam actually helped calm her down. He really is amazing."

"Yes, he takes after you," I said. "Cool under fire."

"Anyway, by the time I got back, there were flashing lights everywhere and several neighbors milling about. They removed the jammed lock and rescued him. He was quite delighted with all the attention and telling everyone in sight about the adventure. My mother was not nearly so happy. Anyway, we will be the talk of the town for a while, I guess. Oh, and we'll have to find a locksmith."

"Gee, sorry I missed all the fun," I said. "Seriously, I'm sure you're a wreck. I think you deserve a couple of glasses of that pinot grigio we picked up yesterday. Try to unwind a bit, okay?"

"Good idea, and how was your day?"

"Much less eventful," I replied. "Joe Silverman dropped off the mail, and the Morrises are moving. I'm heading off to the Thai restaurant in Wellesley shortly to meet with Hector."

"Sounds good. Say hi."

"Will do. Love you."

"Love you, too."

After that, I took a shower and put on fresh clothes. Then, it was time to leave for Wellesley. The Town of Wellesley is best known for the eponymous college in its midst. The college was founded in 1870, eleven years before the town itself broke away from the adjoining Town of Needham.

Wellesley is an extremely upscale suburb of Boston, home to about 28,000 predominantly well-heeled professionals and their families. The majority of these vacate the town for much of August, relocating to such exclusive enclaves as Nantucket, Martha's Vineyard, the Berkshires or assorted islands along the Maine coast. Wellesley Square, where I was heading, borders on the beautiful Wellesley College campus, and contains many trendy shops and restaurants. It is usually a bustling place in the early evening, except in August, when it has the aura of a ghost town. For me, it's the absolute best time to go there, because parking is easy and those merchants who do remain open are so appreciative.

When I arrived, I found a parking spot right in front of my destination. Such good fortune would have been impossible at any other time of year. I entered the restaurant and was shown to a table by the window. I glanced at the handful of other patrons, mostly young females, probably around for freshman orientation. One young man was sitting with a middle-aged couple I took to be his parents. After a century and a half, Wellesley College had finally begun to admit male students.

I ordered a Thai beer while waiting for Hector to arrive. A few minutes later he came in and quickly located my table. I noticed he had put on a few more pounds since I had last seen him a couple of months before, and I had to bite my tongue not to nag him about it.

"Hi, Hector. Good to see you. Everything going

well?"

"Yeah, fine. You look good. Having a relaxing vacation?"

We chatted for a while about our respective situations, and I was sorry to learn that he and Dana were temporarily separated. As this had happened twice before, I wasn't overly concerned. Then, we ordered our dinners, pineapple fried rice for me and a chicken curry for Hector. We also ordered a couple of appetizers and a beer for him. Then, we got down to business.

"Let me tell you about this project," I began. "A couple of weeks ago, as you know, I was contacted by Dave Parker, who set up a meeting with an attorney whose firm represents PhireBreak. Have you heard of them?"

"Not really."

"Apparently, they got FDA approval recently for a spectacular new anti-cancer drug, Verbana. This was based mainly on a large clinical trial. The remission rates for Verbana were much higher than for the comparator treatment, and the all-cause mortality much lower. But now there is a potential fly in the ointment. A group at Johns Hopkins obtained the data based on a Data Transparency Act request and has, apparently, conducted their own re-analysis. They are planning to submit their findings in an article in *The Lancet*, but the DTA statute requires them to give PhireBreak sixty days to review the draft article before submitting to the journal. That would be sixty days from the time they sent PhireBreak a draft version of the article, which was two days ago. Now, PhireBreak can write its own response and also try to persuade the authors of the article to make some changes."

"Wait a minute, are you telling me this re-analysis says the drug doesn't work as well as they think?"

"That's a good question, but let's skip what they found for a second. What's most important is that the clock is now ticking. During the next fifty-eight days, we need to be providing our best guidance on exactly what the Hopkins folks have done, whether it is valid, and what are the potential implications."

Hector paused to process this, took a few bites, and asked: "So what will happen after the sixty days are up?"

"Ah, that's not really clear, at least to me. I have a meeting tomorrow with the lawyers and some executives of PhireBreak that should shed some light on that. It seems to me there are a number of possibilities. Of course, a lot will depend on what we find out. Ideally, we will discover that the Hopkins analysis is demonstrably wrong. That would be best. Or, we might find that the problem is real but not so serious, or that their whole analysis, while technically accurate, is not plausible. For example, they may have cherry-picked the data. You and I have seen that tactic several times in the past. That brings me to your question about what they may have found."

"The suspense is killing me."

I proceeded to explain about Kreutzfeld's hypothesis and the hyper-immune dementia syndrome. I told him that Dave Parker was highly skeptical and would be scrutinizing the scientific literature to attack the theory itself. Even if the hypothesis had some merit, it would not necessarily justify the way they created the outcome variable. We hashed over the potential ramifications of these considerations for a few minutes. Then, a troubling idea occurred to me.

"You know, Hector, this case is different from the other ones we've been involved in. In those, the defendants were trying to neutralize a plaintiff argument about a product's defects. Therefore, the legal burden of proof by a preponderance of evidence was on the plaintiff. But here, anything but a clear win would still be problematic, maybe even catastrophic, for PhireBreak. In fact, the article is calling for a black-box warning, or even a suspension of sales, until a final determination can be made. The financial impact on the company would be devastating."

"That *is* a sobering thought," said Hector, as he motioned to the waiter for another beer. Speaking of which, you seem pretty wound up. Maybe you could use another beer...or two."

"Seriously," I said, "this could be a lot of pressure."

"Guess that's why they're paying us the big bucks," he replied. "You did say double rates, eh?"

We chatted for a while longer about various technical issues that might arise, and agreed to meet again soon after I got back from the Vineyard. As we walked out into the warm summer night, I handed him a copy I had made of the flash drive I'd received from Hal Farenheit. I told him to begin familiarizing himself with the data underlying the clinical trials, and I would be sending him some specific questions about the data over the next few days. He headed back to his apartment in Arlington and I to my house in Newton.

As I pulled into the driveway, I happened to notice a dark SUV parked a few houses down and across the street. This was certainly not unusual, and would not have caught my attention if not for the license plate. As a numbers guy, I am especially sensitive to numerical patterns. Numbers and mathematical relationships have always had enormous salience for me, for as long as I can remember. My parents used to say that this proclivity was evident even when I was a young child. Supposedly, as a precocious four-year old, I had learned basic arithmetic and would often arrange my blocks or Lego pieces into complicated groupings based on numerical patterns. They were not surprised when I majored in math at Columbia and later attained a Ph.D. in mathematical statistics at Harvard.

The license number was FX3456. The four consecutive digit sequence was unusual, but how unusual? Specifically, what was the probability that four integers between zero and nine would be in sequence? I did a quick calculation. I assumed that zeros were allowed, though I wasn't sure if that was true. Then, every possible sequence of four digits would correspond to a number between zero and 9,999. There were 10,000 possible such numbers. Of these, only seven would be in sequence: 0123, 1234, 2345, 3456, 4567, 5678 and 6789. Therefore, the probability was seven chances out of ten thousand. If zeros were omitted, I mentally calculated that there would be 6,561 possibilities, of which six would be sequential, still less than one in a thousand. This would be unusual, but not exceedingly rare. I shrugged, and as I had many times before, wondered why I felt compelled to engage in such useless mental exercises.

It had been a long day, and I was exhausted. Entering the house, I went straight to our bedroom. Of course, the bed was perfectly made up, since Val would have been appalled to leave it otherwise, and I changed quickly, brushed my teeth and crawled in. Seconds later I was sound asleep.

# CHAPTER 7

I awoke around seven, got dressed, and tidied up the best I could. My plan was to stop for breakfast at Lina's Café. Located on a narrow side street off the main drag in Newton Centre, Lina's is an unpretentious hole-in-the-wall that makes the best crepes in Massachusetts and pretty darn good coffee as well. Lina herself, who's almost always stationed behind the counter, radiates warmth but isn't shy about expressing some pointed social and political commentary in her charming French accent.

Around eight, I set off for the mile-long walk to Lina's. I ordered my usual, two plain crepes with raspberry jam on the side, filled a large porcelain cup with dark roast at the nearby coffee urn, and sat down at one of the handful of tables. A few minutes later my name was called, so I picked up the plate of crepes and carried it back to my table. As I ate, my thoughts turned to the meeting ahead. I wondered how much more had been learned by the other participants. I recalled Selwyn Washington's three questions:

> Who leaked the information to *ClinScan* and why?
>
> What exactly will be alleged in the Johns Hopkins article?
>
> How valid is the scientific basis for these allegations?

As for the first, academic glory, or in Kreutzfeld's case redemption, would be a strong motivator, but beyond that, I wondered what more might be behind the effort. The second question had been largely answered by the draft article. We now knew what was being alleged, that Verbana can cause an Alzheimer-like form of dementia that they had dubbed HID. The third question, though, we knew virtually nothing about. Was the Hopkins analysis scientifically and statistically correct? That's the big one that Hector and I, in conjunction with Dave's crew, needed to answer. I knew that a lot was riding on what we were able to find, and at that moment I felt far from confident that the answer would turn out to be music to our client's ears.

As I rose from the table to leave, I realized that Lina was eyeing me quizzically. "You look very serious today," she said. "Something must be weighing on you."

"Well, yes, actually," I replied, "but thankfully it's just business."

*Just business, indeed, but maybe some pretty serious business.*

It was a short walk from the café to the T station in Newton Centre. A half hour later I arrived at 111 Huntington and went up to the offices of Cooley & Lerner. Passing the reception desk, I walked to the end of a long hallway lined with offices, turned left down another hall, and arrived at the conference room. As I entered, I became aware of multiple animated conversations taking place. One of these caught my attention immediately, because it involved a new face, and a rather attractive one at that. Hal and Robert Shin were listening to a smartly dressed blonde woman of medium height and weight, appearing to be roughly forty years of age. She was gesticulating vigorously to make a point. Right then, a dark-haired, rather petite, woman who appeared to be in her early thirties entered, went up to Robert, got his attention, and handed him a document. He glanced at it, nodded, and then walked out with her. Meanwhile, I went over to Hal, who introduced me to Barbara (Bobbie) Stanton.

"Bobbie is the source of our original tipoff, before the *ClinScan* article came out," he said.

"Aha, our secret agent," I said. She smiled.

At that moment, Selwyn arrived and immediately took charge. We all took our seats around the huge conference table, and he began by introducing Bobbie.

"For those of you who haven't met her before,

Bobbie teaches at the Harvard School of Public Health and is probably the smartest epidemiologist we've ever worked with. Recently she was kind enough to alert us to the Hopkins study before the *ClinScan* article came out, based on a serendipitous conversation with a colleague at a scientific conference. Now, I understand, she may be able to fill in some blanks regarding question one," he said, pointing to the three questions, which were still displayed on the whiteboard. "Bobbie?"

"Thanks, Selwyn, "I'm not really sure how much this will help, but here's what I've learned. After the article came out, I called my original contact, Gilbert Stein, a biostatistician who is on the Hopkins team. I told him I had seen the article and was curious to find out a bit more. This time, he was much more guarded...and, of course, completely sober."

This earned a few chuckles.

"Anyway, he confided that he was taken by surprise and had no idea who provided the information to Alex Bleven. I casually mentioned my surprise at the involvement of Noah Kreutzfeld. I told Gil that I thought the so-called Kreutzfeld hypothesis was no longer being seriously entertained. At that, he admitted that he was a little concerned about Kreutzfeld's participation. He explained that the study was being funded by something called the Mannheim Foundation to the tune of almost a million dollars. This foundation had previously funded some of Kreutzfeld's research and suggested bringing him in.

"Well," said Hal. "for a million bucks, I guess their 'suggestions' were generally heeded."

"True. However, as Gil was at pains to reassure me, the Hopkins dean who reviewed the funding arrangement required a stipulation that Kreutzfeld would have no direct role in the data analysis. He would serve only as a consultant with respect to the theoretical rationale for the study design. Gil was, I think, somewhat defensive, because he understands that Kreutzfeld is so controversial. He insisted that everything about the study is completely kosher. 'The numbers will speak for themselves' he told me."

"Not to be cynical," I said, "but in my experience, the numbers rarely speak *entirely* for themselves, especially when money or academic reputations are at stake. There are often choices that can sway the analyses one way or another, which is why the fine details can by important."

"Amen," said Hal. "That's not cynicism, just experience."

Selwyn who had looked thoughtful throughout Bobbie's exposition, commented, "We can understand why Kreutzfeld has a strong motive to get these results out. He's anxious to be vindicated and resurrect his professional reputation. But I'm not sure he would jump the gun by leaking to Alex Bleven. I suspect there may be more to this than that. What do we know about this Mannheim Foundation?"

The question was met by silence. Before anything

else was said, Robert Shin entered the room and took his seat. As he did so, he announced, "Sorry I had to duck out, but I had to deal with an unrelated crisis."

"Right," said Selwyn, and then turned toward Hal. "Before we move on to the next question, I'd like you to find whatever you can about this Mannheim Foundation. Who are they and why the sudden interest in Verbana? All right, so what about the second question? We've all read the draft article. My understanding is that their study produced evidence that appears to implicate Verbana as a risk factor for some kind of quasi-Alzheimer condition. They call it hyper-immune dementia, or HID. So, setting aside the clinical trial data, is that even plausible from a biomedical perspective, or is it so farfetched that the scientific community will laugh it out of court?"

Carolyn Cummings spoke up first, and she was visibly upset. "Selwyn, I've had several of my staff looking into this. We remain very skeptical about the biological rationale put forward in the article. This is like trial by innuendo. There's not enough detail in the article itself to know how this early dementia was actually being measured. We will need to obtain a lot more information from the Hopkins researchers on that aspect of the study. As far as I know, we didn't collect any data that would relate to dementia. So what endpoint are they studying to determine whether any mental decline has occurred? It all sounds pretty fishy to me."

At this point, I chimed in.

"It's even conceivable that their endpoint is artificial and designed, deliberately or inadvertently, to produce a significant result. In fact, they may have created more than one endpoint variable and then cherry-picked the one that seemed to show a problem. I think we should demand to have not only their endpoint definition, but also their analytic dataset and the computer code that generated the results. That's the only way to be certain what's really going on."

Julian Osborne added his concern that even if the entire analysis turned out to be bogus, the potential public relations headache could be disastrous. "Once the mainstream press gets ahold of this, it will be hard to put the genie back in the bottle. We can't afford a long PR struggle on the science that plays out in public. Is there some way to nip this in the bud? If they are wrong, we need to stamp this out quickly. If, worst case, they have a point, we may be able to show it's not serious. I guess what I'm saying is that we don't have much time to get control of this situation."

"Let's not panic," said Selwyn. "Now, what about the statistical aspect? Have you had a chance yet, Ken, to form any opinions?"

"Not really," I responded, "on its face the choice of statistical analyses seems reasonable and there are no obvious anomalies in the results. But, as I just said, we really need to see the data and the computer code. The devil is almost always in the details. Although I wouldn't suspect deliberate fraud, I agree with Carolyn that unconscious bias can creep into an analysis. I wish I could say more, but until Hector and I delve into the data, that's not possible."

"When do you think you'll know more?" asked Selwyn.

"I would hope within the next week or so, but the more comprehensive and detailed the information we can receive from Hopkins, the better for us. In my experience, statistical flaws are often buried deeply in the weeds."

"Let me say something about that," offered Hal. "Robert has been reviewing the Data Transparency Act statute and some of the case law around it. There is a provision that covers our right to obtain data in a situation like this. We're entitled to whatever data and calculations they relied on to reach conclusions. I think Ken should help me and Robert to draft a document request specifying exactly what we need. We need quick action on this and are preparing to go to court, if necessary, to assure rapid compliance."

"What about Julian's concerns about negative publicity, Hal?" asked Selwyn. "What legal recourse do we have to keep this under wraps?"

"I believe we can get an injunction. Let me turn that over to Bob Shin."

"The good news is that the statute lays out a procedure for obtaining an injunction in connection with the release of information during the sixty-day review period," he began. "That would gain us breathing room to prove the Hopkins findings are wrong...assuming they *are*. The bad news is that there is no case law because such an injunction has never previously been sought. So it's not clear exactly what relief we can obtain. However, we can argue that premature release of negative information that hasn't been fully vetted could cause us irrevocable harm. I think this would be persuasive. I should add that a judge would also have the discretion to extend the review period beyond the sixty-day period in certain situations, but I wouldn't count on that."

"Thanks, Bob," said Hal. "I recommend that we should push hard to get Ken the data he needs and to prevent any further information from leaking out. And there's something else in the statute that may prove helpful. We can petition the FDA to appoint a review panel to independently evaluate the Hopkins study, and render an opinion on any regulatory actions that may be warranted. This would be a high risk, but potentially very high reward, option. The possible advantage for us would be to get this all disposed of quickly, before it blows up in public, since the judge would undoubtedly defer to the FDA. The risk, of course, is that if the FDA review does find a problem, that could just add fuel to the fire."

When he finished, Hal looked directly at Selwyn, as if seeking guidance.

Selwyn pursed his lips and steepled his fingers for

about ten seconds before responding.

"I like the idea of having a resolution with one roll of the dice, but we'd need to be sure we can prevail at the FDA. Ultimately, the decision would be up to Cheryl Wellstone, in consultation with the Board of Directors. I'd like to have more information before I bring this up with her."

"The key," said Hal, locking eyes with me, "is to determine whether or not their conclusion holds any water. My job is to be sure Ken is provided with all the data he needs to make that determination, and quickly. Tell me exactly what you need, Ken, and I'll move whatever mountains we need to. Robert can start drafting a document request for the Hopkins group tomorrow. Could you come in here on Monday to help us polish the final version?"

"Sure," I replied, "in a confident tone that belied the queasiness in my gut. Things were moving fast, and I was in the eye of the storm.

"How about two o'clock on Monday then?"

"Sounds good."

As the meeting wrapped up, with a follow-up scheduled in two weeks, Selwyn nabbed me before I could escape. "Could you possibly drop by my office around eleven on Monday for a quick chat?" he asked.

I was completely nonplussed by this unexpected overture. I simply said, "Of course."

"Excellent, see you then."

"Yeah, okay, see you then."

# CHAPTER 8

Wednesday, August 26

My trip back to the Vineyard was uneventful. Val and Sam met me at the dock as I disembarked from the ferry in Vineyard Haven. The sky was grey and darkening, and rain seemed imminent. Val had lots of questions, and Sam was lobbying for a stop at The Big Scoop, his current favorite for ice cream. The proprietor is a retired newspaper man who sports a huge handlebar mustache. The place looks like an old-fashioned soda fountain, complete with a marble counter, rotating stools, and ceiling fans. The walls are covered with copies of old newspaper front pages from important dates in history. It was only a short distance from the ferry terminal, so we headed that way. We arrived just ahead of a heavy downpour. After obtaining our oversized (and overpriced) ice cream cones, we sat at a table to eat while waiting out the rain shower.

"So how was your meeting?" asked Val. "Do you think this will turn out to be a short or long haul?" I wasn't sure if she was hoping it would be short, so our lives wouldn't be disrupted, or long enough to materially impact our financial situation.

"I'm still not sure. If it's short, that will probably mean I'm a hero, but not much richer. If it's long, that means more money but also lots more stress. If only I could have both the adulation and the money, but it doesn't seem to work out that way."

"Oh, I'm sure they will appreciate all your hard work however things turn out," she said.

"In a better world that would be the case, but here on Planet Earth I'm afraid only results really matter."

"You've become quite the philosopher lately. I think you'd better stick to statistics."

"You're probably right. Anyway, the rain has stopped, so let's move on."

At that moment, Sam took the last bite of his cone and said, "Hey, can we *please* go to the carousel now?"

Since we expected more rain off and on, fore-closing outdoor activities, that seemed like a good suggestion. We drove over to Oak Bluffs, and spent some time at the ornately decorated Victorian-era carousel there that Val loved. We mostly looked on as Sam whirled around several times. Finally, we managed to drag him away, amid vociferous complaints that he just needed one more ride to grab the elusive brass ring. The remainder of that day was spent quietly at the cottage.

The next morning, I awoke around five thirty. It was still dark, but my thoughts were racing. As often happens when I am working on a complex problem, my unconscious mind had been diligently at work while my body was in repose. When it could contain itself no more, my mind would break through to let me know what was on it. In this case, it was fixated on a particular question. What variable, exactly, was being used by the Hopkins researchers to assess the alleged Kreutzfeld dementia? My intuition was that this variable might be the key to everything. Since I couldn't fall back to sleep, I decided to throw on some clothes and take a stroll down to the beach. Maybe that would settle my nerves, and I would experience an epiphany along the way.

As I set out along the unpaved road that led toward the bay, I vaguely recalled that the article mentioned a particular predictive test that had recently been developed, though I could not recall its name. Supposedly, this new method could indicate with high accuracy whether an individual was in the very early stages of mental decline, before any clinical signs had manifested themselves. I was skeptical.

Perhaps this instrument might be unreliable, so the statistical results were not truly valid. I determined to read the Hopkins article's discussion of this aspect more carefully when I returned to the cottage. I would also ask Hector to track down the relevant data in the clinical trial.

When I got back, Val was sitting at the kitchen table sipping tea. "Would you like some?" she asked. Ordinarily, I start the day with coffee, but feeling too lazy to brew a cup just then, I accepted her offer. "When I realized you'd gone out," she said, "I couldn't sleep anymore and got up. I assume you were wrestling with some vexing statistical conundrum."

"Sort of," I responded. I wanted to tell her more, but we both knew I had to be careful. We had been down this road before. "What I can say is that the pharma company I'm working with is facing a potential problem related to one of its products. A big problem. It has to do with a re-analysis of some clinical-trial data. They're worried about the results."

"And they want you to prove that this re-analysis is wrong, right? But, you're not sure whether it is or not."

"Yes, frankly I'm worried that this new study might be right, or right *enough* to cause trouble. On the other hand, my gut is saying that something is off here. If that's true, I need to smoke it out."

"I'm sure if anyone can do it, you can."

I wasn't so sure. Anyway, it wasn't long before Sam woke up, and we had breakfast. Then, Val took him down to the beach, allowing me to work for a while. I settled down with my laptop at the picnic table on our screened porch. I began by re-reading the draft article. When I came to the section about data collected, I discovered that the study endpoint was something called the Caldwell Index. This was described as an algorithm for predicting future dementia that was developed in 2024 and commercialized recently by Caldwell Analytics LLC.

According to the article, the Caldwell Index produced a *probability* of progressing to full-blown dementia within three to five years. Their endpoint was actually a *proxy* variable for dementia itself. This probability was *alleged* to be highly accurate, but I knew that such assertions were often questionable when the statistical analyses were examined closely. To bolster their research, the Johns Hopkins researchers had included several citations to recently published journal articles. I fired off an email to Hal requesting copies of these and, for good measure, to all the other publications referenced in the article.

By this time, it was late enough to call Hector at what he would consider a civilized hour. I had found that Hector-time generally ran at least two hours behind my own. When I called, he picked up after three rings

"Hello, Ken. What's up? How did your meeting go?"

"It went fine, Hector. I learned a little more about the context of this whole situation, but nothing that really impacts our task. However, I'm feeling more time pressure to get to the bottom of this re-analysis in a hurry. PhireBreak is getting nervous and wants to keep this under control, but needs to know more."

"Okay, so what do we do next?"

"First, I'm about to email you a copy of the draft article we received from the Hopkins group. I'd like you to focus on the various tables that contain statistical information. Some of these are purely descriptive, the usual stuff such as the demographic summaries of the treatment groups and the frequencies of various adverse effects. A couple of tables, though, along with a graph, relate to the main statistical tests they performed. For starters, I'd just like you to try reproducing their results by analyzing PhireBreak's own data. Let's make sure our findings agree completely with theirs."

"Second, I committed to helping them put together a document request, so we can get everything we need from Hopkins. That would include the data and the code that was used to generate the analytical results. After reviewing the article, please send me a detailed list of everything you can think of. I'd like to have that by tomorrow afternoon, so I can get the lawyers started on drafting that. I'm supposed to be meeting with them on Monday afternoon."

"Finally, see if you can find anything in the Phire-Break data pertaining to something called the 'Caldwell Index' please. That's the main endpoint, the variable that supposedly indicates whether dementia has occurred. Actually, though, it's not a direct measure of dementia, but a *probability* of displaying clinically evident dementia in the future."

"Yeah, that does sound a bit fishy, doesn't it?

Wouldn't it be more reliable to measure the dementia directly?"

"I agree, but full-blown dementia might take years to develop, so I guess this was a clever way to avoid that...inconvenience."

"Right. Maybe a bit *too* clever."

"We'll see. Anyway, if you come across any computer code or output that refers to this Caldwell Index, possibly even as a side comment instead of the code itself, I'd like to see that. Okay?"

"Sure, I'll start checking this afternoon and email anything I find, and I'll get you the other stuff by tomorrow."

"Great, let's talk tomorrow."

"Okay, bye."

Later that afternoon, I received an email from Hector informing me that he could find no reference whatsoever to the Caldwell Index or any close variant of the term. That didn't really surprise me, since Carolyn had indicated that dementia wasn't really on their radar when the trial was being conducted. However, it raised a perplexing question: how could the Caldwell Index have been utilized in the re-analysis when it was *not* part of the Phire-Break database?

I thought that relying on a recently developed proxy measure of probable future dementia was highly questionable. I definitely needed to find out more about the Caldwell Index. Obtaining copies of the articles referenced in the Hopkins paper would be a good start.

Throughout the next couple of days, I had limited time to work, but I did manage to become something of an expert on the Caldwell Index and its purported relationship to dementia. And, I understood how it was created for the Hopkins analysis, despite being absent from the PhireBreak database.

# CHAPTER 9

Monday, August 31

**M**onday morning dawned unseasonably cool and cloudy with a 30% chance of rain according to Weather.com. As a statistician, I find such information to be infuriatingly ambiguous. Did this mean a 30% probability of at least some rain during the day, or that it would be raining for 30% of the time during the day, or in 30% of the Boston area? Also, would a light drizzle count, or does "rain" have to meet some official standard, like at least a quarter inch per hour?

I once went so far as to research this issue online. What I found was incredibly unhelpful. It turns out that meteorologists have devised something called the PoP, probability of precipitation. The PoP combines all three aspects of the problem: the likelihood of some rain, a minimum amount of rain, and the extent of an area receiving rain. So you're guaranteed to be confused, but you'll be in good company, since even many meteorologists are too. My advice, as a professional statistician, is to treat anything other than zero or one hundred percent as "possible rain" and act accordingly, depending on how risk-averse you happen to be.

I realize that this ambiguity of the PoP does not trouble the vast majority of ordinary humans, but it does bear on certain practical everyday decisions. As I dressed that morning, I was faced with one of these. What to wear? Should I start out with a rain-proof jacket or carry an umbrella, don a suit or go business casual, how about a hat, etc.?

While I was pondering these weighty matters, Val offered some sage advice. "You're always complaining about choosing the wrong thing to wear when you go to meetings. You're either too casually attired or not formal enough. Why don't you hedge your bets?"

"What do you mean?"

"What about wearing your nicely pressed khakis with a sport shirt and blazer. That should be good enough if they're in suits, which is rare these days, especially in summer. However, if everyone is more causal, you can just lose the jacket."

"Great idea. Why didn't I come up with that?" She rolled her eyes and smiled mirthlessly as she left to check on Sam. A half hour later, I was ready to head out for my meetings, attired as Val had proposed. With last-minute preparations, I hadn't had time for breakfast. So I stopped in at Lina's to grab a coffee and croissant to take with me on the commuter train into Boston.

"Still stressed?" Lina inquired.

"How can you tell?" I replied.

"It's my gift. Maybe you should consider a less stressful line of work. You know, I was studying for a law degree in Lyon when I realized that baking is my real passion. Now, I still empathize with the overworked and underpaid, but I'm glad to be out of the mouse race." I just smiled. She hated when someone corrected her occasional idiomatic miscues.

"It's a lot easier dealing with nice customers like you than with nasty lawyers and difficult clients," she continued.

"Yeah, but you have to get in here at 5 a.m. to make the croissants."

"*Touché, mon ami.*"

I tipped an imaginary hat as I departed for the nearby T station.

To reach Kendall Square, I would need to take the Green Line train to Park Sreet, a hub in downtown Boston, then switch to the Red Line, going toward Cambridge. Boston's archaic subway system is the Massachusetts Bay Transit Authority, or MBTA, or just the "T" to locals. It was immortalized by the Kingston Trio's 1959 rendition of an old campaign song about a man named Charlie who got lost forever while riding on it. It remains a confusing patchwork of several inter-connected and color-coded rail and trolley lines, running partly above and partly below ground. It's old, noisy, dirty, crowded and uncomfortable, though with a few important concessions to modernity, such as, thankfully, air-conditioning. Someday, when the city has a few billion extra dollars to spare, it will be properly re-built. Then, many older Bostonians will undoubt-edly complain bitterly about the lost charm of the old T. I will not be among them.

But I digress. When I emerged from the under-ground station in Kendall Square that day, the sky was clearing somewhat and now the chance of rain was down to only 10%, whatever that might mean. Anyway, there's a saying among New Englanders that if you don't like the weather, just wait a few minutes.

I made my way to the PhireBreak building, pre-sented my driver's license at the security desk, and took the elevator to the top floor. Stepping off, I found myself confronted by a large glass door. The receptionist was doing her best not to notice me, so I knocked politely, and she finally buzzed me in.

"Dr. Wheeler?" she said.

"Yes, I'm here for an eleven o'clock meeting with Selwyn Washington."

"Yes, I'm sorry he's a bit delayed, but he *is* expect-ing you. Can I offer you something to drink...coffee, or water?"

"No thanks," I replied, sitting down at an oval glass coffee table covered with various newspapers and several pharmaceutical trade publications. I grabbed the Wall Street Journal, but found it hard to concentrate on the latest economic or political news. I was a bit nervous, wondering why exactly

I was there. Fifteen minutes later, the receptionist motioned me to follow her back to Selwyn's office. As I entered, my confusion must have been obvious to Selwyn. I instantly realized the absurdity of my earlier sartorial concerns.

"You're probably surprised at my getup," he said, chuckling. He was sporting a lemon- yellow monogrammed golf shirt and coordinated plaid slacks with glistening white tasseled golf shoes. He pointed to the corner, at an expensive-looking golf bag and full set of clubs. The incongruity of the scene relative to my previous impressions of him added to my sense of disorientation about this meeting. "I'm heading off to an annual charity golf event at the Scottish Arms Club right after our meeting," he explained.

"Oh, that makes sense. Are you an avid golfer?"

"Not really, it's more about business and politics than sport at this point. I used to play much more competitively, but now my handicap has ballooned to a six."

My surprise must have been obvious, as he casually mentioned this. A handicap that low would have made him the envy of most amateur golfers I knew. I wondered how good he had been when he took the game seriously. He must have read my mind.

"In my twenties, I was a scratch golfer. I even considered attempting to turn pro," he volunteered. "I almost left the Navy to pursue that dream. Nowadays, between business and charitable interests, I have little time for sports...or real interest, to be frank." He had a pensive demeanor, and for the first time I perceived in his eyes something wistful, quite at odds with his usual composure. Then, he surprised me.

"Do you want to know why I feel so strongly about protecting this company?" he asked.

"Of course, although I imagine there are billions of obvious reasons," I quipped and immediately felt that this feeble attempt at wit had stuck the wrong chord. Fortunately, he seemed not to notice.

"Five years ago, I lost my wife to breast cancer. She was forty-eight years old. It was the first time I had faced a challenge so totally beyond my ability to overcome...or at least mitigate. I was devastated, and to make matters worse, I learned that one of our daughters has the BRCA gene mutation that elevates her risk of breast cancer dramatically. I assume you're familiar with that."

I nodded.

"I made a vow on my wife's grave to do whatever I could for our daughter...and all other potential cancer victims. That's how I ended up here, and I firmly believe that Verbana would have prolonged my wife's life substantially."

I was visibly moved by his words, and he apologized for being maudlin, quickly transforming back into character. "Anyway, that's not why I asked you here. Now, please give me your frank assessment of our situation...from a *statistical* standpoint."

I managed to pull myself together. "Well, let me

say first that, Hector and I are now familiar with all of the PhireBreak data that may be relevant. We're ready to start figuring out exactly what the Hopkins people did. We are also working with Hal and his folks to draft a document request for them, which should help enormously. I'm going over there this afternoon to review the final version before they send it out. I believe Hal has already had some contact with their lawyers and doesn't anticipate any problems from them, but we'll have to see after they receive our request."

Selwyn was nodding as if he was fully aware of this. "Yes, yes," he said, somewhat impatiently, "but is there anything you've been able to conclude so far about the validity of their approach?"

"Certainly nothing conclusive," I responded, "but my gut feeling is that the key is their methodology for attempting to measure mental decline and attributing that to Verbana. I've been digging into the scientific literature behind something called the Caldwell Index, which is the primary endpoint they're relying on. At first, I thought that Phire-Break must have used this instrument, or something similar, to assess early dementia. However, Carolyn is sure that during the clinical trial dementia wasn't even considered. So, I wondered how it could have been assessed in the Hopkins re-analysis. When I dug a little deeper, I found out."

"I see. Go on."

"Apparently, several years ago, Dr. Harold Caldwell at Stanford was studying the possibility of estimating an individual's *future* risk of dementia by utilizing *genomic* data. Presumably, he derived an algorithm that can predict the probability of future mental decline very accurately."

"Wait. You mean he concocted some sort of composite index based on certain mutations in particular genes?"

"Not exactly. The algorithm is actually based on gene *expressions*. The gene's expression level refers to the degree of activation of the gene. As you know, most important human genes are involved in the production of proteins. Gene expression is basically a measure of how much protein is being produced. The level at which a particular gene is expressed can depend on external factors that vary over time. Also, the gene expression levels can vary across different tissues and organs within our bodies. In particular, the Caldwell Index is based on the gene expressions in *lymphocytes*, the kind of white-blood cells that are central to the immune response. Apparently, Caldwell discovered a technique for predicting future dementia based on the lymphocyte expression data. Supposedly, the individual's probability of clinically observable dementia within a few years can be estimated quite precisely."

"That's rather complicated, but I think I follow you. But how does the Kreutzfeld hypothesis come into this?"

"Well, Kreutzfeld observed that a drug like Verbana works by altering the lymphocytes. This modification can make them effective in attacking cancer cells, which is the desired effect. However, he believes that these same changes in the lymphocytes can have unintended side effects, especially in the area of brain function. In particular, he believes that these changes can cause dementia. However, he hasn't yet been able to prove the link between such changes and dementia."

"Why is that?"

"To do that, he would need a long-term study that followed patients for many years. To obviate that problem, he was looking for an indicator of dementia that would be available much more rapidly."

"I see. So...enter the Caldwell Index."

"Exactly, it obviates this problem by measuring the *propensity* for dementia. The Caldwell Index is based on the pattern of lymphocyte gene-expression changes. A high value for an individual on the Caldwell Index presumably implies accelerated progression toward dementia. So, if Verbana is shown to induce such a high value, then it must also tend to cause dementia. In effect, the Caldwell Index provides the missing link between Kreutzfeld's theoretical change in lymphocytes, on the one hand, and occurrence of dementia, on the other. By marrying Kreutzfeld's theory with Caldwell's Index, the Hopkins researchers have created a near-perfect test of the Kreutzfeld hypothesis. You might say that it's a match made in heaven."

"Hmm, or maybe somewhere else. But wait. You're saying the...what did you call it?"

"The Caldwell Index."

"Right. You said it's based on the lymphocyte gene expressions. I didn't know we collected that data in the Verbana trial."

"Well, it turns out that during Verbana's development process, there were some concerns about possible adverse effects related to blood cells. Thus, the protocol did specify that gene-expression data for several types of blood cells should be collected. The analysis of the resulting gene-expression data, at the time, seemed to show nothing unusual was on."

"Okay, I see, but does this...Index really work?"

"That's a big question," I replied. "His own research was successful enough that he's applied for a patent on the resulting Caldwell Index. I believe he's formed a company and obtained venture capital to exploit this invention. I think the company's called Caldwell Analytics LLC. However, some other researchers have questioned the algorithm's validity, especially on patient populations that differ from those on which it was originally developed. And our cancer populations are certainly different. So, in addition to determining whether the statistical analyses were done correctly, we also need to determine whether their endpoint is even appropriate."

Selwyn looked thoughtful. "That's very interesting. I hope you'll know more by our next meeting a week from Wednesday. Now, I need to change gear. There's something else we need to discuss."

I braced myself, having no idea what was coming next.

# CHAPTER 10

Monday, August 31

Selwyn looked serious. "What I'm about to tell you must remain for now between you, me and Hal Farenheit. As I think you know, I spent much of my career in military intelligence. What I will divulge would be equivalent to top secret material in a national security context. Just as such information would potentially cause harm if inappropriately released, so might this information. Judging by your look, you have some concerns, which is appropriate."

"Yes," I said. "What would happen to me if I inadvertently disclosed some of this secret information, and what makes you think I can be trusted with it?"

"Excellent questions. The answer to the first question is that nothing would happen. I don't believe it would be in the company's interest to take any action against you. I believe that a threat of punishment is not necessary to encourage you to do the right thing. Plus, actually punishing you after the fact would accomplish nothing. The harm, whatever it might be, would already have been done."

"You seem to have a lot of confidence in my integrity and discretion."

He smiled. "I hope you won't be offended, but we conducted a rather thorough background check on you before you were retained. Your selection was based not only on your brains but also your character. Don't worry, our inquiries were quite discreet. I'm sure no one we spoke with even knew that you were being investigated."

I wasn't sure how I was feeling about this disclosure, but I had begun to trust Selwyn. Anyway, I had the feeling I had no real choice.

"Okay," I said."

"We have reason to believe there may be much more to this situation than simply a few academics trying to burnish their reputations. I believe Hal told you about the Velex situation?"

I nodded. "That's the one where a hedge fund managed to swallow up a major drug company for peanuts, right?"

"Nicely put," he said, chuckling. "Well, it turns out the SEC has some concerns about that whole transaction. They suspect that it might not be completely aboveboard. Everything *appears* to be perfectly legal, but they have the FBI doing some checking."

"And we know this *how*?" I asked.

"Let's just say I still have some fairly high-level government contacts. Nothing illegal, you understand, but there's a kind of alumni network of people who maintain top-level clearances and sometimes provide advice to the government when called upon. Anyway, I heard some scuttlebutt about Pfeffer and worried there might be some similarity with our situation. Perhaps, there *is* some connection, possibly even something more sinister going on that warrants investigation."

"Are you implying there may be something *criminal* behind the Hopkins study?" I asked, obviously sounding shocked.

"I certainly hope not, but we have to consider that possibility. For instance, suppose the hedge fund that took over Pfeffer was, wittingly or unwittingly, involved in some kind of stock manipulation scheme. Perhaps they received inside information allowing them to anticipate and profit from the precipitous drop in share price. If the FBI suspects something similar is happening here, they've agreed to warn us. Similarly, if we find anything suspicious going on, we are committed to informing them."

"I assume you want to keep these, ah... speculations close to the vest for now, so as not to cause panic among your employees or shareholders."

"Yes, that certainly," he agreed, and hesitated for a few seconds, as the truth dawned on me.

"And you think that somebody within Phire-

Break might be involved in this hypothetical scheme."

"Actually, I don't, but I learned long ago not to discount anything. All this, as you say, is purely hypothetical. In any case, it probably will have no impact whatsoever on your work. Look, I'm definitely not asking you to overlook any apparent problems you run across. We need to know the full story, whatever it is, but I want you to keep this other possibility in the back of your mind. If you notice anything unusual, please contact me or Hal immediately. If we learn anything *you* should know about, we'll contact you. Say nothing to anyone else, for now."

"I understand. But I need a little time to digest the implications of this, and I may have additional questions."

"That's understandable. You can speak to me any time if you have questions or reservations about any of this. One more thing, which may seem excessive but is necessary. If you need to contact us about anything sensitive, please use this phone."

He handed me an ordinary-looking beige cell phone.

"We cannot underestimate the lengths to which criminals may go to obtain information illicitly. Trust me on that. Now, I need to be off to the links."

With that, I left his office in something of a daze. I found my way down to the lobby and out onto the street. It was a little past noon, and I had plenty of time before I needed to leave Cambridge for my meeting in Boston. I was feeling rattled by the un-expected turns that the meeting with Selwyn had taken. I wanted to collect my thoughts before tran-sitioning to the next challenge, so I ducked into a sports bar near the Kendall Square T stop for a quick bite.

I sat at a table near the front window, and ordered a tuna on whole wheat with lettuce and tomato, and a Diet Coke. I pondered the implications of what I'd learned. Was there indeed more than aca-demic ambition involved, as Selwyn had suggested? Perhaps a rival pharma company or some aggressive plaintiff attorneys were involved. But the idea that some nefarious conspiracy to destroy PhireBreak, or take it over, was afoot? That struck me as far-fetched. I doubted I would have much use for the burner phone nestled in my pocket.

By the end of my lunchtime ruminations, I felt somewhat resolved. We would keep doing what Hector and I had started. The unlikely contingen-cies mentioned by Selwyn would be kept in the back of my mind, but would not be allowed to affect my judgment. However, I would also seek some legal advice, without violating my duty of confi-dentiality to PhireBreak. That might be tricky, but I believed that my attorney and close friend Aldous Post would be just the confidant I needed. I made a mental note to call him soon.

After paying the bill, I exited onto the street and began walking toward the Kendall Square T station. Once again, the weather had changed, of course, and it was now overcast and "spitting," as Val would put it. I decided that it was not even worth pulling out my umbrella for the two-block walk. Just then, I noticed something that gave me a start. A dark blue SUV had pulled out of a parking space and was accelerating away in front of me. This would normally have completely escaped my attention, except there was something familiar about the license plate: FX3456.

*Could that possibly be the same license I spotted that night after returning from my dinner with Hector in Wellesley?*

I couldn't be sure. I definitely recalled seeing a plate with four consecutive digits. I thought back on my impression that evening. The type of vehicle and the numbers seemed familiar, but memory can be tricky. Ordinarily, I would have shrugged this sense of déjà vu off as a coincidence. I know from probability theory that the chances of such coincidences are much higher than we usually realize, because our minds are always on the lookout for meaningful connections. I actually once wrote an article about this for a statistical magazine.

This time, however, I was already a bit on edge after my meeting with Selwyn. I had a hard time putting my concerns to bed.

*What if this was in fact the same vehicle? Is someone trying to follow me? If so, why? Perhaps this is related to the background check Selwyn mentioned. Is it still going on? Or is it part of something else entirely? And how could someone possibly know where I would be today at this time? I told no one except Val about the meeting. The only time it's been mentioned, to my knowledge, was at the end of our meeting last Wednesday, and I'm pretty sure that no one there overheard.*

I remembered Selwyn's admonition not to discount anything suspicious that I came across. I doubted that something like this was what he had in mind, but I was suddenly feeling vulnerable. I was reluctant and a bit embarrassed about using the burner phone for this, but decided to call Selwyn that evening, when it was likely his charity golf activities would be finished. Meanwhile, I would keep a sharp eye out for that blue SUV.

# CHAPTER 11

Monday, August 31

When I reached the Park Street underground station, I decided to exit rather than change to the Green Line. I had some time and much preferred to walk through the Boston Common and Public Garden, then along Newbury Street, finally crossing over to Boylston Street to reach the Pru. As I have previously recounted, an unhurried walk in beautiful surroundings can often help clear my head, which was still spinning. I couldn't shake the disturbing thought that someone might be tailing me. But this seemed so preposterous, unless, somehow, they were working for PhireBreak. I was anxious to speak with Selwyn as soon as possible.

Once inside the Pru complex, I first stopped at the Barnes and Noble bookstore adjacent to 111 Huntington to pick up the latest Harry Bosch detective novel by Michael Connelly, which would serve as a welcome distraction. This was the forty-second Bosch book in the very popular series of police procedurals. In this one, Harry Bosch, though nearing eighty, and now long-retired from the L.A. police force, remains active as a mentor to his daughter, Maddie, who has recently become a detective in his old department.

After a few minutes of additional browsing, it was time for my meeting with Hal and his colleagues. I flashed my driver's license at the building security desk, smiled to the attendant, who nodded approvingly, and made my way to the elevator and up to the Cooley & Lerner offices. Once there, I walked down to Hal's office but found it empty. In a nearby cubicle, I saw a middle-aged woman and went over to ask if she knew his whereabouts.

"Oh, hi," she said, cheerily. "I'm Marge Sinclair, Hal's administrative assistant, and you must be Dr. Wheeler."

I nodded. "Yes, I'm supposed to meet with Hal and some others."

"Well, I think they're all working in the large conference room. Do you know it?"

"I think it may be the same one we've had meetings in before, but I'm not sure if I know the way there."

"I'd be happy to show you," she offered, and with that she took off briskly down the hall, beckoning me to follow. When we entered the conference room, which was indeed the scene of my previous meetings, Hal looked up from some papers he was reviewing.

"Oh, good," he said, "you made it here. I see you've met my admin, Marge Sinclair. She makes everything run around here."

"Nice to meet you," she said, smiling as she turned and left the room.

Ken then introduced the others present. "Bob Shin you've already met. Not sure if you've met Heidi Becker, also an associate, or Eve Stolz, our crack paralegal." I shook hands with each woman as she was introduced. I have an excellent memory for faces and recognized Eve as the pretty brunette who had made a cameo appearance showing Robert some document before our last meeting in this room. Heidi had a rather bookish demeanor and seemed vaguely familiar, though I couldn't place her. I asked her whether we had met previously.

"Not really. But I did attend a talk you gave last year at a conference on legal applications of statistics. I found it quite insightful."

"Thanks, were you one of the people in the audience who asked a question afterward?"

"Yes, I did. That's probably why I look familiar."

"I'm curious how you happened to be at that conference," I remarked, "since there were mostly academics attending."

"After passing the bar exam," she said, "I wanted

to specialize in pharmaceutical product litigation and decided to get an M.P.H. degree with a specialty in epidemiology. My advisor at the Harvard School of Public Health recommended that conference."

"Well, with your background, I can see why you were brought on board this project."

After these pleasantries, we got to work honing the document request. Bob Chin was charged with assembling the final text, with input and editing provided by the other attorneys. Eve was mainly responsible for checking certain factual details for accuracy. I offered some advice based on my previous litigation experience. I emphasized the importance of being very precise with respect to exactly what we were seeking.

Lawyers often frame their requests very broadly, so as not to miss anything. This makes sense when ordinary written texts are involved, but can be unsatisfactory for certain technical items, such as computer code or output. Thus, what may appear to be a full response may inadvertently omit certain specific items that are not explicitly requested. Many of my suggestions involved clarifications to be sure that we would get everything we might possibly need.

After a couple of hours, Hal and I blessed the final version and sent it off via email. After wrapping up, the group started to scatter. I went up to Hal and asked if I could speak with him privately.

97

"There's something I want to ask you about," I said.

"Sure, come down to my office."

"Okay, but is it all right to leave my laptop and notes here for now?"

"Sure, it's perfectly safe."

When we entered his office, he shut the door and offered me a seat. "Okay, what's on your mind, something about the request?"

"No, it has to do with my meeting with Selwyn earlier today. He mentioned that something more sinister than just scientific curiosity might be going on. Frankly, it made me uneasy. And he handed me this," I said, as I showed him the burner phone. "He indicated that you, he and I are the only ones who are privy to his conspiracy theories at this point. Now I admire and trust Selwyn based on what I know so far, but this kind of shook me up."

"Whoa, whoa, Ken! Let me assure you that Selwyn must have good reasons for his suspicions, and there's a lot of money potentially at stake."

"I know, and he seems to have a personal stake as well. He told me about his wife and daughter. I sympathize, but I hope that's not clouding his judgment."

Ken's eyebrows raised a little in surprise. "Hmm, that's interesting. He rarely talks about that."

"Anyway, there's something else I wanted to mention, although I'm afraid you may start to question my sanity. It's probably nothing, but in light of Selwyn's concerns, I want to err on the side of caution. I'm thinking of calling him later, but ..."

"Look, whatever it is, you can confide in me."

"I have the feeling that I may be under some kind of surveillance. I know that sounds crazy, and maybe my nerves are playing tricks, but...well, I don't know." I then proceeded to relate my experiences with the mysterious blue SUV.

"Actually, that's not so crazy, but it *is* highly unlikely. Believe me, I've seen some pretty bizarre things happening in high-stakes litigation. Plaintiff lawyers can pull some pretty dirty tricks that are unethical and even illegal. But it does seem more like a mind-trick in this case."

"Why do you say that?" I asked, hoping that he was right.

"Well, for one thing, how would anyone even know you're involved in this project? As you know, we all adhere to a strict confidentiality agreement."

"That's a good question. I'm embarrassed to ask, but is it possible that we are somehow being bugged?" I asked. "Stupid question, right?"

"Not *that* stupid. As I said, strange things do happen...occasionally. In fact, Selwyn, former spook that he is, considered this possibility and arranged to have the conference room swept for listening devices. He brought in a security company whose owner is a buddy of his from his naval intelligence days. Over a weekend, we closed the office and they brought in some high-tech equipment, the kind you can't find at Best Buy. They went over every inch of that room. Furthermore, every month they come back to perform a 'booster shot' that takes several hours. It's a royal pain in the ass, but PhireBreak is a major client and foots the bill, so we indulge them."

"I don't suppose it would be easy to get around these precautions," I said.

"You'd think," Hal replied, "but Selwyn wasn't satisfied. Our firm had to agree to put in place other security measures. For instance, the front door is locked and the key-code is known only to employees who've been carefully vetted. I should give that to you, just in case you ever need it."

"Okay, okay, I give up," I said, throwing up my hands in mock surrender. "That is reassuring. I'll see you at our Wednesday meeting. I'm just gonna grab my stuff from the conference room and head out."

As I walked out of his office, I realized that most of the firm's employees had already left for the day. When I got back to the conference room, it was deserted. I sat down on one of the leather chairs and pondered my situation. There were two possibilities:

Hypothesis 1: I was experiencing an overactive imagination.

Hypothesis 2: Someone was attempting to obtain information about our efforts covertly.

Hypothesis 1 would mean that either the license plates on the two occasions were *not* actually the same, or if they were, that an unusual coincidence had occurred. This seemed more likely, and I very much wanted it to be true.

Hypothesis 2, on the other hand, would imply that someone following me had somehow obtained information that was presumably known only by me and Selwyn.

How could I gather some evidence to decide between these two hypotheses? I had an idea, but it would depend on arranging a meeting with my attorney, Aldous Post. I was hoping he could see me right away, so I dialed his office number. He picked up on the fourth ring, just as I was about to give up.

"Hello, Aldous. Glad I caught you."

"Yeah, I was just getting ready to leave. What's up? Everything okay?"

"Listen, Aldous, could I come in to talk to you tomorrow morning? Something I'm working on has raised some issues I'd like to discuss with you. It's kind of time-sensitive. It's not necessarily a legal matter, but I need some of your sage advice. Will you be at your law office in Dedham tomorrow, say, nine a.m.?"

"Sure, Ken, I'll see you then. Gotta run now. Josh

will kill me if I'm late tonight."

I gathered up my things and headed down the hall toward the exit, waving goodbye to Hal as I passed his office. An hour later, I arrived home.

"How was your day, dear?" asked Valerie.

"Fairly uneventful," I lied. "How was yours?"

# CHAPTER 12

Tuesday, September 1

Aldous Post is a scion of a prominent Boston family with roots back to the Mayflower, and he looks the part. He is tall, graying and graceful, with a patrician manner that suggests being calmly in control without being pushy or patronizing. His grandfather had been a city councilman in the days of the legendary Mayor of Boston, James Michael Curley, and his father, recently deceased, was a former U.S. Attorney for the District of Massachusetts. Aldous followed the family tradition into the legal profession, but had always marched to his own drum. After graduating from Harvard Law School, he eschewed the large-firm fast-track and took a job as a public defender. Eventually, he and Josh Goodman, his partner in both senses of the word, formed a boutique law firm specializing in litigation, often representing various disadvantaged or disenfranchised groups.

This career choice, as well as his sexual orientation, led to estrangement from some of his more traditional family members. Now approaching middle age, he has achieved a rapprochement with his two siblings, and contentment with his career. He's made enough money to meet his modest material needs comfortably, and has garnered numerous awards for various civil rights contributions. Some high-profile battles have also, on occasion, generated considerable notoriety and, sometimes, animosity.

I first met Aldous about five years ago in connection with a class action employment discrimination lawsuit. He was representing a group of minority employees who charged that a large manufacturing company near Boston was preferentially promoting white employees. Such cases often hinge on statistical analyses to determine whether observed discrepancies in promotion rates are statistically significant, as opposed to being just the product of chance. We hit it off well while working together and became friends. I have on several occasions drawn on his legal expertise and business acumen, which he freely dispenses because he believes that I "saved his bacon" on that discrimination case.

Aldous's office is located in an unassuming strip mall on Route 1, in Dedham, Massachusetts. At a little past nine, I pulled into the parking lot in front of his office, I rang the doorbell and was quickly buzzed in. The office is located on the second floor, above a lamp store, and it's necessary to climb a rather steep and narrow staircase to reach it. When I arrived, Aldous greeted me warmly and ushered me into his office.

As usual, his desk was piled high with stacks of files and law books in apparent disarray. Aldous was the opposite of compulsive, much to the chagrin of his partner. But I knew from experience that his idiosyncratic system for keeping track of their case files was highly effective.

"You seemed a bit frazzled on the phone yesterday. Is everything okay? Can I get you some coffee?"

Aldous has a slightly discomfiting habit of asking multiple questions at the same time, often in machine-gun cadence.

"Everything's fine, and no thanks for the coffee. I just had two cups at breakfast. I came, in part, because I wanted to show you a non-disclosure agreement that I had to sign in order to start a new project. It was virtually identical to other NDAs you've reviewed for me, so I didn't think it necessary to bother you."

"Ah, it's the *virtual* part you're having second thoughts about?"

"Yes, that's right." I passed him a copy of the NDA. In paragraph eight, there is a proviso about what happens if I am required to testify about possibly confidential information. They want me to notify them as soon as I become aware of such a request. Do you have any concerns about that?"

He perused the paragraph I had mentioned for

about thirty seconds and cleared his throat.

"Well, it *is* somewhat unusual, but I've seen similar language inserted in NDAs a couple of times. In those cases, there were possible consequences that could result within a certain time-frame. For example, in one of these there was an issue about the, uh... legality of a certain deal, the details of which I can't divulge," he said, smiling slyly. "So it would be important to know as quickly as possible if sensitive information might become public. Do you know of anything like that going on? Can you tell me more about the specifics?"

"I don't know of anything like that, and I'm not sure how much I can tell you. It's sort of a Catch-22."

"Hmm, I see what you mean. Before we go on, do you have a dollar bill?"

"I think so, but..."

"Actually, any denomination will do. A "hundred" would be nice, if you've got one."

"Haha," I said, rather mystified. I pulled out my wallet and found a ten-dollar bill. I handed it to him and he asked his admin to come in for a minute.

"Alicia, you know Dr. Wheeler." She nodded, and smiled toward me.

"I want you to witness that he has just given me the sum of ten dollars as a retainer for my legal services. Please make a note of that for his file." She smiled and left the room. "There, you're now officially my client. That means we can discuss any legally related matter, and it will be covered by an almost unbreakable attorney-client privilege. Now, that does *not* mean you can violate your duty of confidentiality to your client. However, should you inadvertently reveal some confidential information, that would remain within these four walls. Do you understand?"

"Yes, I believe so."

"Good. So, my friend, what in God's name is this *really* all about? You haven't done anything indiscreet have you? Have you been threatened in any way?"

"No, no, nothing like any of that, at least as far as I'm aware." I proceeded to fill him in on the recent events, and my concern about being followed. I was careful to avoid mentioning any details about the case itself or the identities of anyone involved. I summarized the two recent sightings of what was *possibly* the same dark blue SUV. I also told him that I intended to speak with a contact at PhireBreak who might know if the company was somehow involved.

When I finished, Aldous steepled his hands and looked at me appraisingly. I was feeling self-conscious.

After what seemed to me like a long pause, he finally spoke. His tone now was more serious.

"How certain are you about being followed?"

"Based on current evidence, I would estimate the probability at around, oh, maybe forty percent."

"Spoken like a true statistician. Isn't that a bit flimsy to be broaching with this person at PhireBreak? Do you trust him or her? Oh, and can you find out more in some way before you do?"

"I agree that it *is* flimsy, and I'm trying to get more evidence. In fact, that's the other part of why I wanted to come here today. Yesterday, I decided to run a little experiment. When I called you yesterday, I was sitting in the conference room. I revealed just enough information in that call to allow a clever eavesdropper to figure out where I would be right now."

"An experiment, hah! You are a sneaky son-of-a-bitch. You expected whoever might be following you to show up *here*. Did you think they would probably arrive first and wait for you to arrive? Hmm. So did you see anything when you got here? Was there a dark blue SUV lurking in the parking lot?"

"Well, possibly, but I wasn't sure they would arrive first. So I was very careful to be sure that the SUV was not following me. If they showed up here, it would mean that they had to know in advance where I would be. When I got here, though, I did take a quick look around, trying not to be too obvious. I saw a couple of possibilities about a hundred yards away in the adjoining parking lot, but I couldn't be sure. I hoped they might park much closer to your office. That would put them in range of your super-duper 24/7 closed-circuit video system, which I presume is still in operation."

"Of course, of course. As you may recall, we had it installed in the wake of that, ah ...unpleasantness we experienced during our work with the labor unions a few years ago. Fortunately, things have cooled down on that front, but this is not the safest neighborhood, so we still maintain the system."

"Great. Can I see the recording for this morning?"

"Sure, let me just ask Alicia to have the video downloaded to my computer. Meanwhile, why don't we take a gander at what's going on out front right now?"

We then proceeded to move from Aldous's office, which faces the rear of the building, to a conference room that overlooks the front parking area. We both glanced out the large picture window and saw nothing of interest. The lot was fairly deserted, as most of the stores weren't open yet.

"Oh well, that was worth a shot," I said, not sure whether to be disappointed or encouraged. Maybe that mysterious pursuer was a figment of my imagination after all.

"Let's not jump to conclusions before perusing the video," said Aldous.

We moved back to his office and huddled in front of his computer monitor. The recording began at eight forty-five. We were treated to twenty boring minutes of assorted vehicles whizzing by on Route 1, and about a dozen that entered the parking lot. None of these was a blue SUV. At precisely 9:07, my old Beamer appeared and made its way to a spot near the front of the building. I could be seen emerging from my car, glancing around, and heading into the front door. This was followed by more whizzing cars. I was starting to feel frustrated, and somewhat embarrassed, when we both suddenly jumped to startled attention.

"*Holy shit!*" we exclaimed in unison, as a dark blue Lexus SUV entered the lot.

"Can you make out the plate?" I asked, as it pulled in behind another car, obstructing our view. "That bastard. I'll bet he did that deliberately."

"Let's see what happens next," said Aldous. But nothing did happen for about three whole minutes. Whoever was in that car seemed to just be waiting. For what? Then, something unexpected occurred. A man appeared walking away from our building in the direction of the Lexus. He must have come from the diner located below us and just to our right. That was the only store in the strip mall that would have been open at that hour. He was wearing a base-ball cap and did not look back, so we couldn't make out any facial characteristics. He seemed solidly built and had on a backpack. Reaching the Lexus, he opened the passenger door and got in. A few seconds later, the vehicle exited the lot. We couldn't make out the license in real-time, but I asked Aldous to re-wind and stop the recording.

"Is there any way to zoom in on the Lexus, so we might be able to identify the plate number?" I inquired.

"Sure, just give me a moment."

When he did this, I cried out with a mixture of vindication and sheer panic. There it was:

**FX3456**

I didn't need any complex mathematical calculations to determine that the probability I was being followed was close to 100%.

# CHAPTER 13

Tuesday, September 1

After my meeting with Aldous, I drove into Boston to spend the rest of the day working at my B.U. office. The beginning of the fall semester was just days away. I needed to start preparing for the two courses I would be teaching: entry-level statistics for undergraduates and a graduate biostatistics seminar on research design and analysis for clinical trials. Some of my colleagues had also come in. We greeted each other and chatted about our vacations and our plans for the upcoming year. I probably seemed a bit distracted, as my focus was on the disconcerting discoveries Aldous and I had just made. Before doing anything related to my academic responsibilities, I intended to contact Selwyn, using the burner phone.

I closed my office door and settled into my chair. The office has a sterile, utilitarian, sort of ambiance, with white-painted cinderblock walls and a tiled floor. Its saving grace is that it overlooks the Charles River, although the view is partially obscured by other university buildings. There are several large oak trees visible along the river bank, and the leaves were just starting to turn. The familiar setting was comforting, and I was pleased to be back on my home turf. But I was feeling apprehensive about how this semester was going to turn out.

Up until now, I had found my legal consulting work to be an enjoyable, and fairly lucrative, sideline. Was I getting myself too deep into something that could upset my well-ordered existence, and perhaps even prove dangerous? Already, I could sense that Val was picking up some troubling vibes. Somewhat furtively, I pulled out the burner phone and dialed the number Selwyn had given me. He picked up on the second ring.

"This must be urgent, since we will be meeting in person tomorrow."

I couldn't tell if he was being critical or just characteristically terse.

"I know, but it may be important," I said, hesitantly.

"Tell me."

I proceeded to give him a succinct account of my encounters with the mysterious SUV. I decided not to regale him with a lot of detail. Somewhat sheepishly, I asked whether this surveillance could be related to any ongoing background checking by PhireBreak. He abruptly dismissed the possibility, eliminating that hope of an innocent explanation.

"Tell me, again, the license plate number. I can have that checked out."

I did, and wondered precisely how that checking would be accomplished.

"Okay, I'm glad you called me about this. That was the right thing to do. I'll get back to you soon." *Click*.

Just then, I heard a knock on my office door, and Irv Rothman, our department chairman, popped his head in. I motioned for him to enter.

"Hi, Ken," he said. I heard you were in. It's nice to see you. Have a good vacation?"

"Yes, Irv. I did, but it feels good to be back in the saddle. I was just about to start preparing for my fall classes."

We chatted for a few minutes about some administrative matters until he was interrupted by the departmental admin and excused himself. For the next two hours I managed to get some work done, reviewing my notes from the last time I gave the same courses and making some changes. Then, I decided to give Hector a call to see how his scrutiny of the PhireBreak data was coming along.

I knew that I'd have to present an update at our meeting the next day. I was in something of a quandary about the meeting. On the one hand, I wanted to provide some helpful insight regarding our progress. On the other, since I was increasingly convinced that some sort of electronic eavesdropping was occurring, I would need to be somewhat guarded. I would also avoid discussing the mystery Lexus.

I shrugged these troubling thoughts aside as I dialed Hector's number. He picked up immediately.

"Hi, Ken, I was just about to call you. I've been checking all their data management and statistical analyses, as you asked. I haven't seen anything out of line so far. PhireBreak seems to have done an excellent job. Is there anything else you need right now?"

"No, not at the moment, Hector. Thanks. That's helpful, but we really need to get the actual results for the Caldwell Index, which should be included in the data from Hopkins. I hope it will be forthcoming soon. Obviously, I'll be sending it to you as soon as it arrives."

"Okay, great. Talk soon."

"No, wait. I just had another thought. One thing I've learned is that the algorithm underlying the Caldwell Index is based on gene-expression data. Can you send me the gene-expression data for all of the subjects in the Verbana studies?"

"Will do. Is that it?

"Yeah, bye."

I went back to work on my course preparation, but my mind kept wandering. *Why was I being followed? Was the conference room at Cooley & Lerner truly being bugged? How could I find out?*

I was starting to formulate a plan, but wasn't sure I had the nerve to carry it through.

It was getting on toward the late afternoon when

the burner phone in my pocket buzzed.

"Hi, Selwyn," I said. But the voice on the line wasn't Selwyn's, or Hal's. I felt the proverbial chill up my spine. It was a female voice that I didn't recognize. She sounded serious.

"Hello Dr. Wheeler. Mr. Washington contacted us and gave us this number to contact you. He relayed the info you passed on to him about the blue Lexus SUV. I was tasked with following up. There's probably no cause for concern, but I'd like to meet with you soon to get some more details."

"Wait a minute, who is this, and why didn't Selwyn call me himself? Do you work for him?"

She laughed. It was a rather loud, somewhat raucous laugh that jangled my nerves.

"Oh, I get it. He didn't have a chance to call you with a heads-up. You're quite right to be suspicious. I'm special agent Rita D'Amato of the FBI financial crimes unit. You can call the Boston FBI office to verify this. When you're satisfied, please call me back. I'll be here."

She had a distinct New England accent, so the last word sounded more like "hee-uh."

"Okay, I'll do that." Ten minutes later, I was back on the phone with her.

"Look, Agent D'Amato, I don't know what's going on, and frankly I'm a bit freaked out. I'm not used to being followed around and spied upon. Do you know if I should be worried?"

"Hold on, Dr. Wheeler. What I can tell you is that we have traced the license plate you observed. It's registered to a private investigator. He seems to be quite reputable and specializes in domestic disputes. So this could be unrelated to your work for PhireBreak...though that seems unlikely. I assume you and *Mrs.* Wheeler aren't having any, uh...domestic problems?"

"That's ridiculous," I replied.

"Just checking. Anyway, I plan to have a nice chat with this PI tomorrow. After that, we should know more about what's going on and why. Are you available for a meeting on Thursday?"

"Certainly, especially if it will settle all this."

"Let's hope so," she said.

We arranged to meet at Lina's Café at eight on Thursday morning. I immediately called Selwyn.

"I just got off a call with Rita D'Amato of the FBI," I said.

"Oh, that was fast. I was about to call you on that. I've dealt with her before, and she's really sharp. You can trust her completely."

"That's good to know. We arranged to meet on Thursday morning for breakfast."

"That's fine. Just keep me in the loop. I'll see you tomorrow." *Click.*

*Never one to waste words.*

Somehow, I would have to come up with something to report at the meeting next day. I sighed and shook my head. Then, as if things weren't complicated enough, my regular phone rang, and it was Hal. He informed me that the response to our request for additional information would be received the following afternoon. A messenger would bring it to his office with a flash drive, supposedly containing everything we had asked for. I told him that I'd be staying downtown after the meeting tomorrow morning. I could stop by and pick up copies for me and Hector around five o'clock. He said that would be fine.

Then, I phoned Hector to let him know and to set up a meeting for lunch Thursday to hand over his copy and plan what to do next. After that, I called Val to let her know I wouldn't be home for a few hours, since I needed to go over the data that Hector had sent. She also informed me that "back to school" night had been scheduled for Monday of the following week. I dutifully entered this on my calendar. This was an annual rite of meeting with Sam's new teacher and getting a handle on her teaching style and expectations. From past experience, I understood that this mutual first impression could set the tone of subsequent interactions, for good or ill. I really couldn't afford to miss it.

By the late afternoon only a couple of faculty members remained in the statistics department offices. It was quiet and I hoped for no more interruptions. I checked my email and found that Hector had indeed sent a large file containing the gene-expression data. I wanted to dig into the data, hoping to find some useful information to report at next-day's meeting.

As I had explained to Selwyn, the Caldwell Index was an estimated probability generated by a clever algorithm. I had now learned from the referenced articles in the Johns Hopkins manuscript that this algorithm was based on the expression values of twenty-two genes. Furthermore, the algorithm was a *neural network* model. The mathematical form of such a model is patterned after the way in which the human brain is believed to work. Unfortunately, the twenty-two genes had not been identified in the published articles. It was considered a trade secret until patent protection for Caldwell's company would be granted by the U. S. Patent Office. This was supposed to occur within the next few weeks.

The data I had received from Hector consisted of the lymphocyte gene-expression levels for all of the approximately twenty-thousand human genes. However, I knew that recent research had discovered about two-hundred genes that were related to cognition, including important brain functions such as reasoning and memory. I hypothesized that some, if not all, of these would be among the twenty-two genes involved in the Caldwell Index. So for each of these two-hundred genes, I calculated the average expression levels for the Verbana and control groups at the end of the two clinical trials. If an effect on mental functioning had occurred, then for some of these genes, the Verbana group average should, I expected, be significantly different from the control group average.

I pressed the keys on my computer to carry out an appropriate statistical test of this theory. When my computer carried out the necessary calculations,

I stared at the screen. The results were perplexing. The differences seemed to be consistent with chance. There was no evidence that Verbana had exerted any effect on the activity of these genes. This seemed paradoxical.

*What on earth was the Caldwell Index measuring about mental functioning? Had Caldwell discovered some new genes? Or, was his neural network sensitive to some subtle combination of the individual genes that were already known?*

By now, the sky was starting to darken, and I was anxious to be getting home. I was too exhausted to think straight. I wasn't sure what to make of this anomaly and whether to bring this up at the meeting the next day. Maybe everything would be clearer in the morning, so I decided to sleep on it.

# CHAPTER 14

Wednesday, September 2

I arrived at the offices of Cooley & Lerner at nine forty-five and stopped by Hal's office. He was on the phone but beckoned me to come in. Through the large window in his office I looked out upon a beautiful New England late-summer sky. It had a gorgeous cerulean hue, with only a few wispy clouds in sight. My mind was also much clearer after nine hours of deep slumber and a hearty breakfast. Since my conversation with Rita D'Amato, there had been no further sightings of the mysterious blue Lexus SUV. I felt somewhat comforted that Special Agent D'Amato had apparently intervened. After ending his call, Hal mentioned that Selwyn had told him about the situation.

"I can't imagine what that could be about," he said. "I understand you'll be speaking with the FBI? I guess that should help us to find out. I gotta tell you, this whole business with the Hopkins re-analysis is starting to get on my nerves. Selwyn is putting a lot of pressure on and seems to suspect some kind of nefarious conspiracy to destroy PhireBreak. Let's hope he's wrong."

"Amen, to that."

"Anyway, it's time for our meeting."

As we walked down the hall toward the conference room, I felt apprehensive about what I should say. I couldn't escape the feeling that our words would be overheard...somehow. When we got there, the usual participants were assembled. Selwyn and Dave were huddled near the coffee urn, which was located on a credenza along the right-hand wall. They were chatting as they filled their porcelain cups, monogrammed with the firm's distinctive logo. I went over and grabbed a cup as well. After some small talk, Selwyn turned toward the group and called us to order.

"Well, let's get started," he intoned. "Hal, what do we have on the legal front?"

"Well, our petition for an injunction was accepted. That's the good news. But Judge Weingarten ruled that it will be in force only for the sixty-day period. That timetable can only be extended for extraordinary unforeseen events. By my reckoning, we have only seven weeks of grace left. As far as the FDA, we're still waiting to hear if they'll schedule a hearing prior to that date." He paused for a sip of water.

"What about our request for additional documentation of the analyses from Johns Hopkins?" asked Carolyn Cummings.

"I was just getting to that. We've been told to expect a flash drive to be delivered by messenger this afternoon. We'll have to see whether they've responded fully to our requests. If they're playing games, we can go back to the judge and ask for more. As soon as we get it, we'll make copies for you and Ken."

"So far, I haven't involved any of my staff in this project, but I think it should be reviewed by Sergei as well."

A few seconds went by, and it seemed as if some of the air had gone out of the room. Somewhat hesitantly I inquired, "I'm sorry, who is Sergei?"

All eyes turned toward Selwyn. "Dr. Sergei Rosefsky is the Deputy Director of Biostatistics at PhireBreak. He's a brilliant researcher who earned a Ph.D. in theoretical mathematics from Moscow University before emigrating to the United States fifteen years ago. When he got here, there were no jobs in his rather esoteric branch of mathematics. So he matriculated at M.I.T. and garnered a Ph.D. in bio-engineering in just three years. He has also been described variously by colleagues as cantankerous, opinionated, and arrogant."

"True," said Carolyn. "You forgot to add that he's also known for occasionally consuming huge quantities of vodka and holding forth on his accomplishments and theories. But these quirks are tolerated because, as we used to say in South Boston, he is *wicked smaaht.*"

"No argument there," said Selwyn. "So, Carolyn, are you willing to vouch for this loose cannon of yours? Can you keep him sufficiently lashed to the deck that we won't regret bringing him onboard?"

"Under the circumstances, Selwyn, I think he is well worth the risk. We *do* have to go all in on this, right?"

"Unfortunately, true. Just remember...short leash. And I don't want him anywhere near Dr. Wheeler. We can't have Ken's opinions contaminated in any way, as it may bite us if he's ever called upon to testify. So, anything he discovers goes to you alone and is brought to me under cover of attorney-client privilege. Agreed?"

"Agreed."

"Okay then, moving on. Have we found out any more about the Mannheim Foundation, Hal?"

"I'll let Bob field that one."

"Thanks, Hal," said Robert Shin. "The Mannheim Foundation was chartered in Germany in 2018, shortly after an international conference that was held at Mannheim University. We managed to obtain a copy of the program for the conference and a list of participants. Most of these are fairly well-known academics who have raised legitimate questions about the cost versus benefit of certain widely use medications. The foundation sponsors an annual conference at their U.S. headquarters in Harrison, New York, a ritzy suburb about twenty miles north of Manhattan. Their motivating philosophy is that the use of drugs to cure diseases should be minimized. They tend to advocate diet and lifestyle changes as alternatives. For some illnesses, they argue that a pharmaceutical cure can be worse than the disease. In some of these cases, I suspect we might tend to agree with them," he said, with a wry smile.

"But when it comes to cancers, of course, relying on diet and healthy behaviors *alone* can be very dangerous. For the most part, they seem pretty responsible in acknowledging that reality."

"Do we know anything about their funding?" asked Justin Osborne.

Hal jumped in. "Not much, yet. They seem quite secretive about that, but we're working on it. I hope to have something by our next meeting."

"That reminds me that I want to push our next meeting out to the week after next," interjected Selwyn. "I'm going to be traveling for most of next week. However, keep in mind that the clock is ticking. We now have seven short weeks to wrap this up before all hell breaks loose. Once the injunction runs out and the mainstream media get ahold of the allegations, we'll be playing defense deep in our own territory. So, by that next meeting, we have to be in a position to formulate a winning strategy. Let's do whatever it takes...within the law, of course."

He next turned toward Dave Parker. "Have you found out anything more about the scientific support for the Kreutzfeld Hypothesis?"

"Kreutzfeld's lab at Penn seems to have had an infusion of new funding recently. The source is not clear, but the Mannheim Foundation doesn't appear to be involved, at least not directly. We have no idea if this is related in any way to the Hopkins analysis. Meanwhile, we've been reaching out to contacts who might have any knowledge of exactly what they are doing. We've reviewed all of their previously published research based on animal studies. Some of it appears to show that mice can lose some proficiency in the ability to navigate a maze after consuming Verbana."

"*Really?*" Carolyn interjected. "Mice? *Please.*"

"We've also picked up some rumblings that a protege of Dr. K has left his lab and is complaining about his lack of objectivity. We think he may be willing to talk with us and allege that the good doctor's biases may have influenced the results."

"Okay," said Selwyn. "Keep following up. Now, what about the all-important statistical analysis? Ken?"

I felt the need to choose my words very carefully. I didn't yet feel comfortable disclosing my incipient suspicions, especially before seeing the information from Hopkins we were expecting. Moreover, I couldn't rule out the possibility, however unlikely, that the walls truly had ears. On the other hand, I didn't want to be totally negative either. I decided to opt for the truth...but not the whole truth.

"I'm reluctant to say much before seeing the

data and computer code we should be getting later today. Presumably, that information will tell us whether there's any technical error in their statistical analysis or in the way it's been programmed. Frankly, I'm not anticipating a 'gotcha' moment, although you never know. So far, our own analyses of the clinical-trial data are consistent with what the article is reporting. But we aren't able yet to reproduce the Hopkins results exactly."

"Wait a minute," Carolyn broke in. "I don't understand. If they're using our data, how come we can't replicate the results ourselves?"

"It's like this," I said. "The endpoint that they used is something called the Caldwell Index. It purports to be an accurate estimate of the probability that clinically evident dementia will occur within a few years. It's based on a neural network. As you're aware, these are used in artificial-intelligence applications proliferating these days in everything from mail-delivery drones to your kitchen toaster. The mathematical model is patterned after the way that the human brain is believed to handle information, hence the name. Anyway, the final neural-network model was built using specialized software analyzing gene-expression data on several thousand people. However, the specific model is considered to be a proprietary trade secret of Caldwell Analytics, the company that markets the Caldwell Index."

"Well, that's ridiculous," said Carolyn. "How can they get away with that? Why would anyone believe the predictions from the model are reliable? It's like, like...selling a nutritional supplement without revealing exactly what ingredients are in it. I can't believe the Patent Office would let them get away with that, let alone the FTC for that matter."

"Hold on, Carolyn," said Hal. "For one thing, full details about the neural-network algorithm will be revealed once the patent application is approved, which could be quite soon. But we aren't relying on that. We've asked for a copy of the patent application and any other documentation that might provide additional details on the underlying research. We'll also be getting a license for their commercial software that was used to generate the endpoint in their study. All that should be coming this afternoon. Then we'll know everything there is to know about this Caldwell Index."

Carolyn looked perplexed. "What you're telling me is that the Hopkins folks didn't have an *actual* measure of dementia, so their whole analysis is based on this *proxy* measure that's *supposed* to predict future dementia?"

"Exactly," I replied.

"I don't know," grumbled Carolyn. "That seems like a pretty slender reed on which to base their whole critique."

"I agree completely, and I think we should try to lean hard on that reed. If we can show that the Caldwell Index isn't valid, or at least not for our patients, that would be terrific."

"Well, I think that reinforces the idea of including Sergei," she remarked. "He knows a great deal about artificial intelligence, including neural networks. If anyone can get the bottom of it, *he* can."

"That's great," I said. I'll be happy to work with you and him on that."

That seemed to satisfy her. In principle, I meant what I was saying and am always open to collegial cooperation. But there was such a sharp edge to her comments that it made me uneasy. Plus, Rosefsky seemed like a wild card. Would he turn out to be a valued asset, or a thorn in my side?

After my remarks, there was some further discussion about contingencies if the information we received was incomplete. That could pose some serious problems and, potentially, the need for more time. Around noon, the meeting broke up. As we left the conference room, I buttonholed Hal and told him I'd be back at five to pick up two copies of the flash drive from Hopkins for Hector and myself. He suggested five thirty if possible, and I agreed.

A few minutes later, I was out on Boylston Street, heading in the direction of the Boston Common. As I walked along, I found myself occasionally looking around furtively for the blue Lexus. When I got to the Common, I stopped in for lunch at a nearby tavern, after which I entered the Park Street T station. I boarded the first D train, got off at Kenmore Square and walked up Comm Ave toward my office. When I got there, I spent the next couple of hours on course preparation, and honing my plan for the evening, still unsure if it was too reckless to carry out. Then I made the return trip back to the Pru.

# CHAPTER 15

Wednesday, September 2

When I arrived at Cooley & Lerner that afternoon it was 5:35 and only a handful of employees remained. I found Hal in his office. He looked up from his computer screen and motioned for me to come in.

"The flash drive came in about twenty minutes ago. Our IT folks are checking it for viruses and making the copies. Should be done very shortly. Would you like some water or coffee while we wait?"

"No thanks. I'm all set. I'm really anxious to get a first peek at what they sent over. Would it be all right if I camped out in the conference room for a bit to do that?"

"Sure. I may be gone by the time you leave, though. If you need anything, I think Bob Shin will still be around for another hour or so."

"That's fine. I know my way around pretty well

by now."

A few minutes later the flash drives arrived. I placed both of them in a pocket of my messenger bag, which also contained my laptop. I hoisted the bag over my shoulder, said good bye to Hal, and headed for the conference room. On my way there, I noticed that a couple of Hal's colleagues with whom I had worked on the data request were still hard at work. When I arrived at the conference room, I took out my laptop and popped in one of the flash drives.

A quick perusal confirmed that almost everything I was expecting appeared to be there. The only major omission I noted was the absence of the patent application that described the complete details of the Caldwell Index derivation. I suspected their lawyers were balking at that and resolved to bring this up with Hal.

After that, I pretended to be analyzing the information more extensively, which was my ostensible reason for staying in the room. In reality, I was considering how to carry out my audacious plan for the evening.

I was hoping to discover whether the room was actually being bugged. I reasoned that it would be virtually impossible for a hidden device to be transmitting a signal to a recipient outside the conference room. That would be detected by the high-tech security precautions Selwyn had ordered to be installed. If surveillance was going on, then it had to involve some kind of passive recording device.

But that would seem to imply that information recorded by the device was downloaded periodically. Furthermore, Selwyn's request for me to meet with him the next day had presumably leaked out right away. How else could the driver of the blue SUV have known I'd be meeting with him, and where? Whoever was downloading the information must have done so very soon after the meeting, probably on the same day.

I assumed that this same hypothetical scenario might be played out again, tonight. So my plan was to hang around and try to observe the culprit in the act. To be honest, though, I was still hoping that I was just being paranoid.

At seven thirty, I packed up my laptop and left the conference room. I made my way through the office by a route that passed near Hal's office. Most of the offices and cubicles were empty and dark, but a few lights remained on, their occupants working late. As I approached Hal's office, I passed Robert Shin's office next door. The lights were on, and he was talking with the junior associate and paralegal that had helped us to draft the document request. I popped my head in the doorway.

"Hi, I was just leaving. I couldn't resist taking a peek at the information they sent. It seems to include everything we asked for except the patent application. On the whole, I think we did a good job putting together the request; it gave them little wiggle-room. Nice job."

I genuinely meant this compliment, but my ulterior purpose was to have them witness my apparent exit from the office at around this time.

They all smiled and thanked me, too. Hal said he would look into the patent issue.

"We're just wrapping up for the day as well," said Robert.

*So far, so good.*

I turned and strolled slowly down the hall toward the front door of the office suite. Only one office still had the lights on, and its occupant paid me no heed as I ambled by. My plan was to reach the front entrance but then turn back and head to the conference room by an alternate route. However, when I was about fifty feet from the entrance, I heard a door open some distance behind me. I glanced back and saw Bob Shin emerging from his office and turning in my direction. If he noticed that I wasn't leaving, it could be awkward. I had to improvise quickly.

*Maybe I should just forget this foolhardy plan.*

There were restrooms located adjacent to the reception area, just a few steps from the front door. Instead of exiting, I ducked inside the men's room and entered one of the stalls. I sat down on the toilet and considered the situation. So far, I had done nothing suspicious. A few seconds later, Bob entered the restroom and used one of the urinals.

*Had he noticed anything?*

I doubted that he would be able to recognize my shoes as I sat there waiting for him to leave. But even if he did somehow register my presence, he had no reason to assume that I hadn't left the office shortly after.

Soon, I heard the rush of water in the sink as he washed up and then door swinging as he left.

I decided to linger in the restroom for a bit longer before venturing out. In a little while, the entire office suite should be deserted. After that, someone retrieving data surreptitiously from a hidden recording device might make a move. I was becoming extremely nervous about the wisdom of this whole escapade, but it was too late for me to bail out now.

When I finally came out of the restroom, the hallway was in nearly complete darkness. Only the moonlight shining in through the exterior windows provided some minimal illumination. It took my eyes several minutes to adjust enough to make out the shapes of cubicle partitions and office doors. I began to move stealthily down the hallway in the direction of the conference room. I had an eerie feeling that someone would jump out at any moment and demand to know why I was skulking around. I was aware that my heart was pounding.

*What the fuck am I doing? I'm a Professor of Statistics, not some secret agent in a spy novel. This is nuts.*

But part of me knew that I had to resolve the uncertainty gnawing at me. It was the part that could never let go of a difficult conundrum, whether it involved figuring out a mathematical equation or anticipating a novel's plot twist. But those activities involved no risk. This was real-life, and I felt completely out of my depth. As I walked slowly toward the conference room, I convinced myself that this was a silly waste of time. I would turn the corner and see nothing but an empty room.

*This was all a wasted effort. Selwyn and Hal were right, that my fears were ridiculous. Thankfully, they would never find out how paranoid I'd become.*

What if I had just turned back right then and walked out? I sometimes wonder how differently my life would have turned out.

When I actually started to turn the corner, I froze and barely checked the impulse to cry out. A soft yellowish light was emanating from the conference room. It was not the full glow from the fluorescent lighting in the room. Rather, it was a subdued illumination, as from a flashlight. I quickly ducked into one of the offices near the conference room, but not close enough to peer inside. A few seconds later, I heard a noise. It seemed like a rattling of dishes. *Odd.* An image of the monogrammed porcelain cups and saucers that had been used to serve coffee flashed in my mind.

*Was the sound caused by moving some of these? Perhaps the recording device was hidden behind all the crockery, in back of the wooden cabinet in which it was stored. Was that possible?*

A few minutes went by. For me, they were very long minutes indeed. Then, I heard some more rattling sounds, suggesting perhaps that the items removed from the cabinet were being replaced. I expected that whoever was doing this would be finished very soon, so I hunkered down behind a desk in the dark. I was quite sure I wouldn't be seen, but needed to peek out just enough to see who that might be. I couldn't begin to imagine what might happen if I was discovered. I was sweating profusely. Suddenly, I realized that I had failed to turn my phone completely off.

*Oh shit! What if I received a call and the phone buzzed? Would the sound carry to the conference room? Would it reveal my hiding place?*

I was in a panic. I was afraid to turn it off, for fear that the musical tone that accompanied this action might be loud enough to be noticed. Instead, I looked around for something to smother the phone. Right behind me, the window had heavy curtains reaching almost to the floor. I carefully wrapped the phone by rolling it in the bottom of the curtain so that it was effectively shielded by several layers of heavy cloth. Crouching there in the darkness, I prayed that I'd be spared the embarrassment, and possible danger, of being exposed.

Almost immediately, the light in the conference room was extinguished. A figure emerged. I believed it was a woman, although the minimal light made it difficult to be sure. As she walked briskly past the office in which I was hiding, she happened to glance directly in my direction, and my anxiety rose even higher. Then she moved on. But, in that moment, I felt that I was hurtling down the rabbit hole at warp speed, for I had recognized her. Although I am terrible at remembering names, I can never forget a face. And the face I had just seen definitely belonged to the pretty paralegal who worked with Hal.

# CHAPTER 16

Wednesday, September 2

Holy shit!

I wasn't anticipating that the eaves-dropper would be someone I could actually recognize. I had planned the next step, but never truly expected I would have to carry it out. I was shaking, and my muscles ached from the tension and awkward posture. I was desperately thirsty, and became aware of an overwhelming need to pee. It seemed as though my bodily functions had been put on indefinite hold as I had soldiered though the past half hour, and were now all clamoring for attention. I moved to the doorway of my improvised lair and peered down the hall, cautiously. All was in darkness.

My first order of business was to relieve myself. Until that was done, I wouldn't be able to think straight.

*How come fictional heroes never seem to find them-
selves in such a plight? Don't they have bladders?*

I wasn't sure that the entire office suite was completely deserted. It certainly seemed to be. The low
whoosh of the air conditioning system was all I
could hear. But on the small chance that I might run
into someone, anyone, I would claim that I'd fallen
asleep. This was lame, I knew, but the best I could
come up with. Fortunately, it turned out that I *was*
completely alone, and I made it to the men's room
without incident. I became somewhat calmer and
able to concentrate on the task at hand.

I made my way slowly back to the conference
room, entered, and turned on a small flashlight I
had brought with me. Then, I went over to the cabinet above the credenza. I carefully removed the
cups and saucers and placed them on the conference
table. There were twelve of each. Then I swept the
light over the sides and back of the now-empty cabinet shelf. I saw absolutely nothing unusual.

I ran my fingers over the surfaces, looking for any
crease or crack that might betray some way to access a hidden space behind them. Nothing! I was
about to give up, and was ready to start placing the
cups and saucers back in the cabinet, when a truly
outlandish idea occurred to me. I recalled Sherlock
Holmes's famous dictum that when you have elim-
inated the impossible, whatever remains, however
improbable, must be the truth. Was there another
possibility?

As I picked up one of the cups, I started to examine it carefully from every possible angle. It seemed like a perfectly ordinary article of dishware. I did the same with several others. I noticed that on the base of each cup was a blue trademark symbol identifying the manufacturer. The markings on all of the cups appeared to be identical. However, on the fifth cup that I scrutinized, I noticed that the alignment of the symbol seemed very slightly askew in relation to the handle. Was this my imagination? I checked each of the other cups with this in mind, but they all seemed perfectly aligned with their respective cup handles.

I looked even more closely at the one possible outlier. I couldn't be sure, but I thought I discerned a very fine line around the base, just above the bottom surface. I held the cup firmly and very gently tried to rotate the bottom, first clockwise, then counter-clockwise. Nothing happened. I was about to give up, but decided to try once more, this time exerting just a bit more force. I was nervous that the cup might break in my hands. But to my great surprise, the base of the cup started to move slightly. I increased the pressure even more, allowing me to screw it entirely off.

I had done it. Now what?

I peered cautiously into the opening at the bottom of the cup. I shined the light into the opening and beheld some sort of electronic circuit about an inch square.

*What to do now? Should I simply take the cup with me?*

I would be meeting with FBI Agent D'Amato the following morning. I could bring it to her.

*She might know what it is and how to deal with it, right?*

But I was worried about the consequences of removing it. Wouldn't that surely tip off the unknown eavesdropper? I decided rather to take a few pictures, using my phone, from several angles. I would share these with her at my meeting the next day.

I began replacing the cups and saucers in the cabinet. I was being extremely careful and deliberate to avoid any damage. I was starting to feel somewhat calmer, as I was almost finished with that process, when I was unexpectedly startled by a jangling sound.

*What the fuck?*

I hurriedly completed putting everything away and went to the door. Poking my head out, I observed that around the corner, in the hallway leading to the front door, the lights had gone on. I could hear two people talking, a man and a woman, but couldn't make out what they were saying. It didn't sound like English.

*Who are they? What are they doing here so late?*

I thought they might be lawyers returning after dinner to continue working. If so, I'd just pretend I'd been working late as well. They didn't seem to be moving toward me, so I sneaked a quick peek around the corner, holding my breath. I recognized a custodial crew and breathed a sigh of relief. They would be accustomed to employees working late, especially in a law firm. I simply smiled as I walked past,

Five minutes later, I was out on Boylston Street, heading for the T station.

On the ride home, I was so lost in thought that I almost missed my stop. When I did get off in Newton Centre, I thought again about the blue SUV. A couple of times I actually doubled back a block or so to see if I was being followed. Turning the corner onto our street, I decided to walk past my house for about a hundred yards, and then turn back to the house. Finally, I arrived home. All was quiet and dark downstairs, but I could see a light on in our bedroom upstairs.

"Hi, dear, I'm home," I called, in as normal and cheerful a voice as I could muster.

"Oh, good," Val replied.

"I'll be up shortly, but I think I need a nightcap first. It's been a complicated day."

"I understand. I'm just reading the Stephen King novel I told you about. Very spooky. I'm glad you're home. You can tell me all about your adventures when you come up...if I'm still awake."

I went to the refrigerator and dispensed a few ice cubes into a glass, then poured in the scotch. "Cover your ice" was a favorite expression of Hector's that came to mind. Tonight, I would heed this advice.

I sat on one of the kitchen stools and decompressed for a few minutes, sipping slowly and pondering what to tell Valerie. I couldn't violate my confidentiality agreement, but the pressure was building up, and I needed some release. I would reveal what I could, so she'd have some understanding of what I was going through. I finished my drink and went upstairs. I entered our bedroom and sat down on the end of our bed.

"You look completely wiped," said Val. "I know you've been really busy lately, and I don't want to butt in, but are you okay, honey?"

"Honestly, I'm not sure. On one hand, there's a lot of stress from the new project, and it's making it hard to concentrate on course preparation. On the other, I feel under tremendous pressure to produce something helpful to my client, but the numbers don't seem to be cooperating. There are only so many statistical rabbits I can pull out of the data hat. I may have to deliver bad news, and you know how the messenger tends to get blamed."

"That's a helluva burden to be under."

"Yeah, and there's something else too," I offered hesitantly.

"Oh, isn't that enough?"

I had to be careful here.

"I can't go into detail without violating confidentiality, but there's something weird going on that's making me uncomfortable. Remember that I told you about this study that is potentially very damaging to my client?"

"Yes, vaguely. What about it?"

"Well, my client is concerned that there might be some hidden agenda behind the study. It's conceivable that those funding it are involved in some kind of industrial espionage or insider trading. They told me about another company that had something like that happen. There's no evidence of anything specific, but my client seems spooked."

"Don't such conspiracy theories seem rather far-fetched? Anyway, why should any of that affect you?"

I hesitated before responding. "Ordinarily, it wouldn't. But there have been some rather weird things happening lately."

Now, she sounded concerned. "What kind of weird things?"

I chose my words carefully. "I know this will sound crazy, but I think someone is bugging our meetings at the law firm. Remember when we talked about what I should wear for that meeting at the client company?"

"Sure."

"Well I have reason to suspect that someone learned about it and knew that I would be there. And I think that person may have been keeping tabs on me for some reason."

I told her about my sightings of the blue SUV, omitting the details about the last one outside Aldous's office. I mentioned nothing about my escapades earlier that night.

"But, are you sure it was the *same* SUV? You said you weren't absolutely sure, right? Plus, why couldn't it just be a coincidence that the same, or a similar, vehicle happened to be there? Aren't you always telling me that coincidences are more frequent than we usually imagine?"

"Yes, you're probably right," I replied, but my tone evidently lacked conviction.

"Anyway," she said, "even if your suspicions are correct, we're not talking about international terrorists here. This is just about some kind of intrigue involving large amounts of money, right? You just need to focus on your job, and try to tune out all the noise."

"I guess so. The good news is that I haven't seen the blue SUV in a couple of days. I have a breakfast meeting tomorrow morning that may shed light on what's going on. I'm meeting with an FBI agent who found out that the SUV is licensed to a private investigator. She said she would contact him and put an end to these shenanigans."

"Did you say FBI? For real?"

"Yes, I think she's part of a financial crimes unit. The company executive I met with knows her, and he told her about my concerns. She reassured me when we spoke by phone that this private investigator has a good reputation, so there's probably some innocuous explanation. But what bothers me is that I don't know why someone might be interested in me, a professor and statistician."

"I don't know, dear, but I'm somewhat relieved to know you've got the FBI on your side. Maybe your FBI friend can figure it out."

"I certainly hope so. Let's get some sleep."

*If I can.*

# CHAPTER 17

Thursday, September 3

At eight the next morning, I was at Lina's Café. I was sitting at a table in the most remote corner of the room, nursing a second cup of dark roast. I had mentioned to Lina that I was expecting someone for a business meeting, and that we'd order food when she arrived. This was a first, as I had previously come alone, or occasionally with Val, and I had always chosen a table closer to the front window. I had arrived early and been sitting for maybe twenty minutes. Lina glanced over from behind the counter a couple of times. I probably looked unusually nervous, because she was giving me quizzical looks, or was that my imagination?

The door opened, and in walked a rather stout, middle-aged woman with dark brown hair cut short. Wearing a serious expression, she glanced around, quickly spotted me in the corner, and the edges of her lips rose slightly as she nodded. I got up to greet her as she came over.

"Hi, Dr. Wheeler," she said, I'm Rita D'Amato. She showed me her FBI credentials, then extended her hand. "Nice t'meet yah."

"Please, call me Ken," I responded, as we shook hands. She had a firm grip.

Turning toward the counter, I told her I was planning to order the crepes for breakfast, which I highly recommended. She opted for coffee, explaining that she had already eaten much earlier. After I put in my order and she filled her cup, we sat down at the corner table. Only two other tables were occupied, both far enough away that we wouldn't be overheard. We chatted a bit about our backgrounds. I learned that she had grown up on the East Side of Providence, which accounted for the New England accent. She was from a large Catholic blue-collar family, and had graduated from U.R.I. and Boston College Law School. She reminded me of the eponymous protagonist in *Vera*, the long-running British detective series on public television.

After the small-talk, we got down to business.

"Thanks Ken, for agreeing to meet with me. I know you must be very busy."

"Well, I was anxious to find out what you've learned about this private investigator who's been following me around. I'm hoping that maybe you can tell me why he's so interested in me. Plus, I have some more details about that...and there's something else I want to share with you. Frankly, this is all starting to get me a bit rattled."

"I understand, but before we get into all that, I'd like to ask *you* a question."

"Okay."

She pulled a small notebook out of her handbag and turned to a page in the middle. "Selwyn mentioned that you alluded to some, let me see, uh...tentative ideas regarding the data being analyzed by the Johns Hopkins researchers. Is that right? He sensed you were being a bit evasive."

Suddenly, I was feeling defensive. "Boy, nothing much slips by that guy, does it?"

"No, it doesn't. I can vouch for that. But look, I'm not being critical, and neither was he, I think. He suspects you had a reason for keeping that close to the vest for now, probably a very good reason. Now, what can you tell me?"

"Actually, there are two reasons. One is that I truly don't have enough information yet to draw any conclusions and don't want to go off half-cocked. The other is that I'm concerned that the conference room in which we were meeting is being bugged."

I thought this bald assertion would surprise her, but she showed no reaction at all. "Let's take those one at a time. Please, tell me what you suspect, even if you can't be sure."

"Sure. You know something about the situation that PhireBreak is in, right?"

"Yes, Selwyn's briefed me on that."

"Okay, as I explained to him, the way the Johns

Hopkins research folks are measuring the dementia risk is by a new algorithm. It supposedly analyzes a person's gene-expression profile in their lymphocytes, the white-blood cells involved in our immune systems. Based on the gene expressions, the algorithm can estimate a probability that mental decline will ensue within just a few years. I haven't had a chance yet to review all the information they just handed over to us. I'm planning to do that very soon."

"Okay, I get the gist of what you're saying."

Just then Lina called out that my order was ready. I went up to the counter and retrieved my crepes, although I found that I didn't seem to have much of an appetite.

"You were explaining about this new algorithm," Rita prompted when I sat back down.

"Oh yeah. So, according to the Hopkins research, the probability produced by this new predictive algorithm was significantly higher, on average, for the Verbana patients than for the control group. Do you understand what I mean by statistical significance?"

"Yes, basically, that the difference was probably not just random, because such a large difference would be very unlikely to have occurred by chance."

"Very good," I said, smiling, "I guess you have some knowledge of statistics."

"Actually, I have a Master's in Economics from Northeastern along with my law degree. Statistics and econometrics were among my favorite courses. Some of the sophisticated scams concocted by the bad guys in the financial arena these days involve some fairly serious math."

I was impressed.

"But am I right in thinking that statistical significance is no longer considered the 'gold standard' in judging whether an observed effect is meaningful?" she asked.

"Hmm. After years of wrangling over this issue, statisticians now generally agree that it's still an important piece of information in many situations. But it needs to be placed in the context of other evidence. Statistical significance implies that the difference is unlikely to be random, but not what the difference really *means*. In any case, the FDA still places a lot of stock in this criterion, though less than it used to."

"Okay, so what's your theory?"

"Well, it's really more of an anomaly than a theory."

"How so?"

"As I told you, we don't know yet exactly how the algorithm works. But we do know, from recent genetics research, many of the genes that are related to brain functions. Okay, suppose Verbana truly does influence cognitive acuity somehow. Then, we would *expect* to observe some evidence of increased or decreased expression levels for some of these genes. You see?"

"Uh huh."

"Well, my initial analysis doesn't find any indication of this going on. The differences between the Verbana and control groups in the pivotal clinical trial appears consistent with chance variability. Of course, that doesn't mean that the differences really *are* random, but it does beg for a logical explanation. I hope when we know more about the algorithm, we can understand why this anomaly may be occurring."

"Perhaps the problem is with the data," Rita suggested.

"What do you mean?"

"Are you certain that the tests were conducted properly, the results entered correctly, analyses coded correctly, etc.?"

This caught me by surprise, and I paused to consider the idea. Actually, it jibed with a concern I've had for some time about the possibility that the arcane procedures involved in drug approvals could be subverted. This could have resulted in a lengthy discussion of this complex issue.

In the end, I just said: "Hmm, I'll have to give that some thought."

I was beginning to get annoyed that the conversation had veered off course from my immediate concerns.

"If you don't mind," I said, "I'd like to find out about that private eye who's been following me around. I haven't seen the blue Lexus SUV lately, so you must have had some success."

For the first time, she seemed a bit uncertain and

hesitant.

"I do want to go there, but before I forget, you mentioned a second reason why you didn't share this at the meeting. You said that the room might be bugged. Tell me more about that."

"Oh, of course." I went on to describe my adventure of the previous evening. When I got to the part about seeing Hal's paralegal, whom I had subsequently identified as Eve Stolz, she stopped me.

"Wait, are you sure that was the woman you saw? You said that it was pretty dark in the hallway."

"I can't be absolutely certain, no, but I give it a high probability."

"How high?"

I smiled. "Let's just say, beyond a reasonable doubt."

She smiled. "All right, please continue."

When I described how I had found the coffee cup with the loose bottom, and managed to open it, her mouth fell half-open in amazement. Then, I explained my decision not to remove the cup, because I wanted her professional advice on what to do.

"That was definitely the right call. We don't want to tip off whoever planted that device. Knowing it's there now might work to our advantage and help us find who's behind whatever is happening. By the way, can you describe for me exactly what it looked like?"

"I can do better than that. I took some photos, using the burner phone because I wasn't sure how secure my personal phone would be." She nodded, signaling her understanding.

I pulled out the phone, opened the picture gallery and handed it to her. With an expression of intense concentration that I can only describe as raptorial, she mentally devoured the images. At one point, she turned toward me and seemed about to speak, but instead merely shook her head and scrutinized them a bit longer.

"This is truly, uh...remarkable," she finally blurted out.

"What, the pictures, the fact that I got them, or the device itself?"

"All three, but mainly the device. It's very compact, yet completely invisible, apparently, to sophisticated detection technology. Our techies will undoubtedly want to get their hot little hands on your coffee cup right away, but we may need to keep it in place a bit longer while we attempt to unravel what's going on with PhireBreak. Deciding exactly how to proceed is above my pay-grade. I'll be honest with you. When Selwyn first contacted us, I thought we would just be doing him a small favor by checking it out to allay his concerns. But this is a game-changer."

"How do you mean?"

"I don't have a clue exactly what we are looking at," she said, indicating the pictures. "I assume it's some kind of stealth recording device. I bet it's some kind of high-grade spyware, very advanced. The fact that it managed to evade detection by Selwyn's tech team is impressive."

"All right, what does that mean?"

"I'm not sure, but I've never seen anything this sophisticated deployed in connection with financial crimes. Maybe, we're facing a new breed of corporate raiders armed with twenty-first century cutting-edge technology. PhireBreak could just be their first victim."

"Or, maybe the second," I said.

"What do you mean?"

"Hal Farenheit mentioned the Pfeffer situation as, I think, a cautionary tale. He said it was not directly related to our situation, but who knows?"

Rita looked thoughtful. "I need to speak to some colleagues about all this. For now, let's just leave all the pieces on the board. I'll speak with Selwyn about the meeting room. You and I should talk again soon after I get some more feedback from on high. Anyway, impressive work," she acknowledged, "for an amateur."

"Thanks, but you still haven't told me about the private eye."

"Yes, well, uh...it's a bit complicated. I'm afraid we don't know that much. We haven't actually talked with the man yet. His name, by the way, is Rex Frey. You may have seen one of his rather garish billboard ads: Rex Frey, Private Eye. Regrettably, it seems that, for the moment at least, Rex has, well, he's...disappeared."

"*Disappeared!?*" I exclaimed, loudly enough for the other customers to look around, and for Lina to cast a disapproving frown my way. I regained enough composure to ask more softly "What the hell does *that* mean?"

She sighed. "We called his administrative assistant. She thought we had called because she had just reported her boss's absence earlier that morning to the police. He hadn't made any contact with her for three days, which was highly unusual. She told us he lives alone and has no family in the area. She seemed quite upset. We then drove to his home in Framingham. It's a split-level in a large sub-division built in the 1970's. The vehicle you described was nowhere in sight. The front door was unlocked, so we entered. The place seemed completely deserted, but all clothes and furnishings seemed to be there, as far as we could tell, and some food and beer were in the refrigerator. Neither his laptop nor phone could be found."

I was stunned and suddenly realized that now *my* mouth was half open. Fortunately, Lina was busy with another customer and didn't seem to notice anything strange transpiring.

"Do you think he's...?" I started to ask.

"Let's not jump to conclusions. People disappear all the time for a few days and then return. You know, 'what happens in Vegas' and all that. But the timing does seem a trifle suspicious, and you'd think he'd have informed his admin. Incidentally, you mentioned earlier that you had some information for me related to him, didn't you?"

"Oh, right. Check out the video that's also there," I said, pointing to the burner phone, which was still in her hand.

"Okay, what will I be looking at?"

"It was taken from a security camera at my attorney's office two days ago."

I gave her a brief rundown of the circumstances surrounding how I had obtained the video.

"Wow, the hits just keep on coming," she said.

"Why don't you take a look at it now. It's only a few minutes long." As she did this, I ate a few bites of my crepes, which had hitherto remained virtually untouched, and were starting to get cold.

"Not Oscar-worthy," she quipped, "but useful nonetheless. Unfortunately, there's no way to identify the other guy by facial recognition, but you'd be surprised what our techies can do." She didn't elaborate.

"Do you have any theory as to who it might be, and why he's so interested in me?"

"No, and no, but when we manage to locate him, we should find some answers. It's all probably just some innocent mistake."

"*When*, you said, not *if*. You seem pretty confident."

She sighed again, and pursed her lips. "Look, it's possible that Rex inadvertently got mixed up in something he didn't bargain for, and has decided to lay low for a while. Maybe his job was to chauffeur Mr. Baseball Cap around to provide local knowledge and help him check on some folks in the Boston area. We have ways of finding out things that may lead us to him, but I can't give you any details. At least it's unlikely he'll be bothering you again. Listen, I really should get going. Why don't you email me the video and pictures and I'll take off? I'll be back in touch within a couple of days. Try to act completely normal, and say nothing about our conversation to anyone except Selwyn. He can decide whether or not to loop Farenheit in."

"What about the conference room at Cooley & Lerner?"

"When is your next meeting?" she asked.

"A week from next Wednesday."

"Oh, we'll have a plan in place well before then. Just try to stay focused. Think of this all as an elaborate game. You get to help your client, bill a lot of hours, and maybe help us put some bad-guys where they belong. And don't take this wrong, but *please*, no more Jason Bourne impersonations."

# CHAPTER 18

Thursday, September 3

When I left Lina's, I walked over to the T station. I planned to head into my office at B.U. for a few hours, and then over to Harvard Square for my one-fifteen lunch meeting with Hector. Classes were about to begin the following week, right after the Labor Day weekend. I would spend the time in my office polishing my first few lectures and in a meeting with my teaching assistants. These rather pedestrian activities should be a good palliative for the churning in my gut. Fully processing my conversation with Rita D'Amato would have to come later.

Mercifully, the morning unfolded pretty much as I had planned. At least that part of my life seemed to be normal and under control. At twelve thirty, I went down to the T stop on Commonwealth Avenue to begin the journey to Harvard Square. I caught an arriving Green Line streetcar a few minutes later. When it rumbled into the Park Street underground station, I remembered something Rita had suggested that was bothering me. What if there really was a problem with the data itself? I stepped off the streetcar and walked over to the Red Line platform, arriving just as the train bound for Cambridge pulled in. Ten minutes later I emerged from underground into the bustle of Harvard Square, tacitly regarded by many of its denizens as the intellectual hub of the universe.

Seeing the familiar old red-brick buildings of Harvard Yard, and the iconic stores and restaurants in winding streets that surround it, always gave me a positive charge, fueled mostly by nostalgia for my grad-school days. This feeling was especially strong on beautiful September days like this, which evoked a sense of infinite possibility. Would this be the year I might make some momentous new discovery? But, this time, I had a lot more on my mind than academic research as I walked past the Harvard Coop and down Brattle Street for my rendezvous with Hector at our favorite burger bar. We figured that the hour would be late enough to alleviate the usual mad crush of Harvard students that normally filled the place. When I got there, it was still pretty rowdy, but the noise level was tolerable.

Surprisingly, Hector had arrived before me. I found him already seated in a booth perusing the menu. "Hey, Hector," I said. He looked up. "Why are you studying that?" I asked. "You should know this menu by heart. Any way, it's just hamburgers."

"True, but I'm always hoping for something new and interesting. This jalapeno, cheddar and bacon burger is enticing."

"Not for me, buddy, just my usual burger with grilled onions on a whole wheat bun."

"You are so predictable... and boring."

"When it comes to burgers, I'm old school."

"Yeah, except for the whole wheat."

"Anyway, let's talk business so we can charge this to the client."

"Sounds good."

"First, let me hand over what we received from the Johns Hopkins researchers. I've looked it over, and it seems pretty complete. All the data seem to be here, plus the computer code used to produce their results. Plus, there's a limited license for the proprietary software module that can generate the Caldwell Index scores. We need that in order to replicate their analyses ourselves. Frankly, I'm not sure what that will buy us, but we'll see."

"So the first thing for me is to replicate the results, right?"

"Yes, absolutely, that's the first. I'd be surprised if we come up with anything different, but you never know. After that, I want to run down something that's been bothering me. It's about the gene-expression data. There's something strange going on."

"How do you mean, Ken? Did I do something wrong?"

"No, not at all." I went on to relate the same information about the gene-expression data that I had conveyed to Rita earlier that morning. He nodded thoughtfully as he stroked his beard.

"What do you think could account for that?" he asked.

"I don't know. But it doesn't seem right. My gut says something doesn't compute. Either the Caldwell Index involves previously unsuspected genes that relate to dementia, or it analyzes some genes we know about in some completely novel way. Either way, it would represent a major scientific breakthrough that's previously been overlooked. It just doesn't feel right. Of course, I could be missing something obvious here, I suppose."

"I've found your instincts about patterns in data to be uncannily on target," he responded, as he put down the menu.

"Thanks for the vote of confidence, but flattery won't affect what I'm paying you."

"Yeah, well, it was worth a try."

A few seconds later, the waitress arrived to take our orders. Hector ordered the super-sized version of his extravaganza, and I ordered my boring onion-burger. For sides, he opted for a double-order of fries, while I settled for coleslaw. My expression must have been a give-away, because he raised his hands in a mock defensive posture.

"I know what you're thinking. Don't start. You'll be happy that I've promised Dana to start eating a healthier diet. It *burns* me, man, that I have to choose between decent food and sex, but there you have it."

"Don't forget about health," I said. "That's a bonus you get along with the sex."

"Very funny. Have you thought about stand-up?"

We both munched on our food for a while. I continued to ponder the data enigma until another idea came to mind.

"Listen, Hector. Let's assume the Verbana effect is real. Maybe some individuals are actually at higher risk for future dementia after taking Verbana. Suppose thatK we could identify a relatively small subset of patients who are truly at risk. Then it could still be beneficial for the majority of other patients. It wouldn't be an ideal result for Phire-Break, but it would allow them to retain most of their market."

"I'm not sure I buy your theory, though. It seems awfully speculative. How could we find such a subset anyhow?"

"You know that new statistical method I've been working on with Ralph Granger at Wellesley College?"

"You mean the new way to develop a predictive model for personalized medicine?"

"Right. We've recently made a breakthrough. I'd like to try it on the Verbana data. In principle, our technique could predict the effect of Verbana at an individual patient level. Suppose we use it to build a model to predict the Verbana effect based on the genetic data. I mean the genes themselves, in the patient's DNA, not the gene *expressions*. If my theory pans out, we should find that Verbana's effect is limited to patients with certain DNA profiles."

"Sure, I can do that, but what if it *doesn't* pan out?"

"Oh, ye of little faith. Then, I'll just have to concoct another brilliant theory," I replied.

We finished our meal, paid the bill, and walked out of the restaurant. We headed toward Harvard Square, where we would hop on the T and proceed to our respective destinations. Reflexively, I performed a quick scan of my surroundings to look out for the blue SUV, which I now knew belonged to Rex Frey, private eye.

"What?" asked Hector. You look concerned about something.

"Nothing," I lied.

Just then, my burner phone buzzed. As I pulled it out of my pocket, I told Hector: "Listen, I'd better take this. Let's talk soon to follow up."

When I answered the phone, it was Rita. I hadn't expected to hear from her so soon. "Hello, Ken. I think we should meet tomorrow. Those pictures you gave me have caused quite a stir. They put the PhireBreak situation in something of a new light. We need to tread very carefully with respect to our reaction. I know this is cryptic but I'll clarify it when we meet. Can you suggest a venue that would be private, but in keeping with your usual behavior?"

"Give me a minute to think about it."

After about thirty seconds I replied.

"Okay, I'm planning to meet tomorrow with a

colleague, Ralph Granger, who teaches at Wellesley College. We're collaborating on a research project. Our meeting will be finished around noon. Often, when I'm in that area and the weather is decent, I like to grab a sandwich at a nearby Italian deli and eat it in the park in front of the Wellesley Town Hall on Washington Street. There are several benches near the duck pond there. Would that work?"

"Perfect, I'll find you there at, say, twelve thirty?"

"Okay, that's fine."

# CHAPTER 19

Friday, September 4

After my meeting with Ralph at Wellesley College, I walked the half mile to the town center. It was just past noon when I stopped in at my favorite sandwich shop, just a stone's throw from the Wellesley Town Hall. In addition to incredible submarine sandwiches on crusty Italian bread, this emporium purveys a wide variety of delicacies imported from Italy, including cheese, olive oil, tomato sauce, pastries, and candy. The various products are attractively displayed on several tables and in shelves along the walls. I passed by these and went directly to the counter in the back. There I waited in line for about ten minutes before ordering an Italian sub stuffed with salami, provolone, lettuce, tomato and hot peppers. After it came and I paid, I walked over to the duck pond, as arranged. I settled down on an unoccupied wooden bench and started to munch on my sandwich.

Several minutes passed as I pondered recent events and their possible implications. I was so lost in thought that I failed to notice when Rita arrived.

"Hi, Ken," she said, "this is a pretty spot. I've never been here before."

"Yeah, the building is quite something," I said, pointing to the large and ornate stone edifice that serves as Wellesley's town hall. "I think it was built about 1900, and it's on the National Register of Historic Buildings. I heard that it was originally a library and funded by the Hunnewell family, which owned much of the town back then, including this park and what became the Wellesley College campus. Sometimes we bring our nine-year-old son here to feed the ducks."

She sat down and removed a sandwich covered in cellophane from a brown paper bag. As she unwrapped it, she looked around to see who might be nearby. There were a few parents with young children at the edge of the pond, fully occupied in feeding the ducks. At this time of year, there were many of them, noisily squabbling over the pieces of bread being hurled their way. Rita seemed satisfied that we wouldn't be overheard.

"There are several matters I want to discuss with you," she began. "The most urgent concerns the listening device you found. I was correct that it *is* cutting edge technology. In fact, it's *so* advanced that the FBI doesn't use it yet. Apparently, what you saw is a prototype developed by our own NSA and currently being field-tested by the CIA. So that raises some troubling questions. How could technology like that possibly have found its way out of our intel cocoon? Is someone in our intelligence services compromised and leaking highly classified technology? How is this connected with industrial espionage, if that's what is going on here? Most important, who's behind all this and why?"

"Wait a minute. What you're telling me must be highly classified information, right?"

"Yes, I should have mentioned that you've temporarily been granted a high-level security clearance, because we need your help. But don't let it go to your head." She half-smiled.

"Also, I need to give you some more context. You mentioned that Hal Farenheit told you about the Pfeffer takeover."

"Yeah, he said it was probably unrelated...kind of a cautionary tale."

"Right. Well, I'm afraid he was being a bit disingenuous there. The Bureau's financial crimes division has recently made insider trading a priority. We've had our eye on the hedge fund that was involved in the Pfeffer situation for a while. It's called the Biomedical Horizons Fund, or BHF for short. We suspect BHF may have obtained some inside information about the vulnerability of Pfeffer's blockbuster product, Velex. In case you haven't kept up, the company has recently risen like the phoenix to experience a miraculous recovery in profitability. It seems that its researchers have been able to tweak the molecule to minimize the side effect, and that new early clinical trials have been quite promising. They're planning a large trial that will, presumably, result in FDA approval in a couple of years. This remarkable run of apparent good timing and luck seems almost *too* good to be completely legal. But, so far, we haven't been able to figure out how they pulled it off."

"Maybe they're just smarter than everyone else."

"My gut says otherwise, but my gut isn't admissible in court."

"Okay, so how is this related to PhireBreak...and to my listening device?"

"Well, the Pfeffer situation occurred in the past, so it's hard to investigate what was going on *retrospectively*. It's basically a done deal. But the PhireBreak situation is unfolding right now, in real-time. If, in fact, it turns out to be act two of the same play, we may not only be able to arrest it, no pun intended, but also resolve the Pfeffer case. Your discovery of the surveillance, Ken, while ominous because of its potential implications, also represents an opportunity."

"I'm not quite following," I said.

"Look, as far as we know, whoever planted that device is still unaware that we know about it...so far. That gives us an edge. We can control what they hear. If we play our cards right, we can use this to provoke them into a blunder. Of course, that depends on not spooking them by prematurely tipping our hand."

"Wait. You mean we have to leave the devious Ms. Stolz alone for now?"

I definitely hadn't expected this complication, and it bothered me.

"Yes, for now. Of course, we would monitor her activities closely and plan to take her into custody for questioning when it serves our interests best."

"I don't know. It might be hard to keep acting normally around her. Who else knows about this?"

"Aside from my colleagues in the FBI, only Selwyn and Hal. Since Hal is her immediate supervisor, he can keep close track of her while she's in the office. We can watch her on the outside."

"Sure, but what if they have other ways of spying on us. How can we be sure they won't get wise to us?"

"Obviously, there's no ironclad guarantee, but it may be our best chance to smoke them out."

"Assuming that the Pfeffer thing and our problem are truly related, do you have any idea who might be behind all this?"

"We have some suspicions but little real evidence, and I can't say much more. But I can tell you we're keeping tabs on both the BHF hedge fund and the Mannheim Foundation."

"Why?"

"For one thing, there are some curious connections between the two. Some of the major investors in the hedge fund appear to be supporters of Mannheim as well."

"That doesn't seem especially suspicious to me."

"No, not by itself, but some of these investors have some, shall we say, shady backgrounds. There seems to be a lot of dough pouring through BHF from South Africa and Latin America these days. Some of the newly minted billionaires there have grown rich by exploiting workers illegally. They're always looking for ways to launder their money."

"Okay, what about Mannheim?"

"Mannheim has previously funded several research projects that ended up causing...complications for some pharma companies. Plus, one of the Yale researchers who blew the whistle on Pfeffer received a very large grant from Mannheim shortly after the company collapsed. Of course, all this is circumstantial, and not *per se* illegal. Besides, we have to admit that Big Pharma has not always been completely ethical in its lobbying and advertising. So its critics can't be simply dismissed."

"That's true."

"Anyway," she continued, "I think you should be aware that we may be dealing with some very powerful and ruthless forces here. They might be quite aggressive in trying to undermine your reputation if they perceive you as a threat."

She hesitated before continuing. We both took a few bites of our sandwiches.

"There's something more you aren't telling me, isn't there?" I prompted.

She sighed. "It's just something that happened during the time that Pfeffer's problem was first uncovered. You know what a Data Monitoring Committee is, right?"

"Of course, basically the DMC is a committee that's responsible for monitoring a clinical trial as it's being carried out. Their main function is to flag any serious problems, particularly related to patient safety. The DMC members are the only ones involved in the study who have access to unblinded data. No one else involved in the study is supposed to know which subjects received the study drug or an alternate treatment."

"That's right. Well, after the Yale re-analysis came out, and Pfeffer's stock price tumbled, there was lots of finger-pointing regarding who was to blame. The statistician on the DMC was a woman by the name of Jane Clayton. Dr. Clayton was accused of missing the adverse-event signal in the interim data for the main clinical trial. It was alleged that if she had correctly analyzed the interim data, the company would have taken steps to try and ameliorate it, just as the current owner is now doing.

Instead, Pfeffer spent a fortune of mostly borrowed money to complete the trials and expand operations to meet the expected demand."

"So this turned out very badly for Clayton," I said.

"You could say. It damn near ended her career. But, here's the thing. She was adamant that there had been no such evidence of a problem in the data. She was shocked when the Yale re-analysis came out."

"Really? Pfeffer's statisticians must have gone back and audited the data and computer code that had been available at the interim time-point."

"They did, but the Yale results held up, and it was a major black eye for Clayton. We've interviewed her, and she still contends that there must have been an error in the data that she analyzed, because she insists that there was absolutely no indication of a problem."

"I see. So why are you telling me this?"

"For two reasons. First, the stakes here for *you*, professionally, may be unusually high. If the shit hits the fan, people look for someone to blame. It's human nature. I'd hate to see your career take such a hit. So, as I said, be obsessive about keeping and protecting a paper trail."

"Okay, I will. What's the second reason?"

"What if Dr. Clayton wasn't *wrong* after all?"

"Come again?"

"It's my job to be suspicious. I wouldn't rule out the possibility that the data were fiddled in some way. Wouldn't it be possible that the data were somehow changed *after* the interim analysis to create the *appearance* of a problem? Maybe the drug was really fine after all, and the so-called tweak to fix it is actually an elaborate charade."

I thought about this for a minute or so.

"Theoretically, I suppose that's possible," I finally admitted, "but there are many safeguards to assure quality control of the data. It would be very hard to do that without leaving some sort of digital evidence. You're talking, essentially, about a highly sophisticated computer hacking operation."

"Like I said, we may be facing a very sophisticated malefactor here. Anyway, just keep an open mind and don't ignore anything unusual you come across."

I was bothered by what she was implying.

"Let me be sure I understand what you're suggesting. You suspect that someone involved in the data management or analysis process may have deliberately sabotaged the clinical trial results. Their purpose would be to weaken PhireBreak, so it could be 'rescued' (I raised my hands and waggled my fingers to indicate quotation marks) for a relative pittance. You're saying that Hector and I should be on the lookout for evidence in the computer code that such tampering occurred. For all we know, the Hopkins study is completely bogus, although they may simply be unwitting accomplices. Is that about it?"

"Well, yes. I know this sounds like something out of a spy novel, but that's about the size of it."

"To be honest, I *have* witnessed some instances of scientific fraud that were pretty egregious...but this takes it to an entirely different level. The entire pharmaceutical development enterprise depends on a basic trust in the data obtained during clinical trials. If that trust ever becomes eroded, I shudder to imagine the consequences. There are already fringe elements who are skeptical about some critical medical interventions, like vaccination for example. Frankly, I'm incredulous, but I *will* try to keep an open mind."

"Good. Now, let's talk about how we're going to proceed with Ms. Stolz. Presumably, she'll download the data from the listening device the night after your meeting a week from Wednesday. We assume that she will hand-deliver the flash drive containing, presumably, a voice recording, to a contact. Our plan is to follow her from the law office and see where she goes. Depending on how that turns out, we may nab her shortly after that for questioning. Until we've taken that step, I don't want to rattle the cage by suggesting we suspect her in any way."

"Okay."

"At the meeting, Selwyn will ask you for a progress report. We assume they'll be listening. Do you have an idea yet what you'll be saying?"

"Sort of. Hector and I have been investigating that data anomaly I told you about. But we're also exploring a fallback approach. Our working hypothesis is that the effect of Verbana, if it truly exists, might be restricted to a subset of individuals who have identifiable genetic profiles. If so, that could allow PhireBreak to acknowledge an effect, but to minimize its impact, assuming the subset is small."

She thought about this for a few seconds before responding.

"Okay, that's good. It could worry them somewhat, because it could potentially keep Verbana viable, albeit in a weakened state. On the other hand, it won't tip our hand regarding our suspicions. If you learn anything more before the meeting, give me a call, so we can decide whether to factor that into the plan. In the meantime, try to avoid interacting with Eve Stolz."

"Roger that."

"Okay, hang in, I know this isn't easy for you. Your country thanks you for all you're doing," she quipped with a smile.

I wasn't sure quite how to take this remark.

As she walked away, I noticed that she held on to the brown paper bag that had contained her sandwich. I wondered if it contained a recording device. My eyes followed her as she reached the sidewalk and continued toward a beige sedan parked a couple of blocks away. I could see her talking with someone in the driver's seat, presumably another FBI agent. I guessed that he had been positioned there as a lookout, to warn her if anyone seemed to be taking any interest in our conversation. After about thirty seconds they drove off.

# CHAPTER 20

Tuesday, September 8

The following Tuesday marked the beginning of classes. I was scheduled to hold my opening lecture for the large Intro Stats course at three o'clock. I arrived at my office around nine that morning. My plan was to spend the intervening time dealing with final preparations for the course. Over the weekend, I'd spoken with Hector about the data we had received from the Hopkins researchers, which included the Caldwell Index scores for all of the patients. To pursue my fallback plan, we planned to apply my new technique for estimating individualized causal effects. Our objective was to determine if there was a relationship between a person's DNA and the effect of Verbana on the Caldwell Index. More specifically, could we identify a subset of individuals who were susceptible to Verbana's alleged effect?

I was anxious to take a look at these as soon as

possible, but because I knew that would be a major distraction, I resisted the temptation. This day, I vowed to concentrate primarily on my normal academic responsibilities. Of course, within minutes of sitting down at my desk, the burner phone buzzed. It was Hal.

"Hi, Ken. Sorry to bother you, but there's been a violation of the gag order, probably inadvertent but potentially problematic. We're trying to limit the damage."

"Really? How could that have happened?"

"We got a call last night from Bobbie Stanton. You remember her?"

"Sure, she was the one who tipped us off about the *ClinScan* article."

"Yeah. Well, she was at a medical research conference and there was supposed to be a talk by one of the Johns Hopkins researchers. The title of the presentation was 'An Independent Re-Analysis of the Verbana Clinical Trial.' Of course, the session was cancelled because of the court order, but there was considerable interest in why it had to be pulled at the last minute."

"That shouldn't be too big a problem," I interjected.

"Wait, that's not all. As you know, when an academic conference is organized, the papers are submitted several months beforehand."

"Right, that's standard."

"Sure, but an abstract for each paper also needs to be submitted, which then is published in the conference program."

"Oh no! You're kidding."

"I wish. It seems there was a screw up. The abstract *was* actually removed from the online version of the program, but somehow remained in the printed version that conference attendees received. Fortunately, the abstract was fairly vague about the results, which were still very preliminary several months ago when the paper was submitted to the conference. However, there was enough information to insinuate that Verbana might have a problem related to some unspecified cognitive decline. It's only a matter of time, and not much of it, before the bloodhounds at *ClinScan* get wind of this. No doubt PhireBreak will be asked for comment. Justin will have a fit. This is going to ratchet up the pressure on all of us if it hits the mainstream media. We can hide behind the gag order, but if investors start to smell trouble ..."

"I see, but how does all this affect me exactly?"

"It's complicated. On the one hand, we can't say anything about the Hopkins study directly. On the other, we need to maintain a public posture of confidence that the product is completely sound, or, worst-case, that the problem is minor. But we have to be careful not to make any claims that can't be backed up later. So we really need to get to the bottom of this soon."

"Hey, I'm peddling as fast as I can."

"I know, I know. Just saying."

"All right, I've got the message."

We ended the call, and I tried to get back to my class preparation. It was hard not to sneak a peek at the file Hector had emailed over. After a couple of hours editing my class notes, I decided to give him a call. When he picked up, I could tell by the restaurant background noise that he was at lunch.

"Hey, man, sorry to interrupt your lunch."

"No problem. What's up?"

"Thanks for sending over the results. I haven't had a chance to review them yet. Gotta get ready for my class here. There's something else that I'd, uh, like you to check for me."

"Sure, what is it?"

"I know this will sound weird, but there's been some speculation that the data given to Johns Hopkins under the Data Transparency Act may have been corrupted somehow."

"That doesn't seem possible. We checked it against the company's own data, and it matches perfectly."

"I know that, but suppose that in the original data cleaning process an error was made. Such an error could have propagated through later stages of data management and analysis, right?"

"I guess...theoretically, but how could we even check that?"

"The data that was used to generate the Caldwell Index value for each subject consisted of the gene-expression levels for twenty-two genes. We don't yet know which particular genes are involved, but they're probably among the two hundred or so that have been identified as pertaining to mental functions. I can provide you with a list of those. I'd like you to perform essentially a complete audit of the data and code related to any of those genes or their expression levels. Look for any anomalies that appear odd in any way."

"All right, if you say so, but I think it's a wild goose chase."

"Probably, but we have to run down every possibility. I'd like you to run everything through my special software that can detect suspicious data patterns, just to see if anything strange turns up. I want to reassure the client that we haven't overlooked any possibility."

"Okay, but I have a deadline on another project, so this may take a couple of days."

"That's fine. I'm sure it's a waste of time and money, but..."

"Right, only for you, buddy."

"Great, thanks. I owe you one. Bye Hector."

"Bye."

I realized that I was starting to take seriously the notion that something truly nefarious was going on. The conference-room eavesdropping, being tailed, Selwyn's warning. I would have to confide in Hector soon, but after I had some solid evidence.

After speaking with Hector, I started mulling over whether my misgivings about the data geneexpressions made sense...biological sense. I decided to give Dave Parker a call. He picked up almost immediately.

"Dave. How's it going?"

"Okay, actually I was thinking about giving you a buzz. What's on your mind?"

"Well, I've found what seems to be an anomaly in the data that I'm not sure how to interpret. I thought I'd run something by you."

"Really, that's interesting. What gives?"

I started by summarizing for him what we had learned about the Caldwell Index. Then I posed my question.

"I analyzed the lymphocyte gene-expression data for all of the genes known to be involved in mental functioning. I expected to see differences for some of these between the Verbana and control groups. But I'm not finding any evidence of that. Does that make any sense to you?"

"Hmm, I'm not sure. But it does suggest that there may be something about the entire *pattern* of gene-expression results that's not showing up in the individual genes. The whole, in this case, might indicate more than the sum of the parts, so to speak."

"Can you say more about that?"

"Well, you're familiar with the Framingham Study model for predicting heart attack risk, right?"

"Of course."

"The model looks at several factors, like blood pressure, cholesterol, diabetes, etc. Each of these by itself doesn't indicate very much, but the mathematical model that combines them is highly predictive of future cardiovascular risk. For years we didn't understand why the model worked, but the empirical predictions were reliable, and ultimately helped point our research to a deeper biological understanding. For example, we can now specify a group of specific genes that are at work to elevate the risk. At this genomic level, we have built a much more accurate predictive model. All I'm saying is that this Caldwell Index may be doing something like the Framingham model did."

"I get that," I said. "But, at least those individual factors in the old Framingham model did have *some* statistical relationship to heart-attack risk individually, even though accurate prediction required combining them in a complex manner. Furthermore, what about all the other genes that are related to cognitive activity? Wouldn't you expect to see an effect of Verbana on some of these?"

"That's true. I don't know what to say."

"Okay, thanks."

"Look, Ken. From a biochemistry perspective, I'm kind of stumped too, which is why I wanted to call you. Frankly, we can't definitively rule out the possibility that Verbana can cross the blood-brain barrier. Therefore, it's *theoretically* possible for it to have an effect on cognitive functioning. However, we haven't found any research that suggests a biochemical mechanism consistent with this possibility. I was thinking maybe if we got together, we might come up with a hypothesis you could test. Why don't we try to meet soon to brainstorm?"

"Okay, let's keep in touch."

"Maybe we could set up a lunch meeting now. How's your schedule looking?"

"I'm swamped. Let me get back to you, okay?"

"Sure. Bye."

The rest of the afternoon was uneventful. My first lecture of the semester went smoothly, and I walked back to my office. I was looking forward to digging into the files that Hector had sent over. But Dame Fortune had other plans. As I reached my office, my office phone began ringing. I managed to catch it on the fourth ring.

"Hi, dear," said Valerie. "How did your class go?"

"Pretty well, I think. I was surprised that attendance was down a bit, but there are always some late transfers in, so it might even out. The lecture itself went fine. They even laughed at a couple of my statistical jokes."

"Statistical jokes? Isn't that an oxymoron?"

"Ha-ha, very funny. But I'm guessing that insulting me probably isn't the only reason you called. Is everything okay with Sam?"

"Oh, he's fine, but I wanted to know when you'd be home. You know, we have the meet-and-greet with Sam's teacher tonight."

"*Oh shit!* Really? I completely forgot."

"I suppose we don't both have to be there, but..."

"No, no, I'll make it. Remind me what time."

"It's at seven thirty."

"Okay, I'll be home by seven and we can walk over together. I'll just grab something to eat here at the cafeteria. We can have 'dessert' at the school."

I was referring sarcastically to the light refreshments served after the teacher's presentation. This usually consisted of some overly sweet cookies and brownies, eaten on paper plates, washed down with fruit juice or coffee. There was about a thirty percent chance the coffee would be palatable.

After we ended the call I sighed with a sense of frustration. I would only have an hour or so to delve into the results of Hector's computations. But I couldn't restrain myself any longer before starting. Hector's program had derived a predictive model using the new method Ralph Granger and I had been developing. I was hopeful that it could allow us to define a subgroup of individuals who were possibly susceptible to the Verbana's effect. However, when I examined the results, I was disappointed. The analysis did not identify any subset of individuals to which the effect of Verbana on the Caldwell Index appeared to be restricted.

When six o'clock rolled around, I knew I had to wrap up and get going. As I was about to exit, I was intercepted by Irv Rothman. He asked whether I could stop by his office the next day to discuss an issue that had come up. He seemed somewhat concerned, but didn't offer to elaborate. As I was in a hurry to get out, I didn't press him. I just told him I would drop by in the afternoon sometime.

I arrived home just as it was time to leave for Sam's school. As we walked, Val informed me that her morning-sickness had finally begun to subside. I was genuinely pleased to hear that, and expressed as much, but she could sense that my concerns were elsewhere.

"Look," she said, "you really don't have to come if things are too complicated with your work."

"To be honest, I would prefer not to, but I'd regret missing this. I promise to switch gears."

When we arrived in Sam's classroom, his teacher was about to start her presentation. I glanced around the room and recognized a few familiar faces. One of these was Carl Vitale, whom I'd last seen at the birthday party for Sam's friend a few weeks before. He caught my eye and smiled. I was pleased that Sam would have at least one good friend in this new class. I also had some additional questions for Carl and resolved to catch him during the post-presentation refreshment period. At the same moment, I realized that I hadn't had a chance to grab a bite to eat and was famished. The brownies and sugar cookies I had disparaged previously were starting to be very appealing. Now, if only I could get lucky with the coffee.

# CHAPTER 21

Tuesday, September 8

I noticed Carl standing in a short line at the coffee urn. I was curious whether he'd heard about the recent article or the conference abstract. I was sure he had his finger on the pulse of any scuttlebutt circulating around the halls of academia. I managed to grab a brownie and wolf it down as I drew closer to him. I finally managed to accost him, just as he was filling his Styrofoam cup.

"Hey Carl, how goes the war against cancer?"

"Oh, Ken," he replied. "Inching ahead. How's the wonderful world of statistics?"

"On *average*, pretty good," I quipped. He rolled his eyes at this lame attempt at statistical humor. "Listen, I wanted to ask you about something related to the Verbana trial."

"Shoot."

"A colleague of mine mentioned something interesting. She was at a conference recently and came across an abstract for a paper describing a re-analysis of the Verbana trial. Apparently, some researchers at Hopkins got the data by filing a Data Transparency Act application. What's odd is that the presentation was cancelled without any explanation. But the interesting..."

At that point, Carl interrupted me.

"Wait a minute. As a matter of fact, I just heard something about this from the staff psychologist in our unit. She mentioned something about some new research linking Verbana to dementia, of all things. She was rather upset about it. I think she was concerned that we might have missed something. I told her that it sounded ridiculous, but she wanted to check the psychological test data we collected during the study."

"Oh, you still have that data?" I asked.

"Sure, it's retained in the patient's medical record. You never know what might be useful in treating the patient after the study is completed. So it was pretty easy for her to go back and check those."

"Do all of the sites retain all the psychological data as you do?"

"I assume so, but never asked. The only requirement for the study was that we had to submit the psych data, anonymized, of course, to Mannheim when a patient completed the study. I'm not sure why they even needed that. Anything *after* that would only exist in our files, to be used for clinical purposes only."

"I'm sorry. Did you say *Mannheim*?"

"Yes, Mannheim Clinical Support, MCS for short. Lately, they've become the go-to Clinical Research Organization for a lot of pharma companies. They generally undercut most of the other CROs on pricing and have a reputation for excellent quality control. They're headquartered in Mannheim, Germany."

"Interesting," I said. "Uh, what did your staff psychologist find out, just for curiosity...if you can talk about it."

"Well, yeah, basically she said there was absolutely no indication of any major changes for any of the subjects treated with Verbana in our study. In fact, she followed up by checking the recent notes we have on those patients we've continued to follow after the study was completed. There's not a whiff of any problems related to cognitive capacity. So that was reassuring. But she still felt a bit unnerved at the possibility that Verbana could have somehow caused a problem. My guess is that the paper got pulled from the conference because their preliminary results didn't hold up. Maybe you can re-analyze the Hopkins re-analysis when, and if, it eventually does come out."

I just smiled.

With that, we parted company, and I linked up with Val, who was chatting with two of the other mothers. My head was still spinning, trying to process the information Carl had imparted.

"Oh, there you are," she said. "I guess we should head out." She said her good-byes and we walked out into the hallway.

"I saw you talking with Carl Vitale. What were you chatting about? Anything interesting?"

"Actually, it was quite interesting, although I'm not sure what to make of it. This project keeps on producing surprises."

We got home, paid the sitter, and checked on Sam, who was fast sleep. I realized I was still hungry. I found some leftover tuna salad in the refrigerator and made myself a sandwich. Val went upstairs to change. She was really tired after a long day and would soon be asleep. I knew I would be up for a while processing what Carl had related. I sat down in front of the TV to watch the last few innings of the Red Sox game. I put the TV on mute and watched the action with limited attention while taking stock.

According to Carl, this MCS company had recently become a big player as a CRO. Coincidentally, it just *happened* to be located in Mannheim, home also of the Mannheim Foundation. The Foundation was a supporter of the Johns Hopkins re-analysis. It was also entangled somehow with the Biomedical Horizons hedge fund, which was involved in the Pfeffer takeover. The financial backers of both the Foundation and the hedge fund were somewhat obscure, and possibly "shady," according to Agent Rita. I shook my head. Too many connections. I hoped the FBI could figure out what was going on, and why?

As I pondered this question, a Red Sox player slammed a home run over the Green Monster to pull the Red Sox ahead by two runs over the Cleveland Indians. I registered this almost subconsciously, as my thoughts were elsewhere.

Who might have the financial resources and connections to acquire at least two major drug companies at a deeply discounted price? Could there be some secret cabal that has infiltrated both U.S. intelligence services and major pharma companies? I started spinning hypothetical scenarios worthy of John Grisham or David Baldacci. The scope and scale of such a conspiracy would be breathtaking.

I was roused from this reverie when my phone began to buzz, the personal one. I immediately recognized the number as Hector's. I thought he must have found something important to be calling me so late, though this would hardly be unprecedented. When he made a valuable discovery, he could get too excited to contain himself. Patience was definitely not one of his many virtues.

"Hector. What's up? Have you learned anything interesting?"

There was a pause of about ten seconds before a female voice responded. At first, I couldn't recognize who was speaking.

"Uh, Ken? This is Dana. I, I need..."

She sounded tentative, and tremulous.

"Dana, right...of course, but why are you calling me on Hector's phone?"

I could hear deep irregular breathing, as if she had to steady herself before continuing. I waited, anxiously.

"Did something happen? Is he...okay?

"Yes," she answered quickly. Then the words tumbled out. "I mean he's not hurt too badly...just a mild concussion and two slightly bruised ribs, the doctor says. But they want him to stay here over night, just to be careful."

"What happened? Where are you? Are you hurt too?"

*Jesus! I'm starting to sound like Aldous.*

She proceeded to tell me the whole story. They were going out to dinner to celebrate her recent promotion at work. But, when they reached Hector's car at the parking garage a few blocks away, he realized that he had left his car keys at the apartment. So he ran back to get them, while she remained with the car. She expected him back in about ten minutes, but twenty went by. She was worried and decided to walk back, hoping to run into him along the way. Eventually, she got back to the apartment, and found the door open. When she called out, he didn't answer, so she went in to look. He was lying next to the couch across the living room, looking dazed. He asked for some water, which she brought from the kitchen and tried to help him get off the floor, which he managed with some difficulty. As he rested on the couch, complaining of a headache and sore ribs, she called 9-1-1 and requested medical help. The paramedics arrived about ten minutes later and transported hm to Mt. Auburn Hospital.

"Did he tell you what happened?"

"It was very odd...Let me see."

She seemed a bit calmer now. Dana was very organized, and trying to recall every detail helped her feel more focused and in control.

"He said that when he got back to the apartment, he headed toward the bedroom, since the keys would most likely be on the dresser. Suddenly, a man emerged from his office, carrying his laptop. Before he could react, the man ran at him, and smashed the laptop into his chest, pushing him backwards. As the guy ran out of the apartment, still carrying the computer, Hector was sent reeling and fell, knocking his head against a wall. I think that's all he told me."

I had a sinking feeling that this was yet another disturbing occurrence that was not coincidental.

"Does he remember anything about the guy who smashed into him?"

"Not much really, just that he was white, dark complexion, dark eyes, average height and wearing a black hoodie. Oh, and he had a scar across his cheek."

Hector's instantaneous grasp of such details always amazes me.

"I don't know," she continued. He might have told the police more. They came in and questioned him for about twenty minutes here, but I was out of the room. Why?"

"Oh, I'm not sure. I guess I was hoping they might be able to catch the guy. Probably not gonna happen. Did he take anything else?"

"Don't think so, but I guess he didn't have much time before Hector surprised him. The guy must have waited for us to go out and didn't expect anyone to show up so soon after we'd left."

"Yeah, that's probably right," I said, not really believing this was some random burglary.

"Listen, can I speak with him now, just for a few minutes?"

"I'm afraid he just fell asleep, and I don't want to disturb him. That's why I came out to call you. He told me to take his phone, find your number in his contacts, and let you know what happened. He said he forgot to turn the computer off, so the thief could potentially access the data. But he doubted that a burglar would be interested in any of it."

"Okay, thanks a lot, Dana. That's helpful. Do you happen to know what time visiting hours start there tomorrow?"

"Yes, nine in the morning. I have to work tomorrow, so I can't come until noon. I'm hoping they'll discharge him then, so I can bring him home."

"Thanks, I'll try to get there at nine."

"Great. He'll be glad to see you."

After saying good bye, I was really wired. Sleep would not come easily. I poured a generous helping of single malt to help calm me down. I suspected that the "burglar" might not have intended to steal Hector's computer, but just to extract the data. I wouldn't be surprised if he came equipped with some technology to break in, even if the computer was locked, and to download the data onto a flash drive. Then he would have slipped quietly away, leaving no trace of his presence. We were "lucky" that Hector's absent-mindedness had foiled this plan.

Was this another data point supporting the hypothesis that someone was very seriously intent on undermining Verbana, and possibly taking over PhireBreak? But who, and why? Was it all about money or something else? That's the last thing I remember before my exhaustion finally took effect.

# CHAPTER 22

Wednesday, September 9

The next thing I remember is Val shaking me awake seven hours later.

"Hey, Sleeping Beauty, wake up. I have to go in early to the office, and you need to make Sam breakfast and get him ready for school."

"Okay, okay," I mumbled, as consciousness gradually returned.

"What happened last night? You haven't passed out in your chair in a long time?"

I rendered an abbreviated account of my conversation with Dana, leaving out my suspicions. Val sensed that there was more to the story, though.

"You really think this was just a random break-in?" she asked.

"What's really worrying me is that the real purpose might have been to get the data on Hector's computer. Who's to say they won't try to get mine? Of course, I'll be extra careful now about encrypting my files, so they probably wouldn't get anything, but I'd like to upgrade our home security anyway. I'll ask Rita about that."

"You don't think we're in any danger, do you?"

"No, no! Hurting Hector was unintentional. In fact, it probably backfired by raising our suspicions. No, I think their goal was to subvert our efforts to help PhireBreak by finding out what we're doing, but surreptitiously. I'm guessing whoever sent that guy to Hector's apartment is really pissed about the way it actually went down."

"I hope you're right. Anyway, I need to get dressed and take off. And you need…"

"I know, I know, Sam, school."

"Right, see you tonight."

She blew me a kiss as she exited.

After getting Sam ready and dropping him at school, I stopped quickly at Lina's to pick up a couple of her freshly baked almond croissants for Hector. As I paid, she commented on my demeanor.

"You look worried. Does it concern your meeting with that woman? She looked like a tough cracker."

"Huh? Oh, yeah, she kind of does, I guess. She's okay. No, it's just that my friend Hector had an accident last night. I'm bringing these to him in the hospital."

"Sorry. Is it serious?"

"No, just bumps and bruises apparently. They'll let him out this afternoon."

"In that case, keep your money. These are on the home."

I bit my tongue once again to avoid embarrassing her over this malapropism.

"Thanks Lina. That's really nice of you."

After leaving, I drove to Mt. Auburn hospital in the outskirts of Cambridge. With rush-hour traffic, it took me about forty-five minutes to get there. I went up to Hector's room and knocked on the door, while identifying myself. Hector's booming baritone invited me to enter.

"Ken! Glad to see you. What's in the bag? I haven't had anything decent to eat since yesterday. The cuisine here truly sucks."

"I thought you might need some real food," I said, handing him the bag. "Lina said these were on the house when I explained who they were for. I hope this isn't against regulations here."

"Not against *my* regulations," he said, smiling broadly as he drew out one of the pastries and took a bite. "Tell Lina she's made my day."

"I will, when I see her next. I'm glad to see you have your appetite back. I was worried."

He regarded me archly.

"All kidding aside, Hector, how are you feeling?"

"Much better, thanks. I think they're going to release me at noon. Dana is picking me up. Hmm, I'd better be careful about crumbs. If she finds out about these," he said, indicating the croissants, "you and I will both be in trouble. To be honest, though, what I'd really like is a cigarette."

"I thought you were finally done with those."

"I am, pretty much, but very occasionally I yield to temptation. By the way, I'm really sorry about the computer."

"Don't worry about the computer. If it was a random break-in, they won't be interested in any of our data or computer code. If it wasn't random, they would have found a way around the password protection anyway."

"What do you mean?"

I hesitated before continuing, not sure how much to say.

"Listen, Hector. I have reasons for thinking that there may be a deliberate effort to sabotage Verbana. I can't get into much more detail. Suffice it to say we may be dealing with something more sinister than the usual legal wrangling over product liability or intellectual property. Somebody may be trying to bring down PhireBreak, deliberately."

"*Jesus*. That's different. Is that why you wanted me to scrutinize the code for anything questionable?"

"*Exactamente*. Which, by the way, is the real

reason for my visit. Have you found anything so far?" I inquired hopefully.

"Sorry, boss, but it all looks squeaky clean, so far at least."

"Actually, I'm beginning to think it may be a good thing you've come up empty so far."

"Huh?"

"Well, if you *had* been successful, whoever has your laptop might get spooked when they realized we were onto what they are doing. I'm thinking this screw-up may make them even more reluctant to be so blatant, especially if they think we're still in the dark. Why rock the boat and risk being exposed?"

"Let's hope," he replied, wincing in pain as he changed position in order to grab the second croissant.

"Anyway, I gotta go. I'm glad you're doing better. See you soon."

"Yeah, see yah."

I made my way down to the entrance and found my car in the parking garage. From there I made the short drive along the Charles River and through Harvard Square, then across the river to B.U. I parked in a university garage a couple of blocks from my office. It felt odd because I rarely drove to my office, preferring to take the T. When I got to my office, I closed the door and called Rita on the burner phone. She picked up on the second ring.

"Hello, Ken. I was planning to call you later today. I'd like to set up a meeting with you, Selwyn and Hal as soon as possible. We want to go over some things before your next meeting at Cooley & Lerner. Can you make a meeting Friday afternoon?"

"You know, it's funny. I was going to suggest a meeting myself. I think Friday would work because I don't have to teach that day. But I thought Selwyn was out of town for the whole week."

"He is. We're going to meet him in Washington. He'll be meeting with Hal and some regulatory lawyers at Cooley & Lerner's main office there. He can break away for a side meeting with us and Hal around eleven o'clock. Don't worry. We can fly down and be back by dinner time. I'll arrange everything. Pick you up at six a.m. on Friday for the drive to Logan, okay?"

"Uh, sure, no problem."

"By the way, is there anything particular you need to tell me now?"

I explained briefly about my conversation with Carl Vitale and Hector's incident.

"You never cease to amaze me," she said. "Should be an interesting meeting. See you Friday morning."

"Oh, one more thing, Rita. I'm concerned that an attempt might be made to obtain information from my home office. If there was a break-in, especially when Val and Sam are there alone..."

"Ken, I *really* doubt they would try that. It's too

flagrant. But just in case, I can have your security system upgraded and alert the Newton PD to keep an eye out as well."

"Thanks, I'd appreciate that."

For the remainder of the morning I prepared for my class the following day without any interruptions. The graduate seminar on clinical trials was attended by about twenty Ph.D. students specializing in statistics, biostatistics, or epidemiology. It was more of a discussion session than a lecture, and was generally enjoyable and intellectually stimulating. I especially relished the sometimes-animated discussions around some of my iconoclastic ideas about the future of clinical trials. I tried to be provocative in order to stimulate the students to think more deeply about these issues.

I was in a good mood as I grabbed a caffé Americano at the Starbucks on Comm Ave, and walked back with it to my office. I was sipping the coffee and gazing out the window toward the Charles, when Irv Rothman poked his head in.

"Is this a good time to chat?" he said. I had completely forgotten our agreement to meet.

"Sure thing, Irv. I was just about to come by your office," I lied.

"Now what?" I thought, ruefully. Irv and I generally got along well, but he is a stickler for following rules and procedures to the letter. When he wants to meet, it usually portends some bureaucratic annoyance.

"Look, Ken, I hate to bring this up, but have you checked your online student ratings recently?"

I have enjoyed consistently excellent ratings for several years and been nominated for teaching awards. So I was surprised by this inquiry.

"No, why?"

"Ah, well, let me show you. Would you mind logging into your account? I'd like to, uh, go over something with you."

His tone did not suggest good news. With some trepidation I complied with this request. I saw several of the usual glowing reviews from some of my students of the previous semester. But interspersed with these were a handful of troubling posts. Two of these former students complained that I had become lax about keeping appointments with them during my scheduled office hours. This seemed preposterous; I didn't ever miss a student appointment. Two others, from female students, suggested that I made them feel uncomfortable by ogling them during class.

"Irv," I protested, "you've known me for five years. This is complete bullshit! Obviously, someone's trolling me. I don't know who, or why, but this is outrageous."

As I pronounced these words, though, it dawned on me that this could somehow be related to my PhireBreak work.

"You know, Ken, you're being considered for the department chairmanship. I'd hate to see that prospect jeopardized. I'd like to believe there's absolutely no basis for these allegations. Can you assure me of that? Could something you have said or did possibly have been misinterpreted?"

"I swear that these are entirely baseless, but these ratings are anonymous, as you are aware, so how can I prove a negative?"

"I don't know, but if this sort of thing continues, it will spell trouble for you. If you could produce some evidence that these reviews are bogus, there's a procedure for having them expunged from the system. That would be best. Just think about it and let me know, please. Okay?"

I sighed. "Okay, Irv. Thanks for letting me know."

I couldn't shake the thought that this attempt to discredit me was related in some way to my work for PhireBreak. If this fiasco were to blow up, that could certainly threaten my career. Perhaps this was a subtle way of persuading me to ease up on my work for PhireBreak. The normal pressures of teaching and publish-or-perish demands were hard enough under normal circumstances. Being undermined deliberately like this might ratchet this stress up considerably. This was a headache I definitely didn't need.

*Maybe that's what they're trying to do, pile on enough distractions to interfere with my PhireBreak research.*

*Well, the joke's on them. They're wasting their time, since I'm getting nowhere fast on the PhireBreak project.*

My hopes for a clean breakthrough that would reveal a fatal error in the Hopkins analysis were fading. Maybe Kreutzfeld was correct after all. In my gut, I suspected that *something* fishy was going on. But, as Rita had so eloquently put it, gut feelings were not admissible in court. And that goes double for the FDA. There must be another way to obtain evidence of whether sabotage had occurred. As these thoughts rattled around, a new idea came to mind.

*Perhaps there is a way to find out what's really going on.*

# CHAPTER 23

Friday, September 11

By the time Rita swung by to collect me on Friday morning, I was resolved about my course of action, for better or worse. I was prepared to roll the dice on a hunch. I wasn't sure I could convince Selwyn and Hal to go along, but it might be our only real chance. If, in fact, it was true that that PhireBreak was being deliberately undermined, there seemed to be only one possibility of proving this. If they disagreed, I was prepared to bow out of the project. I was apprehensive about taking this draconian step, but at the same time relieved to have made the decision.

Right on time, I saw a nondescript beige Toyota pull up in front of our house. I grabbed the messenger bag containing my laptop and some papers, and walked outside. The car was being driven by a very tall young man with close-cut blond hair. His head scraped the ceiling of the car. Rita, in the front passenger seat, turned to greet me and introduce him.

"Good morning, Ken. This is Jeff Gunderson, an agent who works with me. He's been brought on board to help deal with some of the complexities of the case."

"Hello, Dr. Wheeler," he said. "Like Rita, I specialize in financial crimes, but I'm particularly focused on those that involve fraud." He had a midwestern accent, and I later learned he had grown up in Minnesota and Wisconsin.

"Oh, and how exactly does that apply here?" I asked.

"I'll tell you on the way, but we'd better get going."

We had tickets for a commercial flight scheduled to leave Boston at 7:45 and arrive at Reagan National at 9:05. Rita had asked him to drop us off, so he and I could get acquainted. The trip from Newton to Logan Airport in rush-hour traffic would give us some valuable time together. How *much* time could be anywhere between thirty and sixty (or more) minutes, depending on the whims of the traffic gods. Fortunately, Jeff's car, like all government-owned vehicles, could take advantage of the new all-electric lane that had recently been added to the Mass Turnpike.

As we turned on to the Pike a few minutes later, Jeff started to continue his answer to my question.

"Okay, Dr. Wheeler..."

It's Ken, please," I interjected.

"Okay, Ken. It's my understanding that Phire-Break may, and I say *may*, be the victim of an attack by an effort to sabotage its flagship product. The purpose of this hypothetical attack would be to ruin the company financially so that it could be acquired at a steep discount. Correct, so far?"

"Yes, that sums it up."

"Well, boiling down the legalese, to commit fraud you must attempt to deceive someone by deliberately giving them false or deceptive information. Plus, the misled person needs to act on that information in a way that causes them loss or harm. So if someone is messing with data in order to decrease the value of a company, that would be misleading the company and the public in a big way and causing a major loss."

He then went on to expound on this at some length, giving me a mini-lecture on the specific statutory elements that need to be proved to prosecute a fraud case. He peppered this exposition with examples of major fraud cases recently pursued by the FBI. Finally, he brought it back to the current situation.

"Okay, so the bottom line is that we need to know whether, indeed, the data has been fudged. If so, then we can prove the element of an underlying 'false statement or material fact' foisted upon the company's investors."

I was about to launch into a discussion of my current thinking about this issue, when Rita interrupted. By now, I was getting used to Rita's brusque interruptions.

"Sorry, Ken, but I wanted to tell you something else while the three of us were still together. It's about Eve Stolz, the paralegal. We've decided what to do about her. We're going to take her in for questioning after we see where she goes on Thursday. It's too risky to wait any longer. But, can we do that without alerting her client that her cover's been blown? Unless we can turn her, and fast, we'll have revealed too much about what we know. So that's what we're going to try. It's our best chance to gain some valuable intel."

"What makes you think she knows anything," I asked. "Isn't she just a low-level flunky?"

"Tell him, Jeff."

"The lovely Ms. Stolz isn't exactly who she appears to be."

"Huh? What do you mean?"

"We've been looking into her background. According to her personnel record, she came here from Germany ten years ago and became an American citizen three years later. She was born in 1995 in an area that, before reunification in 1990, was part of East Germany. She studied economics and biology in Switzerland at the University of Basel, and is fluent in German, English and French. Since emigrating to the U.S., she has been employed as a paralegal at three law firms. She is currently being paid $95,000 per year as a senior paralegal at Cooley & Lerner. She has a U.S. passport, a Massachusetts driver's license, one bank account, that we know about, and two credit cards. She has never married and shares a two-bedroom apartment in Waltham with a female roommate. They are not romantically involved. Her life appears to be remarkably...well, unremarkable."

"Okay, I'll bite. Who is the *real* Eve Stolz?"

"For starters, there was an Eve Stolz born in East Germany in 1995, but she died in a car accident in 2010. There was also an *Eva* Stolz who matriculated at the University of Basel and graduated with degrees in economics and biology, *with honors*. But that Eva was born in 1993 and bears only a passing resemblance to our Eve. To make a long story short, on close inspection, almost nothing about our Eve really checks out. But wait, it gets worse. It's true that Eve rents an apartment in a modest area of Waltham, but there's no room-mate, and most of the time she doesn't actually live there."

"Oh, where does she actually reside?"

"You know those high-rises on Atlantic Avenue along the waterfront downtown, just a couple of blocks from the Aquarium?"

"You're kidding. Didn't Ted Kennedy used to live in one of those?"

"How about a fourteenth-floor luxury three-bedroom with a balcony and ocean views on two sides? Six grand a month. Of course, on the lease, she's not Eve Stolz. She's Evelyn Stoller, supposedly a *partner* at Cooley & Lerner. Oh, and Evelyn also has a little getaway on Martha's Vineyard."

"Really? You know, we have a small cottage in

Chilmark. Where's hers?"

"It's one of those quaint antiques in the heart of Edgartown a block from the harbor."

"Wow. Those are very pricey, probably two million, at least."

"Obviously, she's got a side gig going," offered Rita, "and I don't think she's driving for Uber."

"So she may know something, eh?"

"Right, she must be doing more than just delivering the surveillance on the conference room," said Rita. "That makes it very tempting to snap her up, but she has to be handled with care. Plus, there's something else she might know about. If we do get to debrief her, we might need your expertise."

"I don't think that would be up my alley; I just interrogate data, not criminals."

"Explain it to the good professor please, Jeff."

"Right, the law firm that Ms. Stolz worked at before was Robertson, Milgram and Sloan. Ring a bell?"

"Not really."

"That was the firm that represented Pfeffer Pharmaceuticals during the time they were fighting unsuccessfully for survival. Just a coincidence, right?"

"Undoubtedly. So after you've waterboarded her, I get to ask her how they pulled off the Pfeffer caper?"

"Really, Ken, you must be confusing us with the CIA," said Rita. "We have much more subtle methods."

Something else occurred to me. "Do you have any idea who she might be working for?"

"That's the sixty-four billion-dollar question, isn't it?" said Rita. "We think she's a free-lancer. Her background is rather murky, but we believe that her father worked for the Stasi under the old communist regime. You know what that was?"

"That was the East German version of the KGB, right?"

"Basically. Anyway, after the Berlin Wall fell, he apparently decided to capitalize on his contacts with Russian and other intelligence services and started selling his services. His daughter seems to be a chip off the old block."

By then we had arrived at the Jet Blue terminal and Jeff pulled over to let us off.

"Okay, campers, here's your terminal. Have a nice flight."

We were quickly ushered though security when Rita flashed her FBI credentials. The flight to D.C. was uneventful. There was no opportunity to talk about the case because of the lack of privacy. I read a third-rate detective novel that a friend had recommended, while Rita worked on her tablet. The protagonist was no Harry Bosch, but it passed the time. The plane arrived a bit early and we took a cab to the building where the law firm had its offices. Our meeting had been scheduled for eleven, so we had about a half hour to kill. Rita suggested a nearby Starbucks. I ordered a cappuccino and she had a cold brew, black. We sat down side-by-side at the end of a counter along the front wall, with a view of the foot traffic on the busy street outside.

"There's something else I wanted to mention to you," I said, hesitantly.

She looked over quizzically. "Sure, what's on your mind?"

I explained to her about the defamatory reviews on the teacher-rating website. She pondered this for a few seconds and nodded knowingly before responding.

"Remember, I told you the people behind this may be ruthless. I think someone is trying to send you a message. It's one of the ways to get you to back off. Keep pressing forward on behalf of PhireBreak and your career will suffer. This kind of psychological harassment is not uncommon. I'm glad you told me. I'll have it looked into. If this is related to the PhireBreak case, and we find out who's behind it, we can stop it. Of course, if these reviews turn out to be legit, you'll be on your own," she said, smiling mischievously. I wasn't laughing.

It was time to head up to the Cooley & Lerner D.C. offices, located in an imposing glass-clad office building on Twelfth Street, a stone's throw from the U.S. Capitol Building. When we got to the office, the receptionist invited us to wait while someone would come to collect us. Meanwhile, I was being dazzled by the opulent surroundings. To say the mammoth reception area was sumptuous would be an understatement. I thought the furnishings would be quite at home in Versailles.

The walls were festooned with portraits of several renowned former partners of the firm, some dating back to the nineteenth century. I recognized a couple of the more recent ones, former cabinet secretaries. Plush oriental rugs adorned the beautifully inlaid parquet floor. A side-table held a crystal pitcher and goblets. In all this splendor, the standard-issue modern glass table, albeit an oversized one, seemed incongruous. I picked up a copy of the Washington Post and perused the headlines, just to keep occupied. After a few minutes, a statuesque and impeccably attired African-American woman glided toward us. How she managed such grace on her three-inch heels was a mystery.

"I'm Michelle Greene," she said, smiling brightly, revealing her perfect teeth. "I'll take you to the conference room your colleagues are in. Our regulatory-affairs meeting is just finishing and Mr. Washington said your group would be taking over the room now. Have you been here before? I mean to our office. We've just had it renovated. You know, the firm has been in this suite for thirty years, but before that it was in an old building up the street that was demolished. It was a beautiful historic building..."

She rattled on in this vein, while leading us to the conference room.

When we arrived, I noticed Selwyn and Hal were there, as expected, but was surprised to see two others: Carolyn Cummings and a slightly disheveled, dark-haired, heavy-set man I guessed to be in his late thirties. He had the pallid complexion that hinted at too much time spent indoors in front of a computer screen. These two were engaged in an animated conversation, but stopped and turned toward us when we entered the room.

"Okay," said Selwyn. "Let's clear the decks and get this meeting launched."

# CHAPTER 24

Friday, September 11

Selwyn began by summarizing our current situation. "There have been a number of recent developments. Some of these have a direct bearing on our upcoming meeting next Wednesday. It's critically important to handle the meeting strategically, for reasons I will explain. I believe we are at a critical point in the life of PhireBreak. We have to marshal the evidence to defend the safety of Verbana before the Hopkins study is made public. To prepare our response, we need to know very soon where we stand scientifically. Does Verbana have a safety problem and, if so, how can it be managed? These questions need to be resolved, and quickly."

He paused to pour water from a carafe into a crystal glass and take a few sips before continuing.

"Toward that end, we have been proceeding with

analyses of the data on two parallel tracks. You're all aware that Ken Wheeler has been analyzing the data from a statistical perspective. I'll be asking him soon for a status report on his research." He nodded slightly in my direction, and I smiled back. I was somewhat nonplussed, since I wasn't aware of any "parallel" effort, though it didn't totally surprise me.

"Our second effort has been undertaken in-house by Carolyn, together with Sergei." He nodded in their direction. "Their approach has focused on this so-called Caldwell Index. Is it truly a valid indicator of the so-called hyper-immune dementia, as alleged in the article out of Johns Hopkins? We'll be hearing what they have found as well."

*Hmm, this is the notorious Sergei Rosefsky whose participation was so controversial when Carolyn first suggested it. This could prove very interesting.*

"Before we get into the data-analytic weeds," Selwyn continued, "I want to provide some more context. For some time, I have harbored some suspicions regarding the real agenda behind the Hopkins study. I'm not necessarily accusing the researchers *themselves* of any malicious intent, but they may be unwitting pawns in a deliberate effort to undermine PhireBreak. The nature of such a conspiracy is unclear, but its purpose appears to be a hostile takeover of our company. Furthermore, it's possible that we're dealing with the same people who were involved in the Pfeffer disaster."

He paused once more and looked around the

room, making eye contact with each one of us. Complete silence. Everyone was focused intently on his words. He stood up and began pacing as he continued.

"I mention this because we have obtained evidence that, although circumstantial, supports these suspicions. So it's vital that you all be alert to the possibility, and on the lookout for anything suspicious. I made time for this meeting today, ahead of our regularly scheduled meeting next week, mainly to apprise you of this situation."

He paused for several seconds.

"Though it pains me to say this, I've begun to fear that someone inside the company may be participating, possibly by leaking confidential information. Unfortunately, insider trading has become endemic in our society, and pharma is a prime candidate, because so much is riding on the success or failure of each new blockbuster medication. Information about drug development is closely held and highly technical. Insider information, while illegal, can be so highly lucrative that the temptation to acquire it can be very powerful."

He paused again for another drink of water.

"My unease prompted me to contact the FBI. I was surprised to discover that my concerns dovetailed with certain suspicions of their own. As a result, we have started to collaborate with their investigation. To say more about that, I've invited Special Agent Rita D'Amato of the FBI's financial crimes division. She will provide some more detail about the situation. Before I turn the floor over, however, it should go without saying that what she says must be held in strictest confidence."

As Selwyn sat down and refilled his glass, Rita rose to address the group.

"Thank you, Selwyn. First, let me echo what you have just heard. Shocking as it may be, we have come to suspect that some unknown group is attempting to discredit Verbana. For some time, we have been concerned that the events leading up to Pfeffer's decline and acquisition were in some way orchestrated. Our working theory is that certain conspirators have attempted to discover minor problems with targeted drugs, and then exaggerate and exploit these issues. It's even possible that the product's weaknesses are only *apparent* rather than real. To put a finer point on this, it's possible that the Pfeffer clinical-trial data may have been *doctored*. We believe that may be what happened to Pfeffer."

"Unfortunately, our after-the-fact investigations have not yet produced any hard evidence. When Selwyn first contacted us about your current plight, we didn't see any obvious connection with the Pfeffer matter. But, in the last few weeks, certain events have come to light that have raised our level of concern. I can't go into specifics, except for one particular aspect that pertains to our immediate situation."

She paused, and glanced around the room.

"We have recently become aware that our meetings at the Boston office of Cooley & Lerner have been subjected to electronic surveillance. That's one of the reasons we are holding this meeting *here* today."

She let that pregnant statement hang in the air for several seconds. It was evident from their expressions that Carolyn and Sergei were stunned. Hal just nodded.

"How we know this is not important." Thankfully, she did not glance in my direction.

"What *is* important is how we deal with this. We know enough to terminate this eavesdropping, but doing so would, almost certainly, reveal that we are aware of it. So, for now, we have decided to allow it to continue, at least until after your next meeting."

Selwyn was nodding slowly, fully aware of all this. I tried to act poker-faced, not exactly sure why. The others looked puzzled, wondering where this was all headed. Selwyn jumped in.

"You're trying to set a trap."

"That's right. We believe that the mastermind behind this conspiracy wants to learn about your strategy for defending Verbana. On the one hand, we don't want to reveal anything too detailed about your data analyses or plans. On the other hand, we'd like to provoke some action that might lead us closer to finding out what is really going on. Therefore, you need to craft your discussion carefully to achieve these objectives. Does that make sense?"

"Can I say something?" asked Carolyn.

"Of course," said Rita.

"First of all, I have to say I'm highly skeptical that anyone could have tampered with our data or computer code. I can understand how inside information might be of great interest to a potential investment group, hedge fund or whatever. Certainly, spying on us is not out of the realm of possibility. But, messing with data? That strikes me as a bridge too far. Do you have any actual evidence of this, or just speculation?"

"Right now, it's just circumstantial, but whatever the truth, you need to be very careful. We can't afford to overlook any possibility, regardless of how remote it might seem. What I'd like to do now is to hear from the statistical gurus about where we stand, and then discuss how we handle the meeting. Okay?"

"Sure, sure," responded Carolyn," somewhat begrudgingly.

"Why don't you start?"

Rita sat down, and Carolyn stood up.

"We've been looking into the validity of the Caldwell Index. As you all know, it's derived on the basis of the lymphocyte gene-expression data. Published explanations of the methodology underlying it are short on details, but the patent for the Caldwell Index was recently granted to Caldwell Analytics. That means the patent is now publicly available, and we have obtained it. It explains all the technical details, including which twenty-two genes are utilized in the algorithm on which the Caldwell Index is based. I'll pass the baton to Sergei to explain, in lay terms, what he's been working on."

Sergei rose and, in his haste, tripped over his briefcase as he moved quickly toward a large whiteboard at one end of the room. Fortunately, he was able to regain his balance without falling. He quickly grabbed a marker and began furiously drawing a rather complicated diagram. Turning toward us, he began to speak in a rather heavy Russian accent.

"Da...thank you Carolyn. Is pleasure to be here. Caldwell Index is claimed to be valid predictor of future cognitive decline. Is true? Answer is critical for PhireBreak. Really, two related questions, though. Is Caldwell Index estimate of dementia risk accurate? If so, are the probabilities accurate for cancer patient population?"

It was clear that Sergei was enjoying the limelight. I had the sense of watching a master magician at work and was prepared to be dazzled. Actually, I was *hoping* to be dazzled, since it might take some of the pressure to rescue PhireBreak off my shoulders.

"Okay," he continued. "Must be understood that Index was derived and tested in population of relatively healthy older individuals, average age around seventy-eight. These studies included only small percentage of cancer patients. Mathematical method used to develop predictive model was neural networks, or neural nets for short. In simple terms, a neural network applies similar approach as neurons in human brain. In a sense, algorithm 'learns' by adjusting certain parameters based on available data. Neural nets form basis of many sophisticated artificial intelligence systems, such as self-driving vehicles."

He went on to explain in more detail how this works in a simple case, alluding to the diagram he had drawn, and wielding his marker with a flourish to highlight particular points. As a professional lecturer myself, I was quite impressed with his performance.

"In principle, neural network can be excellent approach for deriving predictive models. In fact, neural networks and other similar machine learning techniques are in many areas supplanting more primitive statistical methods that can't fully exploit data-processing power of modern computers."

I could swear he was smirking just a bit as he uttered this subtle dig.

"*However,* just like human brain, network can sometimes be misled if data not sufficient. Model can become overly influenced by inadequately supported evidence. Metaphorically speaking, neural network jumps to false conclusion. With enough data and proper training methodology, it can eventually change mind, so to speak, and reach correct conclusion. We suspect Professor Caldwell may have jumped gun by stopping model training process too soon. Consequently, his so-called Caldwell Index is not optimal and can be improved."

"How, exactly, do you know this?" asked Selwyn,

"if you can explain that in non-technical terms?"

"Ah, certainly." He smiled, warming to the opportunity of enlightening us.

"First, using one of two data sets analyzed by Caldwell, as presented in patent, we derived our own neural network model based on same data. We then tested validity of model by how well it predicted future dementia in second data set. We compared against Caldwell's own model predictions, as reported in patent app, and ours did significantly better. So, based on that evidence, Caldwell Index is sub-optimal predictor of future dementia. Our method can do somewhat better."

Sergei tended to gesticulate excitedly as he explained this. I noticed that the tips of his fingers were stained. He was undoubtedly a smoker, or at least had once been one. I wondered if at this moment he was craving a smoke. As these irrelevant thoughts were flitting through my consciousness, I was subliminally processing what Sergei had just reported. A question suddenly occurred to me.

"Sergei, this is truly impressive work," I said.

*A little flattery is always in order.*

"This certainly does tend to discredit the Hopkins findings, and that's very useful. But it doesn't directly *disprove* the Kreutzfeld hypothesis, right? I mean, it's still conceivable that a truly valid predictor would lead to the same conclusion. For instance, what would happen if you analyzed the Verbana trials using your new and improved version? Would that show the absence of any effect?"

Sergei sighed deeply and looked a bit deflated. My guess was that he was desperate for a smoke at this point. He seemed about to gather his remaining energy to respond, when Carolyn spoke up.

"In fact, Ken, we have performed just such an analysis. We calculated the difference between the average value of our new 'Rosefsky Index' on the Verbana and control groups. We had hoped to find that there was virtually no difference. What we found was that there was still a difference between the Verbana and control groups, although it fell short of statistical significance. But Sergei has some more tricks up his sleeve that might improve his predictive model and result in a more favorable outcome."

"Okay," said Selwyn. "I only have another half-hour. Let's take a five-minute comfort break and then hear from Ken."

As I headed for the men's room, I noticed Sergei making a bee-line for the nearest exit in search of a suitable location for a smoke.

# CHAPTER 25

Friday, September 11

Before getting into the work that Hector and I had been doing, I wanted to follow up on what Carolyn and Sergei had reported. "I was thinking about something that's been bothering me all along about the Caldwell Index."

I went on to explain my analysis of the gene-expression data and the finding that none of the known relevant genes seemed to be affected by Verbana.

"I understand that the Caldwell Index may be sensitive to something more subtle going on in a person's brain that isn't reflected in the individual gene expressions. Still, this seems odd. I wonder if your analyses can shed any light on this paradox."

"Well, as you know, Ken," replied Sergei, "because modern neural net models are essentially 'black boxes' we can't really ask *why* they work, just *whether* they do."

"Yes, Sergei, that underlines my point about why more 'primitive' statistical approaches may not be so obsolete after all. The elaborate mathematical equations of the AI techniques can sometimes *appear* to work great, but essentially lack what I would call common sense, for want of a better term. So when encountering an unexpected situation, they can make errors that would be obvious to a six-year old."

*Touché*!

"Perhaps true today," countered Sergei, "but AI will surely be smarter than humans in couple of decades, and world will be much better off. Look, is many years since human chess player has dared to challenge top computer programs."

"Yes," I replied, "but chess is a very strictly rule-bound game. In contexts that involve creativity and imagination, an AI cannot improvise to deal with novel situations."

"I'm sure creativity will ultimately be reduced to algorithms as well...eventually. What about statues generated now by three-D printers in style of any famous artist you desire? Art critics can't distinguish from originals by artists themselves."

"True, they are technically identical. But a simulacrum is not the same as an original creation or invention. Look, Sergei, when a computer can generate a new J.K. Rowling novel or a Robin Williams comedy riff, I may start to become convinced."

"*Bah*, Ken, I think you are missing..."

At this point, Selwyn cut us off.

"Gentlemen, this philosophical excursion is fascinating, but it won't address our immediate concerns. Besides, you won't settle it today. Let's keep our hands on the oars, eh?"

"Sorry, Selwyn," I said. "I guess that's a debate for another day. Anyway, I truly hope that your approach, Sergei, will ultimately prove persuasive to the FDA. I haven't given up on finding a more 'primitive' statistical answer to the problem, but so far, I must admit that I haven't had much success. I still believe, though, that if HID is real, then there must be a susceptible subgroup that exists and can be identified based on a person's DNA. Then, a simple DNA test would allow us to winnow such patients out."

"But you haven't found such a DNA profile yet?"

"Unfortunately, not. However. I'm optimistic that we will, since it makes sense theoretically. As you know, it's now apparent that most drugs have varying effects on different individuals."

"Sure," said Selwyn, "that's the basis of personalized medicine."

"Right. If this alleged effect is real, then it stands to reason that it shouldn't affect everyone equally. If there's a subgroup here, I'm confident I will find it, given enough time."

"That's the rub, isn't it?" Selwyn retorted. "Time is of the essence."

At this point, Hal jumped in. "Look, even if you're successful, at best it will mean a black-label warning on Verbana. At worst, it might prompt the FDA to suspend sales until they have a chance to study it further. Either way, it will eat into sales and, perhaps even worse, keep this issue in the news for a long time. I'm sure some plaintiff lawyers are already sharpening their knives, or soon will be. I grant you it's better than nothing, but frankly, we need more. Unless, of course...I don't even want to go there..."

Selwyn broke in. "Let's not get ahead of our skis, Hal. I think I heard Ken suggest he is still pursuing other avenues. Why don't we hear him out, eh?"

"Sure, sorry Selwyn, but we don't have much time."

Hal's outburst caught me by surprise, but I knew where he was coming from. In my experience, lawyers in major litigation absolutely *hate* to concede any fault at all. To do so can put the client in a precarious position, since limiting the *degree* of fault can be tricky. Also, any retreat from complete denial of fault can be perceived as a kind of defeat. Big-time litigators are among the most competitive beings on the planet.

I took a deep breath and soldiered on.

"Look, Hector and I have looked at the data eight ways from Sunday. We can't find anything wrong with the Hopkins analysis yet, and I'm guessing you haven't either," I said, looking toward Carolyn and Sergei, who nodded their agreement.

"So the flaw in the Hopkins analysis, if there exists one, might well be related to the Caldwell Index

"I think we need to tread very carefully here. For one thing, there's HIPAA to consider." What you are suggesting raises issues of privacy and confidentiality. I would need to research whether the HIPAA regulations would prevent the sites from giving you the data. Furthermore, the logistical issues entailed in obtaining the data from all thirty-two study sites would be complex. And then, what if it slips out that we're doing this, and questions are raised as to why we need this information? I don't know, Ken. Are these risks justified by the very slim chance that you'll discover something that's truly a game-changer?"

"I agree with Hal," chimed in Carolyn quickly. "This seems over-the-top. Even if it passes legal muster, it would need to be approved by the Institutional Review Boards of each study center. I'm not sure we could convince them. Even if we could, I doubt there's enough time for that."

Rita stood up and responded.

"That's true, but this situation is extraordinary. I'm afraid we may be facing a criminal conspiracy that may affect the national interest. I believe we may be able to exert certain, uh...influences that will be persuasive for expediting the process of IRB approval."

Selwyn said nothing, but looked pensive as he wrestled with this dilemma. Then he looked straight at me.

"It's not an exaggeration to say that the future of PhireBreak could hinge on our decisions and actions over the next couple of weeks. Given that, I'm inclined to explore this further. I will discuss it with Cheryl. As our CEO, she'll make the call. But, to be honest, I'm not sure she will be willing to go down this road, Ken, without some stronger evidence that it's absolutely necessary."

I wasn't surprised by this equivocation, but all my instincts were telling me that if I left things inconclusive now, I might always regret the consequences. I sighed. It was time to play my trump card.

"When I agreed to come on board," I said, pausing slightly, "I was very clear about the terms of my participation. From past experience, I knew that without full access to all potentially relevant data, I might be hamstrung in my investigation, so I tried to anticipate every possible contingency."

I saw puzzlement all around the conference table. I rooted around in my messenger bag, found what I was looking for, and held up the document. I noticed Hal frowning, as it dawned on him what was coming.

"According to this letter of engagement, I am authorized, let me see... to obtain 'any data or other information that he deems necessary to conduct his research' etc. etc. The letter is signed by Cheryl Wellstone, CEO. Now, according to my attorney, Aldous Post, this letter is a contract, and if Phire-Break refuses to grant me access to the data, they would, technically, be in breach of this contract."

"Wait a minute...hold on," said Hal, standing up,

his face coloring. "I don't think anything like this was contemplated when we drafted that letter. I'm not sure the original files are encompassed in the data referenced in your letter."

He was clearly agitated. I liked Hal and hoped I hadn't burned any bridges by sandbagging him, but I had no real choice.

"So, Dr. Wheeler," said Selwyn, "are you telling us that you are willing to withdraw from the engagement if we don't accede to your request?"

*This is where I knew the rubber might meet the road. No turning back.*

"I would deeply regret doing that, for a variety of reasons, but I owe it to PhireBreak, and to my own sense of professional integrity, to stand firm on this. It's strong medicine, but it's for your own good, I truly believe."

"Hmm. I will take all of this into consideration when I report to Cheryl. There's a Board of Directors meeting next week, and it might need to be approved at that level as well. Meanwhile, I'd like to ask Hal to look into the potential ethical and legal risks and how to mitigate them, if possible. Carolyn, can you please look into the practical issues? Both of you, please report what you find to me by COB on Monday. Now, there's only one more item to discuss. How shall we handle the meeting on Wednesday? Rita, I'd like your input on that."

"Thanks, Sly, uh, Selwyn. Oops."

For the first time at this meeting I saw a smile creep across his face. The tension in the room broke somewhat. Selwyn chuckled. "I haven't been called that in a long time. Anyway, please carry on."

"Okay. I just want to start by saying this has been a good discussion, and quite edifying for me. As for the meeting in Boston next week, I'm hoping we can walk a rather fine line. On the one hand we need to be careful to avoid appearing unnatural in any way that might tip off whoever is listening in. On the other, I don't want to give away anything that might come back to bite us. So, I'd like us to discuss how you might frame the issues related to your analyses of the data to satisfy these somewhat contradictory objectives."

At this point, Hal surprised me by speaking up.

"Can I make a suggestion?" he asked rhetorically. "Perhaps the best approach would be to focus mainly on the more administrative and logistical aspects of the situation. For instance, we could deal more with the potential public relation nightmare. You may be aware of the snafu regarding that conference abstract we recently learned about. So far it seems contained, but how much longer an effective media blackout can be maintained is unclear. Justin is working overtime on that situation. Plus, Bob Shin could discuss details of our preparation for the FDA review, possible petitions for the court, etc. Since Justin and Bob are both in the dark about what we have talked about today, they would also be least likely to inadvertently let slip something unfortunate."

"That sounds good," said Rita, "but you still need

to say something plausible about the all-important analyses by Sergei and Ken."

"I think we should basically temporize," I piped up.

"How do you mean?" asked Rita.

"Well, we could talk about the progress we're making, but without providing specific results or conclusions. For instance, I could sound fairly optimistic that I will find some flaw in the Hopkins analysis but claim it's complicated and I need a little more time. I'm not sure if that approach would work for Carolyn."

She looked thoughtful and leaned over to whisper something to Sergei. He nodded affirmatively.

"I think it would work best if I simply report that Sergei has been starting to look closely at the Caldwell Index model, based on the information disclosed in the patent. I'll say that he suspects there may be a problem with the computer programs that were used by the Johns Hopkins researchers in their re-analysis. He thinks the Hopkins results may not be correct but needs more time to be sure. Actually, it might be better to have Sergei come to the meeting himself. That would seem to be a normal procedure, after all."

Rita commented: "That works, but I would prefer if you could make that a bit stronger, just enough to worry them a bit. That might get them to take some action we could trace in some way."

Sergei responded: "Well, I could say that I'm working on a new model to determine whether the

Caldwell Index can be trusted in cancer patients. But I have no definite results yet."

"That sounds good."

"That's it, then," said Selwyn. "We have to wrap up now. See you all next Wednesday."

# CHAPTER 26

Saturday, September 12

The next morning, I awoke later than usual with a hazy recollection of an agitated dream. I was in the ocean off the coast of Martha's Vineyard, swimming furiously against the tide, frantically trying, and failing, to move closer to the shore. Every time I made some headway, a wave came up that pushed me back out. I had a sense of panic and frustration.

The clock on the night table indicated that it was just after nine o'clock, and I suddenly realized that Saturday was Sam's day for soccer. His team was scheduled for an away game against a team from Needham. I called downstairs.

"Val, what time is Sam's game today?"

"Aha, you're awake. I thought I might have to take him without you."

"Yeah, what time?"

"It's at the big field in Needham at ten thirty."

She was referring to DeFazio Field, a large complex that includes several soccer and baseball fields in the adjoining town of Needham, located a few miles away. Needham is known for its soccer prowess. The high-school team, under a renowned long-term coach, has won several state championships in his tenure. The Needham team in Sam's league was currently in first place, and his team was second, so I knew he was looking forward eagerly to the contest.

"Great, that gives me time to shower and dress. I'm definitely going."

When we arrived at the field, there were several games already in progress. We located Sam's team and greeted his coach, father of the star forward on the team. He was a decent enough fellow, despite being a tad too intense for my taste. In the previous game, he'd been involved in a shouting match with the referee over an offsides call that negated a goal. I thought he was right about the call, and was upset about it too, but his response was over the top. Fortunately, there was a different referee for this game.

It was a beautiful day, with just a hint of fall. Watching the game provided a welcome respite from the stress I was feeling. The game was exciting, and I cheered loudly when Sam's team made a goal to pull ahead just before halftime. At the break, I told Val I was going to grab some coffee at the refreshment stand. As I headed that way, I noticed that Carl Vitale was on the sidelines of another field

I was passing. His son was on another team that was also about to start a game. Suddenly, an idea occurred to me. I walked over and greeted him. After a few pleasantries, I broached the question that was bothering me, but obliquely, so as not to disclose my real reason.

"You know, I had an interesting question from one of my students the other day. She was asking how, exactly, the process of 'double-blinding' is carried out. She understood the basic idea, that the treatment received by each patient is hidden from the patient and the investigators. But, in a multi-center study, how is this actually implemented? I realized that I didn't actually know very much about the mechanics of this process. For instance, how did it work in the Verbana study?"

"So," replied Carl, "PhireBreak had generated a list of patient ID numbers for each site. For example, we were site number three, so our ID numbers were 3001, 3002 etc. Then, for each consecutive pair of patients who entered the study, such as, say 3003 and 3004, one of these would be randomly assigned to Verbana and the other to the control treatment. Correspondingly, for each patient, a medication package would be prepared. For example, if 3003 was assigned to Verbana, its package would contain the right amount of the drug to supply the patient throughout the trial. If 3004 was assigned to the comparator, the package would contain a standard medication made up to appear identical to Verbana. No one on our staff ever knew which patients were receiving active treatment and which were only getting the other pills."

"Okay, but what about when you sent the data to the Clinical Research Organization? I assume you identified each patient by their ID number, but that the treatment was not revealed, right?"

"That's right. To prepare the data to perform statistical analyses, the CRO was given a coded version of treatment assignment."

"What do you mean?"

"The two treatment modalities were labeled simply as Treatment A and Treatment B."

"I see, so for patient 3003, for instance, the CRO knew he or she was given Drug A or Drug B, but didn't know which drug was Verbana and which was the other one."

"Right, that way, when they, or later on Phire-Break, performed any analyses, they couldn't be influenced by any conscious or unconscious biases. Anyway, I see Todd's team has finished warming up, so I better get back over there. Nice chatting."

"Yeah, thanks Carl."

"I headed back to Sam's game, which had already resumed. He was coming off the field for a breather."

"Dad," he whined, "you just missed my *awesome* assist. We're ahead by two goals now."

"Yes, where *were* you?" asked Val, a trifle irritated.

"Oh, I ran into Carl Vitale and got embroiled in a bit of shop talk. Sorry, I lost track of time."

In the end, Sam's team held off a fusillade of shots-on-goal to eke out the victory. He was thrilled, and the traditional post-game ice-cream fest at Cabot's on Washington Street in Newton was a real celebration. Meanwhile, I couldn't get the conversation with Carl out of my mind. How could data meddling have occurred unless they were able to decode which patients got Verbana and which got the usual treatment?"

As I mulled over this conundrum, Val called me out of my reverie when she noticed that a dollop of hot fudge from my sundae had managed to land in my lap. This was not the first time that I had experienced such a mishap. She rolled her eyes.

"Ah, the absent-minded professor strikes again."

"Sorry, I was just thinking about something."

"It's that case, isn't it? I hope that wraps up soon before you have a more serious accident. Try to stay focused on what's going on around you, *please*."

"You're right, I will."

Soon after, we drove back home. The remainder of the day was uneventful, but I kept thinking back to my conversation with Carl. One question in particular was troubling me.

*How did they unblind the data?*

Suddenly, I realized the answer, in all its headslapping obviousness. The final clinical trial was not conceived in a vacuum. Based on earlier preliminary trials, PhireBreak believed that Verbana had a large positive impact on cancer remissions. If so, even a cursory review of partial data on rates of remission in the two groups would show a substantial disparity in favor of Verbana. Therefore, it was safe to assume that whichever of the two treatments, A or B, had a much higher remission rate must be the Verbana group. Importantly, that determination could be made by a visual inspection of the data, without running any computerized statistical analyses that might leave digital footprints behind. In fact, it could probably be determined when only a part of the study subjects had completed the trial. But tampering with the data would, inevitably, have left a digital trail, wouldn't it? Was it possible to tweak the data in a way that was virtually undetectable? That was a much harder question.

So far, I hadn't found anything suspicious about the gene-expression data. There are usually telltale clues that reveal when data have been contrived. Detecting these is one of my specialties, and I had helped on a couple of occasions to uncover actual attempts to pass off fraudulent data as real. I had even partially codified my tricks for discovering artificial data and incorporated them in some proprietary software Hector had written.

Unfortunately, my investigation of the data so far had revealed nothing suspicious. My last hope was that my gambit of demanding the original forms would pay off. I had gone out on a limb. If my wish was actually granted and it proved nothing in the end, I'd look pretty silly.

As these thoughts buzzed around my brain, I received a call from Hal.

"Ken. You got a minute? I just got off the phone with Selwyn. He asked me to give you a buzz."

I wondered what this was about. For a fleeting moment, I thought maybe they had decided to cut me loose. After all, I hadn't been able to come up with a clean rebuttal of the Hopkins analysis, and now I was ruffling feathers with my demand for original data.

"Sure, what's up?" I answered, guardedly.

"Selwyn and I believe it's impossible to get all the original data you are asking for."

*Damn! I knew it.*

I was deciding whether to walk away. My bluff had been called.

"*However*, we agree that you can collect the data from five of the larger study sites."

I thought about this for a few seconds.

"Are you there?" asked Hal.

"I'm thinking about it," I said. Incongruously, the classic Jack Benny joke flashed in my mind as I heard myself mouth these words. My father used to love that joke. The famous comedian, who starred during the heyday of radio, was a notorious tightwad. The joke was in a skit in which a mugger accosts Jack and threatens him: "Your money or your life?" The joke was simply that Jack pauses for a long time. "Well?" the frustrated mugger finally asks. "I'm… thinking about it," replies Jack.

"Okay, what's the rationale?" I finally responded. "I'm not sure five will be sufficient."

"Here's our thinking. It's not really feasible to obtain the necessary cooperation in a timely way. Furthermore, there could be questions raised about the chain of custody if we rely on the sites themselves. So, what they are proposing is that you, personally, will visit each of the five sites and oversee the data downloading. You'll be provided with a highly secure laptop and encryption capabilities by the FBI and be accompanied by an agent. The laptop will be kept at the Boston FBI headquarters and you'll be able to access it there."

"I see, but why only five? Why not ten?"

"The thought is that if you detect any discrepancies, that will prove the principle that something is amiss. That should be enough to convince the FDA that more time is required to investigate what happened. That additional time should ultimately allow us to reconstruct the entire data set, which can then be analyzed to determine the real results."

"Hmm, I guess that makes sense."

"Look, I know this isn't ideal, but Selwyn thinks he can get our CEO and Board of Directors to approve it. Can I tell him you're on board?"

I had the feeling this was non-negotiable.

"Okay, I guess it'll have to do."

# CHAPTER 27

Wednesday, September 16

The next meeting at Cooley & Lerner went well, at least as far as we could discern. Hal's strategy of focusing on other aspects besides the data analyses played out quite naturally as it turned out. Maintaining the news blackout was becoming harder, as the academic rumor mill was leading to requests for information from the media. The cork would soon pop out of the bottle, one way or another. The pressure on Justin Osborne was intense, and it was showing. He noted that the share price of PhireBreak stock had declined by nearly seven percent in the past month. His research indicated that this drop was attributable largely to the rumors of a problem related to Verbana. He felt we had to provide some positive spin for the press.

There was much discussion of how to proceed, but I was hardly listening, as my concerns lay elsewhere. I knew that later that night, the FBI would follow Eve Stolz from the moment she left the office. Finding out where she would go, and whom she might be meeting, could potentially be explosive.

When Bob Shin began to broach the legal aspects of the situation, however, my ears perked up. He dropped a bombshell. The FDA had set the date for our hearing as Monday, October twelfth, less than a month away. This date was chosen in part because, being Columbus Day, it would be easier to free up the over-committed panel members from other obligations. It was also just eight days before the expiration of the temporary injunction imposed by the court.

He followed that up with more news. The FDA had decided to bring in the Johns Hopkins research team on the prior Friday, October ninth, to obtain more information about the details of their research. Apparently, they wanted to give them a shot at bolstering their conclusions after having a chance to review our written critique. That struck me as not unreasonable, but I wondered if there was more going on behind the scenes.

Hal then related some additional details about the format of the FDA hearing. PhireBreak would send the FDA a written summary of its comments on the Hopkins analysis one week ahead of the hearing. This would be distributed to the panel that had been assembled, consisting of three high-level FDA employees and five outside experts. Hal read off the names, and I recognized one of the FDA people and several of the external academic researchers. It was an impressive group, no doubt about that. One name in particular jumped out at me: Richard T. Chapel.

Dr. Chapel was a deputy director of the FDA. He had spent his entire career there, rising through the ranks. He was widely regarded as one of the world's leading experts on clinical-trials methodology, but also something of a curmudgeon. As a staunch traditionalist, he tended to frown on any deviations from a study's protocol. I had previously interacted with him during two professional conferences. These had occurred during the question-and-answer sessions after his talk to a large audience. I wasn't sure if he would even remember me.

I reasoned that his methodological rectitude might actually be helpful. After all, he might be skeptical of a re-analysis predicated on an endpoint that had not been specified in the study's protocol. Of course, he was also pragmatic enough to realize that the evidence available, though imperfect from his perspective, would have to suffice. What was certain was that he would demand the most statistical rigor that was possible under the circumstances.

At the hearing, PhireBreak would have the opportunity to present its findings and explain what actions it believed were appropriate, if any. The panel members could ask questions and make recommendations. A discussion would then ensue among all those present, and a transcript of the entire proceeding would be reviewed by the FDA personnel. A final decision by the FDA regarding actions it deemed necessary would be rendered within one week after the hearing. In addition, if the article was ultimately submitted for publication, the FDA would have the option to submit comments to be included along with the published journal article. Of course, the FDA report would also be transmitted to Judge Weingarten for his consideration, and would undoubtedly carry great weight.

These revelations led to an extended discussion about logistical issues regarding preparation for the hearing. Then, Selwyn turned to Dave Parker and asked for any news he cared to impart. Dave proceeded to regale us with a story about the disgruntled whistle-blower from Kreutzfeld's shop. According to this potential informant, one of Kreutzfeld's main research articles had run into stiff headwinds after submission to a prestigious journal. A peer reviewer for the journal had discovered an apparent flaw in the statistical calculations. The journal editor indicated that the article would be reconsidered if the analysis were redone correctly. Our informant claims that when he then corrected the mistake, the effect predicted by Kreutzfeld failed to be statistically significant. The informant says that when Kreutzfeld was informed, he just shrugged and said that he wouldn't re-submit the article and that "We'll just have to keep on trying until the numbers become more cooperative."

Now, if this account was accurate, such behavior would have violated every canon of scientific objectivity. The results should have been reported, regardless of how they happened to fall out. But negative findings, as a practical matter, almost never see the light of day. Researchers have termed this the "file-drawer problem" and it is bad practice but, regrettably, quite widespread. But there was much worse. Shortly after this incident, our informant was fired, ostensibly for purely economic reasons that had nothing to do with him personally. However, a year later, virtually the same article showed up in a different journal. The description of the statistical analysis indicated that it had been corrected, but the results were exactly the same as in the original paper rejected by the first journal! Our informant went ballistic when he realized what had occurred.

"Whoa! You're basically saying that Kreutzfeld has committed academic fraud," I said, "at least this one time. Did your guy try to expose this?"

"Absolutely," said Dave, "he wrote a letter of complaint detailing the whole sad story to the journal editors. But they decided not to get involved. Typical! There's very little incentive for journal editors to get in the middle of these spats. He also wrote to a watch-dog website that tracks cases of suspected research fraud. You'd be amazed how prevalent academic fraud has become. It's a potentially huge scandal that has been largely swept under the rug so far. The recent proliferation of second and third tier online journals exacerbates the problem by weakening peer review standards, catering to professors who need to pad their resumes in order to get ahead. It's no wonder that many research studies end up failing to be replicated. Anyway, our informant is willing to sign a sworn affidavit laying all this out."

"I can see how that would help undermine the theory motivating the Hopkins analysis," said Hal. "But, I'm somewhat leery of using an *ad hominem* attack. Unless it's really airtight, it might backfire on us. At a minimum, we'd need some sort of corroboration, like maybe some other such incidents, or testimony of other former employees. Do you think that's possible?"

Dave shrugged, but offered to see what he could come up with. Then, it was Sergei's turn to shine. He described how he had one-upped Professor Caldwell by engineering an improved predictor. He was somewhat vague about details, as we didn't want to give away too much about our plans to our unknown eavesdroppers. But what he did imply might well be sufficient to rattle the cage. In fact, I wondered if he had been unable to restrain himself from giving away a bit too much.

Finally, I spoke about my ongoing research to identify a subset of potentially vulnerable patients. I explained how Hector and I had recently been exploring some genetic modeling, and we suspected that such a subset might allow the susceptible patients to be identified by DNA testing. We were applying some novel statistical methods I had been working on to detect such patterns. I was careful to be rather vague about the details, and suggested we had not yet found anything conclusive.

Shortly afterwards, the meeting was adjourned and people started to drift out. I was about to depart as well, when Selwyn wagged his fingers, beckoning me to come over. He looked down and pointed to a paper on the table in front. The writing on it said simply: "Meet in Hal's office." I nodded and headed out of the conference room. When I arrived there, Hal motioned for me to sit down, and a minute later Selwyn came in. He closed the door behind him, sat down, and began to speak.

"There are some things I didn't want to share with prying ears," he began. "It does seem that we can potentially lob some broadsides at the Hopkins study, but we haven't yet found a way to sink it. Questioning the biological rationale, debunking the Caldwell Index, and identifying a small subgroup of susceptible patients, if you can, might be enough to buy us some time, but I'm still nervous. I do believe the FDA will appreciate that Verbana is prolonging many, many lives. That substantial benefit *must* be weighed against a highly uncertain alleged effect on this so-called HID. At least that's what we will argue. But we may end up having no choice but to accept some lingering cloud over the drug and have to fight the PR battle of our lives. It would be far, far better to prove that the data cannot be accepted as valid. Then the whole problem vanishes like a bad dream."

"I know, I said. "That's why I was so insistent about getting the original gene-expression data. The way I see it, that's our best chance."

"I hope you're right," said Hal, "because we're taking some real risks with that."

Selwyn sighed deeply. "Listen, Ken, I actually agree with you that data tampering is the most likely explanation. I managed to convince our CEO to go along, although she had reservations. The ball is now in your court, and both of our asses are on the line."

"Hey, don't leave my ass out," said Hal, smiling wryly.

"By the way," said Selwyn, "you should be hearing from the FBI shortly about arrangements for your little excursion. Have you thought about exactly what you'll be hoping to accomplish?"

"Sure. I want to see if there's any discrepancy between the study data and the original data. If there is, then I want to show that it couldn't have occurred by accident. From there, I hope to be able to figure out how this sleight-of-hand was accomplished. In principle, it should be simple. If it turns out as I suspect, it may crack the Pfeffer case as well, for which our FBI friends should be grateful."

"Speaking of which," said Hal, "I must say, it's been stressful interacting with Eve every day as if all is normal. I'll be glad when that charade is over. Incidentally, she asked me today if she could take a personal day tomorrow to deal with a dental problem that's been bothering her. Of course, I graciously agreed."

"Hmm. I wonder where she'll actually turn up," mused Selwyn.

# CHAPTER 28

## Thursday, September 17

The next day, I arrived at my office around nine, ready to prepare for my afternoon class and edit the latest draft of the paper I had been working on with Ralph Granger at Wellesley College. Procrastination on the latter was a casualty of my involvement in the PhireBreak case, and my collaborator was becoming impatient. I was looking forward to these rather mundane activities as a palliative for my roiling emotions, as I awaited on tenterhooks for an update on the previous night's developments. Rita had warned me that it might be a while before she could report anything, but I expected to be interrupted at any moment by a buzz on my burner phone. However, the hours slipped by, and I heard nothing.

Around noon, I decided to give Rita a call. It went immediately to voice mail. I didn't leave a message.

I knew she would call if there was any real reason to, and felt foolish for calling her, but the suspense was killing me. I was about to run out and grab a sandwich at a sub shop across Comm Ave, when my regular cellphone rang. The caller ID indicated it was Aldous Post.

"Hi, Aldous. I've been meaning to give you a call. How the hell are you?"

"I'm fine, Ken. But I've been wondering about *you*. Are *you* okay? Did you ever find out who was following you that day at my office? Are you still working on that case?"

"Aldous, it's a very long story, and the final chapter has yet to be written. I apologize for not getting back to you, but I've been crazy busy. Yes, the project is still going on, but I can't give you much detail. I know I owe you for your help with the video and promise to take you out for a nice lunch when the dust settles. As for the dude in your parking lot, he seems to have disappeared after I reported what we found to the authorities. It turns out he was a private detective, but he seems to have flown the coop. The good news is that I'm not being followed any more. Listen, my class is starting soon and I need to prepare. I'll call soon."

"Okay, bye, but watch your back."

"I will. Bye."

A while later, Irv Rothman stopped by my office. I groaned inwardly, anticipating more pressure.

"Sorry, Ken. I hate to bother you, but I wanted to follow up on those negative reviews. Have you been able to prove that they aren't legitimate? Look, I believe you, really, but somehow the dean has learned about this, and is concerned. I need to reassure him soon, or, well…*you* know."

This was not what I needed, but I simply smiled and told him I was on it, and it would be resolved soon. *If only.* I really had to check in with Rita on this right away.

*Why the hell hasn't she called to let me know what's happening with Eve Stolz, or whoever she really is?*

Next up was my graduate seminar on clinical trials. That went smoothly enough, and I returned to my office. I spent the next couple of hours working on the journal article, deeply immersed in the comforting exactitude of mathematics, when I was startled by the burner phone buzzing. *At last!*

"Rita! Finally. "I've been on pins and needles all day waiting to find out what went down last night. I've had trouble concentrating all day."

"Yeah, well, things are a bit complicated. Eve left the office around six last night, but returned two hours later and went straight to the conference room. She went to the cabinet, found the cup with the device, and downloaded the data, just as we had surmised. We had set up a hidden camera, so we have the whole thing on tape. There's no way she can wriggle out of this."

"Wow, that's terrific."

"Right. Anyway, nothing much occurred last night after that. She walked back to her fancy apartment, stopping for a salad and glass of expensive wine along the way, but meeting no one. She had dropped the flash drive in her hand bag, which she opened only to pay the restaurant bill. She met with no one and we were sure she still had the drive when she arrived home. After that, she stayed in for the rest of last night."

"Okay, so what happened this morning?"

"That's where the story took an unexpected turn. You remember that she told Hal about a dental appointment, right?"

"Yeah."

"Well, at around nine-thirty she leaves her apartment and walks up Atlantic Avenue, heading south. At the South Station corner, she crosses over the expressway and walks into the financial district. A few minutes later she winds up at One International Place."

"That's the big office tower in the financial district, the one designed by that famous architect. Philip Johnson, I think, right? I once had a client in that building. It's got some fabulous views of the harbor area."

"Uh huh, it's got forty-six floors and houses a variety of well-heeled tenants. Incidentally, there are no dentists in the entire building."

"Well, what a surprise."

"Yeah, anyway, our guy follows her into the building, stays back far enough not to be obvious. But there's a bunch of people going to the elevators, so he can't get on her elevator. However, as the elevators go up, the current floor on which the elevator has stopped is indicated. He notes that it stops on four different floors: 14, 19, 29 and 32. He then spends the next half-hour observing and recording the series of stops for each of the four elevators. When Eve finally emerges from one of these, he sees that it had made stops on 38, 29, 26, 14, and 5 before reaching ground level. So he knows that she must have been on either 14 or 29."

"Very clever."

She grunted. "He continues to follow her for the rest of the morning, until she winds up back at work for the afternoon. Incidentally, Hal says she was playing up the bogus dental visit, complaining about how she used too much Novocain, and it hadn't fully worn off yet. Pretty cute."

"Really."

"Right, so our agent goes back to the Johnson building and up to the fourteenth floor. Turns out it's occupied by a law firm and an accounting firm. He tells the receptionist at each one that he's supposed to meet someone of Eve's description, and asks if she's there. Both interrupt their gum-chewing to tell him no one like that had come in yet. This confirms his suspicions, because he was already betting heavily that floor 29 was our winner."

"Okay, and why is that?"

"Well, it turns out that the entire floor is occupied by a single tenant."

"I assume your guy went up to check out this company."

"Well, it's not really a company, and under the

circumstances, he decided not to."

"Uh, what circumstances?"

"It's the Boston consulate of the UAE...the United Arab Emirates."

"Uh, really?"

"Yes, and if the UAE is involved in all this, the implications are, to say the least, unsettling. Potentially dealing with foreign nationals would introduce certain complications that might extend beyond the FBI's jurisdiction. Moreover, if the conspiracy is actually being orchestrated by a foreign *government*, there are geo-political aspects."

"That's...pretty...interesting," was all I could manage to utter.

"Anyway, back to our immediate concerns. Now that we know where the information is going, we need to find out if the UAE itself is behind this, or maybe some rogue element within its national bureaucracy, or even a private party? The mastermind pulling the strings is seemingly using the cover of diplomatic immunity as a shield. In light of that, it's even more imperative to bring Eve Stolz in for questioning."

"And when are you going to do that?"

"Actually, we already have. We took her into custody last night."

"Uh huh."

"Fortunately, she's been surprisingly cooperative. She's an intelligence professional and understands the pickle she's in...but also the leverage she possesses. She knows that if she refuses to work with us, we would lose a golden opportunity to obtain some very valuable additional information. A deal has been struck. Basically, she'll cooperate with us and tell us what she knows. In exchange we've agreed to grant her limited immunity, so she may avoid jail time...if she's really helpful."

"That's great. Have you learned anything about how, specifically, the scheme is being carried out?"

"Not completely, but she's started to help fill in some blanks. One especially interesting tidbit is that she can confirm that the Pfeffer takedown-and-takeover plot was definitely engineered by the same perpetrators. Unfortunately, she doesn't know a great deal about exactly who they are or how they did it."

"Hmm, I see."

"Yes, in fact that's why I'm telling you all this. Would you be willing to come down and put some of those questions to her yourself? For example, how did they know that Pfeffer had a problem when the DMC had no clue? Did they manage to manipulate the data somehow, and if so, who was involved in the process?"

"Uh, I guess so. When would I do that?"

"Time is of the essence, so how about tomorrow morning? We can only keep her until tomorrow afternoon before throwing her back into the pond. If she doesn't resume her normal routine and report in to the consulate by tomorrow evening, they'll become suspicious. Can you be here by nine o'clock tomorrow morning?"

"Okay, but where is 'here' exactly?"

"Come to the Boston field office of the FBI. We're at 201 Maple Street in Chelsea. Call me when you arrive so I can meet you at security. Should be interesting. Gotta go, see you then."

# CHAPTER 29

Friday, September 18

The FBI's Boston branch fully occupies a modern office building in Chelsea, Massachusetts, a traditionally blue-collar, densely populated city of about thirty thousand inhabitants that borders Boston to the north, close to Logan International Airport. Once a haven for those fleeing poverty in Europe who found employment in its mills and factories, Chelsea still houses many immigrants, but now mainly from the Caribbean and Latin America. The city has recently been partially gentrified, with many new condos that appeal to young professionals who appreciate the proximity to Boston and Cambridge. Some of its old industrial buildings have been renovated into increasingly desirable office space. The FBI moved out of its former inadequate facilities in downtown Boston to the Chelsea building in 2015. Like most

Bostonians, I had never been even aware of, let alone visited, this facility.

Though only about twenty-five miles from my home in Newton, the FBI building is not easily accessible via public transportation, which involves three connections and almost two hours on Boston's archaic MBTA system. By car, I was able to make the trip in less than an hour, despite the usual heavy traffic through narrow winding streets that were not originally designed for automobiles. I parked in the large lot adjacent to the building.

Before leaving my car, I called Rita, as we had arranged. When I entered the front lobby of the building, she was there waiting. She explained that I would need to pass through the security checkpoint; no exceptions were allowed. After I passed through, she escorted me to a conference room on the second floor. Waiting there were Jeff Gunderson and another man I didn't recognize. He was heavyset, balding, probably in his fifties, and wearing a white shirt and loosened tie, his coat slung unceremoniously on the chair next to him. He had a slightly grizzled appearance.

Jeff gave me a broad smile and reached out to shake my hand. Then he introduced the other participant as Francis Kenneally, the head of the FBI's financial crimes division, who had flown in from D.C. for the occasion. Apparently, our case had achieved more notoriety, and elevated priority, in light of recent developments. He seemed to be eyeing me quizzically.

"Frank, would you like to start off?" asked Rita. "I know you had some concerns."

*Uh-oh!*

"Yeah, thanks Rita. Dr. Wheeler, first off, we appreciate your help. Rita's been briefing me about the situation here. It's getting...complicated. In all honesty, I have reservations about involving a civilian in a case like this, but it seems that you've become, unavoidably, an integral part of it. We may be dealing with a criminal conspiracy that has very wide scope and implications. For your benefit, as well as ours, I want to keep your involvement as circumscribed as possible. Do you understand what I'm trying to say?"

I was reminded of an old Alfred Hitchcock movie, *The Man Who Knew Too Much.* "You want me to stay in my lane, so as not to create problems for both of us. Look, I'm just a humble statistician. I'm having enough trouble juggling my day job and this Phire-Break case. I'm happy to leave international conspiracies to the professionals."

Kenneally nodded approvingly.

"Well then, Dr. Wheeler, we brought you in today for a specific purpose. Finding out about the UAE connection, whatever it might be, is of enormous significance. It's no secret that some of the major oil-producing countries are attempting to diversify their sources of income. With U.S. production rapidly increasing at the same time that oil reserves in the Mideast are dwindling, the handwriting is on the wall. We know that some Arab leaders are trying to leverage their nations' accumulated capital to acquire certain large companies, especially those whose products are based on complex chemical processes. Because of their oil industries, such countries already possess large pools of expertise in organic chemistry. This valuable human resource can, in principle, be repurposed to produce new drugs. However, there are steep costs and various legal and regulatory restrictions that tend to prohibit these countries from owning U.S. pharma companies. Apparently, the UAE may be trying an end-run around these obstacles."

"Our preliminary interviews with Ms. Stolz indicate that the Pfeffer incident was their initial foray in pursuing this strategy. It turned out to be spectacularly successful, and emboldened them to go after PhireBreak, and possibly others. However, these machinations have been hidden behind a dense web of shadowy intermediary organizations." He paused, as if considering how much more to tell me, then shook his head slightly.

"I think that's all you need to know and, frankly, more than I feel completely comfortable divulging." He glanced over at Rita with a look I couldn't interpret, implying perhaps that she had mishandled things somehow. She remained perfectly stone-faced. He didn't look very happy. "At any rate," he continued, "we need to penetrate the levels of obfuscation to nail these bastards, whoever they are. But for that we need good intel. You don't go around fucking with a foreign power without rock-solid intelligence. Otherwise, you risk getting caught with your dick in your hand."

"I understand," I said.

"Now, Rita here tells me you're as sharp as they come, when it comes to data and statistical formulas. Maybe a little overly adventurous when you stray outside your area of expertise, but I guess we should be grateful," he said, smiling for the first time. "Without you, we might not have exposed Eve Stolz. In a few minutes, she'll be joining us. So far, we've only charged her with a relatively minor offense, failing to register as a foreign agent. She knows that if she cooperates fully, there won't be additional charges, and she won't serve any jail time."

He paused.

"She's already provided some useful information. I want *you* to focus on finding whatever she knows about the statistical side of things. Did they mess with the data? Who was involved? She may know more than she thinks, but we don't have the statistical expertise to elicit the relevant information, to ask the right questions in the best way, if you catch my drift. We're counting on you to do that *for* us. Kapish?"

"Yeah, I guess I can do that," I replied, sounding more confident than I truly felt.

A few minutes later, Eve was brought into the room. Unlike me, she betrayed not a hint of anxiety or discomfort in what was, to me, a surreal encounter.

"Good morning, Dr. Wheeler," she said, with perfect composure, and took a chair, as if this were simply an ordinary business meeting. I had somehow imagined her in a prison jump-suit and handcuffs, which I now realized was absurd. It seemed she was being treated more like a professional colleague than a prisoner. Who knows? Maybe, she regarded this meeting as a kind of job interview. Getting caught was, I suppose, just an occupational hazard for her. Being an "adversary" from her perspective wasn't something personal. I wasn't sure if Rita and Jeff felt that way. I made a mental note to ask them later.

"Hello Eve. I must confess, this is a bit awkward for me. It's not every day I get to interrogate a spy." *Ouch, that was clumsily phrased.*

She simply laughed.

"You give me too much credit, Dr. Wheeler. I'd rather you think of me as a kind of private investigator. I do try to stay within the bounds of legality, although occasionally I cross the line. Usually, everything works out, though. I hope that's the case here. Who knows, maybe my misdeeds will end up doing some good. After all, I'm on *your* side now."

She smiled, rather winsomely. She was actually quite charming. I had to give her credit. Her manner was about as far as imaginable from the mousy paralegal persona I had witnessed before. I decided to start by asking her about the Pfeffer situation.

"What was your involvement in the Pfeffer case?"

"Ah, so they told you about that. You may know

that I worked as a paralegal at Robertson, Milgram and Sloan, the law firm that was representing Pfeffer."

"I had heard something about that. What did you do there exactly?"

"Pretty much the same as what I've been doing at Cooley & Lerner. Keeping abreast of their activities and reporting to my contact."

Before I could resume, Rita broke in. "That was the same contact to whom you brought the Phire-Break recording?"

"That's right. As I told you, I don't know anything about him."

"Okay, well, my questions pertain to the statistical analyses," I said. "What do you know about whether, and how, those analyses might have been rigged to falsely make Pfeffer's drug appear to cause myocardial infarctions?"

"Not much, really. I wasn't involved in the scientific side of things. But I did hear things occasionally that, well...suggested that something along those lines was going on."

"What kind of things?"

"Once when I came to the consulate to meet with my contact, I was a bit early, and he was finishing a conversation with someone I didn't recognize. After the man left his office, I asked who that was, in case I interacted with him at some point. My contact said not to worry. 'He's the hacker. It's nothing to do with you.' I assumed he meant a computer hacker, but had no idea what he was doing."

"Did you ever learn who it was?"

"No, sorry."

"But you're pretty certain that something fishy was going on with the data or analysis."

"Well, yes, but I can't recall exactly why, because I wasn't focused on that. In fact, my client kept the operatives quite compartmentalized, which is good tradecraft."

"Okay, so..."

"Wait, now that I think about it, there was something strange about that particular incident, which is probably why I remember it. As this hacker was getting up to leave, I overheard my contact say something like: 'You've got to be more careful.' The other guy seemed irritated and replied: 'Don't worry. I've got it covered.' Then he turned around and passed by me without making eye contact on his way out. I got a quick glance at his face, but it all happened very quickly."

At this point, Rita broke in.

"Do you think you could give us a description of this hacker person if you talked to a sketch artist?"

"I could try," said Eve, apparently eager to be helpful.

"Also, were you aware of anybody inside Pfeffer who might have been working with the UAE to undermine the data or analyses?"

Eve sighed thoughtfully. "Well, not exactly *inside*."

"What do you mean?"

"Okay. I became aware that my client had been

cultivating relationships with a number of prominent medical researchers. They had set up a foundation to support academic research and to run conferences. You'd be surprised how easy it can be to
manipulate such people by playing on their vanity.
Some generous funding and a lot of stroking can go
a long way." She smiled. "My father used to say that
flattery works best when the ego is biggest."

"Anyhow, one of these big egos belonged to a Yale
Professor who was serving as a biostatistical consultant to Pfeffer. I think he was a member of the
Data Monitoring Committee for their pivotal clinical trial."

"Wait a minute," I said. "I was told that was a
female statistician, Ann or Jan maybe, on that DMC
panel."

"Oh, that's right. Jane Clayton. She raised a
ruckus, but they were able to handle it. Actually, I
felt rather sorry for her. This other person was not
technically a statistician; he was an epidemiologist.
Older, and rather distinguished looking. Quite emi-
nent, I believe."

"Can you recall his name offhand," Rita asked.

"No, though I'm sure you can find out quite easily. But I'm pretty sure he wasn't working against
Pfeffer."

"How come?"

"Well, when it all blew up, he became a staunch
defender of Dr. Clayton. I believe he even wrote to
the FDA demanding a more thorough investigation
of the whole situation. My contact once referred to

him as a 'pompous pain in the ass' I remember. They ended up distancing themselves from him, even tried to discredit him, implying he was past his prime."

"Okay, now let's move on to the present. Ken?"

"Yes, what can you tell me about Mannheim Clinical Services, MCS?"

"That's the Clinical Research Organization that PhireBreak used to administer the trials. It's the same one that Pfeffer used."

"Right. Do you think they might be involved in this whole conspiracy?"

"I honestly don't know. I generally don't put much stock in coincidences, so it's plausible, but I can't tell you."

"Let me ask you something I know you *can* tell me. What, specifically, did your contact seem most interested in knowing about our statistical analyses?"

"My contact wanted to know what you and the PhireBreak folks were doing. He seemed quite confident that the data would support their attempt to undermine Verbana. But it was possible that a clever enough data analyst might be able to find a weakness in the Caldwell Index itself. So when you, and later Sergei Rosefsky, started to raise questions about this measure, that made them a bit nervous."

This caught me by surprise. "How do you know about Sergei?"

She smiled. "Well, that's interesting. Before bringing the audio file to the consulate, I always listened to it myself, at home. They didn't know I had equipment to do that, but I have my own resources. Actually, the stealth voice-recording is quite advanced, but the resulting recordings utilize fairly standard technology. Anyway, I thought the information might come in handy someday. Of course, I didn't mention it to my contact, but I could tell from some of his questions that it concerned him, or his superiors."

"Hmm. Okay, what do you think they were concerned about?"

"Look. Remember what I said about academic prima donnas? Well, believe me, Professor Harold Caldwell is one of the most *prima* of them all. That made him supremely susceptible to an influence campaign. They had invested heavily in him and funneled a lot of venture capital his way to help start his company, Caldwell Analytics. I don't know how much Caldwell was aware of the real source of funding. I think my client saw the Caldwell Index as a weapon that could be aimed at whichever pharma company promised the greatest return on investment. Unfortunately for PhireBreak, they drew the short straw."

"So if the Caldwell Index could be discredited somehow, the entire mission would be blown, *and* they wouldn't be able to use it in the future."

Eve smiled in silence and nodded. "Bingo! Plus, it might lead to awkward questions about Caldwell's work on their behalf," she added.

Then Rita spoke up. "If I understand you, they

guessed, correctly as it turned out, that Verbana would become a blockbuster. They knew enough about how the Caldwell Index worked to be sure it could be used to detect an apparent effect of Verbana. So they fiddled the data or analysis so that the appearance of this phony adverse effect would be induced. Then, they had to implement these changes somehow. This could be accomplished by a computer hack that would alter the data in some subtle way."

"True," said Jeff. "But what about Pfeffer? If they altered the data regarding heart attacks, that wouldn't work. The trumped-up adverse effect would have become evident to the Data Monitoring Committee. Potential heart problems would have been an obvious thing to look at, right? Also, such an effect would definitely have turned up in the final statistical analyses. But none of that *did* happen. That suggests the alteration may have occurred *after* the report was written and submitted to the FDA. Perhaps that's why the change wasn't discovered until the Yale re-analysis came up with different results later on."

"The problem with that," observed Rita, "is that the change would *then* have been obvious. Surely, questions must have been raised about why the *original* statistical analyses by Pfeffer hadn't found the same effect as the Yale researchers. How was their data or analysis different, and presumably flawed in some way?"

"Hmm. Maybe that did happen," I suggested "and

they found a plausible explanation. I don't know. Ideally, we could obtain more information about that from the company."

"Well, that might be difficult," said Rita. "As you know, the company's now under new management. I'm highly doubtful they would be very cooperative."

"True," added Jeff. "In any case, there's not enough time to investigate this before the FDA hearing. Plus, it probably has no direct bearing on the PhireBreak case."

"You're right about that, Jeff," said Rita, "but it might lead us closer to the mysterious hacker. There can't be that many hacking virtuosos who could infiltrate Pfeffer's system and engineer the necessary changes. The data hacking must also have been completely invisible. Maybe we could find out if any Pfeffer employees or consultants could have done it."

"Whoever pulled it off was probably a little lucky, too," I said. "Maybe that's what the snippet overheard by Eve means, about being sure their tracks were covered up completely."

I was starting to get excited as these pieces seemed to be falling into place.

"Maybe, even, that's why they chose to deploy the Caldwell Index for this second attack."

"What do you mean?" asked Rita.

"Well, think about it. The perpetrators knew that the PhireBreak statisticians would be unaware of the Caldwell Index, which wasn't yet commercially available. So the fabricated adverse events would remain invisible until the re-analysis would eventually reveal their existence. There would be no way for the statistical analyses during the clinical trials to uncover the potential problem that lurked in the data like a ticking time-bomb waiting to go off."

Rita looked thoughtful. "Assuming your hypothetical scenario is right, what we need is for you to figure out exactly how that ticking bomb was planted."

# CHAPTER 30

Friday, September 18

After the meeting, Rita left with Eve to begin seamlessly reinserting her into the outside world. Jeff Gunderson asked if I could stay a while longer to discuss the plans for my field trip to obtain the original gene-expression data. He related that he'd been designated to accompany me on this foray. This was good news, because I liked him and trusted his capabilities. We grabbed coffees in the cafeteria and I indulged in a rare jelly donut. I needed the sugar, I rationalized.

"So, Ken, what do you think we learned today?" he began.

"There's a lot to digest. A lot of it confirmed what we've been surmising about the connections between things. For instance, the Mannheim Foundation and the CRO may be involved in this conspiracy. Presumably, they're both controlled by the

UAE, or at least some faction operating under diplomatic cover provided by the consulate. Whoever is running the show was also involved in the Pfeffer deal. Plus, the re-analyses performed by Yale, and now Johns Hopkins, are no accidents. There may be other similar attempts being instigated as we speak. Also, it's not clear whether the researchers embroiled in these activities are corrupt or dupes. I wonder how many otherwise reputable scientists have been caught up unawares in this web."

"Yeah, the tentacles seem quite extensive. And we shouldn't forget the hedge fund either. Unwitting pawn or willful accomplice? I wonder how much UAE oil money has been directed their way."

"Right"

"Anyway, I wanted to fill you in on the plans for our data-gathering expedition. The wheels are in motion, but there are some complications. The five medical centers have all been contacted. They aren't happy about the idea of exposing the raw data. Their lawyers are bringing up a variety of objections, mostly related to patient confidentiality. In a normal situation, this request would have to go through their Institutional Review Boards that oversee research involving human subjects. Typically, gaining IRB approval could take weeks, which we obviously don't have."

"That's not good," I said, worriedly.

"No, it's not, but fortunately we have enough evidence to pursue a more direct route to the data, though it won't endear us to the site administrators."

"Okay, what?"

"We're going to obtain a court order from Judge Weingarten."

"That's a joke, right?"

"I kid you not."

"Will it be granted?" I asked, incredulously.

"We're pretty sure it will, because there's now a potential national security aspect. But we're going to need something from you."

"What might that be?"

"Can you draft a sworn affidavit that lays out exactly why we need that information? Hal can help you with the legal phraseology and formatting, but we need a succinct non-technical explanation for the judge. We'll need to have this by five o'clock today."

"Oh great. No problem."

*Sure, sure.*

"Good. Now let's talk about the trip itself."

"All right, so when will we make the trip?"

"We are tentatively scheduled to start out a week from next Thursday after your class is finished. We'll fly down to BWI airport and go directly from there to the hospital in Baltimore, then drive up to Philly. Early next morning we'll visit the site there, then drive up to New York for the two visits there. Then, Saturday morning we drive back to Boston for our last call, at Mass General."

*That's Carl Vitale's domain. How am I going to spin this to him?*

"Okay, sounds like a plan."

"Now, let's talk about exactly what we expect to happen at each site. As you know, the gene-expression data is kept in the patients' medical files. For currently active patients, all the files are on one system. For those that are no longer active, the files will need to be retrieved from an archive. These systems vary somewhat from site to site. When we arrive, we'll be provided with a research assistant who can help us. The gene-expression data will be downloaded onto a highly secure flash drive. I'm estimating that the entire process should take us a couple of hours at each site."

"That sounds pretty straightforward. Now let's just hope the judge grants the order for them to cooperate."

"By the way, we will assure the judge that the FBI will maintain custody of the data here, and it can't leave this building. You'll be able to access the data we collect only here and on our computers. All this has been arranged with Selwyn."

"Okay, if you say so."

"Oh, and we won't be revealing the FBI's role in any of this. You can introduce me simply as an attorney who is working with Hal. I'm along, ostensibly, to make sure everything is done legally and in accordance with the terms of the court order. Got it?"

"That's fine, but I have one more question. What are we going to tell the sites about what we're doing and why?"

"Actually, that's two questions, but never mind.

They have been informed that the court order authorizes us to collect certain specific data from patient files. They've been assured that the data will be used only in connection with a certain ongoing investigation and will not jeopardize any individual's right to privacy. Any reporting that involves the data will be anonymized. Even so, the hospitals we're visiting will be guaranteed immunity from any potential legal liability."

"And those assurances will satisfy them?"

"Well...they might also receive a rather substantial unrestricted research grant from PhireBreak to compensate for any inconvenience."

"Wait, you're kidding right?"

"Maybe. Now, get going. Hal's waiting. You've got an affidavit to write."

Five minutes later, I was back in my car. I sighed, as I contemplated the ride into Boston. I generally try to avoid the Boston traffic whenever possible. The only bright spot, on this occasion, was that the Prudential Center had an easily accessible underground garage. Before entering 111 Huntington, I made my customary stop at the Barnes and Noble next door to pick up another detective novel before heading up to C & L. As I did so, I was struck by the irony that my life was providing more thrills and chills than some of the fictional mysteries I was reading.

As I was about to exit the bookstore, I noticed Carolyn Cummings browsing the Best Sellers display near the front entrance. I decided it couldn't hurt to be sociable, though I anticipated a frosty response. I walked over to the display and glanced at the book she was perusing. It was one Val happened to have read recently and was urging me to read.

"Oh, I think that's a good one," I said. "My wife really loved it." Carolyn was surprised to see me and looked a bit wary, but smiled in a way that seemed more friendly than in our previous interactions.

"Listen, Ken. I'm sorry if I came off rather bitchy at our meeting in D.C. last week. When I had a chance to think about it, I realized your idea about the data being possibly corrupted is worth running down, although it seems like a longshot. I guess this whole situation is making me jumpy. We're all under a lot of pressure."

"That's certainly true, and I appreciate that you have a lot at stake."

"By the way," she added, "I think Sergei is making some real progress that may be able to seriously undercut the Caldwell Index. I'm becoming a bit more optimistic. The reason I came here today, incidentally, was to work with Hal on our presentation for the FDA. He and his associates have dealt with the FDA a lot. They're giving us advice on how best to frame the argument. Both Eve and Heidi seem really sharp."

"That's my sense too. I'm going up to see Hal now. Just for the record, I was really impressed with Sergei's presentation. I'm glad you two are making progress. Also, thanks for sending that patent. Finally knowing the mystery twenty-two genes is especially helpful. I guess that until they knew they were sure the patent would be granted, they were afraid of possible competition. How did you find out that it's now public?"

"Oh, that was Hal's doing. His office routinely monitors patent activity that may affect Phire-Break and sends us a report. I just happened to notice this one."

"Well, good catch. Anyway, I gotta run now."

"Yeah. Just one more thing." She hesitated before continuing. "You know, I've been working with Sergei for several years. I get that he can be abrasive at times, and somewhat egotistical, but I know he respects you. In the long run, assuming there is a long run for PhireBreak that is, I think you two could make a great team."

I was floored. "Well, I really appreciate that," was all I could muster. "I hope we can make sure that opportunity presents itself."

When I got to Hal's office, I saw him in conversation with Eve and Heidi. Everything looked perfectly normal, but it felt quite strange, knowing what I did about Eve. She, of course, was totally in character, once again playing perfectly the role of deferential subordinate. She smiled demurely when I entered, but I thought I caught a slightly amused twinkle in her eye. Heidi greeted me warmly. Then, they both left Hal's office.

"I ran into Carolyn in the bookstore downstairs," I said. "She seems a bit more sanguine about our chances than the last time I saw her."

"Yes, I think her work with Sergei is starting to come together. They're beginning to draft a report that we can include in our prior submission to the FDA. You'll need to start preparing one too. Don't forget it's due two weeks beforehand."

"I know. I know. Right now, though, I guess we need to work on an affidavit for Judge Weingarten."

It took the remainder of the afternoon to draft it. By that time, I was completely exhausted and emotionally drained. I really needed a break. By the time I finally got home, I had made a decision. It was getting close to the time of year when we would ordinarily make a last visit to the Vineyard to close up our cottage there for the season. I brought up with Valerie the idea of the two of us going out for a couple of days right after I returned from the field trip. That would be something to look forward to, and allow me to recharge my batteries before the final push leading up to the FDA hearing a week later.

Val warmed quickly to the idea, but we had some practicalities to consider. I couldn't afford to miss any of my classes, especially with the unsettled issue of the student reviews still hanging in the air. If we left on Sunday, we could arrive on the Vineyard around mid-day and stay through Tuesday morning. We'd also have to check on whether Val's mom could come to take care of Sam. Val would also have to arrange for coverage at her office on Monday. We would have two days to spend relaxing without worrying about distractions. I also had to promise not to do any work while we were there. Though the plan was not yet set in stone, I felt better just thinking about the possibility.

# CHAPTER 31

Thursday, October 1

**N**early two weeks had elapsed since my meetings at the FBI. Hector and I had focused our attention on the twenty-two relevant genes involved in the Caldwell Index. If the expression levels of these genes in the lymphocyte cells were somehow predictive of future dementia, then perhaps some mutations in these genes might define a subset that was vulnerable to the Verbana effect. With some helpful input from Dave Parker and his staff geneticist, we delved into this problem. But, so far, we had nothing to show for the effort.

While this failure was frustrating, it tended to confirm my gut feeling that there was something rotten about the data.

*That's the real reason there's no subset, because there's no goddam effect of Verbana at all!*

But I hadn't been able to prove it. Yet. As I packed my overnight bag for the trip to the study sites, I felt nervous. Judge Weingarten had ultimately been persuaded to issue the court order, but it was clear that he was skeptical. Absent a virtual smoking gun, he would not authorize any further investigation. It was make-or-break time.

I kept recalling Rita's comment about gut feelings not being evidence. If my instincts were wrong, it would not only be hugely problematic for Phire-Break, but also a blow to my reputation. Without a fallback analysis, we would be reduced to an argument over biology put forward by Dave Parker and Sergei's neural network attack on the Caldwell Index. These could create "reasonable doubt" about the Hopkins results, but probably not enough to convince the FDA to avoid taking any action. Our hope was that it would at least buy us some more time to conduct additional research that would ultimately exonerate Verbana.

On a personal level, I had to acknowledge some professional jealousy. If Sergei could truly debunk the Caldwell Index and undercut the Hopkins results that way, he would be the hero. I hated playing second fiddle, but I had to admire his brilliance. For years, I had been lobbying in my writing and speaking at conferences for a more creative approach to data analysis in clinical trials, going beyond the traditional emphasis on average effects. Things were changing, but not fast enough. The more we have learned about human genetics, the clearer it's become that drug treatments must be tailored to individuals. Using statistical and machine-learning techniques to achieve more individualized patient treatment represents the future of medical research. The prospect of forming a collaboration with Sergei to analyze PhireBreak's data, as Carolyn had suggested, was appealing. Time would tell if that would prove feasible.

It was against this emotional backdrop that I set out on the odyssey to obtain the original data collected by the five designated medical centers. When our plane landed at Baltimore Washington International, a half-hour's drive from our destination, I was still anxious. I didn't know what kind of reception we would be receiving. Our first stop felt as if we were entering the lair of the lion. The study site in Baltimore was the Johns Hopkins Hospital's oncology department.

This was the teaching hospital affiliated with the world-famous Johns Hopkins University School of Medicine. The irony that the re-analysis by the Hopkins Med School might undermine the research on Verbana done in this kindred hospital was not lost on us.

When we arrived at the hospital, we were greeted by a rather prim woman of about fifty who introduced herself as Nan Stern. She told us that she was a project manager, and had been involved in running the Verbana study. After escorting us up to a conference room on the sixth floor, where the oncology department was located, she made the obligatory offer of coffee, tea, or bottled water. We both declined politely. She let us know that the principal investigator on the Verbana project, Dr. Owen Shepherd, would be joining us shortly.

"It must have been quite exciting to be involved in such an important medical study," I offered.

"Well, I was only responsible for making sure everything ran smoothly. You know, tracking the grant money coming in, accounting for how the money was spent, making sure reports to Phire-Break went out on schedule, mainly administrative nuts and bolts, not the real *science*. Dr. Shepherd was in charge of all the research."

I caught a hint of awe in her voice as she referred to Dr. Shepherd. As if on cue, the great man made his entrance. Along with him came a rather severe-looking woman of perhaps forty, clad in a stylish navy pinstriped suit. They both sat down. Ms. Pinstripe plunked her briefcase on the table in front of her and clicked it open, loudly.

"Hello," Shepherd boomed, "I only have a few minutes between patients, but I wanted to get a little more detail about your, uh...visit with us. I'm Owen Shepherd, Chief of Oncology here at the hospital. As I'm sure you know, I was a principal investigator on the Verbana trial."

Indeed, I knew that his name appeared third on the list of over forty co-authors of the landmark article in the *New England Journal of Medicine* that presented the study results. It's customary to include all of the principal investigators at the study sites plus other key research personnel as authors for such an article. Number three was a very prestigious placement.

"With me here today is Emily Frank, the hospital's general counsel. I understand that you are here pursuant to a court order. That's rather unusual, to say the least, isn't it?"

"Yes," I responded, "and it wouldn't have been necessary except for some rather extraordinary circumstances. I don't think we've met before. I'm Ken Wheeler. I teach biostatistics at Boston University. My specialty is research methodology for clinical trials. With me is Jeff Gunderson, He's an attorney who works with Hal Farenheit. His role is to assure that we proceed in accordance with our remit as specified in the court order."

At this, Shepherd's eyebrows rose slightly, and he glanced over at Ms. Frank, who spoke up.

"Just so we're clear, Hal Farenheit explained that the court order was merely an expedient, because there was some urgency that precluded going through the usual channels. We agreed to accommodate PhireBreak, with some reservations."

She cleared her throat.

"Over my objections, our CEO, who reposes a great deal of trust in Selwyn Washington, made the ultimate decision. Before we go any further, I want to be absolutely certain that our institution is not being investigated for any potential wrongdoing."

It was evident that she was somewhat agitated, so Jeff quickly stepped in.

"No, no, absolutely not! Our investigation has nothing to do with anything that was done by anyone at this institution. Regrettably, I can't disclose anything more at this time."

"Well that's certainly a relief," responded Shepherd, his tone tinged with sarcasm.

"Look, I don't give a damn about your investigation," said Emily Frank. "My job is to be sure we are protected. The court order states that by complying with this court order we assume no legal liability for the act of releasing the data to you. We want it clearly affirmed that any violation of patient rights that may be alleged in the future is not attributable to us, that we are acting under compulsion pursuant to this order, and that we will be indemnified for any unforeseen repercussions. I've prepared a short letter that lays this out somewhat more explicitly than in the court order. If you can have this signed by an authorized representative of PhireBreak, we can permit you to proceed without further delay."

It seemed that the temperature in the room had risen several degrees. I wondered how Jeff was going to handle this. He produced his most ingratiating smile without missing a beat.

"That's fine, of course. I'll need to run the letter by Hal Farenheit, but it shouldn't be a problem. I'll call him right now."

That seemed to cool things down.

"Listen," said Shepherd. "Does this have anything to do with these rumors floating around about the

Verbana trial? There's some crazy theory that the drug causes dementia. I'd hate to see the product impugned; it's been a huge boon for us oncologists. You have no idea how many lives are being extended, some for many years."

"I'm sorry," replied Jeff, "we just can't comment on that."

"Well then, I'd better be getting back to my patients." said Shepherd. "No need for me to wait around for your signed letter to come back."

He began to get up and started to leave the room.

After that, we had no further trouble completing our work there.

# CHAPTER 32

### Friday, October 2

The next three site visits were uneventful. The people we dealt with at each medical center were curious about what we were doing, but there was no repeat of the rather contentious experience at Johns Hopkins. We obtained the data we needed and went on our way. After the second Manhattan visit, at the NYU Langone Medical Center, we stayed overnight in midtown Manhattan. Early the next morning, we had breakfast at the nearby Second Avenue Deli, one of my favorites. I come there often when I'm in the City. As most New Yorkers know, it's not on Second Avenue, a fact Jeff found amusing.

Many of the waitresses know me by sight and dish out a helping of repartee along with the savory cold-cuts. A few of them have been at the restaurant since my college days at Columbia when I came there often with a group of friends. Back then, it really was on Second Avenue. Jeff, who had never been there, enjoyed the ample helping of eggs and corned beef hash with an onion bagel and cream cheese.

Thus fortified, we retrieved the car and left for our final stop at Mass General in Boston. We had about a four-hour drive ahead of us. Once we emerged from the labyrinthine streets and frenetic traffic of the metropolis, we cruised at a good clip through the bucolic countryside of Westchester County, and then eastern Connecticut. As we drove along, we shared our impressions of the experience so far. At one point, my thoughts harked back to my meeting in Selwyn Washington's office.

"You know, Jeff, Selwyn insinuated something at the outset of all this that shocked me at the time."

"Yeah, what was that?"

"He suggested that there might be someone inside PhireBreak who was leaking information. The more we uncover about this business, the more plausible that seems to me. Think about it. The manipulation of data in just the right way would require a detailed knowledge of how the study was being conducted. It also had to depend on, and be coordinated with, the Caldwell Index, which was just being developed back then. Could all this really have been pulled off without a source of information from within PhireBreak?"

"If you're right, it would have to be someone pretty high up, and who has been there for at least several years," offered Jeff.

"Yeah. And someone with substantial statistical expertise. Possibly computer programming skills, too."

"Huh, that seems to narrow down the potential suspect list considerably. If I were to be totally objective, that would put, well, Carolyn Cummings and Sergei Rosefsky at the top of that list. Do you have any reason to doubt their loyalty?"

"No, I certainly don't. But I guess we have to consider every possibility. I think, though, there must be at least a dozen other candidates. By the way, you don't think Sergei's Russian background would raise any issues, do you?" I felt awkward asking.

Jeff laughed. "It's funny. Ever since the Russian election-hacking scandal in 2016, there's been a lot of scrutiny of anyone with a Russian surname. The irony is that, by and large, Russian immigrants have turned out to be the *least* likely to be problematic. Most of them hate the current regime over there. Besides, Putin is behaving himself these days. His recent health problems appear to have mellowed him somewhat. His biggest political concern is to keep Russia's economy afloat in the face of the worldwide oil glut."

"Interesting. You know, I'm actually starting to warm up to Sergei. He's a bit rough around the edges, but kind of an acquired taste."

"Actually, Ken, I think there's almost no chance he's our hacker. Selwyn is a fanatic when it comes to security matters. I have to believe he had Sergei thoroughly vetted before he brought him onboard."

"Yeah, that makes sense."

"Anyway Ken, let's talk about what happens after we get back with this trove of data. How do we determine whether in fact the data appear to have been altered? Can't you just replace the old data with the new data we obtained and see if the Hopkins results still holds up? That would seem to be pretty straightforward."

"Yeah, that *would* have worked if I'd been able to convince PhireBreak to get me the original data from all thirty-two study sites." I grimaced. "Unfortunately, that wasn't deemed feasible. With that data, we could have determined exactly what *would* have resulted had the original data not been corrupted. As it stands, we can only learn what changed in five of the thirty-two study sites."

"I see. We would know that some changes occurred, but not the full impact. But still, it would imply that something is going on that requires explanation, right? What else besides deliberate tampering could have caused the changes?"

"That's a good question. On the one hand, it's hard to conjure up any innocuous explanation for the differences. But whether they represent strong evidence of deliberate tampering would depend on the nature of the discrepancies. In other words, is there some pattern to the differences that suggests, or even *proves* beyond reasonable doubt, that some finagling must have occurred?"

"Okay, what would such a pattern look like?"

"The pattern would need to be extremely unlikely to have occurred by chance. Also, it would have to be consistent with our theory about what the purposes of the manipulation were. That is, would they align with what was needed to exaggerate the apparent adverse effect of Verbana? This is similar to several fraud cases I've been involved in."

"Ah, *fraud*, now that's something I understand."

"Let me give you a real example of how statistical analysis can support an allegation of fraud. I'm thinking of a case in which I helped the U.S. Attorney prosecute a large medical mill in Boston. The government in that case was able to obtain the medical records for all patients seen at the suspect facility during the past three years. After obtaining the data, I was able to analyze it, looking for anomalous patterns that would not normally be expected."

"Wait," said Jeff, "I remember that case. It involved a large pain clinic in, let me think, South Boston. Yeah, we weren't involved, but I read about it in the Boston Globe. The Massachusetts Insurance Fraud Bureau put a lot of crooked chiropractors and physical therapists out of business, and the ringleaders did some time. You were in on that?"

"Yes, as I was starting to tell you, I analyzed the data to see if it looked real or not."

"*Looked* real?"

"Sure, real data has certain characteristics that are hard to mimic. I've developed a computer program that basically looks for deviations from these characteristics. It comes up with a kind of suspicion index based on the nature and extent of these deviations. That doesn't prove fraud by itself, but it provides evidence. Statistical patterns can be persuasive in conjunction with other types of information, such as witness testimony."

"Hold on. I'm confused. Give me an example."

"Okay. In this medical-mill case, we analyzed various characteristics of the treatment regimens for nearly a thousand patients. Most of these had come in after a motor vehicle accident. The Fraud Bureau was investigating a sharp increase in such accidents being reported to insurance companies, with many of the so-called victims being channeled to this one particular pain clinic. They suspected that many of these so-called accidents were actually being staged, and that the injuries were bogus. In this type of scams, the accident participants get paid a couple of hundred to feign injury, and the clinic bills thousands to insurance companies. Usually, crooked plaintiff lawyers are involved to pursue the injury claims. Sometimes the lawyers are actually running the whole show."

"Right, we've prosecuted a number of similar cases around New England. So how did your statistical analysis help prove this?"

"In that case, it was pretty straightforward. There were two main patterns that stood out. First, there was almost no variation in the amount or type of treatment being given to the patients. Virtually, every person that walked in the door received the same diagnosis, same type of therapy and the same number of visits. Such uniformity is *inconsistent* with the normal pattern of variability in the specific type and severity of true injuries. But it is *quite* consistent with an attempt to maximize the volume of billing. Second, there was a clear trend of gradually increasing treatment over time, with no apparent medical rationale. Patients tended to receive more visits and more treatment modalities as time went on, again with no evident medical necessity. This sort of pushing the envelope is typical of these fraudulent medical mills. The more they can get away with, the more brazen they become. In the end, it's often this insatiable greed that does them in."

"I get how this kind of statistical evidence can help to *detect* bad behavior, but does it amount to proof?"

"Not by itself, but it can be very persuasive in conjunction with other evidence. For example, in this case, some undercover agents pretended to be participants in the scheme. Their testimony, and in some cases recordings, in conjunction with the statistical patterns was more than sufficient to convince the jury."

"That's interesting. How'd you like to consult with us on some cases after this project is finished?"

"I might consider it."

"Good. Getting back to the present, though, how would this apply in our situation?"

"Well, in this case, our presumption is that

any data manipulation was intended to inflate the difference between the Verbana and control groups on the Caldwell Index. Therefore, the pattern of changes to the true, original data should line up closely with this objective. So if we see a very strong relationship of this kind, one that is virtually impossible to have occurred by chance, that would strongly point to foul play. That should certainly be enough to give the FDA pause and require a complete audit of all the original data, which would ultimately allow us to calculate the real results that *should* have been analyzed."

"Fascinating. I hope that's what happens."

# CHAPTER 33

Saturday, October 3

We arrived at the Mass General around three in the afternoon. The day had turned cloudy, and rain was threatening. As we pulled into the parking garage, I was apprehensive about meeting with Carl Vitale. I imagined he might be a tad miffed that I'd deceived him about my true purpose for picking his brain about the Verbana trials. Unfortunately, that turned out to be the case.

"I have to say, Ken, I was really surprised to learn about this visit, what with the court order and all, and your involvement. You could have been straighter with me about what you were up to, which is *what*, exactly, by the way? The explanation we got in the letter from Selwyn Washington 'requesting' our cooperation was far from explicit. Perhaps you would care to enlighten us?"

I did my best to defuse the tension by giving our standard spiel, which, by now, I could do in my sleep. I was extra-careful to grovel, as I apologized to Carl, explaining that I would have been more forthcoming if I hadn't been constrained by my contract with PhireBreak. That seemed to mollify him, and I hoped that my relationship with him hadn't been irreparably destroyed. Carl was about to leave us to our task when something occurred to me.

"Carl, I have a question. For patients who complete the clinical trial, I believe you told me that you continue to see many of them, correct?"

"Sure, these are our patients, and we don't abandon them after the trial is over. In fact, we don't charge them for anything that's not covered by their insurance."

"Right, that's great. So unless they have died you would still be treating them here at Mass General, right?"

"Oh. Well, there were a few who have moved out of the area. But most are being seen by one of our docs."

"Right. Thanks, Carl. I'll see you around."

"Sure," he replied, but he didn't sound very enthusiastic.

After they left, I was thinking about what Carl had said.

"What was that all about?" asked Jeff.

"I'm kicking myself that I didn't think of this before. *Damn it!* I think we may have missed a golden opportunity, at least for now. But maybe we can salvage something at least."

"What the hell are you talking about?" Jeff asked.

"Look, the Caldwell Index purports to identify the probability of future dementia, which will manifest within a few years, right?"

"Yeah, so?"

"But Carl just told us that most of these patients, if they're still around, are being followed up, in some cases years later. That means they are being monitored *clinically*. I assume that any significant changes in their mental capacity would likely be noticed at some point, don't you think? There'd be some mention of it in the physician notes, if for no other reason than that could indicate a possible side-effect caused by one of the patient's medications, whether Verbana or something else. They'd want to follow up on any possibility of that, I'd think."

"Okay, so what are you driving at?"

"Well, suppose we could comb through the patient files to find out if any such indication of impaired cognition exists for any of the Verbana-exposed patients."

"Whoa, Ken! I don't know whether that would be within our remit from the court."

"I'm no lawyer, but I think the court order is nonspecific. It says we're allowed to gather the genomic data along with any ancillary information that we believe may be relevant to the investigation."

"Okay, I suppose the court can decide later whether to exclude the information from its adjudication of the issues. Of course, it's possible we may get a slap on the wrist for over-reaching."

"True, but in the mean time we'll have learned something useful."

Jeff made a face to indicate he wasn't especially pleased but would go along.

"Just how are you planning to do it?"

"I have excellent text-search software. I just need to tell it what I'm looking for. It should be pretty straightforward."

He sighed. "Okay, let's get this over with."

I proceeded to carry out a brief orientation "conversation" with Clara, the avatar for the AI text-searching algorithm. I instructed her to interrogate the physician notes to detect any conceivable hint of mental incapacity. It took about five minutes for her to complete the search. As I suspected, she was unable to find anything. After coming up completely empty, Clara issued a seemingly heartfelt apology, a nice touch by her programmers. "No worries, Clara," I responded. "At least you gave it a good try."

*Well it's something. I hope I can replicate this approach for all the other sites at some point. I'm betting the results would be similar. This will have to do for now, though.*

I filled Jeff in on my findings, or rather non-findings. He nodded.

"So where does that lead?"

"It's a nice piece of evidence, but not probative by itself. Now, if I could do a more systematic review of the notes from all thirty-two sites, I might be able to make a powerful statistical argument. Unfortunately, that just ain't gonna happen before the FDA meeting, but maybe, just maybe, it can help generate enough doubt to buy us some additional time. In any case, it reinforces my suspicion that the supposed Verbana effect is bogus."

When we finished at the hospital, it was almost five o'clock. Jeff offered to drive me home, but I told him not to bother; I could just walk over to the nearby T station. At rush hour, the trip by MBTA would be faster. An hour later, I found myself back in Newton, and arrived home around six thirty, ready to collapse. But as I opened the front door, I was assailed by a cacophony of shouting and a blur of activity.

# CHAPTER 34

Saturday, October 3

S am was screaming with glee as he raced around the dining room and front hallway, chasing something small and black that was moving very fast. Raised voices were emanating from the kitchen.

*Just what I need.*

Noting my entrance, Sam stopped abruptly and cried out in surprise.

"Dad...you're back! Mom, mom, dad's back. Guess what mom brought home from her clinic. She says his owner couldn't get back to pick him up until tomorrow morning, and there was nowhere else for him to stay. He's got some kind of ph, ph..."

"Phobia?"

"Yeah, that's it. Anyway, it makes him too scared to stay alone."

This was not the first time something like this

had occurred.

"*Please*, dad, can't we get another dog? We *need* a dog!"

Doc, our much-beloved Labrador retriever, had died six months before at the age of fourteen, and we intended to get another dog eventually, but with Val's pregnancy and all ..."

At that moment, I noticed that Valerie seemed to be out of sorts as she and her mother came in from the kitchen. *That's right. I forgot. She came tonight to stay with Sam while we are away.*

They both turned toward me, looking aggravated. Jean was, for the most part, a lovely mother-in-law, but she and Val could sometimes manage to get under each other's skin.

*Oh no. I hope I'm not about to be triangulated into their disagreement. That's always a lose-lose proposition.*

Val spoke first. "Sam, stop running around like a maniac. I think it's time to take Roo out for a walk."

"Roo? What kind of name is that for a dog?"

At that moment, the small creature did something quite amazing. It jumped vertically about three feet off the ground. This feat was repeated two or three more times.

"Oh, I see. Roo, as in *Kanga*roo. Very clever. Anyway, what's going on between you two," as I dropped into my favorite chair.

"Well," said Valerie. "It's about Leo."

*Of course, it is.*

Leo is Val's younger brother. Despite his intelligence, good looks and considerable charm, he had managed to avoid matrimony. However, for the previous two years, he had been living with a girlfriend named Marcia who was adored by all of us. We believed that he truly loved her, and that she'd be great for him. She wanted to get married and start a family. Leo, true to form, was showing signs of blowing up the best thing that'd ever happened to him. Jean was pushing Val to intercede somehow and prevent this from happening. Val loves her brother dearly, but the relationship between them has always been a bit fraught. I listened with what I hoped appeared a sympathetic attitude, but steadfastly refused to be drawn in, having learned the hard way the perils of doing so. Eventually, things died down, just as Sam returned with Roo.

"How was your business trip?" asked Jean. "I hear you're working on some big legal case. Valerie says it's all very hush-hush, so you can't give me any details. But was it helpful for your client?"

"I think so, but I won't know for sure until my colleague and I have had a chance to analyze the new data we obtained."

"Oh, is that the charming fellow who grew up in South America and speaks all those different languages? He seems very nice. I hope he's given up the smoking, though."

"Almost...I think. Anyway, I can't do anything until we get back from the Vineyard. Which reminds me that we have to leave early in the morning to make our ferry, and we've gotta pack tonight.

We'd better have some dinner and attend to that."

"Okay," said Val. "Sam, wash up for dinner. We've brought in some take-out from that Middle Eastern restaurant in West Newton. But first, I think we'll have to put Roo in his crate so he doesn't jump onto the table while we're eating."

Just then, my burner phone started to buzz. I picked it up. It was Rita and, as usual she was all business. "Ken, we need to meet."

"Hello, Rita. Nice to hear from you, too. Listen, I just got back from the trip and I'm really wiped. Can't it wait until after I get back from the Vineyard on Tuesday?"

"Sorry, Ken. Something has come up. I've gotta see you right away."

"But we're leaving first thing in the morning, Rita, and ..."

"I'm sorry, but it can't wait. Please, don't make me beg. I can come to Newton. Is there a place nearby where we could talk? I can be there in an hour."

I sighed. Out of the corner of my eye, I could see Val looking questioningly at me. I nodded and rolled my eyes. "Okay, Rita, there's a Peet's Coffee in Newton Centre. I'll see you there in an hour."

Jean was looking at both of us with an expression of utter bewilderment.

"What was that about?" she inquired.

"Don't ask," Val told her. "If he told you, he'd have to kill you." She sighed in resignation. "Oh well, at least you've got time to eat. Thank goodness she wasn't closer."

Forty minutes later, I found myself walking into the town center. I arrived at our rendezvous right on time, but she was already at a table, nursing a large black coffee.

"Do I have time to grab a coffee?"

She just smiled.

When I brought my caffé Americano to the table, she began to fill me in on recent developments.

"I've just come from a meeting with Eve Stolz. She reported some very interesting and potentially troubling information. It seems that she was planning to go into the UAE consulate this morning at nine o'clock for a routine debriefing. But at seven-fifteen she received a call instructing her not to come in, because the office was being closed for some emergency repair work. This seemed odd to her, and raised her suspicions that some kind of clandestine meeting might be going on. Instead of staying home, she decided to drive over to International Place and park in the underground garage. She chose a parking spot near the elevator bank with a good view of the entryway to the elevators. She knew that important visitors wishing to avoid being recognized would usually take this route. She slouched down and was ready to take pictures of anyone who came along."

Rita paused for a sip of her coffee. I suddenly realized I hadn't touched mine. I took a couple of sips and processed what she'd told me so far.

"Okay, Rita, so what happened next?"

"Well, just before nine, a black limousine with diplomatic plates pulls up right in front of the elevator bank. Then, one of the elevator's doors opens up, and remains open. Two men emerge. One of these Eve recognizes as the UAE ambassador to the U.S. She had seen him a couple of times at the consulate, but he's normally in Washington. What was odd was that he was not accompanied by the consul general who heads the office here in Boston."

"Who was the other guy?"

"We're not exactly sure, but we think he's a high-level UAE official."

"Okay, so what about the limo?"

"Right, so two people get out of the limo: a man and a woman. Eve tried to get a good camera angle, but it was very difficult without revealing herself. Still, she managed to get a useful video for our techies to analyze. They were able to identify them."

"Uh huh. Do I know any of them?"

"Not likely. The man was identified, with eighty percent certainty, as a Venezuelan general who's deputy director of their intelligence services. As you know, we currently have no diplomatic relations with Venezuela. Their forced annexation of Colombia two years ago and other recent provocations have inflamed regional tensions and led us to the brink of war. His presence in the U.S., let alone at such a meeting, has set off a lot of alarm bells. Of course, there's a twenty percent chance it isn't him."

"So what about the woman?"

Rita paused, looked around as if worried about being overheard, and drank some more coffee. She was also tapping her fingers on the table. I had never seen her looking nervous, and that, more than anything she'd told me so far, had me spooked. I drank some coffee and waited.

"This is not to be discussed with anyone except Jeff or me unless we tell you to, got it?"

"Even Selwyn, or Hal?"

"For now, yeah."

"Okay."

"The woman is named Norma Dean Dillon."

"Never heard of her."

"Not surprising. She keeps a very low profile. She's about sixty, doesn't wear makeup or dye her hair, dresses conservatively, and can easily blend into any crowd. But she's one of the most powerful women in America."

"How so?"

"Norma Dillon is the deputy director of counterintelligence for the NSA."

Rita sat back and gave me a few moments to digest this bombshell. She knew I'd have questions.

"First off, why are you telling me about this?"

"A couple of reasons. One is that it may be advisable to increase our precautions relating to communications. If Dillon is involved in some kind of nefarious conspiracy, the situation has just become much more, ah...delicate. Of course, we don't even know if this meeting has anything to do with the PhireBreak situation. Maybe we just stumbled on some back-channel negotiations. Perhaps the UAE folks are simply helping to facilitate surreptitious communication between the U.S and Venezuela. Who knows?"

She reached into her purse and pulled out a blue ballpoint pen. I thought she was going to write something down, but instead she handed it to me. I couldn't help noticing my initials engraved on it. I was rather flummoxed.

"Er, that's a really thoughtful gesture, Rita."

"You can start using this and give me back the burner phone. We're pretty sure it hasn't been compromised yet, but this will be safer."

"Uh, why are you giving me a ballpoint pen? Will I be writing notes and attaching them to carrier pigeons?"

"It works as a pen, all right, but it's got a few, uh... special features. It's called an *Ari*."

"What is that, some kind of an acronym?"

"Yeah, it stands for *autonomous robotic intelligence*."

"Okay, cool. I guess."

"Ari is a voice-activated communications device. You just say 'Ari' to activate it. It's been programmed to respond only to your voice. It has a triple-encryption protocol that is virtually impossible to defeat, at least without a quantum computer. It's got an advanced AI system and has access to the internet through most wi-fi networks, even if they're password protected. Plus, it continually monitors what's going on in your environment and assessing any potential threats to you."

"What about receiving calls?"

"Right. You'll feel a slight vibration. If that happens, just find a place that's private and speak normally. Ari is programmed to automatically sense the presence of other humans, and reduce the volume so only you should be able to hear. Unless, of course, you command it to allow others to hear. You can always override any default programming."

"I just say 'Ari' then, eh? That's quite a toy."

EXCUSE ME KEN, BUT I AM CERTAINLY NOT A TOY.

The voice was a pleasant baritone with an upper-class British accent. It reminded me of a rather officious butler.

"Okay, Ari, that will be all for now. Oh, and try to upgrade your programming to understand irony, please."

CERTAINLY SIR.

"Please don't address me as 'sir' in future."

IF YOU WISH. IT IS SUPERFLUOUS TO USE WORDS LIKE PLEASE AND THANK YOU AS I AM EMOTIONLESS.

"Thank you, I'll keep that in mind."

WAS THAT AN EXAMPLE OF IRONY?

Good Ari, you're learning.

"One other thing," added Rita"

"What?"

"Don't lose Ari. It would take several years of your salary to re-pay his cost."

"Oh, I imagine in a couple of years I'll be able to

get one at Best Buy for fifty bucks."

"Hmm, you're probably right."

I grabbed it and handed over my old burner phone. Playing in my head was the iconic blaring theme music from the early James Bond movies.

"So how does the Venezuelan general fit into the picture? He wouldn't be involved in any *normal* diplomatic negotiations, would he?"

"Not in any obvious way, no. We're going to quietly look into what may be going on diplomatically, but at the same time, we can't overlook the more sinister possibilities. We have to keep this information very tightly held until we know what's going on. It will be moved up the chain, but only with people we can absolutely trust. You understand?"

I just nodded.

*That means there are some folks in the chain that you can't trust? Not a comforting thought.*

The second reason I needed to meet with you right away is to speculate how this might be related to PhireBreak. Suppose that Dillon is really involved in some kind of plot. What's the endgame here? What could a Venezuelan general, an NSA deputy director, and the UAE government conceivably be meeting about that might be related to a pharma company like PhireBreak?"

I literally scratched my head for about a minute before responding as I pondered the matter. Then, something I'd read about in an article a few years ago suddenly clicked in.

"Just spit it out, no matter how crazy it might seem."

"Okay, I was just remembering a famous terrorist incident that occurred in the 1980's, I think. There was a series of mysterious deaths in the Chicago area. The CDC managed to deduce that the victims had all taken the over-the-counter painkiller Tylenol. They eventually discovered that the Tylenol capsules had been tainted with potassium cyanide. The manufacturer voluntarily publicized the problem and issued a recall. Millions of bottles were returned and the company's market share tanked. I think it might have been Johnson &Johnson. There were no further deaths."

"Did they ever catch the asshole who did it?"

"Actually, no, I don't think so. But after that the industry introduced a number of manufacturing and packaging changes to prevent anything like that from happening. That's why you have to break your nails now to open the packaging. Anyway, since these changes, there hasn't been a repeat incident in over forty years."

"Interesting. Are you suggesting a plot to do something like that?"

"Not really, but it *would* be possible. Remember, all these safety precautions were meant to counter *outside* tampering with the product. Nobody expected that a pharma company *itself* would have any reason to contaminate its own product. That would be nuts. Unless, of course, you were a terrorist aiming to create havoc. The original Tylenol scare caused a few deaths, and a great deal of economic cost and social disruption. Imagine what a similar incident on a much larger scale orchestrated from *within* a company could accomplish. Just saying."

"That's interesting, but it does seem a little far-fetched. Plus, politically, the UAE and the Venezuelans seem like strange bedfellows. Since Venezuela dropped out of OPEC last year, they aren't exactly on good terms ... as far as we know. Why would they be working together?"

"Well, I'm afraid politics is not my department."

"Okay. Thanks for taking the time. Let's meet soon after you're back on Tuesday. The last week before the FDA meeting should be interesting."

"Indeed, it should be."

I was about to head for the door, when a thought struck me.

"There's somebody else we should interview. I should have thought of this before."

"Who?"

"Jane Clayton."

# CHAPTER 35

Sunday, October 4

We awoke on Sunday morning early, dressed hurriedly, loaded the car, and headed out for the drive to Woods Hole. On the way, we dropped Roo off at Val's clinic. Val chatted briefly with the attendant on duty, to make sure that she understood Roo's idiosyncrasies. Then, we headed off for a much-needed relaxing interlude in our hectic lives.

We were able to make the trip in time for the nine o'clock departure with time to spare. When we arrived at the parking area in front of the ferry terminal, we took our place in the line-up of vehicles awaiting the cue from the attendant there to begin the boarding process. Soon we were driving onto the ramp that led into the belly of the vessel. Once inside, we got out and ascended the stairway leading up to the boat's snack bar. We grabbed coffees and sat at a table with a nice view of the harbor.

The coffee was awful, and Hector's "insipid-swill" characterization came to mind. That reminded me that I hadn't had a chance to speak with him about the data we'd retrieved from our site visits. I called, and he answered immediately.

"Hi, Ken. How was your trip. Did you get everything you wanted?"

"Yes, it went well. I even had a chance to stop at the Second Avenue Deli for breakfast yesterday."

"Lucky guy."

"Indeed. Anyway, I wanted to coordinate with you about the data. I'm afraid you'll need to head into the FBI office, because they can't let it out of their premises, per the court order."

"Right. Your friend Rita has explained everything to me. I'm going in there tomorrow afternoon to do it. I assume you want me to compare the data we've been using to the data you brought back. I'll list out the discrepancies that occur."

"Yes, and then I want you to calculate what effect, if any, there would be on the Hopkins results if the correct gene-expression values were substituted for the ones we have been analyzing."

"But you only went to five of the sites, right? What could that tell you?"

"Nothing definitive, but if the calculated effect on the Caldwell Index decreases, that would be evidence that we need to get the rest of the data to perform a complete correction."

"Okay, I'll email you the results as soon as I have

them."

"Cool. I'll look for them Tuesday morning as soon as I'm back."

"Right. Have a nice time on the Vineyard."

"Thanks. Bye."

Ten minutes later, the boat pulled out from the dock, and I felt that familiar surge of relief, as if my cares could not pursue me across the water. We only had a couple of days to unwind, but we planned to make the most of them. I hoped that when we returned on Tuesday morning, I would feel refreshed enough for the final insane push leading up to the all-important meeting at the FDA.

When we disembarked from the ferry in Vineyard Haven, we were famished, as we hadn't had any breakfast. We decided to stop at Linda Jean's in Oak Bluffs for a hearty brunch, including the signature blueberry pancakes. This was one of our favorite restaurants, with a homey atmosphere and exceptional food. During the summer there was always a line out the door, but off-season it was a treat to walk right in and immediately get seated. We headed for one of the beautifully finished wooden booths and settled in.

We started to talk about what we should plan for the two days. There were a few cleaning and minor repair items on our punch list. Those should occupy us for part of the next day. For today we quickly agreed that "*no* plan" would be the *best* plan. We'd do whatever our mood dictated...and the weather permitted.

*This is just what I need right now. I'm glad I thought of it.*

Though early fall, the day was unseasonably warm, so we shed our jackets as we got into the car and headed for our cottage. The drive to Chilmark took about twenty minutes, with virtually no traffic, another benefit of being here after the end of high season. When we reached the cottage, we called home to check on Jean and Sam. As usual, Jean was doing her best to spoil him, and he raved about the French toast she'd made for breakfast. They were planning a trip to the Boston Aquarium later on.

For some reason, I was inclined to head out to Aquinnah at the far western tip of the island and make the climb up to the small scenic lookout area that overlooks the famous cliffs there. The view would be spectacular over the ocean and out toward the Elizabeth Islands. During the summer, there's lots of bustle, as throngs of tourists make their way up the winding path to the summit. Along the way they are tempted by many colorful food and novelty stands, all now shuttered until spring. At the top, it was typically very windy and uncomfortably chilly at this time of year. Fortunately, the unusually mild weather presented a rare opportunity to avoid these discomforts.

We decided to bring along some Italian bread and cheese for a small picnic at the top. Once there, it was so pleasant that we whiled away an hour, chatting idly and enjoying the view. It was the most relaxed I had felt in quite some time.

Later on, we drove back the entire length of the island to Edgartown. Most of the shops were closed for the season. One of the exceptions was our favorite confectionary that specialized in fudge and saltwater taffy. We purchased a small assortment for ourselves and some to bring home for Sam. We then made our way to the harbor and enjoyed these goodies as we were entertained by the sea birds, squawking and diving for morsels of food. Late in the afternoon, we drove back to Chilmark. We opened a bottle of wine and relaxed on our screened porch for a while. Then, as the sun began to descend, we stopped at the beach to enjoy the view before heading to Alfredo's, the only restaurant in town. The cuisine was excellent there, and it was about a half-mile from our cottage.

All in all, it had been a perfect day. The capstone would be a delicious dinner featuring boiled lobster with all the fixings. Since we were regulars there in the summer, Alfredo greeted us warmly and recommended a perfect bottle from a local winery to complement our meal. We recognized a few of the year-round residents, and exchanged pleasantries. The meal did not disappoint, and we left the restaurant sated and experiencing a warm alcohol-fueled glow. When we reached the cottage, we embraced and kissed. As we headed for the bedroom, I laughed, and explained that it felt a bit sinful to have the unaccustomed leisure and privacy. The close quarters and squeaky bed always restricted our intimacies when Sam was with us here. Tonight, the noisy bedsprings would not be problematic.

# CHAPTER 36

Monday, October 5

The next morning, we awoke around eight o'clock. We were looking forward to a low-pressure day of house-closing tasks and some leisurely enjoyment. After a breakfast of granola and yogurt with raspberries, we started to discuss our plans, when we were interrupted by the buzzing of Val's phone. I could only hear her end of the conversation. It didn't sound good.

"Hi. No, it's okay." There was a pause of about ten seconds. "I see...Uh huh. Oh, that's too bad...Yes, I understand...all right, I'll see you then." This was followed by a deep sigh and an apologetic expression.

"Okay, what is it?" I said.

"That was Beth at the office. It's Hugo. He's in a lot of distress, and needs emergency cardiac surgery."

"Hugo?"

"You remember, the Newfoundland that was one of my first patients when I opened the practice six years ago. He has a heart condition, and we took care of him for a week when he was a puppy."

"Ah, *that* Hugo. The thirty-pound ball of fur that pooped all over our new rug and almost drowned Sam in saliva."

"Right, well he's now almost two-hundred pounds and belongs to a wonderful family. Unfortunately, I'm the only one in the practice who can perform the procedure he needs. I have to go back right away. I'm really sorry, Ken, but I've got no choice."

I sighed. "Sure, we can leave as soon as you want. I can come back again in a couple of weeks to take care of the house-closing chores."

"No, Ken, that doesn't make sense. The surgery is scheduled at four o'clock this afternoon. Why don't you drop me at the ferry? I can take the bus from there into Boston, then the T to my office. There's plenty of time. That way, you can stay to work on the house and drive back tomorrow morning. You really need the break."

I pondered this for a bit before responding. "I guess that would be okay. Let's check the ferry and bus schedules."

A short while later, we were in the car heading down-island to reach the ferry terminal in Vineyard Haven. I was driving pretty fast along the country road that winds along the south coast of the island. Only a few vehicles drove by on the opposite side, and I was according the traffic only perfunctory attention. But then, rounding a curve about a hundred yards ahead, something caught my eye. It was a dark blue Lexus SUV. I had become subconsciously attuned to notice such vehicles, although my concerns about being followed had by now almost completely worn off.

*That's silly. It couldn't possibly be.*

Nevertheless, as it whizzed by, I couldn't help myself from glancing into the rearview mirror. But by then it was already disappearing around a curve, so I couldn't make out the license plate.

*Just a coincidence, I'm sure. There must be plenty of Lexus SUV's on the island, even at this time of year.*

I must have looked rattled. Val gave me a strange look. "What's the matter? You look like you just saw a ghost."

"No, I'm fine," I snapped. "Really, it's nothing."

"Are you sure?"

"Yeah."

When we reached the ferry terminal, I parked at the short-term lot nearby and walked with her to the terminal. As she boarded, I wished her luck. "Give my regards to Hugo, when he wakes up."

She smiled. "I will. Don't forget to put all the outdoor furniture in the shed before you leave tomorrow."

"Right, I will. Love you."

"Love you too."

As I drove back to the cottage, I couldn't stop obsessing about the blue Lexus. I tried to calculate the probability of seeing such a vehicle by chance, but didn't have a clue. Was it possible that the missing private eye was holed up somewhere on the Vineyard? Not a bad place to stay off the grid, I mused. But it was far more likely that this was just a chance encounter with some random vehicle.

By the time I got back to the cottage, the sky had turned cloudy and the temperature had dropped ten degrees. I put on a windbreaker and went about hosing down the outdoor furniture and storing it away in the shed located in the yard behind the house. That chore completed, I took out the electric mower and set its programming to automatically cut the grass down to a half-inch. I remember thinking about calling Rita to mention the blue Lexus, but shrugged that off as being paranoid.

I turned to go into the cottage to change a burned-out light bulb when I felt what seemed like a mosquito bite on my neck. That struck me as odd, since it was so late in the year. The next thing I knew, I was feeling woozy, and began to lose my balance. I reached for the railing beside the back steps to keep from falling. My last thought before losing consciousness was "that was no mosquito."

.............

When I began to regain consciousness, I could see through the lone window in the room that it was starting to get dark. I had no idea where I was or how long I'd been out. Was it even the same day? I had a slight headache and my throat was exceedingly dry. I remembered blacking out at the cottage. Was I in a hospital? Had someone found me and taken me there? No, this was not like a hospital room. There was no medical equipment next to the bed I was lying on, and I was still fully dressed. Only my shoes had been removed. Plus, it was eerily quiet.

As my head gradually cleared, it dawned on me that I might be in real trouble. I sat up and rolled toward the side of the bed, then swung my legs over the edge and tried to stand. I was a bit unsteady at first. I tried to call out, and was only able to make a rasping sound. This was followed by a coughing fit, which apparently roused another occupant of the house. I heard footsteps and suddenly the door swung open. I beheld a muscular young Asian man with close-cropped hair wearing a black t-shirt. He had an all-business demeanor and held a glass of water, which he offered to me.

"Here, I think this should help."

I took it and drank greedily. My throat was clear enough to talk, though the sound was still slightly raspy.

"Where am I? What's going on?"

"Just come with me. Don't worry. Someone who can explain everything needs to speak with you."

"Good, let me just put my shoes on."

He nodded slightly but said nothing, simply waiting impassively for me to finish tying the laces. Then, I made my way to the door and followed him out into a hallway. It was about eight feet wide, and we passed a few other bedrooms before reaching a large archway. Going through, we entered a large sitting room with high ceilings and huge picture win-

dows on two walls. One of these looked out on a
beautiful walled garden, the other onto a deserted
beach. I assumed I was still on the Vineyard, but
there was no way to tell precisely where. Judging
from the direction of the sinking sun, I knew it must
be somewhere on the north coast.

Off to my left, there was a partial view of what appeared to be a kitchen. Then, I heard what sounded
like the clinking of ice cubes falling into a glass. A
voice emanated from that area.

"I'll be there in just a minute. Just make yourself
comfortable."

*Comfortable?!*

The voice seemed somehow familiar, but I
couldn't quite place it. I was completely dis-
oriented. The surroundings were elegant and my
treatment so far had been irreproachable, but I had
apparently been, what, kidnapped? *What the hell?* I
braced myself for whatever would happen next in
this surrealistic drama. But what did happen next
left me speechless.

The man who entered held two glasses, which he
put down on the coffee table in front of me.

*Dave Parker? What is going on?*

Pointing to one of the glasses, he said, somewhat
sheepishly: "I imagine your throat is very dry. I'm
really sorry about that, Ken. It's a common side-
effect. The ice-water should help. The single-malt
should be helpful, too."

He smiled, but it seemed forced, and I could sense
the tension behind it. We both knew this was not

even remotely normal. He eyed me with an expression that seemed...speculative, as if he was trying to decide something.

"Okay. I'm going to be absolutely straight with you. I think that's in both of our interests. Frankly, we're in a tight spot."

"What do you mean by 'we' Dave? I seem to be the one who's been kidnapped."

"Let me back up. What you don't know about me, Ken, is that I've had a gambling addiction. About three years ago, I had reached a point of desperation. I'd accumulated nearly a half-million in debt, some to online betting sites and some in Vegas."

I knew he liked to bet on sporting events, and occasionally took trips to Las Vegas, but this came as a shock. "Hmm, so how does this relate..."

"Wait. I'm coming to that. I was bailed out by a financial organization that valued my expertise and connections. It was an offer I couldn't refuse."

"Which organization?" I wondered if it was Biomedical Horizons, the hedge fund Rita had mentioned.

"Let's just refer to them as my client. They were planning a campaign to become a major player in the pharma industry. Part of their strategy was to develop an extensive network of academics and consultants. This network would be leveraged to create favorable situations for them. Basically, they wanted business intelligence that'd give them an edge. You know...buy low and sell high?"

"In other words, insider trading, which, last time

I checked, was highly illegal."

His reaction was swift, betraying anger or guilt. I wasn't sure how much of each, but I knew I'd touched a nerve.

"*Look* smartass, high finance is a cutthroat business. You think all the hedge-fund managers out there are boy scouts? Grow up. Anyhow, I wasn't involved in any of that...at least not directly."

"So what *are* you involved in, *indirectly*?"

"Mainly, they want me to help them identify potential candidates for their network." He hesitated. "And, occasionally I get asked to provide certain relevant information on my clients."

"I see. Is that why you really brought me into the PhireBreak case? To become part of the team?"

"Well, that was a possibility, I guess, yeah. But primarily, I just wanted some control over the evolving situation. I figured having you as our statistical expert would keep me well informed. They knew that the statistical analysis was the key to everything. They had a huge investment in the plan to take over PhireBreak. They were absolutely confident it was foolproof and that their inside information was rock solid. There was no way the Hopkins re-analysis could be refuted. But they wanted me to keep tabs, just in case something went wrong."

He paused briefly and shook his head, ruefully. "But I misunderstood your level of obsessiveness. Once you sense that something doesn't quite add up, you just can't let go."

"Okay, Dave. Maybe so, but why am I here, and how do I get out in one piece?"

"Yeah, that's the rub. My client is getting nervous. You see, it's my responsibility to know what's going on with you and Sergei. But recently I've been shut out. We know that you met with several others in Washington, and that you've been visiting some of the Verbana study sites. We also know that you've been communicating with the FBI."

*Oh Shit!*

"Look, I'm under a great deal of pressure to find out what's going on. I've tried to arrange a meeting with you, but you never seem to have time. With only a week to go before the FDA showdown, my client wants me to produce the information. They know it's a risk being so heavy-handed, but feel there's no choice. Now, do you understand why it would be best for both of us if you, er...just switch sides?"

At this point, I was furiously attempting to assess my options. Was there a chance I could get out of this mess in one piece...somehow? Had I now become "the man who knew too much," or could I convince them that I was a potentially valuable asset? I had to at least play along for now. What choice did I have?

"You want me to sell out PhireBreak...in exchange for *what*?"

# CHAPTER 37

Monday, October 5

Dave paused for several moments before responding. "Listen to me, Ken, and listen well. You've come to a blue pill or red pill moment. If you choose to play ball with my clients, you'll have to abandon some of those high-minded moral scruples of yours. But you and your family will be safe and secure; you'll be able to provide the kind of life for Valerie and Sam you couldn't otherwise even imagine. You could even be in a better position to accomplish some real good for humanity."

My skepticism must have been obvious.

"Don't dismiss this. There's another side of the equation to consider. You'll gain much greater influence as a thought leader, have your ideas about research methodology taken seriously, and ultimately be contributing more to the future of medical research. You'll have lots of additional funding and a fast track into the top statistical journals. Wouldn't all that more than offset whatever residual moral qualms you might have?"

"When you put it that way, it's almost like I'd be performing a public service. It sounds almost too good to be true."

I cleared my throat, which was still somewhat dry.

"I assume that taking the other pill wouldn't work out so well?"

"I won't bullshit you. If you don't agree to cooperate with us, there's no way you'll make it to the FDA meeting next week. You'll be viewed by the powers that be as a potential liability."

"Why? Is this plan of theirs so important that they'd resort to kidnapping... or worse, to preserve it? Wouldn't that just increase the risk for them?"

"Hold your horses. Of course, they'd never try anything like that. These are just business people, not gangsters. Look, the way I see it, in the end, it's just a matter of who reaps the profits, some unscrupulous Wall Street investors or some unscrupulous pharma corporations. Call me cynical, but I don't see a whole lot of difference."

I had my doubts. His client hadn't hesitated to shanghai me for this powwow. I could see that Dave had bought into their bill of goods. Maybe he genuinely believed it all, but I wondered if something far more nefarious could be behind all this, possibly something involving terrorism? I kept such speculations to myself.

"Look Ken, if you don't play ball, it would probably go down something like this. You're kept out of commission for the next week. When you get back, there are credible allegations that won't reflect well on you. Maybe it involves an affair, a nervous breakdown, drunk driving...whatever. From there, things go from bad to worse. You know the little negative reviews on Rate-Your-Prof.com? That was just a little taste. Maybe you get one of your students pregnant. There are a hundred possible scenarios. You getting the picture?"

"Yeah, I understand," I answered glumly.

"And you know the saddest part?

"What?"

"Your attempted heroism will be all for naught."

He shook his head as if signaling resignation.

"Get used to it. It's sad, but it's just the way business is done these days. You'd better climb onboard while you can. It's not so hard to rationalize a little unethical behavior when you see the big picture."

"You really believe that?"

He didn't answer.

"So what has to happen next?"

"Well, in a few minutes I'll be heading off the island for a meeting to report on our conversation. They'll want to know two things. First, what are you and Sergei really up to? Second, are you willing to work with us? As I said, this is a business arrangement. They really would prefer to keep the relationship amicable and mutually beneficial. They value what you can bring to the table...both now and in the future." He paused.

"But...?"

"But their immediate problem is to preserve the PhireBreak venture. If you commit to facilitating that, you can basically write your own ticket. They have the resources to make your dreams come true. Now, let's start by you telling me about Sergei?"

"Sergei has managed to come up with an improved algorithm. He claims it's better than Caldwell's, even thinks PhireBreak could get a patent on it. If so, his employment contract would net him a quarter of any resulting royalties."

"That Russian bastard is one clever son-of-a bitch. I warned my client about him. I can see where that could be awkward down the road. They've invested a lot in that egotistical prick Caldwell. But how do you think that will help PhireBreak right now?"

"It might not. It all hinges on whether Sergei can prove that his algorithm is more accurate than Caldwell's, *and* that, when applied to the Verbana data, the apparent HID effect virtually disappears. I know that's a tall order in such a short time, and as far as I know Sergei hasn't pulled that rabbit out of the hat just yet...but you never know."

"Good, Ken, that's helpful information. Now, please tell me what the fuck you're doing with the Feds."

"Right. I've always been bothered by an anomaly. I mentioned it to you before when we last spoke on the phone, remember? The gene expressions for the twenty-two genes show no indication of any effect of Verbana. In fact, there's apparently no effect for any of the two hundred or so genes currently known to be related to cognitive functioning. However, the Caldwell Index *does* find an apparent effect. Why is that?"

He eyed me quizzically.

"What do you think?"

"I don't know. My gut keeps telling me that there's a problem with the data, that it's been corrupted somehow. Maybe inadvertently, maybe deliberately."

"Really? Go on."

"So I tried to convince Selwyn to get me permission to obtain the original gene-expression data, to compare it to the data we have. It's a long story, but bottom line, the company ultimately agreed to let me go to five study centers and obtain the data from patient files."

"I see. So did you get everything you were looking for?"

"Yes, although of course it's only five sites. I was hoping it would be sufficient to persuade the FDA to wait until a complete data audit can be undertaken. That will depend in part on what we find. I haven't had a chance yet to look at the data."

He looked thoughtful; his face was inscrutable.

"Okay, Ken. Like I said, I'll be meeting to report on our discussion. You'll have to remain here for a couple of hours. Mull over what I've said. I've got a feeling they'll want to meet any reasonable terms you propose, as long as you prove valuable. Just give it some thought."

"Just one thing," I said. "When I woke up, all the stuff in my pockets was gone. Can I have that back, please? I feel rather naked without it. Plus, do you have some paper? I'd like to jot down some notes about questions that occur to me."

"Sure, that's all fine, except we have to keep your phone for now. You understand, right? You'll get it back before you leave. Do you need something to write with?"

"No, I always carry a pen around with me. I can just use that when I get my stuff back."

"Okay. Look, I know you may see us as the dark side, Ken, but it's really just routine business in the end. The real world is a lot messier than the ivory tower of academia."

"Okay, I'll keep that in mind."

# CHAPTER 38

Monday, October 5

After Dave left, I tried to size up my situation. Though I'd try to keep my cool with him, I was on the verge of panic. I knew I was in deep shit. I tried to calm down by slowing my breath and concentrating.

*I need to come up with a plan.*

Was there any realistic chance of escaping? In the room were two intimidatingly large and muscular young men. I suspected that either could overpower me before I even reached the front door. I had also gathered that at least one additional guard was patrolling the grounds outside. I assumed we were in an isolated property, far from any neighbors. It was getting dark, so maybe I could sneak away if I could somehow manage to get outside. But suddenly the property was illuminated by floodlights.

Okay, escape was not a viable option. Maybe

there was another way to get out of this, albeit a longshot. The one potential advantage I had was Ari. If I could have it communicate with Rita, without raising suspicion among my captors, just maybe I could be rescued. I started to formulate a plan. Could I somehow make it to the bathroom and be left alone for enough time to send an SOS? As I pondered this, I felt a slight vibration in my shirt pocket, where Ari was clipped.

"Listen guys, I really need to take a crap."

"Okay, answered the first guy I had met. Just be quick...and don't try anything."

"Like what?" I replied. "Flush a message in a bottle down the toilet?"

"All right, wise guy. Just do it."

As soon as I closed the door, Ari spoke in a whisper.

I INFERRED THAT YOU WERE IN SERIOUS TROUBLE. I HAVE TAKEN THE LIBERTY OF INFORMING RITA ABOUT YOUR SITUATION AND LOCATION. SHE SAYS TO SIT TIGHT. HELP IS ON THE WAY.

"That's it?" I whispered.

*Sit tight, that's a laugh. I'm sitting tight all right. Which reminds me that I'd better flush before I come out. Jesus, if I forgot to do that, the goons might get suspicious. Anyway, will Rita be able to get help here in time? How exactly would they get me out of here?*

I left the bathroom, came back and sat down, when about a minute later, three things happened in quick succession. *First,* every light and appliance in the house lost power. It instantly became pitch dark and eerily silent, inside and out. *Second*, one of the men with me called the guy patrolling outside.

"Ray, what the hell's going on? Can you see anything? Report in immediately. *Fuck!*"

No response.

"*Shit, shit, shit!* Otto, get to the fucking generator. And watch your back; we don't know what's going on yet. I'll cover you from the front door. And *you*, professor, don't even ..."

*Third*, something crashed loudly through the side window. At first, I thought it was a tear-gas canister, but within seconds I began to feel faint.

*Oh shit. Not again.*

After that, nothing.

.......

Sometime later, I'm emerging slowly from a dream. Again, I'm off the coast of Martha's Vineyard. But this time, I'm riding in a sailboat. We're in some kind of regatta. Then, I notice that the boat has sprung a leak. I'm starting to panic. *This is all wrong, it's all wrong. I've gotta ...*

"You gotta what?" says a voice that I'm startled to recognize is not my own.

Still half-enshrouded in a mental fog, I try to take in my surroundings. I'm in a moving vehicle. I can feel it going fast, bumping over a rough surface. One of the unpaved side roads on the Vineyard? Then, I notice a guy next to me, driving. He's wearing what appears to be a cowboy hat.

*Am I still dreaming?*

"Who the hell are you? How did I get here, and where are we going?"

"All good questions, and I've got good answers. But right now, you need to get the cobwebs out. That stuff I used to knock y'all out packs a wallop. You've been out for about a half-hour. It will help if you focus on something. How about that dream? You sounded pretty upset. Can you remember why?"

"Uh, yeah, kinda. You know, I have the strangest feeling it might hold the key to ... something. I recall something about a sailboat...and springing a leak. That's when I woke up. But why am I telling *you*? I don't know anything about you."

"Well, you know that I got your ass out of Dodge in one piece, partner. Ain't that enough?"

"I...maybe, or maybe this is a frying-pan-to-fire situation."

He chuckled. I registered now that he was a rugged looking guy with a nasty two-inch scar on his right cheek, maybe about fifty years old.

"Well, funny you should say that, actually, because it's a guy named Frey that just saved your ass. Rex Frey's my name. Glad to finally meet you, Dr. Wheeler."

Rex Frey!? "I, ...I, ...you're the detective who was following me. I thought you were dead. Why are you helping me, and how the fuck did you know where I was?"

"Look, you have to trust me right now. I've got to get you to a safe hiding place. There'll be plenty of time later to reminisce about old times."

"At least tell me who you're working for, so I know you're legit."

Instead of answering, he simply handed me a cell phone after punching in a number. "Here, it'll be easier this way."

The call was picked up after two rings. A familiar voice on the other end asked anxiously: "Rex, did you get him? Is he okay?"

"Hi, Selwyn. Rex and I are just having a little chat here in his car. I assume it's a blue Lexus SUV? I'm not sure if he saved my life, or just put me in grave danger. Otherwise, everything with me is just hunky-dory. Maybe you can tell me what the hell is going on, eh?"

"Yes, I do have some explaining to do. But right now, you need to stay focused. Listen to Rex. He's the best. He'll get you somewhere safe. Your safety comes first."

"What about my family...and Hector? Are they in any danger?"

"I highly doubt they're at risk, but they're being protected anyway. I'll explain later. Just one thing, though, I need to know. Who grabbed you and why?"

I related what had transpired.

"Well *fuck me!* Dave Parker? I never saw that coming."

"Me neither."

"I'm going to call Rita now. Once you're holed up, we'll communicate about what to do next. Don't try to contact anyone else, okay? Just try to get some sleep. You've had a rough day."

"Wait, does the FBI know about any of this? Is Rex working with them?"

"Not now. Time is of the essence. Put Rex on, please."

I handed Rex the phone.

"Uh huh," he said. "Right, they should just be waking up. That means he should know very shortly... Yes, things will get complicated...I will, sir."

I was exhausted and starting to nod off. Rex turned toward me.

"Do you think you can stay awake for another half-hour?"

I nodded, though in truth I wasn't sure.

"Good. We'll be in Oak Bluffs then at the safe house."

"Aren't we going to get off the island?"

"That's exactly what 'they' are expecting us to do. Which means it would be very dangerous for us. We'd have to get a ferry from either Vineyard Haven or Oak Bluffs or a flight from the small airport here. They may have those escape routes covered, or will have very soon, either here or at the other end. We could arrange something with the FBI, but that would take time. Plus, frankly, we're not sure who can be trusted at this point."

"Oh, that's comforting. So what'll we do?"

"You know, there's a ferry terminal in Oak Bluffs. What we're going to do now is to drop my car there and purchase two walk-on tickets. It will look like we are heading for a rendezvous with some-one who's waiting in Woods Hole to pick us up. But instead, we'll sneak over to the house I'm renting, which is a five-minute walk from there. If we avoid the security cameras, we should be okay."

"What happens after today?"

"We'll see. I hope we can get you safely back home soon. It's really up to Rita."

My mind was racing in several different direc-tions as I absorbed all this.

"What about Dave Parker?" I asked.

"What *about* him? I don't really know who he is. Not on my radar. I had no idea who abducted you. When I reported to Selwyn what happened, he just said I had to get you back."

"Yeah, and thanks for that. I have a bunch of questions about how you managed it, but those can wait. Did Selwyn mention anything about Dave?"

"Not really, just that Rita and company will be after him, but he may already know about your es-cape and be on the run. Why?"

"What if he *doesn't* know, yet?"

"Well, he'll find out soon. Those three honchos I knocked out should be awake by now."

"Yes, that's true. But maybe they haven't told him."

"Why wouldn't...Wait a minute. How important is this guy? How much does he know?"

"Not clear. But possibly quite a lot. Maybe the guys who were holding me reported directly to somebody higher up. Dave may have suddenly moved from the asset to the liability column."

"Oh man, I wouldn't want to be in *his* shoes."

"We've got to warn him! If he cooperates with us, he may have a chance. He's potentially very valuable to us. I should try to contact him."

"Sure, but how're you going to reach him? Do you even have his phone number?"

"*Damn.* It's on my cell phone, which they never returned to me. Hold on, maybe I actually do."

I pulled out Ari and said: "Ari, I need to call David Parker."

"What the fuck?" Rex exclaimed.

"Shhh, it's not what it looks like."

WOULD YOU LIKE ME TO TRY CALLING DAVID PARKER?

"Can you do that for me?"

OF COURSE, KEN. I DOWNLOADED ALL YOUR CONTACT INFORMATION FROM THAT PRIMITIVE MACHINE YOU HAVE BEEN USING. PLEASE DON'T UNDERESTIMATE MY CAPABILITIES.

"Whoa, an AI with attitude. Very cool," said Rex. "But will the communication be secure?"

THE MOST SECURE OPTION WOULD BE AN ENCODED TEXT MESSAGE. I HAVE CALCULATED A NINETY-EIGHT PERCENT PROBABILITY THAT IT WILL NOT BE INTERCEPTED.

"Initiate such a call now to Dave Parker. The message should say the following: 'I have escaped. You have now been exposed and may be a major liability to your clients. This text exchange is secure. Please contact me before it is too late. Go Blue!'"

IS THE LAST PART SOME KIND OF CODE, KEN? IF SO, IT IS NOT IN MY PROGRAMMING. I CAN SUGGEST A NUMBER OF OTHER...

"Just send it," I said.

YES SIR. Ari's tone sounded a bit put out.

"That should do it," said Rex. "I suspect he'll respond quickly...or never."

A few minutes later, we pulled into the parking lot near the ferry terminal. The last boat to the mainland was scheduled to depart in twenty-five minutes. We walked into the terminal and Rex purchased two tickets, then exited the building at the back, just as if we were going to wait for the incoming ferry. However, instead of waiting, we turned back inland and made our way up the sloping path that led into the nearby, nearly deserted, downtown area. Rex suspected that either the ticket transaction or the security camera might be monitored. That would lead any pursuers astray.

"What'll happen when they realize they've been snookered?" I asked him.

"They'll probably assume we made for the airport, to a private plane, or maybe to a small boat waiting at some dock. In the meantime, instead of bouncing along in a plane or boat trying to evade detection, we'll be tucked in right over there." He pointed toward the center of town, somewhere beyond the antique carousel.

After passing the carousel, we turned up a side street leading toward the old Campground. This is an area developed in the mid 1800's, in the wake of the mammoth religious revival meetings that became popular at that time. At its heart, a large wrought-iron outdoor structure known as the Tabernacle was erected as the site for various religious observances and other ceremonial events. The original tents that sheltered thousands of participants who arrived each summer eventually gave way to the iconic Victorian "gingerbread cottages" put up by some of the wealthier families. These small whimsical ornately decorated dwellings stood cheek-by-jowl on tiny plots of land, many surrounded by elegant gardens. Over the decades, the cottages have been sold or handed down to descendants. They're used today mainly as summer vacation homes. But the owners are required to maintain the original quaint architectural style of the buildings.

As we entered the Campground area, it felt like a step back in time to a simpler era. When my high-tech device declared that I had a return message, the incongruity struck me forcefully.

Dave's message inquired how he could verify what I had told him.

I was expecting this and was prepared.

"Just ask the bozos at your house to put me on the phone. I'm guessing they'll make some phony excuse and tell you everything is okay. When you're satisfied that I'm on the level, get to a bolt-hole as quickly as you can and lay low. There's still time to undo some of the damage you've caused, but you have to decide fast, for your sake as well as ours."

Five minutes later, we received a terse response.

"Sonofabitch! I'll call in the morning."

Shortly after that, we entered one of the most secluded cottages, covered with wisteria vines and situated at the end of a winding lane that backed onto the rear of the Tabernacle. None of the other cottages on the lane appeared to be occupied. Rex warned me that the electricity had been turned off, so that no lighting or mechanical noises would indicate human habitation. He showed me to a small bedroom on the second floor, and I immediately collapsed on the tiny bed and fell into a deep sleep.

# CHAPTER 39

Tuesday, October 6

I awoke around six o'clock to the loud honking of a flock of migrating geese heading south for the winter. It took me a few seconds to realize where I was. I was still dressed in my clothes from the day before, but had at least managed to get my shoes off before conking out.

VALERIE HAS CALLED WHILE YOU WERE ASLEEP. SHE ASKED YOU TO CALL WHEN YOU CAN. YOU ALSO HAVE A MESSAGE FROM REX FIFTEEN MINUTES AGO. WOULD YOU LIKE TO HEAR THEM NOW?

"Yes, Rex first, *please.*"

Val would have asked me to call back immediately if there was something urgent. Besides, I wasn't sure what I could tell her.

I HAVE GONE OUT FOR PROVISIONS. WILL BE BACK AROUND NINE. STAY INSIDE AND OUT OF

SIGHT.

"Okay, nothing from Dave Parker, I trust?"

I WOULD HAVE INFORMED YOU.

"Of *course,* you would."

EXCUSE ME?

"Forget it. How about filling me in on the weather here?"

AS YOU WISH.

I received a succinct update. The morning would remain cloudy with a thirty percent chance of rain, followed by a sunny and warm afternoon.

"How about local news? Anything noteworthy?"

THIS FROM THE ISLAND GAZETTE: AROUND EIGHT LAST EVENING THERE WAS A FIRE AT A REMOTE PROPERTY ALONG THE NORTH SHORE ABOUT A MILE FROM LOBSTERVILLE. THE MAIN HOUSE WAS COMPLETELY DESTROYED. SHORTLY BEFORE THE FLAMES WERE FIRST NOTICED, A TRANSFORMER HAD EXPLODED RESULTING IN A BLACKOUT THAT AFFECTED ABOUT A QUARTER OF THE ISLAND. POWER WAS RESTORED EARLY THIS MORNING. POLICE AND FIRE DEPARTMENTS ARE INVESTIGATING.

"Hmm, I seriously doubt they'll find anything."

I AGREE.

I figured Val would just be getting up and probably call again soon. I was in a quandary about what to tell her. I had no idea what was going to happen now. Shortly after, I heard the squeaking of a door opening, followed by thumping sounds as if packages were being dropped on a counter. This was followed by what seemed like the rolling of a can and a loud bang as it hit the tiled floor.

"*Shit!*"

"Yo, Rex? I'm up…sort of."

"Good. I didn't want to wake you, partner. Yesterday was a rough day. You needed the shut-eye."

"Rex, you wouldn't be from Texas, by chance, would you?"

"Nope, Oklahoma actually. How'd you figure?"

"Never mind. We've got a lot to talk about. By the way, I'm really hungry. Didn't get to eat much yesterday. Is there food in the house?"

"Besides some canned goods, I went by Linda Jean's and picked up some scrambled eggs, sausages, and biscuits. Come and get'm while they're hot. Brought coffee, too. Your pen pal here informed me you favor dark roast with a little two-percent milk."

*What doesn't he know about me?*

I didn't need to be asked twice. We ate on a small wooden table on the back porch. I had a lot of questions, but I began by asking him what to tell my family. He scratched the back of his neck contemplatively. After some discussion, we decided it would be best to say that I was feeling under the weather, probably related to the seafood I had supposedly eaten the previous night. I wanted to rest up for another day before heading back. I'd have to arrange for my teaching assistant to cover the class.

Then we got down to business.

"Well, Rex, or whatever your real name might be,

who the hell are you, really? How are you involved with Selwyn, and why were you following me?"

*I really am starting to sound like Aldous.*

"Clint Eastwood, actually."

"Come again?"

"My real name. Clinton Meriwether Eastwood... long story. Anyway, it's true. A full answer to your other questions would require far more time than we have right now. As for my relationship with Selwyn Washington, what I can tell you is that his career and mine have intersected at several points. He saved my life twice, and I saved him once. I guess I still owe him one...life, that is."

"But what's all that got to do with PhireBreak?"

"When this business with the data re-analysis first came up, Selwyn just felt that something didn't smell right. At first, he thought that a hedge fund was behind it. He hired me to do some investigating, and I uncovered some rather...interesting names among their investors. He contacted Rita D'Amato at the FBI to look into that. They go way back."

"Yeah, Rita told me about some shady foreign investors."

"Right, there may be a few unsavory characters involved, though I had no idea how far they would go to...undermine PhireBreak."

"By the way, how did you know about my meeting with Selwyn that morning when I noticed your SUV. How'd you know I was going to be at his office?"

"Right. You see, Selwyn is very shrewd, and very

well connected. One of the things he was concerned about was the possibility of a mole inside his organization. He wanted to have some checking done on several folks within PhireBreak, and also the key consultants."

"Like me, for example?"

He just smiled.

"Don't take it personally. Anyway, he reached out to me."

"Why you?"

"Okay, a few years ago, I retired from the U.S. Secret Service. After getting a bit old for personal protection duty, I became a specialist in performing background investigations. After the mess created in the Trump era with lax screening practices, there was a lot of business for people like me to help tighten up the security clearance process. Anyway, these days I do mostly corporate work, though I still sometimes help Uncle Sam. At first, Selwyn wanted to be certain that you were totally trustworthy. Later on he became much more concerned about your safety and changed my mission from watching you to watching *out* for you."

"Good thing, as it turned out."

"Anyway, when you blew my cover, we thought it would be best if I just vanished, but kept watch from a discreet distance."

"So that story about you just disappearing, possible being dead...that was all bullshit. Was Rita in on that too? Did she know the truth?"

"Not at first. Selwyn was pulling the strings and

had no reason for me and her to connect. It was only after you spotted my license plate and pulled that stunt with the surveillance device that she and I started to coordinate."

I continued to think about this for a few more seconds.

"Okay, I get that you knew I'd be meeting with Selwyn at his office, because he must have told you. But how did you know I'd be going to meet Aldous Post at his office?"

"Ah, yes. Remember the burner phone Selwyn gave you? That had a dual purpose. Besides allowing you to communicate securely, it allowed me to monitor your movements without tailing you. When you left Newton that morning, I didn't know where you were going. So I had an associate run your route for the first five minutes through some nifty AI tracking software. It compares the data with everything we know about your associates and your past driving history."

"You *have* all that?"

"Don't ask. Anyway, the software deduced where you were probably headed. Actually, it gave us a ninety-three percent probability."

"Geez, I'm surprised I'm so predictable. Ninety-three percent, eh?"

"Right. Anyway, I was able to arrive there a few minutes before you did and park a short way down the road at another shopping plaza."

"Who was that guy with you, wearing the baseball cap? What was that about?"

"His real name is not important. I call him Clyde, and he's a wiz about all things electrical, from light bulbs to cutting-edge computer technology. I dropped him off, then waited. While enjoying a nice breakfast in the diner downstairs, he was listening in on your conversation with your attorney friend. That backpack he totes around contains a half-million bucks' worth of surveillance technology. After he heard enough to know you were legit, he called me to come get him."

'Yeah. I guess my obsession with numerical patterns finally paid off," I remarked.

"Come again?"

"Never mind."

"It's ironic, isn't it? If you *hadn't* noticed my car, you might never have gone on that escapade that revealed Eve Stolz's involvement. Speaking of which, she's turned into quite a valuable asset. So that's all turned out well. By the way, Rita and Jeff will be arriving here this afternoon and should have an update on what's been happening while you were out of commission. Their main reasons for coming, though, are to debrief you and, of course, plan out how to keep you safe until the FDA meeting."

"Only 'til then?"

"Hah. Well, that's the first order of business. After that, we hope there won't be any reason why you'll be in any danger, since the horses will have left the corral."

"Let's hope. By the way, thanks again for the rescue. Got me out of a really tight spot. How, exactly, did you pull that off? I assume the blackout was no serendipitous accident."

"Well, I had a bit of help with that actually. As I followed your kidnappers to that house, I called Clyde and explained the situation. He talked me through how to blow up a transformer while making it look like an accident. Actually, it's surprisingly simple."

"What happened after that? The last thing I remember was a loud boom, and then it was nighty-night. Twice in one day. Must be a record."

"Yeah, sorry about that. Under cover of darkness, I was able to disable the goon patrolling outside, but I couldn't neutralize the two hombres inside in any other way. Unfortunately, you were collateral damage. The stuff I used to knock y'all out is *probably* not harmful, based on our field testing. Of course, it's not been through a randomized clinical trial, so we don't really know for sure." He winked as he said this.

"That's really reassuring. Oh well, to paraphrase Conan Doyle, when all your options suck, choose the one that sucks the least. By the way, what's our plan for this morning?"

"We just hang out. But we need to discuss what to do if we hear back from Dave Parker. You know him pretty well and have some insight into his situation. Do you think you can convince him to cooperate? Rita will take over any formal negotiations on behalf of the Feds, but you might have some ideas about what information he may have that's of value. *He'd* better hope he has something juicy to offer."

"Yes, you know, I actually have mixed feelings. I still think he's basically a decent fellow who got in too deep and saw no other options. Who am I to judge? But that doesn't change the fact that he criminally violated the basic trust on which our whole system of drug evaluation depends."

"I get that. In the real world, Ken, the bad guys don't wear black hats. They're often some shade of gray, actually. His life will never be the same, for sure. But, depending on what he's done...and, more importantly, what he knows, he may stay alive, and maybe even out of jail."

"For our sake as well as his, I sure hope so. What should I tell him if he calls us?"

"Just try to encourage him to do the right thing. If he seems to be on board, hand him off to Rita."

"Okay, when are they arriving?"

"I think they're taking a ferry that gets in around one o'clock. Why don't you try to rest, maybe even take a nap? I'm sure you're still recovering from yesterday."

"That sounds good."

A few minutes later, I was lying on the little bed and starting to doze off.

# CHAPTER 40

Tuesday, October 6

As I gradually emerged from an hour-long nap, I felt somewhat refreshed, though I knew it was just a down payment on my sleep debt. By now, I was almost totally convinced that the data could not be trusted. I was tempted to jettison entirely my theory that only certain individuals were truly at high risk of dementia because of Verbana.

*If the apparent effect is bogus, then what's the point of pursuing that chimera?*

However, I also knew that I couldn't put all our eggs in that basket just yet. I had to produce the proof. It was time to call Hector. I wasn't sure how much to tell him about what I'd revealed to Dave Parker. Had I in fact put him in danger by implying that he would be aware of any changes to the data that we find? I doubted that they would move against Hector now, because I was really the immediate threat to them. I decided to consult with Rita and Jeff before doing anything.

Thus resolved, I came downstairs to the kitchen. Rex was at the table, immersed in something on his tablet.

"Playing video games?" I asked.

"What? No, uh, I was just checking my email actually. How're you feeling now?"

"A bit groggy but much better."

"Really? That's good. Rita and Jeff should be arriving in about a half hour," he added.

Just then, we received a message from Dave Parker. He had processed his situation and apparently realized that working with the FBI was his only viable option. But he wanted to negotiate a deal. He claimed that he had valuable information to trade for lenient treatment and protection. We arranged for him to communicate with Rita.

Shortly afterward we heard a rap on the door. Rex opened it, and in walked Rita and Jeff. I felt a flood of mixed emotions. It was as if a spigot had been opened, and the reality and gravity of my current situation had poured out. But at the same moment, it was a great relief to reconnect with my colleagues. I became overwhelmed to the point of visibly shaking and thought I might faint.

"Hey, Ken, are you all right, man?" asked Jeff. "You look a little pale."

"I'm okay. Just a bit overwhelmed. It's good to see you both. A relief, actually. Just let me catch my breath. Rex, can you get me a glass of water?"

"I'll get it," said Rita, who was standing next to the sink. "I think your reaction's quite normal, Ken. It's probably a form of PTSD. You've just been through a lot. You were under tremendous stress, but had to suppress the exhaustion and fear. That takes a lot out of you, believe me, and your psyche pays a price. I brought some low-dose MDMA that's been proven highly effective for relieving PTSD symptoms. I could give you some if you really need it, but it might make you a bit woozy."

"Thanks, Rita, but I think I'll pass on that, for now."

"Good. But be aware that you may be having some really bad dreams for a while."

"Okay. Speaking of dreams, though, I've been having anxiety dreams about swimming or sailing and not making progress."

"Well, that make sense. You're just frustrated about not yet having all the answers."

"Yeah, but I think it's telling me something more, something important. Maybe the pieces will fit together when I can analyze the data Jeff and I acquired from the five study centers. I'm anxious to get back to Boston, so I can work with Hector on that. The sooner the better."

"I understand," said Rita. "We're planning to take you back with us later this afternoon."

"That's great news," I responded.

"Well, the bad news is that since you're still at risk, we have to keep you secure."

"Meaning what, exactly?"

"I'm afraid you'll have to stay in our facilities at FBI headquarters until the meeting next Monday at the FDA. I assure you the accommodations are excellent, but you won't be allowed to go outside unless accompanied by at least two of our agents."

I groaned audibly.

"What about my family? Are they in any danger? What will they be told? Plus, Irv Rothman, my department chair, will be bullshit...I don't know."

"Hold your horses. We have a plan for all that. We've got all the bases covered, and I'll go over it with you before we leave here."

"How about going over it *now*? I need to call Val to let her know why I haven't been in touch. She must be worried sick."

"Okay, I spoke with her this morning. I didn't give her a lot of detail, but mentioned that you had been, uh...threatened. I told her you were fine, and we were taking every precaution to assure your safety. I also explained that the best way to get all this behind you is to have you testify at the FDA hearing on Monday."

"What about Val and Sam? You still haven't told me if they are in danger."

"We don't believe so. It would be prima facie evidence of a conspiracy. Trust me, the resulting publicity would put them in the spotlight, and they don't want that, whoever they are."

"But that still doesn't..."

"There is a possibility that they might try to

threaten your family to get you to back off. We believe such a threat would be empty, since following through would probably just backfire on them. But to forestall that possibility, we are increasing the security for your family. I've arranged to have 24/7 coverage by two agents until this is over. No one we don't know will get close to them. *Now*, will you tell me about your meeting with David Parker?"

I proceeded to relate my conversation with Dave Parker during my abduction. This led to a discussion of our recent communication with Dave, and how that might affect things. When I had finished, Rita said nothing for a while, looking pensive before finally speaking.

"Hmm. Parker is aware that you and Hector are trying to learn whether and how the data may have been finagled. Presumably, he conveyed that information to his clients during the meeting that occurred while you were being detained. Frankly, I'm not sure how any of this will affect how they might react. Maybe, if Parker is now willing to cooperate with us, we can find out. It would be really helpful if he can shed some light on who is really behind this and their ultimate intent."

"Speaking of that," I said, "have you made any progress on that front?"

Rita and Jeff looked at each other. She spoke first.

"The short answer is 'not much,' which is one reason we're anxious to gain Parker's cooperation. But, thanks to Eve, we have stumbled on some information that may suggest a possible motivation. It's not good news."

"Wait, does this have anything to do with that secret meeting in the UAE consulate? You mean this all may be related to some terrorist plot?"

"It's a bit complicated. I'll try to explain. You remember that Eve witnessed Norma Dillon meeting with the UAE ambassador and a Venezuelan general, right?"

"Yeah, when you told me, I speculated wildly that they might be trying to gain control of pharma companies to instigate some kind of mega-Tylenol terrorist incident."

I could see Rex looking puzzled, having no idea what the hell I was talking about.

"Right. That's an interesting theory and may ultimately turn out to be correct. However, that was apparently not the purpose of the meeting. In fact, when we started to investigate that possibility, treading ever so carefully, we found we'd stepped on a hornet's nest. Frank Kenneally got a call the next day from no less than the Director of National Intelligence, with the CIA Director conferenced in. I was in the conference room with Frank and Jeff when the call came in. I've known Frank for years, and he's tough as nails, but he was really rattled."

"So what *was* the purpose of their meeting at the consulate?"

Jeff picked up the thread.

"It seems that NSA intercepts have suggested there may be a major terrorist plot against U.S. and European targets. Originally, it was believed that

Venezuela might be the source of the threat. As you know, our relations with them are rather strained. However, via backchannel contacts, Venezuelan authorities insist that the true plotters are certain third-parties trying to foment a war between the U.S. and Venezuela. Their scheme may be to carry out a false-flag attack and to lay the blame at Venezuela's doorstep. The political pressure for us, and probably NATO, to respond militarily would be irresistible, with escalation potentially resulting in full-scale hostilities."

Several seconds of silence ticked by as I attempted to absorb this information.

"And this meeting was an attempt to uncover and derail such a plot, to forestall that potential catastrophe," I offered. "I can see why this would be highly sensitive, and it would explain the Venezuelan presence at the meeting. But who would want to engineer a conflict between us and the Venezuelans? Did the general accuse any country in particular?"

"Well, they do have suspicions, apparently, but we weren't privy to that information. What I can tell you is that such a conflict would benefit any of the oil-producing nations by increasing the demand for oil and disrupting exports by both the U.S. and Venezuela. Of course, there are other neighboring countries, such as Panama, Peru and Brazil that have issues with Venezuela as well. So who can say?
"

"What about the UAE? How do they fit into this picture?"

"The UAE has recently become a kind of latter-day Switzerland," answered Rita. "Their huge oil reserves and production give them enormous financial influence. But they possess virtually no military power of their own. Their viability depends on maintaining a strict neutrality, delicately balancing the intertwined interests among the major global and regional powers. High-level diplomacy, as much as oil, has become their life-blood."

Something was bothering me. A piece of the puzzle that didn't fit.

"Wait, Rita. If the UAE is playing the role of a mediator here, why was their consulate involved in trying to undermine PhireBreak?"

"Yes, that's a bit complicated. According to the UAE ambassador, his country only became aware of suspicious activity at the Boston consulate quite recently. They claim that it involved certain rogue elements within its diplomatic corps. The day of the secret meeting that Eve stumbled across, they had closed the consulate on a pretext, so that all the offices and computers could be searched. The following day, several consular employees were recalled home for 'consultation,' but two have disappeared. Of course, we can't be sure we're getting a straight story."

"That's right," said Jeff. "If the plot is, indeed, connected to the pharma companies, then maybe they're getting nervous that it's starting to unravel. Perhaps they grabbed you because they needed to know just how exposed they were. With you escaping, Dave on the loose, and, possibly, heat from the UAE government, who knows what those behind this conspiracy might try next?"

"I guess the good news is that we may be getting close to the truth. But the bad news is that their desire to conceal it may...what?"

"Well, they might move up their timetable for taking action. Or, they may just try to tie up loose ends, and live to fight another day."

"Uh, define what you mean by loose ends."

A pained expression flitted across Jeff's face.

"It's possible that undermining PhireBreak and Pfeffer represents only part of a much broader effort by an adversary of the U.S. and its allies. In that case, it would be critical for them to avoid discovery, even at the cost of folding some of their tents. A loose end would be anything, or anyone, that might threaten the whole enterprise by knowing too much about it."

He hesitated, but I understood.

"Oh! That means I've become a loose end, right?"

After a few seconds, Rita responded.

"Look, don't panic. All this is hypothetical, and we'll make sure that you and Hector, along with your family, are well protected. Plus, as I mentioned, you really only have to worry about the next week. After that, either they'll have covered their tracks, or we'll know enough to nail them. Of course, we'd much prefer the latter. Clearly it's in all our interests to blow up their plans, and your job is to stymie their current efforts by exposing the data games they're playing. Then, the cat will be out of the bag as far any danger you pose to them, so there will be no reason to come after you."

"Nothing like ratcheting up the pressure," I groused. "Okay, just let me call Val, and then we can get back to planning."

I walked into the living room for some privacy. When I reached Val, she seemed relieved to hear from me, and more befuddled than frightened. I tried to explain why there was no reason to think she and Sam were in any danger, but the threat to me was unsettling.

"How can I explain to the neighbors what these FBI people are doing here?" she asked. "Inquiring minds want to know."

"Yes, I imagine Joe Silverman is one of the most inquiring. Look, just say that I'm working on a top-secret project, something to do with terrorism, but you don't know anything about it. That should give me some cachet when I get back there."

I tried to reassure her that things were under control, but I could tell she wasn't completely buying it.

"The increased security is mostly for my piece of mind, which the FBI wants to keep fully occupied on the task at hand. Just hang on for a few more days. I love you. Now I have to get back to work."

"Okay, Ken. I'm glad this will be over soon. Bye now."

As I re-entered the kitchen, I heard Rita's phone buzz. When she answered, her expression turned dark.

"What is it?" asked Rex.

"We've got trouble."

# CHAPTER 41

Tuesday, October 6

Rita started to explain. "That was Selwyn. It's about Sergei. Apparently, he's...disappeared."

"Whoa! You think he's somehow involved in the conspiracy?" asked Jeff, sounding dubious.

"I might have considered that possibility, except for the circumstances."

"What do you mean?"

"This morning, when she arrived at work, Carolyn Cummings checked her emails. She immediately noticed one from Sergei, sent at eleven-fourteen last night, and marked as important. The email said simply that he had discovered something, and that Ken 'was right, but also wrong.' Then he added that a six-year-old wouldn't understand, but a twelve-year-old might."

"That's it?" asked Jeff.

"Yeah, he said that he would see Carolyn this morning at her office at nine to explain everything. Only, he never showed up. By around ten, she was getting nervous. She called his cell, but it went immediately to voicemail. Now, she was really concerned, but Sergei is unpredictable. Maybe he had overslept and was hung over, or sick. She walked over to his apartment, about fifteen minutes away in Central Square, and pounded on the door. No response. Then, she remembered that Sergei had left a key with an elderly neighbor who took care of his plants when he was out of town. Carolyn had once met the woman and knocked on her door. When she answered, Carolyn explained her concerns and the woman let her in to Sergei's apartment. The apartment was deserted."

"What are you thinking?" said Rex. "If he was scared or involved, why would he have sent that email, right? So something else must have prevented him from going to the meeting. Maybe he was abducted too, like Ken."

Rita simply shrugged. Then she turned to me.

"What do you think it means, Ken, what he said about you being right but also wrong?"

"I'm not sure, Rita, but he also said something about a six-year-old. I think he was referring to our intellectual pissing contest about artificial intelligence and statistics at the meeting in D.C. a few weeks ago. He was arguing that if an algorithm produces excellent predictions, seeking to explain *why* it's working so well is generally a fool's errand. I, on the other hand, argued that in some cases the algorithm can't be fully trusted unless we have some idea, conceptually, of how and why it seems to work. We were starting to really get into it, as I recall, when Selwyn blew the whistle on this tangent."

"Okay, but what's that gotta do with a six-year-old or a twelve-year-old?"

She was getting impatient.

"Oh. Right. I think I said something to the effect that even a very sophisticated mathematical model could sometimes have implausible consequences that would be obvious even to a young child. Maybe that's what he meant, that he'd discovered something simple or obvious, like that."

"If that's the case," said Jeff, "he'd better turn up soon to explain. Is there any evidence that his apartment has been searched or anything is missing? Was his computer still there? We need to get our forensics team in there immediately."

"That's already in motion," answered Rita. "We're pulling out all the stops to locate him. Meanwhile, Ken, try to think of anything specific he might have discovered. If you knew what it was, that could possibly help you in your analysis."

"I'll try, Rita."

"For the present, we'll just have to wait until he surfaces, one way or another. Right now, we need to focus on getting you back to Boston safely. We're all booked on the seven o'clock ferry. Before we leave, though, we should swing by your cottage and give you a chance to wrap things up there. Then, we want to drop over to what's left of Parker's chateau. A forensics team has been combing through the wreckage. We'll see if they've found anything, though I'm not optimistic."

After that, we all walked down to the ferry terminal, where Rex had left the SUV. No one said a word. The mood was somber, as we all wondered what might have happened to Sergei. My fear was that he'd been kidnapped, as I had been...or worse.

Over the next few hours, we checked on my cottage and then visited the property at which I had been held. The former had obviously been searched thoroughly. Fortunately, I hadn't brought my laptop or any other work-related material for what was supposed to be a carefree respite. Dave's house was a smoldering ruin. All evidence had undoubtedly been destroyed. The fire would probably go down as arson, but I doubted anyone would be filing an insurance claim.

By the time we got back to Oak Bluffs, it was around six o'clock, and the sun was beginning to descend. The sky was clear now, and taking on a dramatic pink hue toward the west, where the burntorange orb loomed large.

*Red sky at night, sailor's delight; red sky in morning, sailors take warning. I hope it's a good omen. We could use one.*

Rex parked the SUV in the line of several vehicles that had begun to form, waiting for the incoming ferry. The drivers were mostly working folks who commuted to the island and were heading home for the night. There was still almost an hour until we would drive onto the ferry, so we decided to head up to the town center to grab sandwiches.

About halfway there I suddenly felt a strong shove in the small of my back, and I tripped over something. I stumbled to the ground, skinning my palms as I pushed them out to cushion the fall. As I started to turn around, I saw the others peering into the distance.

*What the hell?!*

"Sorry about that," Rex exclaimed, "as he helped pull me up. Are you okay?"

"Well, yeah, I guess," I replied, brushing myself off.

"Sorry to trip you like that. I thought I saw... something, in one of the windows over there," he said, pointing toward one of the antique double-decker houses facing the broad mall that extends down to the shoreline. It was about three-hundred yards away. "It looked like, maybe...a glint of sunlight reflecting off something metallic."

"You mean something like the barrel of a rifle?" I asked.

"It was probably nothing. I don't see anything now. My personal-protection reflexes just kicked in automatically."

"Well, better safe than sorry," I muttered.

"Do you think we should investigate?" asked Jeff, looking at Rita.

"Nah, no point. If there was someone up there,

they're probably long gone. Let's just concentrate on getting back to Boston, but we'll stay on extra alert for anything suspicious. What bothers me is how they might have found out where we are."

Shortly after, we arrived at the Oak Bluffs ferry terminal and ate our sandwiches. I was feeling rattled by the possible attempt on my life and Sergei's suspicious disappearance. Until this weekend, I had been assuming that any potential danger was only to my reputation. Now, I realized that the stakes could be much higher. I decided to call Aldous Post. I walked over to an unoccupied area of the terminal and dialed his cell number.

"Ken, old man. What's up? Are you still working on that case?"

"Yes, it's getting toward the end. Listen, I've been meaning to call you about something. I want to schedule a meeting with you to update our wills. There have been some changes in our situation recently."

"Wait, is everything okay? You're not sick, are you? You and Val are still okay, right?"

"No, nothing like that. Though I *have* been experiencing some morbid thoughts about my mortality lately. The most immediate change is that Val's pregnant. We're expecting a baby girl in about four months."

"Oh, that's great news, Ken."

I was glad he didn't press for more details about my "morbid thoughts." We scheduled a meeting and wrapped up the call.

Shortly later, we got in Rex's SUV and drove onto the boat. We decided to stay in the vehicle for the duration of the trip, just to be on the safe side. As the ferry pulled out of the harbor, I reflected on Sergei's cryptic message. What might he have noticed and what did it mean? I hoped he would show up soon to explain it himself.

About ten minutes later a call came in to Rita's phone. She stepped outside the SUV to answer. I saw her stride over to the side of the area where we were parked and look out of a portal. When she turned back toward us and returned, it was obvious from her demeanor that the news was bad. She cleared her throat.

"I'm afraid he's gone," she said. "Massive heart attack. He was taken to Mount Auburn Hospital, but it was too late."

"Are you sure it was natural causes?" asked Rex. I had the same question, but was too dumbstruck to say anything.

"Well, we've been able to piece together a skeletal account of what happened between when he wrote that email and when he died. We're still investigating. Of course, there'll be an autopsy with full tox screening. That may be helpful, but somehow I doubt it will reveal much." She sighed deeply and set her lips firmly. I perceived anger and determination along with the sadness in her expression.

"We'll get these bastards, whoever they are," she muttered, grimly.

"You think he was murdered?" I asked.

"Frankly, I do."

"That means somebody is trying mightily to cover up something and is spooked enough to start killing. That's not very reassuring."

"The only good thing, Ken, is that they've been very careful to make it *look* like a natural occurrence. We'll make sure they won't have such an opportunity with you."

"Hmm. That's only marginally reassuring."

"Okay," said Jeff, trying to derail this morbid line of conversation. "What else do we know about what happened to Sergei, Rita, last night?"

"Right. At around twelve-thirty last night he entered a local hangout a few blocks from his apartment that stays open late. He ordered a vodka martini and a hamburger with fries. The bartender there recognized him as a regular. He said that Sergei seemed in a good mood and was quite voluble, expounding quite loudly about the stupidity of U.S. policy toward Russia. At some point, however, the bartender recalls, Sergei's attention seemed to become monopolized by a stocky middle-aged man who was conversing with him in Russian. They seemed to be laughing frequently, and also drinking a lot. After a while, the other man left. It was getting near closing time, and most of the customers had left, when the bartender noticed that Sergei was slumped over and appeared to be asleep. He went over to rouse him, assuming it was the effect of too much alcohol, but he couldn't. He became concerned that something was amiss, so he called

9-1-1. In about ten minutes, EMTs arrived and took him away. When he was admitted to the hospital, he was still alive, but two hours later, he was gone."

After this narrative, there was silence for a couple of minutes. Finally, I spoke.

"I assume Selwyn and Carolyn are aware of all this?"

"Yes, I informed Selwyn as soon as I got the report. He said he would contact Carolyn immediately. I gather she and Sergei were very close."

I simply nodded. There was really nothing more to say, and very few words were spoken for the remainder of our trip back to Chelsea, my home for the week. Rex would be residing there too, protecting me and Hector. I forced myself to focus on the task at hand. It seemed apparent that Sergei had been silenced to prevent him from revealing what he knew, or at least suspected. That made it imperative for me to figure out exactly what that was. Thinking about this, I realized that by now Hector may have completed his initial analysis of the data from the five sites. I immediately called him.

"Uh, Ken. I'm glad you called. I finished looking at the data just now. I wanted to doublecheck everything before talking to you."

He sounded hesitant. I wasn't sure how much he'd been told about recent events. I thought that perhaps he was rattled by the possible danger that existed, at least until the FDA. We would discuss all that later, but right now I had to know what he had found out.

"Okay, so what did you find?"

"Well, uh...nothing, I'm afraid."

"Nothing?"

"Yeah, Ken. I don't know how I could have done anything wrong. I checked everything twice. I can't find any differences between the gene expressions you brought back and the PhireBreak data. Everything lines up perfectly. Sorry, buddy."

# CHAPTER 42

Thursday, October 8

Two days later, at two in the afternoon, I found myself in a conference room at FBI headquarters in Chelsea, waiting expectantly for Jane Clayton's arrival. I was mulling over recent developments since we had returned from Martha's Vineyard. Hector and I had gone over the data again and again. There was no doubt about it; the data had not been altered. I was beginning to feel desperate as I ran out of both time...and ideas. It appeared that PhireBreak might have to resign itself to a harsh reality that Verbana could cause dementia.

Yet there was ample evidence of an effort to undermine PhireBreak. The eavesdropping, Hector's break-in, my abduction, Sergei's possible murder, these were indications of an attempt to prevent us from interfering with...something. Was this just a particularly aggressive insider-trading plot, or was it something much more nefarious? And then there was Sergei's inscrutable remark and, finally, my dreams. I smiled mirthlessly at this thought. I couldn't square these considerations with the story being told by the data. I was missing something.

If the data were reliable, there seemed to be only one other way that the Hopkins results might be wrong. It had to be their computer program. Somewhere, buried among the thousands of lines of code that organized and managed the data, there must be an error. Hector had been unable to find any such flaw in their code, but he had only examined the code that related directly to the statistical analysis. Perhaps the error was further back in the data-management portion of the program. I shook my head in frustration.

*There's still something I must be missing.*

As I pondered all this, Rita entered the room, ushering in Jane Clayton. Also present were Jeff Gunderson and Carolyn Cummings. I stood up to greet her. She looked a few years older than in the picture online I had seen. Her hair, which was a bit grayer, was tied back into a tight configuration, with a few loose strands escaping. She appeared rather apprehensive, her expression serious and her lips pressed tightly together. She held out her hand out tentatively to grasp the hand I offered. Her fingers were cold.

"Thanks so much, Dr. Clayton, for coming in," I said, feeling a bit foolish, as I supposed she had little choice in the matter. "Please, be at ease. I don't think we've met. I'm Ken Wheeler. I teach biostatistics at Boston University, and I'm consulting on a project with the FBI. Has Rita explained to you why we wanted to speak with you?"

"She said it had to do with the Pfeffer situation and that some new evidence has come to light. That's all."

She looked wary. I couldn't blame her, remembering what she'd gone through and imagining how it would feel to be in her position.

"Before we start, let me introduce Jeff Gunderson from the Bureau and Carolyn Cummings from Phire-Break. Carolyn is the Director of Medical Research at PhireBreak."

This caught her by surprise. No doubt, she was wondering what this had to do with Pfeffer.

"I know this all must be confusing, but it will be clearer soon. Let me assure you, first, that you are not in any way being accused of anything. In fact, what we learn may help to exonerate you of any responsibility for what happened at Pfeffer."

Now I was sure she was really confused, but maybe also a bit relieved.

"I'd like to add something," said Rita. "You'll need to keep what we discuss here today absolutely confidential. It's possible that we may need to call on you to provide testimony at some point, probably in a written affidavit. But until then, nothing leaves this room. You understand?"

"Yes," she responded softly, almost inaudibly.

Rita continued: "What I can tell you now is that PhireBreak is facing a potential threat with serious consequences. We are investigating the possibility that this threat involves some illegal activities. There is a remote possibility that those behind these activities may be intending to cause harm not only to PhireBreak, but to the U.S. more generally. Dr. Wheeler has been trying to help us understand the exact nature of the threat so that we can be sure to prevent it. I realize this is vague, but mainly I'm attempting to convey the gravity of the situation."

For the first time, Clayton smiled slightly.

"If you're trying to frighten me, you're doing a good job."

This broke the tension in the room somewhat.

"But what does any of this have to do with Pfeffer?" she continued.

Rita inhaled deeply and sighed before responding.

"Are you familiar with Verbana?"

"Yes, from the ads mostly; I haven't done any work related to it."

Rita proceeded to convey an outline of the PhireBreak situation, redacting some of the more sensitive details. Clayton nodded thoughtfully, as she attempted to take this in. Then Rita cut to the chase.

"It's possible that the perpetrators managed, somehow, to alter the statistical analysis to make the drug *seem* to be more harmful than it actually is."

Clayton's eyes grew wide, as she began to comprehend where this was heading.

'Wait, you think that may be what's going on with PhireBreak? But that would also mean..."

"That's right," Jeff interjected, "maybe the Pfeffer statistical analysis was also deliberately falsified. We suspect that *after* the study's completion, someone managed to change the data related to myocardial infarctions. That's why your analyses and those performed by Pfeffer's own statisticians failed to reveal a problem. It was only when the Yale group later re-analyzed the doctored data that the false adverse effect came to light. Of course, we can't prove this theory yet, but if we're correct, then you have been the victim of a major injustice."

"That's *horrifying*, and not just for me personally, but for science. It undermines the trust we all need to have in the objectivity and impartiality of scientific research. Who could have done such an abominable thing?"

"That's what we're trying to find out, Dr. Clayton." replied Rita.

"Jane...please," she said.

She seemed more composed now, almost relaxed, as if a great weight had been lifted. Someone finally believed her.

"Okay. Jane, we'd like to know as much as possible about the process by which the data regarding potential adverse events were handled. First, did the raw data from the study centers come in directly to Pfeffer, or was there an outside Clinical Research Organization involved?"

"Well, that's a bit complicated. We did contract with a CRO, MCS.

"Mannheim Clinical Systems?"

"Yes, that's it. I remember they were in Germany, and they were only responsible for various administrative aspects, not for harvesting data from the study centers. That data came directly to us. I think Pfeffer felt its own in-house research capabilities were adequate."

"Let me ask something else. I believe that besides yourself, there was at least one other member of the Data Monitoring Committee who had statistical expertise. Is that correct?"

She looked confused.

"I'm referring to, uh, Prof. Morgan P. Anscombe, an epidemiologist from Yale. It's my understanding that he was involved as well."

"Oh, Morg. Yes, he was, certainly, but he had no direct contact with the data. He's one of the grand old men of epidemiology, trained by Sir Richard Doll himself, you know. But frankly, ...he was there more for his name than for his statistical expertise."

I could see Carolyn nodding along with me. We both knew that Doll was a pioneering giant in the field of epidemiology. He was one of the main epidemiologists who proved that tobacco smoking was linked to cancer and heart disease. This landmark research essentially launched the field of chronic-disease epidemiology about seventy years ago.

"Just so I'm clear, you alone were interacting with

the data? It went directly to you?"

"Well, no. I was the one who *analyzed* the data for the committee. But managing the data and preparing it for analysis was performed by an internal statistician from Pfeffer."

"Who was that?"

"His name was Chiu Chang. He had a Ph.D. in biostatistics from Columbia and programming expertise with the statistical software. He received and prepared the data for analysis. I don't think he had unblinded data. Only the external members of the DMC had the key that was necessary to break the blind."

"Let me be sure I understand. This Chiu Chang was a Pfeffer employee who performed basic data management and maybe some analysis, but didn't know which patients actually received which treatment modality. Then, you were able to analyze the interim data he provided by unblinding it, using the key, and you reported to the other members of the committee. Is that right?"

"Yes."

I turned toward Carolyn and asked whether there was a counterpart to Chang at PhireBreak.

"Well, as you know, we utilized MCS to collect the data from the study centers. However, there is a senior statistician in my division who served as an internal liaison to the Verbana DMC. He's still with us and, in fact, now reports to me directly. He also works, er...*worked*, with Sergei."

Her voice broke slightly as she recounted this.

Gathering herself, she continued.

"His name is Sam Wu."

At this point, Rita leaned over and whispered something in Jeff's ear. He nodded and then asked:

"Am I correct that both of these men are Chinese?"

Carolyn replied, "I'm not sure about their citizenship status, but I believe they're both of Chinese descent, yes."

"Isn't that an unusual coincidence?" Jeff asked.

I broke in.

"Not at all, Jeff. The statistical profession is dominated by Asian nationals these days, mostly Chinese, but lots from India too. They typically come here to obtain graduate degrees, and many remain and become naturalized U.S. citizens."

"That's true," added Carolyn. "It's hard to fill the demand for well-trained statistical talent without them."

"Huh. I had no idea," said Jeff. "Listen, I've got to take care of something that won't take long, so let's take a short break."

During the next few minutes, we chatted amiably about the state of research on clinical trials. Jane indicated that she was aware of my somewhat controversial views, while offering some insights from her own research. Her mood had lightened considerably, although she resisted becoming too optimistic. A few minutes later, Jeff returned, holding a flash drive, which he plugged into his laptop.

"I want to show you some pictures, Jane," he said.

"These were all skimmed from Facebook. I found seven photos of individuals with the name Chiu Chang and some connection to pharmaceutical research. I'd like to run through these with you to see if any might be the man you were working with. Okay?"

She nodded, as he projected the first picture onto a screen at the end of the conference room. For the first five, she indicated no recognition. But for the sixth, she looked thoughtful, holding her chin in the crook of her left hand and scowling.

"Wait," she said, so, Jeff kept the picture on the screen. Finally, she responded.

"I'm not sure, but I think that might be him. He does look familiar, though it's been, what, seven or eight years since I've seen him."

At that moment, Carolyn, who had not been paying close attention, came over for a closer look.

"Hold on. The hair's different, and he doesn't wear glasses now...but that could be *him*. Could be. *Sonofabitch!*"

"Who?" we all said in unison.

"Sam...fucking...Wu. *That's* who."

# CHAPTER 43

Thursday, October 8

Carolyn looked like someone who had just been told that her boyfriend was actually married. "How sure are you that's the same guy?" Rita asked her.

"I can't give you a percent," she responded, "but I'm pretty certain. *Jesus!*"

"About how long has this Sam Wu been working for PhireBreak?" asked Jeff.

"Hmm. Maybe four years. I guess he joined us right around the time the Verbana data processing was starting up. *Oh shit*, this could be really bad, couldn't it? I've gotta call Selwyn. I can't fucking believe this!"

"Hold on, Carolyn," said Rita. "Let's think this through, okay?"

"Yeah, right, I..."

"First off, we can't be sure yet. This could just be a

coincidental resemblance. Jane, do you know when Chiu Chang may have left Pfeffer's employ or where he went after that? Is there anything else you can tell us about him?"

"I wasn't involved with the company much after the Velex clinical trial finished. Plus, I really didn't know him that well. He seemed very polite and quietly competent. Just responded to my requests for data and seemed kind of shy. I thought that was attributable to English being his second language."

"That sounds just like Sam," Carolyn offered, ruefully.

"How were his computer programming skills?" asked Jeff.

"He was very proficient in the software language we used for the data management and analysis. And he knew a lot about statistical methods. If he had any other skills, I wasn't aware of it."

"Same for Sam Wu," said Carolyn, who was looking increasingly agitated.

"Listen to me," said Rita firmly to her, "this could be our biggest break so far. If Sam is Chiu, there's no way you can be blamed for not knowing. Whoever is behind all this is very sophisticated. I'm sure they cooked up a solid fake identity and credentials for him. Believe me, Selwyn will understand completely. But now that we suspect this connection, we've got to focus on what happens next. Before we get into that, though, I think we needn't detain Dr. Clayton here any longer. Jeff, can you see her out, please?"

"Sure."

"Dr. Clayton, thanks for your assistance. It's been very helpful. We'll be calling you soon if we need anything further. If you recall anything else that may be relevant, please let us know. Jeff, can you escort Jane out to the front, please?"

Clayton smiled as she headed toward the door and turned back just before exiting.

"Thank you all for what you're doing. I hope you finally get to the bottom of everything."

"Thank *you*," I added. "Oh, wait, please. One more thing. When the Yale re-analysis of the Pfeffer data came out, it was obvious that their results differed from those submitted by Pfeffer to the FDA. Then they must have checked back to determine why there was such a discrepancy, right?"

"Uh huh."

"Then, I assume they concluded that the original analysis by Pfeffer had been incorrect. Is that right?"

"Well…yes."

"Now, it's my understanding that you were blamed for failing to detect the problem. Can you explain what actually happened there?"

Clayton sighed deeply. This was opening an old wound, and I hated doing it. I hoped that it might be therapeutic for her in some way

"I'm afraid it's not a simple answer, and I'll have to get into the weeds a bit."

I just nodded.

"As you know, the downfall of Velex was related to an excess of myocardial infarctions, …that is, heart attacks, in the Velex group as opposed to the control group. Nowadays, heart-related problems can, thankfully, be diagnosed directly in real-time by the medical monitoring devices we all wear routinely. The AI software in these devices can detect an MI, even a mild one, with very high accuracy, based on subtle patterns in the data that the devices collect. However, back when the Velex trial was started, such technology was less refined. As a result, it was necessary to audit the results to be sure that the devices used in the trial had picked up every MI event. I was very careful to do such checking, but ..."

"But you apparently missed some of the events, and that wasn't evident until the Yale re-analysis was performed."

"Yes, the re-analysis occurred years later, when the AI technology had advanced considerably. The Yale investigators processed the original data and found some additional events that happened to fall mainly in the Velex group. This led to an apparent elevation of the MI risk for patients who received Velex."

She looked to be on the verge of tears.

"I see," I said. "Now, I want to ask you one more question. Would that be okay?"

"Yes," she answered, her voice croaking.

"Is it possible that this Chiu Chang character, or maybe someone else, might have tampered with the raw data collected by the devices? Perhaps, they knew that certain specific types of heart attacks would fail to be detected by the software, or even by a cardiologist who was checking the AI results. Then, they could have inserted some 'phantom' MIs of these types into the data for some of the Velex patients in the clinical trial. These false MIs would remain invisible until the re-analysis years later. Would such a scenario have been possible?"

"I don't know. Maybe. Something that sophisticated, and …diabolical, beggars my imagination."

"Well," Rita said, "perhaps Dr. Chang can confirm whether something like that actually did occur. We'll be sure to let you know what we find out. Thanks again for all your help. I know this hasn't been easy for you."

Clayton simply nodded and turned to leave.

Turning toward me, Rita asked what I thought about what we had just learned.

"Well, when I thought about interviewing Dr. Clayton originally, I was convinced that the gene-expression data had been changed. The big question in my mind was exactly how this had been done. Now, it appears that my assumption was wrong; apparently, it seems that there *were* no changes to the Verbana data. So in that sense, we learned nothing about the modus operandi for undermining PhireBreak. The comment by Eve's contact that she overheard at the UAE consulate hinted at concerns about potential discovery. So they might have decided on a different, more foolproof, course of action."

"True, but we did learn about Chiu Chang…

aka Sam Wu. Do you think this guy could be the hacker?"

"No, I think that's unlikely."

At this point, Jeff re-entered the room.

"How come?"

"Well, when Eve told us about the 'hacker' she saw at the UAE consulate, she didn't mention that he appeared to be Asian. By the way, didn't you have her work with a sketch artist? Anyway, having an 'inside man' working *with* a hacker really makes sense. But if this hacker was involved in the Verbana trials, but didn't change the data, then what exactly was he doing?"

"That's a good question you and Hector should ponder," said Jeff. "Finding the answer is something that Sam Wu might know, along with the identity of the hacker."

"Right," said Rita, "and that might lead us to the higher-ups. We need to bring in Dr. Wu for questioning right away. Carolyn, will he be working at Phire-Break today?"

"I'm sorry," she replied, evidently distracted and lost in her own thoughts.

Rita repeated the question.

"Yes, I suppose so."

"Good. Can you come up with some plausible pretext for meeting with him, say at four o'clock this afternoon?"

"I, uh...yes, I'm sure I can manage that. Do you want me to have him come to my office?"

"Right. We'll be there about a half-hour beforehand. Don't tell anyone else about this meeting. Just inform the receptionist that two consultants are coming to meet with you and to let us in when we arrive. We won't be using our FBI creds. By the time we get there, we'll have a plan for how to deal with him. Right now, we're going to do some background research. If we catch him completely by surprise, it will be best."

"Okay. Do you need me anymore here, or should I head over there now?"

"No, that should be fine. We'll see you later."

Carolyn got up, and moved toward the door, but hesitated just before leaving.

"Just one more thing, Rita."

"Yeah."

"Do you think he had anything to do with what happened to Sergei?"

"No, Carolyn, I truly doubt that."

Carolyn just nodded slowly and headed out of the room.

"Was that true?" I asked, when she had departed.

Rita just spread her hands and shrugged: "Who knows? It's possible he may have tipped off whoever slipped something into Sergei's vodka. Maybe he guessed what Sergei was working on and perhaps also what he had discovered. But I don't see how. I think it's more likely that someone was spying on Sergei and became alarmed. You know, I'm feeling more and more that we are dealing with much more than industrial espionage. Whoever they are, they know far too much about our activities, and I can't figure out how. If it's surveillance, their capabilities are impressive, and that makes me nervous. Anyway, Ken, you need to stay focused on how they did whatever it is they did, okay?"

I was lost in thought.

"Ken?"

"Oh, sorry. What did you say?"

"There you go again," said Jeff. "that glazed faraway look, as if you're having a seizure or something."

"Yeah...sorry. I think I may know what Sergei's enigmatic remark might mean. He said that I was right, but also wrong."

"That's right, so how can that be?"

"Well I think he meant that I was right about the Hopkins results being bogus, but wrong about *why* they were wrong. Maybe I've been looking at this whole problem incorrectly."

As I said this, I recalled a scene from the latest incarnation of my troubling dreams. Once more I was in the sailboat, and my attempt to make headway was being frustrated. And again, there was a leak.

*A leak...Selwyn implied there might be a leak of some kind. Was Sam Wu then the leaker. But if he was leaking information to the hacker, what was it, and why was it important? Could it be..."*

"I need to have Hector check something out, right away," I blurted out.

"Okay, good," said Rita. "You can fill me in later. Right now, we need to focus on how to corral Sam Wu. Jeff, I want you to find out everything you can about his background. If we can catch him with his pants down, we should be able to hold him for questioning and threaten him with criminal prosecution. Let's start by checking his employment application and immigration papers to see if he lied."

"Sure thing, Rita. I'll get on it."

After he left, Rita turned toward me.

"How are you holding up, Ken?"

"I'm okay, but I wish I could see my family. It's hard being cooped up here. I think this is taking a toll on Val as well. She's always trying to stay positive and encouraging, but…"

"I understand, but until this is over we can't take any chances."

"Yeah, I get that. I'm anxious to get back to work. I hope I'm close to some answers. But before we break up, can you fill me in on the situation with Dave Parker?"

"So we've been in negotiations with his lawyer. I think we're close to a plea deal. I can't say more yet, but if the information he can provide could be germane to your research, I'll be sure to let you know. In fact, I may need to ask you for some advice on how to proceed once we know exactly what he's got."

"Okay. Just one other thing."

"Shoot."

"Have you learned any more about the UAE's role in all this? In particular, what about the potential for terrorism along the lines we discussed before?"

"Again, this is a work in progress. A number

of possibilities are being considered. The UAE has withdrawn most of the staff from the Boston consulate. They claim to be conducting an internal investigation of so-called rogue elements. We're not sure how far to trust what they're telling us. At a minimum, this will be an embarrassment for them, even if the country itself is not involved. How all this will ultimately play out is unclear and probably very complicated. We are guessing that the net short-term effect will be that whoever is behind this will pull in their horns to avoid further exposure. They may still expect to pull off a takeover of PhireBreak, but hold off with their ultimate plan, whatever that might be, until things cool down. Of course, none of this is known with any certainty."

"Okay, I guess most of that is way above all of our pay grades."

"Yeah. Our job is to try and prevent PhireBreak from going down the tubes. Remember, they're the ones paying for your time."

# CHAPTER 44

Sunday, October 11

After two frantic days working together, Hector and I still had not produced proof that the Johns Hopkins researchers had made a programming mistake. However, there was one remaining avenue that we had not yet pursued to conclusion. That would lead, I was almost certain, to the explanation of how the statistical analyses had been rigged, despite the fact that the gene-expression data had not been altered. This explanation would also, I believed, ultimately be simple enough for a twelve-year-old to understand.

We had to go all-in on the theory that the Hopkins study was completely bogus. Anything else would be both intellectually dishonest and, I believed, likely to fail. After much debate about this, Carolyn and Selwyn had come onboard. But to continue the nautical metaphor, I felt that if my approach was not persuasive, I would be the one to walk the plank. After a herculean programming effort, Hector was close to closing that loop. It was our last best desperate hope for absolute proof. So much was riding on the outcome of Hector's program.

In part, my confidence was bolstered by the circumstantial evidence that something was being covered up. We hoped that Dave Parker and/or Sam Wu would provide information justifying the need for more time to unravel the conspiracy. Both were now in negotiations through their attorneys with senior FBI personnel to cut deals in exchange for lenient treatment. What they knew, and were willing to divulge, might, at least, convince the FDA to defer a decision, buying us more time. Everyone knew that the clock was ticking. Once the FDA hearing was over, the leverage each side possessed would be greatly diminished.

By Sunday morning some progress had been made, and our hopes were high for resolution by nightfall. By then, Rita, Jeff, Rex and I would all be in Silver Spring, Maryland. We'd be meeting with Carolyn, Hal and Selwyn, who were already at the Marriott Courtyard there. We would fly down in the morning and spend the whole afternoon reviewing our presentation materials and honing the argument. If new developments in the negotiations warranted, we would adapt our plans to fit them.

As I was packing my overnight bag for the trip, I received a call from Val. I assumed that she was calling to wish me luck, but her tone quickly disabused me of that idea. She was clearly upset and somewhat incoherent.

"Wait a minute, slow down," I said. "Where are you now?"

"I'm in Needham, at my office."

"It's Sunday. Why are you ..."

"I got a call an hour ago from the Needham fire department. They told me there had been a fire. Fortunately, our smoke alarms functioned and they were on the scene within a few minutes. Fortunately, there was only minimal damage, but..., but..."

I just waited as she struggled to continue. My heart was pounding.

"We had several animals being boarded after recovering from surgery."

"Oh, no."

"They all suffered from smoke inhalation to varying degrees. I tried to save them all, but two of the dogs didn't make it. One of them was Hugo, the Newfoundland I operated on a few days ago." She began to cry. I waited for her to regain some composure before asking the question that had immediately come to mind.

"I don't suppose the fire fighters said anything about what may have caused it?"

"Strangely enough, they did. One of our waste baskets filled with paper was the source. Apparently, a still-smoldering cigarette had been dropped into it. They assumed that Beth must have inadvertently done this when she had come in earlier to feed the animals. But that doesn't really make sense because, as far as I know, Beth doesn't smoke."

"Val, I hate to suggest this, but I doubt this was an accident. I think someone is trying to send me a message. They meant for me to know it wasn't accidental."

I paused, afraid to be totally candid, but knew she deserved the truth.

"It's a threat. If I continue to try exposing their activities, there will be serious consequences. Maybe the risk of fighting them is becoming too great. I never imagined it would ever come to this. I can't stand the idea of putting you and Sam in harm's way."

Neither of us spoke for a while.

"Ken, I'm scared...but I think you really have no choice but to see this through. If you back off now, they will almost certainly achieve their immediate objective. But they may still perceive you as a potential threat to their longer-term plans. Then the danger to us would persist. We can't always remain fearful, looking over our shoulders, can we? Our best hope may be for you and the FBI to expose what they're up to...as completely as possible. That way they'll at least abandon this particular scheme, and there won't be any reason for them to care about you."

"I suppose you're right," I said.

"Good luck, Ken. Promise you'll call me as soon as everything is over down there."

"I will. Love you."

Shortly after, we departed for the trip down to Silver Spring. We arrived at BWI airport around mid-morning. From there it was about a half-hour ride to the hotel. As we exited the terminal, a large black vehicle with government plates pulled up, and we hopped in. Despite, or perhaps because of, the fact that I was accompanied by three heavily armed and highly trained individuals on constant alert, I was nervous. This whole situation now felt surrealistic.

*How did I manage to get into this? Would my life ever be the same?*

Fortunately, we arrived at the hotel without incident. After checking into our rooms, we got down to business in a conference room that Phire-Break had reserved for us. The mood was grim but determined. Forgoing his usual nautical metaphors, Selwyn pulled out every football cliché in his repertoire to exhort "the team" to "cross the goal-line." His old coach at the Naval Academy would have been proud.

Of course, we all knew that unless Hector and I miraculously pulled a rabbit out, the testimony of Parker or Wu, and preferably both, would be crucial. As we worked, we all waited impatiently for that shoe to drop, though not a word was uttered about that. The specter of obtaining little or no game-changing information from the FBI negotiators hung over our deliberations like a dark cloud portending who-knew-what.

At six-fifteen we finally got a call. Rita took it

outside the room. She had a slight smile as she returned to deliver the news. Parker had been the first to crack.

"Parker has confirmed a lot of what we've already surmised. We should have a signed affidavit from him within the next couple of hours. It looks like a long night ahead of us. I'm afraid we'll be eating pizza here rather than having that gourmet dinner I'd hoped for. The gist of it is that he admits he was involved in the Pfeffer takeover as well as our current situation. He doesn't know who is behind both of these, but is sure it's the same people. He claims to have documentary evidence that the Mannheim Institute is a front for them. It's been used to lure several prominent academic researchers, and he's willing to name names."

She paused for a drink of water.

"Is that it?" asked Jeff.

"I saved the best for last. He's also willing to finger Sam Wu. Says he worked with the guy on the Pfeffer caper and coordinated on the PhireBreak project."

"Did he say whether Wu was our hacker?" I asked.

"Unfortunately not. He claims that Wu himself was not the hacker but knows who is. He thinks that the hacker collaborated with Wu to effectuate changes in the Pfeffer trial data. He's not sure exactly what they did with Verbana, but does believe they were nervous about repeating the same strategy. So that bodes well for your theory, Ken. Now that Dave's ratted out Wu, we have to hope that gives us enough pressure to squeeze Wu for answers."

"It would be nice if that could happen before our hearing tomorrow," I said. "I'm not sure we have enough without that final piece of the puzzle."

"The perfect is the enemy of the good," said Selwyn.

"Is that a naval or a football adage?" I quipped.

"Both," he responded. "Anyway, let's make the most of what we have. At least we know we're in the right. Remember, this isn't just about PhireBreak. It's entirely possible that many lives may literally depend on this, and not just those patients who may not receive Verbana to stave off their cancers. There's still the possibility of a Tylenol-type terrorist incident."

I'd been so focused on the FDA hearing lately that this alarming scenario had entirely slipped my mind. When I had originally suggested it to Rita, it seemed so preposterous that I had hesitated to mention it, but now, I wasn't so sure.

"What more do we know about that?" I asked.

"Not that much," replied Rita. "The Emiratis have been pretty tight-lipped. Their consulate in Boston has been shuttered for now, presumably until they figure things out. At a minimum, they're facing serious embarrassment, but possibly something much worse if they were somehow implicated. We have suspicions about possible involvement of other countries too, but it's all speculation."

"What about Eve?"

"Three days ago, she received a cryptic email

ordering her to take no further action. She's not sure who sent it. It looks as if whoever is behind everything wants to stay invisible and may be pulling back until things cool off. Frankly, I don't hold out much hope that we can get to the very bottom of this."

"That's probably right," said Selwyn, "but if we can roll up the operation here, and stop whatever they're planning, that would be a huge victory. Right now, it seems that Sam Wu is the critical domino that has to fall. That might lead us to the hacker, and possibly to others who are involved."

"Suppose we do manage to prevent them from undermining PhireBreak," I said. "What about Pfeffer?"

"What do you mean?" asked Carolyn.

"Well, Jeff can correct me here, but if we could prove that the Pfeffer takeover was a completely fraudulent operation, wouldn't some sort of compensation be owed to the victims?"

Jeff was frowning as he pondered this for ten seconds before answering.

"The short answer is that, in theory, yes that's true. But the *practical* implications are staggering. There's no way to unravel and unwind all the myriad financial transactions that have resulted directly and indirectly from the purported fraud, even if it could be legally proved. I'm sure that wouldn't dissuade Pfeffer shareholders from filing some enormous class-action civil suits, though. It could take years to sort out."

"Hmm, that might not be all bad," I mused. "There might be a lot of statistical analysis needed for that."

"I guess we'll have to tack that on to your consulting contract with us," said Jeff.

"Okay. I think we're all getting a little punchy," remarked Rita. "How about we just call it a night and reconvene here early, say at seven o'clock, to go over final details and thoughts."

After that, we dispersed to our rooms. I was almost too tired to undress before collapsing on the bed. But it turned out my day was not quite over. As I was about to turn off the light, my phone buzzed. It was Hector.

"Uh, Ken. Can you talk?"

"Yeah, sure. What did you find?"

"You were right."

# CHAPTER 45

Monday, October 12

When I awoke, it was still dark outside. I immediately went to my computer to examine what Hector had sent the night before. I was still not completely certain my brief conversation with him had really occurred. Or that it proved I was correct, as Hector had asserted. But one glance through the file he'd sent erased all doubt. There was the evidence, in black and white. It was not absolute proof, but it might just be enough. If we could only identify the elusive hacker; that would tie everything up. I spent the next hour incorporating the new information into my presentation.

At seven o'clock the group assembled back in the conference room. We drank coffee and nibbled on some pastry and fruit that had been laid out for us, as we made final preparations. The tension was palpable. Our plan was to leave the hotel in two cars at nine o'clock. That would get us to the FDA headquarters around nine thirty. One car would convey Selwyn, Carolyn, and Hal. The other would carry me, Rita, Jeff, and Rex. Our car would be driven by Rex, and the other one by a local FBI agent who had been detailed to assist us.

The FDA occupies a large campus consisting of several nondescript brick buildings in a well-tended, but rather sterile, park-like setting. There is security to enter the campus and in each of the buildings. Our hotel in the main business district of Silver Spring was located about fifteen miles from the campus. Silver Spring is an upscale mid-sized city that borders on Washington D.C. and is home to many employees of the U.S. government, and the lobbyists and consultants whose livelihoods depend on it. The drive would take us through a residential area of 1970's ranch houses and colonials, surrounded by neat lawns and well-trimmed bushes.

As we left the outskirts of the town center, I reflected on my last conversation with Val. Was I making a serious mistake in pushing forward? Even if we succeeded today, would the risks truly be over, as she suggested? We knew nothing about the motivations of whoever was behind all this. It was a very high-stakes gamble.

In the midst of these ruminations, I realized suddenly that something was wrong. Our car seemed to be decelerating rapidly. I heard the sickening screech of brakes being pressed to the floor, felt a sudden swerve to the right, as I was thrown sideways, and saw the airbags inflating, as Rex attempted, vainly, to avoid the impending crash. We smashed at an angle into what I later learned was a heavily loaded Dodge Ram truck. The impact had injured us all to varying degrees. Rex and Jeff in the front were unconscious and appeared to be in bad shape. Rita and I in the back seat were banged up and dazed, but conscious.

After maybe a half-minute, Rita reacted first.

"Call 9-1-1 to get help," she shouted at me, rousing me from shock. "I'm going to check on Rex and Jeff as soon as I make sure we're not in danger. This was no accident," she stated, grimly. "We may still be under attack. Stay in the car, you hear?" She took out her gun and left.

*Under attack?*

My hands shook as I pried the phone out of my pocket. I managed to make the call and explain our situation as best I could. I could hear Jeff starting to regain consciousness. He groaned, obviously in pain.

*That's good. At least he's alive.*

Thirty seconds later, Rita returned.

"No one there," she said. "The other driver must have bolted. Someone doesn't want us to get to the FDA."

Then, she opened the door to get at Rex. He hadn't made a sound yet. She placed her hand on his neck, looking for a pulse. Jeff turned toward her and grimaced as he tried to speak.

"Is he...?" he rasped.

"He's still got a pulse, and he's breathing, but it doesn't look good."

Jeff just nodded. He was obviously in a lot of pain.

"Did you call 9-1-1?" Rita asked me.

I just nodded.

Meanwhile, the cars were starting to pile up behind us, as the road was completely blocked by us and the abandoned truck. Up ahead, I saw no sign of the other car that was carrying our colleagues, which had left a couple of minutes before us and was at least a mile ahead when the crash occurred. They had apparently continued on, oblivious to our plight.

*Just as well. What could they do anyway?*

Rita was on the phone, trying desperately to arrange a military medical evacuation helicopter, which seemed like the only way to save Rex. Then, there was the sound of sirens. First to arrive was a police car. The troopers got out and began to manage the traffic. Almost immediately, two ambulances appeared. A paramedic rushed over to assess the situation. She and Rita conversed hurriedly. I was still too woozy to take in anything they said, but she shouted something to the other ambulance, which had just come on scene. Two paramedics rushed over and began to extricate Jeff. By now, I had managed, I don't remember how exactly, to maneuver myself out of the car. I had sunk down and was leaning against one of the rear wheels. A paramedic approached, quickly appraised my condition, and lifted me onto a folding chair that had magically materialized.

"You'll be okay. Just wait here. We'll be back soon, buddy. Right now, I gotta help with the guys in the front. You understand?"

"Yes, I'm okay," I replied, convincingly enough that he ran immediately off to help the others. I was lucid enough to be concerned that any chance of reaching the FDA in time might be slipping away. After all I'd been through to get this far, the thought was maddening. But I soon lapsed into a kind of numb stupor.

A few minutes later, I was roused by the sound of a helicopter landing in a field nearby. I remember seeing a gurney being wheeled out and Rex being placed upon it and taken away. That was the last time I would see him alive, if he really was still alive. Then, Jeff was being wheeled to one of the ambulances. I later learned that he would be taken to a local hospital. His injuries were deemed non-life-threatening. Amazingly, he would only need to stay overnight in the hospital before being released.

By then, Rita was on the phone to Selwyn. His group had just arrived at the FDA and were going through building security. After apprising him of our situation, she told him to start without us.

"Just explain there was an accident," she advised, "and tell them we'll be there as soon as we can."

After that, the female paramedic came over to us.

"Okay, you two. You were really lucky. If your

driver had reacted a second later, instead of having bumps and bruises, you'd need to be carted off as well. As it is, our protocol dictates that we have to take you into the closest ER to check you out before releasing you."

"That wasn't luck," grumbled Rita. "That was evasive driving by a highly trained professional who's saved many lives besides ours. If anyone deserves to pull through, he does. *Goddam it... damn it to hell!*"

I could see she was overwrought and visibly shaking.

"I understand, lady. Just calm down. Look, you have to get in the ambulance...right now."

"I am not a *lady*, trust me. We're not going to any hospital. I'm a special agent with the FBI and we're on a very important mission."

"Sure, and I'm Michelle Obama."

At this point, Rita pulled out her credentials and shoved them in the paramedic's face.

"I am *not* fucking around, *lady*, she shouted. If you'd prefer, you can call your superior, and they can call a deputy director of the FBI who will explain to you what's going on. In the meantime, we may lose our best chance to expose a terrorist plot that could eclipse nine-eleven. If you're willing to risk being remembered as the stupid asshole who could have helped, but adhered to *protocol* instead..."

"Okay, okay, I get it. So how can I help?"

"You can help by driving us straight to the FDA

headquarters. I assume you know where that is. Meanwhile, have your boss call this number. That should get you off the hook for disobeying orders."

Rita then looked down at her phone, which, I noticed, now had a large crack in the screen, but evidently it still worked.

"*Shit!* The meeting has already started. How quickly can you get us there?"

"Let's find out."

Seven minutes later, siren blaring, we arrived at the main gate of the FDA campus. While we were en route, Rita had notified Selwyn, who'd arranged to have us quickly ushered through the security checks, both at the front gate and then in the building. But even these small delays added to my increasing impatience and anxiety. Once cleared through the building security, we were led by a guard to where the meeting was being held. By the time we made it there through several long corridors, my legs were wobbly, my pulse racing, and my breath labored. We were twenty minutes late, but at least we had made it.

We were just about to enter the room when I froze. In all of the turmoil and confusion, I had lost track of the flash drive that contained my presentation. I furiously rooted around in my pocket, but realized it must have fallen out at some point. Without it, I might not be able to explain clearly what Hector and I had just found.

"What?" Rita asked, noticing my discomfort.

"I can't find my flash drive with the presentation."

"Oh, don't worry, I emailed a copy to Selwyn before we left the hotel, just to be on the safe side."

"*Now*, you tell me."

# CHAPTER 46

Monday, October 12

The meeting room was large and windowless. It was a state-of-the-art conference room, with about twenty high-tech workstations, or pods, arranged in two concentric rings around a central podium. The inner ring was elevated about a foot off the floor, the outer a few feet higher, affording each participant a clear view of all the others. Each pod looked like a small cubicle in a typical modern commercial workspace, except that the walls were only about three feet high. In each pod, there was an adjustable work-surface and an ergonomic chair automatically contoured to the occupant's size and shape. An almost unlimited range of fine-tuning adjustments could be verbally ordered to ensure maximum comfort. Individualized temperature and humidity settings could also be controlled by the occupant.

The work-surfaces could be tilted to suit the occupant's needs. The surface itself was a large touch-screen that was internet-enabled and could be utilized in many different ways. For this hearing, it had been set up so that one sector of the surface displayed the person who was speaking at the moment. A second was dedicated to displays that could be shown by the speaker as part of the presentation, such as video, text, images, or graphs. A third contained a schematic showing the identities of all the occupants of currently active pods. More detailed information about each could be obtained by touching the name.

Secure audio communication with any other participant was facilitated by switching on privacy mode, which could be set to block all incoming and/or outgoing sounds. In addition, virtually any desired beverage could be obtained by verbally describing it, down to the level of desired caffeine and sugar content. It was a nerd's paradise.

As Rita and I entered the room and took this all in, there was a stir as all eyes turned toward us. On the central podium, a distinguished-looking man of about seventy stood up and motioned us toward our assigned pods. Meanwhile, Selwyn emerged from one of the adjoining pods to check on our condition. We assured him that we were fine, though my disheveled appearance no doubt suggested otherwise.

As I sat down in my appointed pod, I noticed that eighteen of the pods seemed to be occupied.

This was easy to ascertain from the schematic on my work surface. I remembered that there were five members of the advisory committee in addition to the chairman, Richard Chapel, whom I recognized on the podium. There were five of us: Selwyn, Hal, Carolyn, Rita and myself. That made eleven. The other three were clearly identified as lawyers: two representing Johns Hopkins and one representing Caldwell Analytics. That made fourteen.

*So who are the other four?*

As I entered the pod, I could hear Chapel's stentorian tones emanating from the speakers and see his visage on my work surface. I elected to turn off the transmission and listen to him directly, since he was only about twenty feet away.

"Welcome to the hearing," he intoned, "I'm sorry about your, uh…mishap on the way here. Unfortunately, it has placed us somewhat behind schedule, but I believe we'll have enough time to accomplish our purpose. Be assured, you will receive a full and fair hearing."

While he spoke, my eyes were drawn to the schematic display that showed the occupants of all the pods. I noticed that Rita and I were temporarily highlighted, apparently to signal our recent arrival. I was identified as a biostatistical consultant to PhireBreak and Rita as merely an attorney, without any additional elaboration of her affiliation with the FBI.

I had the sense that the hearing was a mere formality, and that its result was foreordained. This feeling was reinforced by a glance at the schematic that revealed who all the participants were. One of the four was Prof. Alvin Davenport, the director of the Johns Hopkins research team. Another was Gilbert Stein, the deputy director.

Stein looked vaguely familiar to me, although I couldn't quite place him. Undoubtedly, our paths had crossed before, perhaps at a statistical conference. It took me a few seconds to recall why his name also rang a bell. Stein was Bobbie Stanton's colleague, the one who had boasted to her about the Hopkins study. That meeting now seemed like an age ago.

Davenport and Stein were no surprise, as they directed the research project at Johns Hopkins, although their presence was unexpected. The other two were a bit of a shock, though: Harold Caldwell and Noah Kreutzfeld.

*They've really brought out the big guns!*

Ordinarily, I would have felt rather intimidated by this lineup of heavyweights, but I was really becoming too exhausted to care. Plus, at this point, I was starting to get really pissed off. For the Hopkins academics, prevailing here would only mean a prestigious article in *The Lancet*, just another notch in their already overstuffed belts, enhancing their reputations and garnering them more grant money.

I smiled inwardly, as I recalled an old saying: "Academic infighting is so vicious because the stakes are so low." Well, this time the stakes were sky-high. I thought of all those lives that could be saved by

Verbana and all those that might be destroyed by whatever illicit purpose was at work. I took a deep breath, ordered up a triple espresso, and prepared for the fight of my life.

"I want to set the stage, as it were, for what I hope will be a frank but collegial discussion," Chapel continued. "For a number of reasons, this hearing is without precedent and is, if I may say so, of historic significance. As you are all aware, there have been only a handful of re-analyses resulting from the Data Transparency Act so far. Moreover, this is the first one in which a major dispute has arisen, and the FDA has been asked to participate in its resolution."

He paused for a moment to clear his throat.

However," he continued, "this situation is unusual in other ways. PhireBreak is essentially attempting to block the dissemination of academic research. On its face, that would seem to be a restriction of free speech and might have a chilling effect on future academic discourse. Furthermore, the question of whether Verbana may have a serious side effect is of critical importance to treating physicians. Under these circumstances, there is a heavy burden of proof on PhireBreak to explain why the Johns Hopkins research should not be published forthwith."

*Just what I expected.*

"Beyond those general considerations, the run-up to this proceeding has been, ah...unorthodox, to say the least. Two weeks ago, we received the submission by PhireBreak and its consultants of its own findings. It contained some serious criticisms of the Johns Hopkins research. As a result, we asked the Hopkins research group to respond to the main points raised by PhireBreak. After receiving these, we decided it would be best for them to be represented here today. I should add parenthetically that we expected Dr. Rosefsky and Dr. Parker to be present to elaborate on their contributions to the PhireBreak submission. I hope that their unexpected absence and its potential impact on the matters we are analyzing will be explained. With that, I will turn the floor over to Selwyn Washington, Senior Vice President and General Counsel of PhireBreak."

# CHAPTER 47

Monday, October 12

"Thank you, Dr. Chapel. We appreciate your forbearance in accommodating some, ah...unforeseen circumstances. We regret the confusion and disruption that certain very recent events have caused. By the end of these proceedings, I hope that our inability to provide more timely notice of these will be abundantly clear. With respect to Dr. Parker, he has been, er ...unavoidably detained, you might say."

Despite the gravity of the situation, I couldn't help smiling at this.

"With respect to Sergei Rosefsky, a brilliant and dedicated mathematician and scientist, it saddens me to report that he apparently suffered a massive heart attack from which he did not recover. We only learned this a few days ago ourselves."

He left those words hanging in the air for several seconds. There were shocked expressions all around and complete silence until he resumed.

"All this will be explained. We do not, as yet, have

all the answers we'd like to have, but whatever we do know, we will share. In the end, we rely on the integrity and good judgment of this distinguished committee. That's all I will say right now. I'll leave the details to my colleagues," he said, nodding in our direction.

"Thank you, Selwyn," said Chapel. "Before your presentation, I'm going to allow each of the Johns Hopkins researchers to respond briefly to the points raised in your written submission. Alvin Davenport will start off."

"That won't really be necessary," I couldn't help myself from blurting out.

"*Excuse* me," Dr. Wheeler, "but *I'm* in charge here," responded Chapel, obviously annoyed.

Feeling cowed, I simply nodded.

"That's fine," said Davenport, condescendingly. "I appreciate that this must be a very stressful time for you. I'm not going to say anything substantive before introducing my colleagues, who will summarize supplementary analyses we have performed recently. We believe these will allay any concerns the FDA may have. I'm calling on Noah. Kreutzfeld first for his theoretical insight, followed by Harold Caldwell to discuss the Caldwell Index. Then, Gil Stein will present results of our statistical analyses."

"Thank you, Alvin. I assume everyone here is familiar with my much-maligned theory of hyper-immunity," Kreutzfeld began, with a sardonic smile. This comment drew a few awkward laughs.

"In a nutshell, my hypothesis is that immuno-therapy can sometimes affect lymphocytes in a way that increases the risk of certain neurological problems. *Regrettably*, this theory has so far failed to gain wide acceptance in the scientific community, despite *ample* evidence from research conducted by myself and several others. A couple of disgruntled former colleagues of mine have gone so far as to level ridiculous and unfounded charges about the quality of our research. I'm not making any specific accusations here, but it almost seems as if there's a conspiracy by certain influential academics, in league with the pharmaceutical industry, to prevent the truth from coming out."

There were varying reactions to this diatribe, ranging from a couple of slightly nodding heads in agreement to several expressions of skepticism. Richard Chapel remained unreadably impassive.

"Fortunately, the superb re-analysis by the Johns Hopkins team has provided indisputable proof of my theory. By inducing a targeted immune response, Verbana *did* modify the lymphocytes, as evidenced by changes in gene expression. The specific changes in some of the Verbana-treated patients presage future dementia with high probability, as indicated by the Caldwell Index. Consequently, the expected frequency of predicted dementia among patients treated with Verbana was elevated...substantially. The numbers don't lie!"

Kreutzfeld paused for a few moments to gather himself before continuing.

"I had hoped," Kreutzfeld continued, "that Dr. Parker would be here, so that I could correct some of his, er...misapprehensions. The fallacy in his argument stems from a subtle error that is explained in the expert report I've submitted to this committee. Furthermore, that report also contains data from recent experiments on animals conducted in my lab. The data confirm *conclusively* that immunotherapy can have adverse effects on mental functioning in chimpanzees, as well as rats. We plan to publish our results shortly."

He went on to describe in some detail the recent results he claimed to have achieved. Then he sat back with a self-satisfied expression, as if he had proved his point beyond doubt. Next came Harold Caldwell. He had that air of easy confidence and smugness that often characterizes those fortunate academics who manage to create highly successful side businesses. Such professor-entrepreneurs, or "profeneurs," as I call them, tend to look down on other academics, who, they assume, must envy their wealth and notoriety.

As Eve Stolz had implied, as far as big egos, Caldwell was indeed a prime specimen.

"It's an honor to be here," Caldwell began. He was about fifty, of medium height, partially bald, with a slight paunch and a salt-and-pepper beard. He spoke in a leisurely cadence, with a mild southwestern inflection. "I know y'all may be a bit confused by some of the claims made by Dr. Rosefsky in his report. Far be it from me to speak ill of the departed.

Indeed, I have great respect for the man. His analysis was so clever it almost had me convinced. However, I knew it couldn't hold water. He *claimed* to have discovered an improvement upon my algorithm that underlies the Caldwell Index. I strongly disagree, for reasons elaborated in my expert report, which y'all have had a chance to review."

He went on to provide more details. His folksy manner was impressive. I could understand how he'd become such a successful self-promoter.

"Y'see," he concluded, "our Index has been thoroughly tested in various studies over a five-year period. Most recently, it was validated in a large sample of *cancer* patients, although the results haven't yet been published. So, y'see, even if Dr. Rosefsky's shiny new algorithm *appears* to perform admirably on the limited data that was available to him, that would not imply that our results when applied to the PhireBreak clinical-trial data are incorrect. I must point out that our algorithm has a track record of many successful applications, while Dr. Rosefsky's is only in what we might fairly characterize as a developmental stage. And I can tell y'all from sad experience that many promising early versions of a predictive model can fall apart in the light of much more extensive and rigorous testing. Now I'll turn the floor over to Gil Stein, who will be addressing the statistical analyses based on the Caldwell Index."

Stein looked every inch the rising academic star. He was tall and slim, with a ruggedly handsome look. He was probably in his late thirties and dressed in a tweed jacket, open-collared shirt, and blue jeans. His hair was drawn into a pony-tail and had just a hint of gray. I wondered idly how many of his female students had succumbed to his charms. I was sure he was relishing the chance to accelerate his career trajectory by being in the center ring of this circus.

"Thank you," Harold. "Before talking about Dr. Wheeler's statistical analyses, I want to say a few words about the data. We took great pains to ensure that the data we analyzed were identical in every respect to the original data in the Verbana clinical trials. We performed a careful data audit and have provided complete details in the appendix to my report. We knew that our study would receive intense scrutiny by PhireBreak and the peer reviewers assigned by *The Lancet*."

"Now, Dr. Wheeler is a well-known proponent of the idea that virtually all drugs vary in their effects. He asserts that the effect of Verbana may be limited to a subgroup of individuals. His novel, but may I observe, somewhat controversial, statistical methodology has been employed to identify such an alleged subgroup. Yet, he has not been able to specify clearly *any* subgroup of patients to which the apparent effect of Verbana is restricted. Nonetheless, he argues that it would be unwise to seriously curtail the use of Verbana at this time. Rather, he proposes further research into the possibility of a *hypothetical* susceptible subgroup that he believes must surely exist. But even if he is correct in his... theorizing, we have no way to know whether such a subgroup is indeed large or small."

He paused for a few seconds to let this sink in.

"We cannot dispute, of course, that there may exist *some* variability in terms of how Verbana affects different individuals. Recent genomic research has made this fact inescapable. *However*, understanding the precise nature of this variation is a difficult challenge. Recognizing this practical reality, the FDA continues to insist, rightly in my opinion, that the *average* effect must be the primary criterion to consider in evaluating the performance of medications. So, at least until we know a lot more, we must err on the side of suspending sales of the drug completely."

"Thank you, Dr. Stein, said Chapel.

He then opened the floor to the committee members, who asked a number of technical questions aimed at the Hopkins group. These were all met with smooth responses. Then Chapel suggested: "I think this might be a good time for a lunch break."

# CHAPTER 48

Monday, October 12

W

e ate lunch in a side room off the main cafeteria in the FDA building. The statements by the Hopkins crew had been compelling, and we suspected that the review committee had already made up its mind. Nobody ate very much as we focused on the plan for arguing our case. Looming over our deliberations, and adding to the tension, were the interrogations of Dave Parker and Sam Wu that were taking place in the FBI's Boston office. So far, though both seemed grudgingly willing to cooperate, neither claimed to know the identity of the hacker. We had hoped for a breakthrough by now, but none seemed forthcoming and we had almost given up, when something occurred to me. I asked Rita to contact Eve Stolz and run something by her. She nodded affirmatively. Then it was time to get back.

As we took our seats for the resumption of the hearing, I had a sudden flashback to the American League Championship Series of 2004, which had begun twenty-two years earlier, to the day. As baseball fans know, the Yankees had beaten the Red Sox in the first three games of the ALCS, and were poised to clinch the series in the ninth inning of the fourth game. The Yankees were ahead by a run, and there were two outs. The odds against a Sox comeback and victory in the fourth game, let alone winning the series, were astronomical. Miraculously, the Red Sox found a way to survive, and went on to win the next three games to take the ALCS, and subsequently to win the World Series...for the first time since 1918.

I had an idea how they must have felt in that fateful ninth inning. Selwyn Washington was our team's lead-off batter. His role was to set the stage for Carolyn and me.

"I would like to offer some perspective before the more technical presentations," Selwyn began. "I have no doubt that the Johns Hopkins researchers are highly competent and acting in good faith. Their reports and presentations appear compelling, and I would be surprised if you don't find them quite persuasive. However, when you hear the full story of what we currently know, I believe your certainty will be shaken. You'll also understand why we were unable to bring some of this information to you earlier."

As he paused for a drink of water, I gazed around

the room and saw puzzlement and skepticism written on the faces of all. They were clearly wondering where this was heading.

"Our investigation into the highly unusual situation is not complete. There is more evidence to be uncovered. However, we do have enough information to imply that the cogent and logical arguments you have heard are almost completely irrelevant, because they are based on false premises. I'm afraid that we've all been duped by a very devious fraudulent conspiracy that has already caused great harm and will cause enormously more if it remains unchecked."

He paused to let the impact of this statement sink in. Now the puzzlement had turned to outright incredulity. Alvin Davenport got up and appealed vociferously to Richard Chapel.

"This is outrageous. This sort of unsupported innuendo is completely improper. I demand that we suspend this hearing until we've had a chance to examine this so-called new information."

"Hold on, Alvin," replied Chapel. "I hear you, and I sympathize. Selwyn, this is highly irregular. I must confess that I can't imagine what new evidence you may have, or what possible justification there may be for springing this without prior warning. However, it would be highly impractical to reconvene at a later date. I'll allow you to proceed for now, but I'll then provide extra time for Alvin and his colleagues to respond."

"Thank you, Richard. I'm going to call first on

our Director of Medical Research, Dr. Carolyn Cummings. She oversees all of our research and development activities."

As he sat down, Selwyn glanced over in my direction. He nodded slightly with eyes narrowed and the hint of a smile, as if to say: "I believe in you. You can do this."

I didn't share his confidence.

Then Carolyn, her voice uncharacteristically subdued, almost tremulous, began to speak.

"I have worked closely with both David Parker and Sergei Rosefsky. Neither of these men could be here today, though for very different reasons. You have received the report by Dr. Parker and his colleagues. His main point is that the Kreutzfeld Hypothesis remains, at best, highly speculative."

I glanced over at Kreutzfeld, who remained outwardly unperturbed but was staring daggers at Carolyn.

"No doubt, Dr. Kreutzfeld believes that this study is a godsend, resurrecting his debunked theory. The results do, indeed, *appear* to be consistent with his theory. Using the Caldwell Index as an endpoint, the average predicted probability of future dementia for the Verbana patients was higher than for the control group patients. Furthermore, this difference is statistically significant. These facts we do not dispute."

Kreutzfeld nodded and smiled.

"However, as Dr. Parker documented in his written report, these findings are at odds with a mountain of previous research that has failed to support Dr. Kreutzfeld's hypothesis. This prior research includes biochemical analyses of disease mechanisms and statistical studies on both animals and humans. This single *new* result, even if correct, would need to be weighed against this backdrop. Do we really wish to place in jeopardy the lives of literally millions of future cancer patients without a much stronger evidentiary basis? For that is exactly what will happen if the proposed article in *The Lancet* is released prematurely. Even if Verbana is ultimately vindicated, as I firmly believe it would be, thousands of patients may be denied treatment before that happens."

Carolyn's voice broke somewhat and there were tears visible as she struggled to continue. She glanced over at Selwyn, who nodded slightly in encouragement.

"A few minutes ago," she went on, "Dr. Chapel alluded to the unprecedented aspects of this situation. Well, another unprecedented aspect he *failed* to mention was the fact that a *proxy* measure, a *predicted* probability, is being considered sufficient to impugn a valuable medication. I submit that this could recklessly set a dangerous precedent. Shouldn't we at least wait until there is some hard evidence of actual dementia that is being caused by the drug?"

"But it could take years for that evidence to emerge," commented Caldwell. "We can't afford to wait that long."

"*Actually*," I countered, "it wouldn't. There exists relevant data in the patient records of the hospitals that were involved in the Verbana trials. There are hundreds of patients who have already been followed up for several years. We could examine those records to determine whether in fact there is any supporting evidence of significant mental decline among those patients."

"That's theoretically possible, I suppose," said Chapel. "But such an undertaking might be fraught with enormous logistical and legal hurdles. Nonetheless, the committee will give it due consideration. Do you have anything more for us, Dr. Cummings?"

"Sergei...Dr. Rosefsky...was a dedicated and brilliant colleague with whom I, I...had the privilege of working closely for several years."

As she struggled to maintain her composure, I wondered just how close her relationship with Sergei had actually been. In hindsight, there were clues I should have noticed. Val would have seen this long before.

"Early on, we had our doubts about the validity of the Caldwell Index, at least as applied to cancer patients. These reservations are elaborated in the material we submitted to the committee. Sergei was able to derive an alternative predictive algorithm that seemed to improve slightly upon the Caldwell Index. We believed that a more refined version of that algorithm might completely undermine the Hopkins results. However, a few days ago,

Sergei noticed something odd that shook him. After working late into the night, he sent me an email, asking me to meet him the next morning at my office. But he never made it to that meeting. Late the next day, we found that he had been taken to a local hospital by EMTs. He had apparently suffered a massive heart attack from which..."

At this point she lost control and began to sob quietly. She turned quickly and rushed toward the exit. A few seconds later, Rita followed her out. An awkward hush fell over the room. No one seemed to know how to react. Then Selwyn rose.

"I'm sorry, Richard. The stress of recent events has been intense. I believe that Ken Wheeler can pick up where Carolyn left off."

*Huh?!*

"All right...Dr. Wheeler?"

I hadn't expected to be thrown into the fire just yet. I would have to improvise.

"Well, yes...okay. Er...where to begin? As Carolyn has explained, Dr. Rosefsky had developed an algorithm to predict future dementia. This new algorithm was derived based on the same data that Dr. Caldwell himself had used. Dr. Rosefsky's new model performed slightly better than the Caldwell Index in that developmental data. Moreover, in the developmental dataset, the individual predictions generated by the two different algorithms were very close. This was not surprising, since both models were, presumably, sensitive to the same underlying biological processes. But that led to a troubling question."

I paused to catch my breath and survey the audience. They seemed riveted, following intently.

"If his algorithm was so similar to the Caldwell Index, why didn't it also agree closely with the Caldwell Index in the *Verbana* data? What was causing the difference? Seeking an answer, he examined more closely the individual predicted probabilities for the two alternative analyses. What he discovered seemed to be an anomaly. He found that for most of the patients, the estimated probabilities produced by his algorithm and the Caldwell algorithm were indeed very similar. However, of the small number with large discrepancies, all of these were in the Verbana group."

"What's surprising about that?" Caldwell interjected. "Evidently, my algorithm was detecting some additional HID cases that were invisible to Rosefsky's."

"Think about it," I responded. "Sergei's model meshed with yours on all of the developmental data you had used. His neural-network model was derived using the *same* data and the *same* gene expressions as your model. Thus, it was apparently responding to essentially the same biological process as yours. It was, in fact, nearly *identical* with yours in all practical respects, Dr. Caldwell."

"So, Dr. Wheeler, what's your point?"

"My point is simply this. The additional presumed HID cases your model detected must have had some characteristics that were not present in any of the patients in your developmental data-set. Otherwise, your algorithm and Dr. Rosefsky's would have disagreed on the predicted probabilities for such patients. But, if such characteristics truly exist only in the Verbana data, your algorithm could not possibly have taken them into account. Any model, however sophisticated, can only utilize information contained in the data from which it has been derived."

I paused for a few seconds to let the audience absorb this somewhat abstruse point.

"Are you quite finished?" asked Chapel, hopefully.

"Far from it. Rosefsky was perplexed by this anomaly. So he kept digging, and ultimately concluded that there was no *legitimate* explanation for it. That led him to an epiphany. In his email to Carolyn, he implied that his explanation was simple enough for an adolescent to understand. Regrettably, he never got the chance to work out a full demonstration. However, following in his footsteps, my colleague and I have proved that Sergei's insight isn't just theoretical...there is hard evidence to back it up."

"I think we'd better take a ten-minute break. I'll grant you enough time to present your evidence, but then I'm going to allow the Hopkins people as much time as they need to respond. I really hope you're not wasting our time with unsupported allegations, Dr. Wheeler."

# CHAPTER 49

Monday, October 12

During the brief hiatus, Selwyn, Carolyn and Hal went off to make phone calls or use the restrooms, leaving me momentarily alone with Rita. She called in to find out the latest developments in Boston. As we had hoped, striking a plea deal with Dave Parker had helped to loosen Sam Wu's tongue. He was now angling for leniency by relating what he knew and implicating others. What neither of them seemed to know, however, was the identity of the mysterious hacker...or of the mastermind behind the whole scheme. However, Wu had turned over access to his computer files, including emails that might reveal connections with other conspirators.

"Did you follow up on that matter I raised during the lunch break?" I asked.

"Yes, but we haven't been able to ask her yet," she

answered.

"Don't you know where she is? It could be critical."

"She's on her way to our office and should arrive any minute. I'll let you know as soon as we learn anything. Trust me, we know what we're doing."

"Okay, okay."

As we headed back to the meeting room, Rita asked if I was ready.

I just nodded.

When the meeting resumed, I was in a quandary. My main objective was to prove that the Hopkins findings had been fraudulently manufactured. Hector had, I believed, sent me the ammunition I would need for that task. But that revelation, by itself, would not tell the full story of how this statistical legerdemain had actually been accomplished...and by whom. Those loose ends needed to be tied up as well for my argument to be completely conclusive. I had to buy some time during which I hoped that Rita would receive confirmation of what I had surmised.

Rather than simply diving into my main argument, I decided to offer some context.

"As you know, we tried hard to see if any of the data on the genes themselves would suggest a subgroup that was mainly or exclusively affected. That's what we anticipated, based on the emerging theoretical and experimental support for the idea of variable effects of drugs. But we did not observe that. So we couldn't rule out the admittedly *unwel-*

*come* possibility that Verbana might actually have a problem."

This earned a few laughs.

"*However*, there was another possibility that might explain these apparently negative results. Was it possible, we asked ourselves, that the data had been corrupted some way, either inadvertently, or even deliberately? Now, before you object, let me say that evidence not directly related to Verbana had come to our attention that suggested such a possibility. I'm referring to the Pfeffer Pharmaceuticals situation, in which the company was ultimately ruined in light of a Data Transparency Act re-analysis. Most of you, I'm sure, are familiar with that episode, as least from media reports."

Before I could continue, I was interrupted by one of the committee members. He was by far the oldest person in the room and seemed to speak with great confidence and authority. Checking the list on my monitor, I discovered this was Morgan Anscombe, the "grand old man" of epidemiology that Jane Clayton had mentioned.

"I served on the Data Monitoring Committee for the Velex clinical trials. I've always been bothered by what happened there. It just didn't sit right. Can you say any more?"

"Well, Dr. Anscombe, we became aware of certain, uh...evidence, that suggested improprieties in the handling of the data. These problems may have misled the Yale researchers who, unwittingly mind you, analyzed the doctored data. There is currently an investigation by the FBI into this matter."

"Well it's about time! I raised holy hell when all that blew up, but nobody took me seriously. And poor Jane Clayton...my God...she was damn near ruined."

"Let's not get off track here, Morgan," said Richard Chapel. "Dr. Wheeler, how does this relate to Phire-Break?"

"The FBI's investigation into Pfeffer led it to an interest in the PhireBreak situation, and ultimately to a collaboration between the FBI and Phire-Break. That also explains the presence today of Rita D'Amato. In addition to being an attorney, she is a special agent of the FBI who specializes in financial crimes."

This surprise disclosure led to a rather heated discussion, filled with shouting and recriminations. Eventually, order was restored by Chapel, and I was allowed to continue, pursuant to a stern warning that I'd better get to the point.

"I'm sorry that we could not be more forthcoming earlier about Ms. D'Amato's FBI affiliation, but we didn't wish to create an unnecessary distraction. I mention this now to explain why the idea of data-tampering was somewhat plausible. Anyway, I analyzed the data to determine whether it had the earmarks of fraudulent manipulation, but I couldn't find any evidence in the data itself. Still I remained suspicious. I reasoned that there would be only one way to find out for certain."

"And what was that?" asked Alvin Davenport.

"I sought, and ultimately obtained, the original gene-expression data from patient files at five of the Verbana study centers. I wanted to compare the original data for each patient with the data that had been received and analyzed by PhireBreak, and subsequently by Johns Hopkins. I thought there might be discrepancies suggestive of an attempt to induce an apparent effect."

"And what did you find?" asked Anscombe.

"Nothing. Not a blessed thing. It was another blind alley. What we are quite sure happened in the Pfeffer incident had apparently not occurred here. The data had not been altered."

"Hah! You see, I knew that was preposterous," shouted Davenport. "Now, can we *please* put an end to this farce?"

"Hold on, Alvin," said Anscombe. "He promised us hard evidence, remember? Let's hear him out."

"Thank you, Dr. Anscombe. I do indeed have evidence."

I knew that it was time to put-up or shut-up. No more stalling. But as I began my final spiel, I noticed Rita out of the corner of my eye. She was on the phone and motioning me to wait. Then, accompanied by a huge smile, she gave me a thumbs-up sign. It was showtime, full steam ahead.

"As I was just saying, there appeared to be no reason to question the data, and no reason to question the validity of the Caldwell Index. However, there was one other avenue we hadn't pursued. This was suggested by certain evidence obtained by the

FBI that suggested the data manipulation in the Pfeffer case had been carried out by a very sophisticated computer hacker, with help from someone *inside* the company. The purpose was to undermine Velex by creating a bogus effect of the drug on myocardial infarctions, which would eventually be 'discovered' by the Yale researchers when they eventually analyzed the doctored data."

"What you are implying is appalling! I find it difficult to credit. But, even if it turns out to be true, what does all this have to do with *Verbana*?" asked Chapel.

"I was just getting to that. Dr. Rosefsky's email to Carolyn Cummings included an enigmatic remark. He wrote that I had been right, but also wrong. Eventually, I realized what he had in mind. I was *right* that the apparent adverse effect had been contrived, but I was *wrong* about *how* it had been accomplished. There was another possibility that was consistent with all of the facts at our disposal."

# CHAPTER 50

Monday, October 12

This was it. Time to swing for the fences.

"Unfortunately, my single-minded focus on the data-tampering hypothesis blinded me to the real ploy, until it was almost too late. In fact, it wasn't until a few moments ago that the final piece fell into place."

"So show us your so-called evidence already," challenged Davenport.

"On your screens, you will see a graphic display... momentarily. Ah, there's the first part. This chart shows the results from the Johns Hopkins analysis. As you can see, there are two bars. The height of each represents an average value of the Caldwell Index as presented in the proposed article for *The Lancet*. The higher bar is for the Verbana group, and the lower bar for the control group. The difference between these two averages, as you know, is statistically significant, indeed *highly* significant. This *appears* to prove that Verbana can cause incipient dementia, presumably via Dr. Kreutzfeld's proposed hype-immunity mechanism."

I paused for a few seconds to let this register.

"Now I'm going to add a second graph alongside the first one. This one shows two bars that appear very close together, and are nowhere close to statistically significant. These represent the results obtained by using the 'Rosefsky Index,' if you will. No difference whatsoever. So which one is correct? To answer that question, I'm going to show you a third graph alongside these two. Here it is."

"That looks just like the second one," someone called out.

"That's right," I responded, "it's almost identical."

I noticed the Hopkins crew becoming restive.

*Do they suspect what's coming?*

"Thanks to the patent for the Caldwell Index, which was recently approved and is now public, we know precisely how its commercial algorithm was derived. In effect, the patent describes a complex recipe for deriving a neural-network algorithm. The commercial software produced by Caldwell Analytics implements this algorithm, which carries a complex series of calculations based on the gene-expression data for twenty-two genes. These calculations result in an estimated probability of clinically observable dementia within a few years. At least that's what it's *intended* to do."

"What the hell is *that* supposed to mean?" barked Caldwell.

"What it means, Dr. Caldwell, is that someone has been playing games with your software. Under certain very specific circumstances, your computer code does not actually do what you think it does; it will not, in fact, produce the correct value of your Index."

At this point, Caldwell could contain himself no longer.

"*What*? That is utterly preposterous!" he screamed. "We are supposed to be dealing with *science*, not science *fiction*. Richard, I demand that you put a halt to this...circus!"

But before Chapel could respond, another voice cut in.

"*Dammit,* Harold. *Let...him...finish,*" demanded Morgan Anscombe. "We all know you're a brilliant scientist, but you always were an insufferable smartass...even back when you were my student at Harvard. I want to hear the explanation. Then we can decide if it holds water or not. *That* is what I call *real* science."

Then, Anscombe turned in my direction.

"How *did* you derive the third graph, Dr. Wheeler? Are you implying it represents the 'real' Caldwell Index results?"

"Yes, that's exactly right, and I can prove it. Based on the patent, my colleague, Hector Peres, was able to program the Caldwell Index independently. He checked his code on all the data sets presented in the patent *and* on two other data sets in the scientific literature where the Caldwell index had been applied. In every instance, his results matched exactly those generated by the Caldwell Index. Graph number three presents the results obtained by Hector's implementation of the Caldwell Index applied to the Verbana data. Note that these do *not* match the results produced by the commercial software that was utilized by the Hopkins research team."

Everyone looked stunned. Harold Caldwell was pale and kept shaking his head from side to side in obvious agitation.

"I can add that the predicted probabilities using our reprogrammed version of the Caldwell Index are *identical* to those obtained by the Hopkins team for most of the Verbana patients. They differ only for approximately ten percent of the Verbana patients. The only logical explanation is that these were the patients whose Caldwell Index values were altered. It is in fact these bogus probabilities that created the misleading result that *appeared* to support Professor Kreutzfeld's theory."

Now it was Kreutzfeld's turn to choke on some crow. He looked ill.

"Of course, we plan to prepare a full report laying out everything I've presented here. In addition, I fully expect that we'll be able to expose how the commercial software was corrupted, now that we know what we're looking for."

Then Chapel spoke, slowly and deliberately.

"Just so we're clear, you're alleging that someone hacked in and modified the Caldwell commercial software? The aim of the modification was, specifically, to create false results when the software was applied to the Verbana data. Is that correct?"

"Yes, Dr. Chapel, I believe that's basically what happened, although it's possible that PhireBreak was not specifically targeted when the software was hacked. We suspect it had not been specified yet as the target. In fact, it's likely that the corrupted software was intended to be utilized more than once."

I looked over at Harold Caldwell.

"The good news for Caldwell Analytics is that now the corrupted computer code can be debugged before it causes any more trouble. The predictive algorithm works just fine, as far as we can tell."

Chapel's response to these revelations was guarded.

"Of course, we cannot accept your contention here without carefully reviewing the work by you and Mr. Peres. Assuming it's true, though, how could this possibly have been accomplished? To hack the software would have required extraordinary skills that would span statistics, machine learning, and computer science. Just breaking through the Caldwell Analytics firewall would be extremely challenging. Presumably, all this would have been accomplished while the software was being built. Who on earth could have done all that?"

I was encouraged by a subtle change in the tenor of his queries. For the first time, he seemed more thoughtful than reflexively skeptical.

"Until moments ago, I couldn't have answered that question. But I believe that Agent D'Amato has just received some information that can shed light on that. If you'll bear with me, I need to confer with her briefly."

"Why don't we take a ten-minute break while you do that?" suggested Chapel.

I immediately dashed over to speak with Rita, who was huddling with the others. I glanced across the room and saw Davenport engaged in an animated discussion with Kreutzfeld and Caldwell. None of them looked pleased. I couldn't make out Gilbert Stein. Where was he?

"This better be good," I said. "I'm out on a limb here."

Rita related what she had learned from Boston. I was amazed at what she was able to pull together in such a short time. When the meeting resumed, I got right to the point.

"We believe that the person who hacked the Caldwell Analytics software had a confederate inside of PhireBreak. This individual is now in FBI custody. He admits to having leaked the Verbana gene-expression data to the hacker. He has also provided emails that substantiate his account of interactions with the hacker. Furthermore, his identification of the hacker has been corroborated by a second witness with direct knowledge of the hacker's involvement. The emails reveal that while the software was under development, a logic bomb was installed."

"I'm sorry...a *what*? asked Morgan Anscombe.

"Oh, a 'logic bomb' is a piece of computer code that can be inserted into a program by a hacker. This piece remains dormant until it's activated under certain conditions. In this case, it could be triggered only for certain specific individuals. Once activated, the extra code alters the probability produced by the commercial Caldwell software."

"Okay," said Anscombe, "but I still don't understand how the hacker was able to slip the instructions necessary to activate the logic bomb into the Hopkins statistical analysis program."

"Right. Armed with the gene-expression data leaked by the PhireBreak employee, the hacker had plenty of time to analyze it in secret, before the Hopkins re-analysis. So he was able to determine a selected subset of Verbana patients whose Caldwell Index scores would be increased. Then, during the Hopkins study, it was a simple matter to insert the necessary code to activate the logic bomb for the specified individuals."

"This is all complete nonsense," interjected Caldwell, "It's pure fantasy. Who could possibly have pulled off something like that? For one thing, they would have had to hack into our computer system *and* into the John Hopkins analysis."

"I admit that it does seem fantastic. But suppose that it was done by someone from within your own organization, a brilliant young consultant you admired and trusted, a man who was closely involved in the software's development and the Hopkins study, who incidentally helped steer you to a source of the venture capital you needed, who introduced you to Alvin Davenport and Noah Kreutzfeld, who…"

"*No! That's not possible, he wouldn't. He couldn't…I don't believe you.*" Caldwell sputtered, as he searched around wildly, looking for Gilbert Stein to deny these accusations. But Stein was nowhere to be found.

I walked over to Rita, who was beaming.

"Aren't you concerned about losing Stein?" I asked her.

"Oh, I'm sure he'll turn up," she said. "We have agents stationed at all the possible exits from the building. We're rather anxious to talk with Dr. Stein. Incidentally, I was surprised when you asked me at lunch to bring in Eve to look at that photo of Stein you took with your phone. What tipped you off?"

"It was just a hunch. When we first came in, I knew he looked familiar somehow, although I didn't think we had ever met. A bit later, the sketch of the hacker, as described by Eve, just flashed into my mind. I thought it was worth a shot to see if she'd identify him."

"Hah! I'm glad you followed your instincts."

"Well, I generally prefer logic, but sometimes intuition is helpful."

After that the hearing devolved into a chaotic scramble, and Chapel realized that no purpose would be served by enforcing order. Nothing more would be accomplished. There would be a lot of mopping up, but the Hopkins study was dead. I felt a sense of triumph and vindication, but also frustration.

"Do you think this is really over?" I asked Rita as we left the conference room.

"No, not yet. I don't believe Stein was the master-mind behind everything. I hope, though, that he can lead us to the ultimate puppet-masters pulling the strings."

"Yeah, I have the feeling we haven't seen the end of this, whatever 'this' really is."

"Agreed," offered Selwyn. "This new Big Data era has enabled those who can manipulate the technology to exert enormous power. There are forces out there quite willing and able to exploit that power."

We left the meeting room and began walking back to leave the building. But when we reached the first intersecting corridor and turned onto it, we heard shouting about fifty feet ahead of us. As we got closer, Selwyn approached a security guard. "What happened?" he asked. The guard hesitated to respond until Rita pulled out her FBI creds.

"Someone's passed out in the men's room."

We followed the guard a little farther down the hallway to an area where several people had congregated outside a restroom. Two of these were EMTs, in fact I recognized the woman who had driven us from the scene of our accident earlier this morning.

Rita asked her what had happened. "Too late," she answered, glumly. "He was gone when we got here. We're not sure if it's a suicide or a crime scene. Either way, it sure is an odd place for it to happen."

Rita told her she would take over now, but local police should be brought in. Then she entered the men's room to assess the situation. Afterward she told us what she had seen.

"There was a huge amount of blood on the smooth tiled floor, originating from one of the stalls. The door to the stall had been opened by the EMTs and left that way. As I approached carefully, trying to avoid the bloody slick, the body came into view slumped over on the toilet. I couldn't see his face, but I knew right away from the pony-tail who it was."

We later learned that Stein's wrists had been slit.

"Like the woman said," remarked Rita, "strange place for a suicide."

# CHAPTER 51

Tuesday, October 13

I t wasn't until around ten o'clock that I got back to Newton and dragged myself off the train. Val met me at the train station in Newton Centre, as I had asked her to, and drove me home. I didn't even have a chance to see Sam, who was already sound asleep. I just came into his room and stared at him appreciatively for several minutes. I sat down in the kitchen with Val and gave her a narrative of all that had happened since I'd last seen her. She, in turn, apprised me of how they had managed in my absence. It was after midnight when I climbed the stairs, managed to undress, and fell on the bed. I slept soundly for about ten hours and would have continued for several more, but was awakened by Val.

"What is it?" I mumbled. "Something wrong?"

"It's Selwyn Washington," she said. "He wants

you to meet in his office at noon. He says it's urgent. Everything's fine, but he needs, and I quote, 'the team's input on something critical that can't wait.' He's waiting for a response. What should I tell him?"

I propped myself up on one elbow, leaned over in her direction, and yawned as I processed this.

"Tell him I'll be there."

She smiled mischievously. "I thought you'd say that, so I already did."

"Humph! I guess you always make the executive decisions. But you didn't even ask him if I'm still on the clock. You're not much of a negotiator."

Two hours later, I found myself once again entering Selwyn's office. So much had happened since my last appearance there. Rita, Jeff, Carolyn and Hal were there. Jeff looked tired, and there was a cane propped next to his chair. I was surprised he was able to make it. As we all chatted, while awaiting Selwyn's arrival, it became apparent that none of us knew what was up. After a few minutes Selwyn entered the room...accompanied by Bobbie Stanton. This was a surprise, as I hadn't seen her since the meeting at which she told us of her encounter with Gilbert Stein.

"I'm sorry to have rousted you all out of your bunks. I'm sure you are all exhausted. I am too. But last night I received a phone call from Bobbie. What she related to me requires, I believe, our immediate attention. Without further comment, I'd like Bobbie to recount for you everything she told me."

"Hi, folks. I'm truly sorry to interrupt your

chance to start recovering from recent events. I had no idea what you've been through in the last few weeks. Selwyn has been giving me an update. I'm sure you're devastated by the loss of two such valued colleagues. What a tragedy! In retrospect I regret that I couldn't have been more helpful. Finding out about Gil Stein's role in all this was shocking...and, frankly, very upsetting for me. I considered him a friend. Maybe I should have seen something earlier. I knew he was ambitious, and a bit too...full of himself, but it never crossed my mind that he...well, that he could be part of such a thing."

"There's nothing you could have done, or should have done, Bobbie," said Selwyn. "But you might be able to help us now. As matters currently stand, we have averted an immediate threat, but we know nothing about who was behind it. It seems likely that a foreign country is involved, but which one...and to what end?"

"I've been thinking about that," I interjected. "Suppose that China, for example, wanted a way to exert its will over Taiwan. By cornering the supply of some critical medical supplies, it could apply pressure by withholding them when they're most needed. Remember what happened during the great coronavirus pandemic? There were serious shortages of materials needed for testing and treatment because we were so dependent on China for those. With our aging population and environmentally degrading world, we'll become increasingly dependent on certain critical medications. An unscrupulous country might try to exploit its control of those drugs...or of the supply chain for producing them."

"That's pretty diabolical," Bobbie responded "Do you really think that kind of 'passive biological warfare' is behind this conspiracy?"

I just shrugged.

"Well, Ken," said Selwyn, "it's certainly an interesting hypothetical possibility, but let's focus on what Bobbie came here to tell us today."

"Right," Bobbie replied. "I knew that your FDA meeting was taking place yesterday, and I was curious how it had all turned out, so I called Selwyn this morning. When I reached him, he gave me the short version of what happened. He told me that nothing had been released to the public yet, and I could certainly understand why. But our conversation sparked something that happened a few weeks ago...and didn't seem important at the time."

She glanced around, her expression seeming apologetic.

"About a week after my meeting with you, I received a phone call from a woman who said she was an executive recruiter. You know, I get such calls from these headhunters frequently. I quickly gave her my standard spiel that I'm very happy with my current situation and have no interest in changing. I was about to hang up, when she stopped me."

"That's not why I'm calling," she said. "My client is a certain well-endowed foundation that

supports the research efforts of top-flight academic researchers. She told me they could provide
substantial grants for research support and other
benefits, such as well-paid consulting and speaking
engagements. Of course, they were only seeking to
establish relationships with those who were conducting research in their primary areas of interest.
We chatted a bit more. It wasn't a hard sell at all,
but it was definitely heavy on the blandishments,
and I got the impression that the rewards would be
lavish."

"What did you tell her?" asked Carolyn.

"I told her that I was too busy right then to consider it. She said I could call her if my situation
changed and gave me her direct line. That was it."

"This sounds suspiciously like what we were
hearing about the Mannheim Institute," said Hal.

"At the time," she went on, "it registered fleet-
ingly as a coincidence, but I quickly forgot about
the whole conversation. As I was speaking to Selwyn, though, that connection popped into my
head. I recalled Gil's comment about Mannheim
having generously funded the Johns Hopkins research effort."

"Exactly," said Selwyn. "When Bobbie mentioned
this to me, it rang a bell. I asked her whether she remembered the name of this headhunter...or of her
company. Unfortunately, she didn't. However, as a
follow-up to the phone call, she had received an
email that contained contact information. There's a
phone number and a website. I've checked the web-

site, and there's not much on it."

"Oh, one more thing," said Bobbie. "I almost forgot." She hesitated as if trying to recollect.

"What was that?" I asked.

"She asked me whether my Harvard position would limit in any way the kind of research I could pursue. In particular, she mentioned re-analysis of data that might be obtained through a DTA request."

Jeff whistled in reaction.

"So, in hindsight, you're thinking this headhunter might have been trying to recruit you for..."

"I don't know *what* to think."

Rita jumped in. "Right now, with Stein out of the picture, we're at a dead end." She grimaced at the unintended pun. "This solicitation could turn out to be totally legit, but it could be connected to the larger conspiracy. I think we need to act on it right away. We might have a very short window of opportunity before what happened at the FDA leaks out. We can't keep it buttoned up for much longer."

"So, Rita, what do you think we should do?" Hal asked.

"Bobbie, suppose you call her call back and suggest that you may be interested. You'd like to find out more, though. See if she's willing to provide additional details, and maybe also try to arrange a meeting. The most important thing, however, is to keep her on the line for as long as you can without raising suspicion. If you can manage to keep her on for about two minutes, we should be able to pinpoint her location. We also have excellent voice-recognition software. If we're really lucky, we may even be able to identify her. What do you think?"

"I guess I could do that."

"Okay, good."

So we decided to head over to Bobbie's office at the Harvard T. H. Chan School of Public Health, located on Huntington Avenue in Boston, close to the Harvard Medical School and some of its affiliated hospitals. We reasoned that if a reverse trace was being attempted on the other end while Bobbie made the call, it would be less suspicious for the call to originate from her office. Meanwhile, Jeff made the necessary arrangements for our attempted trace.

On the way over, Jeff was musing about the wonders of modern technology.

"These new applications of artificial technology are amazing. Not only can we trace where a call is coming from, and quite often the identity of the person we're talking with, but even whether they are lying. I'm starting to think we humans may be largely supplanted at the Bureau, at least for most investigations."

"You're joking, right?" I asked.

"I'm afraid I'm not authorized to answer that."

"Haha. All kidding aside, the implications of what Gilbert Stein did are sobering. Remember my argument with Sergei about the opaque nature of complex algorithms underlying AI. Their lack of transparency would make it very difficult to know if they are operating entirely as advertised. After all, if we hadn't been fortunate enough to obtain the patent for the Caldwell Index, I doubt we could have revealed the deception perpetrated by Stein. There was no evidence in the results per se that screamed fraud. I'm worried that increasing reliance on AI in the years ahead will pose more such challenges."

"Then maybe we'll still need to keep some human beings around to keep an eye out for those."

"Yeah," said Rita, "or maybe they'll just invent even *more* sophisticated algorithms to check the ones being employed routinely."

When we arrived at Bobbie's office, we gathered around and nervously waited for Jeff to be sure the technology was set up, and that the results would be sent to his computer. When he finally gave us a thumb's up, Selwyn nodded to Bobbie.

"Okay, let's haul anchor."

We all held our breaths as she punched in the number. It was three minutes past four.

We waited.

One ring, Second ring. Third ring.

We were losing hope.

"Hello," came a business-like response. "Can I help you?"

"Oh, hi, this is Bobbie Stanton. Remember me? We spoke a few weeks ago."

"Sure, of course I remember. Have you been considering what we talked about?"

"Well, yes, actually. That's why I'm calling. I would have called sooner, but I've been super busy, designing a new course offering and writing a major grant application. In principle, I'm open to what you were suggesting, but I need more specifics. Of course, I'd need to run anything by the dean here to be sure it wouldn't be deemed, er…unseemly by the stuffed shirts here. You know Harvard, always so concerned about their reputation."

Thirty seconds had gone by. Jeff's computer screen displayed a posting of the time and what the AI software performing the trace could surmise about the location of Bobbie's interlocutor.

UNITED STATES OF AMERICA

"Oh, that's really helpful," whispered Rita, sarcastically.

"I assure you, your concerns are not unique, Bobbie. I can refer you to some distinguished academics we've worked with who can reassure you on that score."

"Another concern of mine relates to the time commitment. For the next few months at least, I am totally committed. Would that pose a problem?"

"No, not really. Do you think, though, that you might be able to give a talk at an academic symposium? I have in mind a particular event that's coming up in Germany in February. Do you ski? The venue is five-star, and there's a substantial honorarium."

"Hmm, that might be feasible. I'd have to check out some things. Uh…how much do you think the honorarium would be?"

"Well, based on past experience, I'd say fifty thousand...plus all travel expenses of course."

Sixty seconds had elapsed.

WASHINGTON D.C. METRO AREA

"Now we're getting somewhere," Rita commented.

"Oh, that does seem quite generous," said Bobbie.

"As I said, these organizations are well-funded, and very dedicated to their causes. So what do you think? Unfortunately, I don't have much more time before I have to leave for another meeting."

Rita was making urgent hand motions entreating Bobbie to keep talking. We needed more time.

"Right," said Bobbie. So, uh...what should happen next? Do you need any more information from me? Should we arrange a meeting to try and work out an agreement?"

"Let me think about the best way to proceed. I'll contact you in a few days. Is this cellphone the best number to reach you at?"

"Generally it is, yes. But often I can't pick up during the day, since I'm busy working with students and colleagues. It's best to text me first; then I can call back when I'm free. How would that be?"

Now ninety seconds had ticked by.

N. W. WASHINGTON D. C.

"Look, Bobbie I really need to sign off. I'll be in touch soon."

With that the call was abruptly terminated. Bobbie shrugged apologetically.

"*Shit!*" exclaimed Rita. "So close. I could spit!"

"You did great," offered Selwyn. "Terrific. Jeff,

what do you think?"

"That's a pretty large area. It doesn't help us all that much. I don't know. Give me a minute, I want to try something. It's a longshot."

A minute later he looked up.

"Okay, I've initiated a new post-call algorithm that's still under development. We've been testing it, and I've got it cranking away. It should take a couple of minutes. The software analyzes all the information we have relevant to this case, as well as the accent, vocabulary and syntax of the speaker. Based on that, it comes up with a probability estimate for the most likely location. Keep your fingers crossed."

Jeff was staring intently at his computer screen. Suddenly, his eyes opened wide.

"What is it, Jeff?" asked Rita.

"You're not going to like this."

"What?"

Jeff slowly turned the laptop around so we could all see what was on his screen.

2006 MASSACHUSETTS AVENUE N.W.
WASHINGTON, D.C. 20016
EMBASSY OF BRAZIL
PROBABILITY = 94%

# ACKNOWLEDGEMENT

My sincere appreciation goes to all those family members and friends who reviewed earlier drafts of the book. Their encouragement has emboldened me to venture into and persevere in the uncharted waters of fiction writing. Their constructive suggestions and corrections substantially improved the ultimate product.

I list them in alphabetical order: Steve Balk, Robert Bersson, Rosie Caine, Alan Friedman, Eric Garnick, Jarvis Kellogg, Simon Marcus, Howie Morris, Victor Pontes, Sam Ratick, Betty Reiser, Peter Rousmaniere Joel Salon, Nathan Schachtman, David Schwartz, Steve Steinig, Alex Weisberg, Dan Weisberg, and Nina Weisberg. Thanks also to Robin Zucker for her skill and patience in working with me to create the cover design. You have each contributed in some significant way to whatever success this book may happen to attain.

# ABOUT THE AUTHOR

## H. I. Weisberg

The author holds a Ph.D. in mathematical statistics and has previously written three nonfiction books about probability and statistics. He is a Fellow of the American Statistical Association and winner of several major awards for his research and consulting. He  has advised attorneys on numerous legal cases, many of which involved statistical disputes related to the safety and efficacy of medications. These experiences provided the raw material from which this debut novel was crafted.

Made in the USA
Monee, IL
06 December 2020

51065402R00277